TORTURED
Souls

NIKKI J SUMMERS

Copyright 2020 by Nikki J Summers
All rights reserved. No part of this work may be reproduced,
scanned or distribute in any printed or electronic form
without the express, written consent of the author.
A CIP record of this book is available from the British
Library.

Cover Image: Michelle Lancaster
Cover Designer: Lori Jackson Design
Editing: Karen Sanders Editing
Interior designed and formatted by: Irish Ink Publishing

OTHER BOOKS
By

NIKKI J SUMMERS

Rebels of Sandland Series

New Adult Romance

Renegade Hearts

Stand-Alone

Grey Romance

Luca

This Cruel Love

Hurt to Love

Joe and Ella Series:

Contemporary Romance

Obsessively Yours

Forever Mine

All available on Amazon Kindle Unlimited.

Only suitable for 18+ due to adult content.

TRIGGER WARNING
A Message from the Author

This story is for readers 18 years and upwards due to sexually explicit content. It also deals with issues that some may find difficult to read and may cause distress. There is also bad language throughout.

That being said, I hope you enjoy this enemies-to-lovers, New Adult Romance.

PLAYLIST
Available on Spotify

Available to download on Spotify

https://spoti.fi/32Vpkh4

The Trick Is To Keep Breathing – Garbage

Army of Me – Bjork

In Your Room – Depeche Mode

Tear Down the Wall – Art of Dying

Bury a Friend – Billie Eilish

We are the Enemy – Aranda

Soldier – Eminem

Notorious – Adelitas Way

Feel Invincible – Skillet

Monster – Skillet

Are You Not Afraid – Deadmau5 ft. Shotty Horroh

Wicked Game – Grace Carter

Demons – Imagine Dragons

Breaking the Model – New Medicine

Kick Ass – Egypt Central

Mug – Lunar C

One Too Many – New Medicine

Terrify the Dark – Skillet

This Year's Love – David Gray

Waking Lions – Pop Evil

Leave It All Behind – Cult to Follow

Fake It – Seether

My Demons – Starset

Take It Out On Me – Thousand Foot Krutch

My Ex's Best Friend – Machine Gun Kelly

Warrior Inside – Leader

The Kill (Bury Me) – Thirty Seconds To Mars

CHAPTER One

HARPER

"It's the saddest day of their lives. Heart-breaking."

"No one should ever have to bury their own child."

We kept our heads down, sheltering from the drizzling rain that misted around us on our slow walk through the gothic darkness of St. Anne's church gates. Without glancing up, we moved past the old women who were gathered at the old wooden doorway, gossiping over my brother's death like a gaggle of fish wives.

This was a day out for them.

An event to chat about over their piss-coloured weak cups of tea and stale biscuits.

A reason to get out, and if they were lucky, maybe score a bit of buffet food to save them making their own dinner later on. They didn't realise their throwaway comments meant something to us.

Yes, it was the saddest day of our lives. They didn't need to state that fact. We knew. We felt it with every sharp, searing pain that punched us in the guts at the memory. The thrum of adrenaline drowning our veins with unspeakable sorrow and dread. And the twisted, knotting feeling strangling our lungs, making it difficult to breathe. Putting one foot in front of the other was enough for today. It was all my family was capable of. Get through the day and get out the other end.

This was the worst day of our lives, and my mum and dad shouldn't be burying my twin brother, Brodie, at such a young age. He was only twenty-three. He had his whole life ahead of him. And yet here we were, saying a goodbye we never wanted to utter. And it was all down to one man.

Brandon Mathers.

The devil himself would've been more welcome in the town of Sandland than he ever would.

He'd killed my brother in cold blood. Snuffed him out like the scum of the Earth, brain-dead assassin he was. Brandon Mathers murdered my twin brother, and like a spineless piece of shit, he ran. Hid underground to avoid facing the justice Brodie deserved. No parent should have to lose a child in such a brutal way, but after what we'd been through the past few weeks, I'd made it my life's mission to ensure Brandon Mathers' family faced the same heartache we did.

He didn't deserve to live.

He didn't deserve to breathe the same air as the rest of us.

I wanted him dead, and I wanted to be there when he took his last breath, so I could tell him what a low-life shit-bag he really was. Remind him there was a place reserved for him in hell, courtesy of the Yates family.

We walked into the cold, eerie church, with its stomach-churning scent of mothballs and furniture polish, and made our way to the pews at the front. Our heels clicked on the tiled floors, making every guest turn and look our way, giving us sympathetic smiles. They were thanking their lucky stars they weren't in the position we were in. Counting their blessings and pitying ours.

I was flanked by my mum and dad, as if they were trying to protect me from the sorrow that shrouded us; like a thick cloth of smoke that choked all three of us with the weight of carrying such a burden. A weight we never thought we'd ever be free of. They put their arms around me and the three of us sat as a unit, ready to pay our respects to Brodie, but blocking out the rest of the congregation. We weren't here for them. We had no interest in anyone else. We'd always been a close-knit family, and today was no different. We'd get through this together.

"You're doing well, angel. We're so proud of you." Dad kissed me on the top of my head and gave my shoulder a squeeze. "Brodie is here, you know. He'll never leave us."

I nodded, unable to form any words through the tight ball of pain bunched in my throat. I knew Mum and Dad were going through their own hell. Brodie was their baby boy; the son they worshipped. The one who made us all laugh and would do anything for anybody. But for me, the grief was unbearable.

He was my twin.

Even as kids we felt each other's sadness, bore each other's pain. If Brodie fell over and scraped his knee, I was the one who cried. On that night, when we lost him, I felt it. I felt the blinding shock of pain in my head as he went down, like white lightning blurring my vision and making me feel nauseous and dizzy. I almost threw up, but that bond we had, it kept me focused on him.

I blinked past the tears that welled up in my eyes. Dwelling on that night wouldn't help me now. It'd only make me angrier, and I didn't want to give any more headspace to those negative thoughts. Today was Brodie's day. A day to remember everything wonderful about him. He was all I wanted to think about.

The church organs started to groan out their morose, morbid notes, and we heard the murmurs, sobs, and collective sigh from the congregation as Brodie's casket was carried down the aisle. I couldn't turn around and look. The only aisle I'd ever wanted to see my brother go down was the one on his wedding day, not this. Never this. I kept my head facing forward and focused on the decrepit, worn pulpit and the dark wooden altar, anything but the swell of grief I was drowning in. But everywhere I looked, I felt death. Even the church looked like it was decaying around us.

My parents tensed beside me, and when I saw Brodie's coffin being laid onto the plinth beside where we stood, I cracked, feeling like a freshly healed wound had been savagely ripped open again.

Would it ever heal?

I doubted it.

It felt like my life from this moment on would always be played out in a fog of misery and regret, hurt and pain.

My heart lurched, and I shook with the effort of trying not to break completely. My tears fell freely now.

Why did life have to be so cruel?

He didn't deserve this.

None of us did.

Jensen Lockwood, his younger brother, Chase, and a few of Brodie's other friends had carried the coffin. I was beyond grateful for them today. They'd made it easier for my dad to stay with us and look after his girls, a term of endearment he'd used for the first time this morning. He didn't have his boy anymore.

If I was completely honest with myself, I did harbour some feelings of resentment towards Jensen for what happened to Brodie. He could have stopped it, but he didn't. However, since everything that had happened, he'd stepped up when we'd needed him, and I couldn't deny we owed him for that.

The service went by in a blur of emotions. I somehow managed to stand with the help of my parents to sing the hymns. Blinking through the tears that welled in my eyes, I stumbled through each verse, even though I could barely read the words on the order of service. When the vicar spoke about Brodie, reminiscing over his short life, I stayed locked up in my head, thinking about the Brodie I knew and the memories that were mine alone. No one could take those away.

When the service was over, I felt exhausted and mentally drained. Numb to what was happening around me but crippled by the pain of my reality. I needed to get out and get some fresh air.

Brodie was being buried in the graveyard of the church, so the ordeal wasn't finished yet, but we'd got through this first part. That was something.

We stood first and followed the vicar as he led us through a side door. He was wittering away to my father about the impressive turnout, but I zoned him out. The rest of the congregation followed, and we all headed to where the grave was situated, pre-dug and covered with a cloth that lay around the hole to try and make it look less harrowing. God forbid we should see it for what it was, a hole in the dirt that we were about to lower my brother's body into. It didn't matter how much you dressed it up, that's what it was.

I took my place at the edge of the grave. Despite staring at the ground for the majority of the day, I found it hard to look there now. So, tentatively, I lifted my head, feeling the soft wet drizzle of the English rain mist over my face. Seemed like the weather mirrored the mood of the day. It was sombre, gloomy, and looked like the heavens were about to open at any minute to drench us to the bone. The perfect day for a funeral.

I scanned the faces coming out of the church; Jensen, Chase, a few aunts and uncles that we only ever saw at Christmas, and then I went cold. Zak Atwood, Finn Knowles, and Ryan Hardy strolled out like they belonged there. Ryan was holding hands with Danny Winters' little sister, Emily, and they all wore the same fake, sorrowful expression on their faces. I wanted to march over to them and tell them to leave.

Why had they come?

To gloat?

The reason we were here at all was because their friend had murdered my brother.

I gritted my teeth, taking deep, fortifying breaths as I realised they had to know where Brandon was hiding. They were probably the ones protecting him. Coming to give a fake show of support and then heading back to Mathers to tell him all about it. Let him wallow in the pride he felt at taking another man's life. The thought sickened me.

They weren't welcome, and I wanted to tell them to leave, but when my mum whispered, "Are you okay, Harper?" into my ear, I snapped my head away from them. I wouldn't give them the satisfaction of knowing how they got to me, or of telling Brandon how truly broken I was.

"I need this bit over with, Mum." I kept my breathing deep and steady, needing that panting rhythm to keep me sane. "This is the part I've been dreading."

The pallbearers positioned Brodie's coffin over the grave and the vicar said his final words. Dad pulled me into him as they lowered Brodie's body into the ground, and Mum came behind us so we could shelter from the hurt together.

People around us snivelled and cried into their tissues. I wanted to tell them to shut the hell up. What were they bawling over? Tomorrow, they'd go on with their lives as if nothing had ever happened. It might've been a bad day for them, but it was a bad fucking life for us. Their fake tears and weak support were no help. If anything, it drove me more insane, thinking this day was all about their grief and their feelings. We barely saw most of them from one year to the next. This had zero impact on their lives, and they needed to stop acting like it did.

Then came the ashes to ashes part, and the vicar led the tradition of throwing a handful of dirt onto the casket below. I didn't want to do that. I couldn't bear the thought of it. Why would I want to throw mud down to say goodbye to someone so precious? Instead, I took a white rose from the flower arrangement I'd had made in the colours of Brodie's favourite football team, spelling out 'brother', and threw that down.

"He's always with you, Harper, love." Dad repeated his sentiment from earlier, and I wiped away the deluge of tears that drenched my face and soaked through to my collar.

"I know, Dad. I feel him."

I didn't.

Not since the day he'd left me.

I felt nothing but pain.

I'd stayed awake night after night, willing him to come to me or speak to me in some way, but it never happened. My other half was gone, and I was all alone.

I stood back and watched my dad take a handful of soil and drop it carefully down, and then it was my mum's turn. She grabbed the soil, but when it came time to let go, she couldn't do it. She broke down right there at the graveside, sobbing as my dad caught her and pulled her into him. In that moment, watching my parents huddled together on the ground in their combined grief, my own misery was replaced with fury, and I turned to look at the traitors standing at the foot of the church drive. They were huddled together and no doubt picking over the pieces of my brother's death like the vultures they were.

Why should they get away with it?

They were as guilty as he was. They had blood on their hands and they needed to know.

Staying focused, I stomped over the uneven dewy grass of the churchyard. Finn Knowles looked up, and when he saw me charging towards them, he said something that made them all stop and turn to watch.

"We're so sorry about Brodie," Finn blurted out once I was in front of them. "If there's anything we can do-" He sounded contrite, but I knew it was bullshit. His eyes were sincere, but his actions were useless. As pointless as his words.

"If you wanted to help you wouldn't have come here today." I was shaking but trying not to show it, so I folded my arms over my chest to stop them from seeing me tremble. How could they stand there knowing what they'd done? "Are you spying? For him? I know you know where he is."

Ryan stepped forward and went to touch my arm, but I pulled away. I didn't want anything to do with them. The bloody Renaissance men, as they liked to call themselves. What a joke. More like Satan's spawn. The devil's lackeys. Evil really didn't give a fuck and neither did they.

"If we knew where he was, we'd tell you," Finn said, then turned to look at the others, probably willing them to back him up.

"I don't believe you." I stood firm. I would never believe a word that came out of their mouths. Not where Brodie was concerned, and certainly not when they were trying so hard to hide the truth about Brandon fucking Mathers. "You'd do anything to save one of your own."

"No, we wouldn't. Not with this. What happened was... awful."

I scoffed and shook my head at Zak Atwood's woefully inappropriate description of my brother's murder.

"Awful? You want to know what's awful? The fact that you came here today thinking you deserved a place in that church. Neither of you deserve to be here. You've got blood on your hands and you know it. You might not have been there that night, when Brodie died, but you had a hand in it. You could've stopped him at any time, and you can stop him now. Don't act like you're all innocent." I looked each one of them in the eye, but apart from Emily, they couldn't look back. "If you really want to help, tell the police where he is, or better yet, tell me. I'd rather see my own form of justice served, anyway."

Emily stepped forward, rubbing Ryan on the arm as she did, as if he were the one who needed consoling.

"Harper, I don't know you that well, but I know what it's like to lose a brother. I think I understand a bit about what you're feeling right now."

Was she delusional?

Who the hell did she think she was?

"You don't know shit, little girl. Your brother died in a car accident. He wasn't knocked out right in front of you and bled out in your lap. I still have the clothes I wore that night, you know. Soaked in my brother's blood. It's a harsh reminder of what happened and keeps me focused on what I want. Revenge. You know nothing, so keep your fucking nose out of my business," I sneered at her, but she didn't flinch, just gave me a fake-ass smile and nodded to herself knowingly.

"That anger will need channelling somewhere. And when you need to talk and let it all out, just know you have me in your corner."

She needed to wake up and smell the bullshit.

"Oh, fuck off. I don't need your sanctimonious crap. Go and sort your own life out before sticking your nose into mine. I hear daddy has his trial soon. Might want to save some of that fake humility for the cameras when you do your press conference. You know, to save your family name and make yourself look good."

Like everyone else in this town, I'd heard about the money laundering her dad was involved in. Not the best advertisement for his political campaign. Her innocent act was lost on me.

Ryan put his arm around Emily and glared angrily my way.

"That's enough."

"Enough?" I laughed sarcastically. "It'll be enough when he is in a grave in this churchyard. Until then, nothing will ever be enough. So, do me a favour and go. Leave. All of you. You're not helping me or my family, gloating over the scraps your friend left behind."

I went to walk away but had to get one last shot in before I left.

"Tell him it was a lovely send-off. The church was full, and everyone was there because they loved Brodie. When his turn comes, there won't be anyone to see him off. Except me, that is. I'll be standing there making sure they bury him as deep as they can. I'll even spit on his grave."

And with that, I turned and left.

CHAPTER
Two

HARPER

"Why are we doing this? Why are we here? You know I hate these nights, Brodie. It makes me feel sick. I wish you wouldn't do this."

The barn we were packed into was stuffy and full of rowdy groups shouting over at the two men fighting in the middle.

Bare-knuckle boxing.

I hated it.

But my brother, Brodie, he lived for nights like these. All of his friends did, although there was only Brodie and Jensen who'd ever fought. I blamed the overload of testosterone. I didn't see the appeal in smashing your fist into another human being, but what did I know?

"Chill out, Harper. I'm down to fight and you know I've got this. I'm undefeated..." He huffed, clearly annoyed with me, and he ran his hands through his hair. *"Just let me have this, okay? I need to let off steam. If you don't like it, you don't have to watch."*

Brodie hadn't fought the last time we went out; he'd given that honour to Jensen. But now, it was his turn, and the familiar bile rose up in my throat as we made our way towards the middle of the barn. Since splitting up with his girlfriend, Sally, he'd been more reckless. I think boxing was his way of letting some of the angst and frustration out. If Sal were here, she'd have been able to talk him out of it. She always did. But not me. He never listened to a word I said. I didn't know why I still came to these things. It was bloody torture.

I saw Jensen nudge his brother, Chase, and turn to give Brodie a wicked stare. When I saw who stood beside Pat Murphy, the organiser of the fight, I knew why.

Brandon Mathers.

He was a few years younger than us, but that didn't mean shit. The guy looked feral, unhinged, and his eyes were glazed over like he was on something. Even crazy people would give Mathers a wide berth if they met him.

I prayed to God he wasn't fighting Brodie. They had history, and if they were pitched against each other, it'd be a bloody massacre.

Their feud went way back to primary school. I had no idea what had gone on, but I knew Brodie and the others hated Brandon. He was that kid. The one who looked like he needed a good wash and a decent meal growing up. The boy that looked one step away from totally flipping out. An outsider, a tear-away, and the last boy you'd ever invite to your home, because he'd probably steal from your mum's purse while you weren't looking and vandalise your bedroom before he left. In short, he was bad news. Always had been and always would be.

"Please tell me you're not fighting him, Brodie. He fought Jensen a few days ago and look how that turned out." I gestured over to where Jensen stood in front of us, sporting a still nasty bruised and swollen face. The guy was making the effort not to hobble, but I knew he was in pain. He couldn't hide it, no matter what.

"I am, and he needs taking down a peg or two, Harp. I'll do it for Jensen, and you."

He kissed the top of my head and left me standing there as he sauntered over to where the others stood. I followed, reluctantly, but kept myself hidden in the crowd. I didn't want any part of the ridiculous taunting they'd engage in to get a rise out of Brandon. Like he needed goading. He looked like he wanted to take on every man in this shithole barn.

Jensen called out Brandon's name, and he turned to face them. I could see a slight smirk creeping out of the corner of his mouth, but he soon turned that shit off and did a really good job of looking dangerous and soulless. The guy was like a machine, primed and ready to attack. Horror movie bad guys had nothing on him. He was the real deal. The bogeyman that kept kids in Sandland awake past their bedtime. I hated him.

"No friends tonight, Mathers? They finally seen you for

the loser you are?"

Jensen was playing with fire, talking to Brandon like that. The guy always did have more bravado than brains. Brandon had given him the pasting of his life, he still held the evidence of it for everyone to see on his beaten up face, but that switch in his head that was slightly off kilter didn't register what the rest of us knew. He was making things worse for Brodie by firing Brandon up. He wasn't doing a great job at saving his own ass either, because that switch that the rest of us had, that told us when to stop, Brandon lacked it too. Pitting those two against each other was a lose-lose situation. Nothing good could come from them verbally sparring before Brodie's fight.

"That's funny. I seem to remember beating your ass just a few days ago, Lockwood. I'd wait for the bruises to fade before you come at me again. You might sound more convincing," Brandon spat back, looking like he was ready to give Jensen a reminder of what it felt like to be on the receiving end of one of his punches.

I knew the night wasn't going to end well. The whole aura felt off. Knowing both Brodie and Brandon were undefeated on the bare-knuckle boxing scene meant someone was going home fucking shredded to pieces. I prayed it wouldn't be Brodie.

I went to reach forward to grab him, maybe pull him back from the crowd and talk him out of it, but I was jostled out of the way, and all I could do was watch as they all went

24

toe-to-toe in their stand-off before the big fight. Jensen was snarling and getting into Brandon's face.

"All I see is a lonely, washed-up nobody. A wannabe Tyson Fury without the charisma. You're less gypsy king and more shitty king. You know, like the shit they found you in when your mum left you to bone every drug dealer she could get her hands on."

We all held our breath as Jensen said that, spilling truths we'd all heard whispered around Sandland.

Brandon snapped and lurched towards Jensen, and in that split second, I saw the fear in Jensen's eyes. He knew he'd gone too far. He'd woken the beast, and now my brother was going to step into the ring with it. I say ring, but they didn't fight in the usual boxing ring. A tower of hay bales and a referee was all that kept them from the baying crowds that jeered and shouted as each punch was thrown. Jensen had done a great job of riling up Brandon, and now, we all had to watch as Brodie dealt with the fall-out.

Pat Murphy whispered to Brandon, probably hoping to calm him down, and Brandon nodded then pulled his shirt off.

"Hot damn, that boy is fine."

I turned to where a group of women were standing just to the side of us, eyeing-up Mathers like he was the half-time snack. I looked back and tried to see what they saw. Okay, so he was ripped, and his abs looked like a work of art. Not to mention the tattoos that covered his body. If he wasn't the unhinged psychopath I knew him to be, I might've joined in on the eye-fucking, but he was a psycho. One look at the dead eyes and fearsome snarl and I felt nothing but revulsion.

I watched as Brodie walked into the fight zone and smiled at him.

'Don't goad him, Brodie. Stay focused.'

I hoped my subconscious message got to him. I was fully channelling my twin power of telepathy, but from the way he glared as the ref fed them the rules, I knew he wasn't in-tune. He wouldn't listen.

He held his fists up ready to fight and then I heard the final nail in the coffin.

"Come on then, you pussy. Show me what you've got. Or did Jensen wear you out the other night? You've always been a disappointment. All these people here tonight to watch you fight and look at you, nothing but a weak ass fucker with a chip on his shoulder."

Oh, Brodie. Why couldn't you keep your big mouth shut?

He never was very good at engaging his brain before he spoke. Tonight was a perfect example. He'd just given Brandon the fuel he needed to stoke the fires. Not that he needed much more to get him going. The guy was demonic. Focused on his opponent and using that tunnel vision I'd watched him use before to drown everything out and analyse the fight.

Brodie was a scrapper, but Brandon was methodical.

Where Brodie used power and brute force to gain the upper hand, Brandon used strategy powered by a deep-seated anger. Brodie had played right into his hands.

The fight started and the crowd booed as Brodie smacked his fist into Brandon's face. Brandon could've easily ducked away from the hit, but he didn't. He smirked as the blood coated his teeth. He wanted Brodie to hit him. That told me one thing; he needed to feel the pain. It spurred him on and fired him up.

Brandon took a few more hits to the body and everyone started chanting, thinking Brodie had this wrapped up, but I could tell from the fire in Brandon's eyes that he wasn't out of it yet. This was foreplay for him. The way he tightened his abs as Brodie punched him showed he was absorbing the pain. The way his mouth quirked up at the edges meant he was enjoying the build-up. The attack was all part of his plan.

I shouted out to Brodie, scared he was wearing himself out too soon. He had a large frame, but he wasn't built for stamina. My brother was more of a knock-em-out kind of fighter. Brandon had staying power. I knew that. I'd done my homework.

Suddenly, the air in the barn shifted as Brandon threw a punch into Brodie's face. He hit him with so much force that Brodie staggered backwards and then wiped over his face as the blood began to pour from his nose. Blows to the head were my biggest fear, and I grew dizzy as Brodie shook his head and tried to regain his balance. Something didn't feel right, and I pushed through the crowd, trying to get as close to the action as I could. A few people complained and shoved me back, but when I snapped at them that I was his twin sister and pointed at Brodie, they moved. Don't piss off the angry sibling. If I wanted to be in the heart of the action, I would.

I felt a surge of energy, and the crowds cheered as Brandon charged into Brodie and pinned him to the hay bales, raining down blow after blow on his body. Brodie tried to cover himself as best he could, but he lost his footing and fell onto the ground. I shouted for the ref to intervene and he did. Jensen and Chase were standing beside me now and judging from the look on their faces they weren't as confident as they had been in their pre-fight verbal knockout. They looked as green as I felt.

"He's going to fucking kill him," Jensen whispered to himself, but I heard, and my stomach turned over. "Come on, bro!" Jensen cupped his hands around his mouth and shouted. "Get up and take him out."

I tried to shout too, but my throat had closed up. All I could do was watch everything unravel in front of me. I knew as soon as it was over, I'd be leaving this barn and I never wanted to watch another fight for as long as I lived.

Brodie pushed himself to stand up, stumbling a little as he did, but his eyes were unfocused, dazed almost. The ref said something to him, nodded, and then stood back. And then my heart fell from my chest right onto the cold, hard floor of the barn. Brandon had caught Brodie with an almighty punch to the side of the head, knocking his jaw and making him stumble and miss his footing. Brodie fell backwards and crashed to the stone floor. The way his head bounced as it impacted on the dusty cobblestones made me howl in pain. I pushed Jensen out of the way, as he screamed over the noise of the crowd for Brodie to get back up.

Was he for real?

My brother had just been knocked out cold. He wasn't going to get back up and fight. Not if I had anything to do with it. This was over.

As I pushed my way into the fight zone, I saw the blood trickling out of the back of Brodie's head, covering the floor in a dark red puddle that made me feel physically sick. Brandon was leaning over my brother as if he wanted to finish the job he'd started, but the ref pulled him away.

I knelt at the side of where Brodie lay and picked up his head, cradling it in my lap. The blood soaked through my jeans, but I didn't care. He was lifeless, and in that moment, I felt helpless. I put my fingers against his neck to feel for a pulse, but there was nothing, and the blinding pain in my head told me all I needed to know.

I looked up at Brandon standing over us like the demon he was.

"I think he's dead!" I cried, wanting to take a knife and finish this guy off myself for what he'd done to Brodie. "You

killed him! You fucking killed him!"
You killed him...
You fucking killed him...

I woke up with a start. The sweat from my body drenched my bed covers and my heart was racing so fast I felt like my chest would cave in at any moment. Frantically, I threw the covers off to try and cool myself down and took deep breaths to regulate my breathing.

I had these nightmares most nights, and I usually woke up when Brandon got the first punch in, but not tonight. Tonight, I'd lived through it all. The hell that was my brother's last moments on Earth. The twist in my stomach felt as fresh as it did on that night, and I wondered if it'd ever get any better, or was this my new normal? A life where every waking moment was filled with the pain of loss and the guilt that I could've done more. I should've done more.

Squeezing my eyes closed, I tried to block out my guilt-ridden thoughts, dragging my nails over my thighs in the hope that the sting from my skin would ease the pain in my heart. Everything felt disgusting, dirty, and wrong. I lifted myself off the soaked bedcovers. My silk nightie was stuck to my skin, and I peeled it away to waft some coolness over me. Having long hair wasn't always great when you were hot. Mine was currently dripping wet and plastered to my neck, so I pulled it into a ponytail and then used a band from my bedside table to keep it in place. I felt heavy from the weight of emotions that still plagued my waking mind, a cruel gift from the nightmare I'd just clawed myself back from.

I headed to the window to open it up and let in some fresh air. At the same time, I hoped it'd release the stifling demons that were swirling around me in the musky darkness of my room. The flicker of menacing shadows from the trees outside danced across my walls, as if they were trying to reach out and grab a hold of my soul and drag me farther and farther down to hell. But they didn't need to try, I was already at rock bottom.

That was when I saw it.

The orange glow of a cigarette at the bottom of my garden.

Someone was down there, hiding in the midnight shadows.

I gasped as my adrenaline spiked and my nerves went into freefall. Moving to the edge of the wall, I plastered my body against it, praying they didn't see me. God, I hoped they didn't see me. My heartbeat drummed fast in my ears, and I tried to steady myself as best I could, but how could I? When there was a psycho standing in my garden, ready to do God knows what. My nightmares were becoming a fucked-up reality.

Cautiously, I peered slowly around to see if they were still there. My throat pulsed with fear, and I held my breath as I saw the dark, hooded figure take another drag of their cigarette, momentarily lighting up their face. A man's face;

rugged, unshaven and sinister. Whoever was down there was dressed all in black and had the hood of his jacket pulled low over his eyes. But he was watching. That much was clear.

Was it him?

Had he come back to finish the job?

He'd destroyed one twin, so now, was he hell-bent on finishing the other?

The sweat that soaked my skin only moments ago had turned to ice, and I was shaking. I didn't know what to do. I could open my window, maybe shout and alert my parents and the neighbours to our silent stalker, or I could stay hidden and watch him. Try to figure out what he wanted and why he was doing this. I decided I'd wait it out. In some sick, perverted way, I wanted to lure him in. Maybe this was the best way to catch him?

I kept my back flush against the side of the wall, and I watched. I watched him put out his cigarette and light another only minutes later. All the time, he stayed rooted to that spot; looking up at our house and my window, but never taking a step into the moonlight that might illuminate his features and give his identity away.

I knew it was him, though. It had to be.

This figure had the same build and emanated the same macabre aura.

I should've known he wouldn't be able to stay away. Evil always did return to the scene of the crime. They lived off the grief and fear of their victims, and that's what he thought I was.

A victim.

Like a demon feeding off the weak, he'd come for sustenance, but he wouldn't get it. I wasn't weak and I'd never be his prey. He might have gotten to Brodie, but I was still alive, here to fight back. I'd always fight back when it came to him.

I heard shuffling coming from the hallway and then the bathroom light came on, bathing the back garden in a blanket of light. The orange tip of his cigarette hit the floor fast and he faded into the thick set of conifer trees, slipping into the darkness to become one with the shadows. I heard Dad finish up in the bathroom, then the light went off again, but he didn't come back. The dark figure from my waking nightmares was gone.

But he'd return.

I knew that much.

And when he did, I'd be ready for him.

CHAPTER *Three*

HARPER

I didn't sleep much that night. Thoughts of revenge consumed me and made my mind whirl with the possibilities. In the light of day, I knew I needed to speak to Jensen and the others. My own strengths were limited, and when it came to Brandon Mathers, I'd need more than a sharp mind and a grudge to beat him. I needed power too. Knowledge and power. That was something I felt sure the Lockwood brothers could give to me. They had enough dirt on Mathers, and when the time came, I knew I'd need everything I could use against him. I needed a fully loaded arsenal.

I managed to drag myself out of bed, shower, and change. I felt proud of myself for making the effort, but I had to. If I stayed in bed all day crying, it wouldn't do any good. I needed to keep myself busy. Wallowing wouldn't bring Brodie back, but action might help to stop me from staying trapped in the well of despair I was currently locked into.

I headed downstairs to the kitchen where I could hear Mum and Dad chatting over their morning coffee, discussing the wake and how proud Brodie would've been. Mum started to cry, and when I walked in, Dad was holding her. When she saw me, she pulled away, trying to paint on a fake smile.

"You don't have to pretend with me, Mum. If you want to cry, cry." She reached over to me and pulled me in for a hug.

"You were so brave yesterday. We will get through this. It might not feel like it now, but someday... a long, long way off, we'll heal. We'll learn to live again. It'll never go away, but we'll get better at dealing with it. At least, that's what Doctor Meredith says."

Mum had been seeing a counsellor since Brodie died. Doctor Meredith O'Neill was her lifeline most days. Mum had her number on speed dial and used it readily.

"You should come with me today. I'm seeing her at two. She could help you too, Harper. It helps to talk."

I shook my head. I wasn't ready to talk to anyone about what'd happened, least of all a complete stranger.

"Thanks, but no thanks. I have work." Both of my parents scoffed as soon as I spoke.

"You can't go to work. Not today. You only buried your brother yesterday. They won't expect you in," Dad said, and they frowned at me, but I wasn't going to be swayed.

"I can't sit around here all day moping either. I want to go to work. It'll keep me busy. I love my job." I gave a weak smile that didn't reach my eyes and my parents huffed out their annoyance, but surprisingly, they dropped the subject.

"At least let me make you breakfast." Dad sighed, opening the cupboards and pulling out a frying pan.

"I'm good, Dad. Fruit will be fine."

I picked up an apple from the fruit bowl and bit into it, wincing as the sourness hit my taste buds and the juice ran down my chin. I wiped my face with the back of my hand and then I headed for the patio doors that led out to the garden. In the distance, I could see the conifers swaying in the breeze, and I felt a tug of curiosity, willing me to go down there. I needed to know how he'd got in. Did he scale the fence? Or was there some other more perverse way that he moved around? Like a demon in the dust, appearing and disappearing on the gasp of his victim's breath.

I left my parents to their hushed conversation and made my way outside. The morning was fresh, and when I stepped down onto the grass, I took a deep breath in to try and fill my lungs with the goodness of the day and suffocate the bad.

I wandered down to the bottom where my night-time reaper had stood. When I got there, I noticed a small collection of cigarette butts on the ground. Fucker couldn't even pick up his shit. He'd left it all there like a sick calling card.

I pushed my way through the trees to get to the high fencing that ran around the perimeter of our property. I couldn't see any signs of forced entry. The fencing panels were all intact, and apart from some disturbed ground right by them, you wouldn't have known anyone had been here.

He'd obviously scaled the fence to get in, and it crossed my mind to get Dad to install barbed wire at the top, but in a twisted way, I didn't want to. I wanted him to get comfortable coming here. When you're comfortable, you let your guard down. An unguarded, vulnerable Mathers was a weakened one. One I could manipulate and destroy, with a little help from my friends.

I left the devil's hiding place and made my way back up to the house. I wasn't going to tell my mum and dad about our unwelcome visitor. They had enough on their plates, and I needed to digest everything and form a plan myself. I couldn't do that if they were scared out of their minds about our crazy murdering stalker. I needed space to think and clarity of mind. But that wasn't the easiest thing to get. Not after Brodie's death. My mind was like a thick fog weighing me down. That's why I knew going to work would be good for me. I needed some degree of normality to my day.

-

I pulled into the carpark of Sandland Primary School just after eight-thirty. The children were starting to filter into the building already and parents were dotted around the playground, chatting and doing a really shitty job of managing their offspring as they climbed on every surface they could find. I guessed being on the school premises meant a lot of parents switched off, seeing it as our job to police their little hellions. I saw Izzy, one of the teachers, standing at the door, and when she saw my car, her eyes went wide.

I grabbed my bags and made my way through the playground towards the building, feeling like I was encased in a bubble. The sounds around me were distorted and I couldn't quite focus on anything other than the ground ahead of me.

A few of the younger girls ran over to hug me and then didn't come up for air as they prattled on about their pets, games, T.V. shows, and anything else they thought I needed to hear about. I gave them the appropriate amount of oohs and ahhs to keep them happy and make it look like I was paying attention. I wasn't. But they didn't need to know that.

I'd always loved my job as a teaching assistant. Every day spent with the kids made me smile. I liked to think I made a difference in their lives, even if I wasn't their main teacher. I got all the fun parts without the stress. I was the one who'd take them out of class and spend quality time with them, helping them achieve the goals they wouldn't reach if they were left to fend for themselves in an overcrowded classroom.

"Harper, what are you doing here?" Izzy asked in an exasperated tone as she held the door open for me and ushered the over-enthusiastic girls away to play. "We can manage just fine. You need to be at home. Concentrate on you and your family. We'll still be here when you're ready to come back. School isn't going anywhere."

I understood what she was trying to say, but my mind was already made up.

"But I'm ready now. I want to be here, Izz. The kids will help take my mind off things and I know we have a ton of stuff to do. We're short staffed on a good day."

Izzy nodded, but the way she bit her lip told me she didn't agree. She wanted to argue but didn't want to upset me either.

"How are you?"

I hated that question just as much as I hated people saying how sorry they were. It was a weak response to a catastrophically awful thing that'd happened in my life. Sorry was something you said when you bumped into someone or forgot something trivial. When people said it in regard to Brodie's death it set my teeth on edge, but I was getting better at not biting back.

"I'm okay," I answered, keeping the statutory 'fine' for the next person who asked.

"I really don't believe that, but I'll let it slide." Izzy gave me a smile filled with pity and then relented. "Well, I'm happy to see you. I have been worried. But I'm not giving you Tommy and Scott today. Those two have been shockingly bad this week. You can work with Stevie, and Abigail could do with some help with her phonics."

"Izz, I can take my usual groups. You don't have to mollycoddle me."

She sighed but let it go. I wasn't there to be treated differently. I already got that at home. I just wanted a day to be Miss Yates, business as usual.

However, my day got progressively worse from there on in. It was one of those days where I was pulled from pillar to post; dealing with sick children, classroom problems and not having a minute to come up for air. In the last lesson before lunchtime, I was taking a small group in the library area, and I could feel myself starting to struggle.

"I hate reading. I'm not gonna do anything you say." Tommy was pushing his luck and refusing to even open the book we were working on. Usually I'd have some strategy I could call on to deal with him, but my well had run dry. I had nothing.

"Open your book and sit down, Tommy. If you don't, I'll send you to the head teacher."

I was shaking, trying to keep the rest of the group on task as Tommy swung the chair around dangerously close to the others and smirked at me. I took deep breaths, but it did no good. His outburst just made my anger escalate.

"My mum said your brother was a thug and he deserved to die. I hate you," he spat back, throwing the chair across the library, narrowly missing Alice who sat close by, and making her cower and silently start to cry.

"I hate you too," I said without thinking, and as soon as it was out, I knew I'd lost control.

Instantly, Tommy started screeching. "You're the worst teacher in this school. I hope you die like your brother."

He flung his arm across the bookshelves, emptying them of the books, and then picked them up to throw them at me.

"GET OUT!" I shouted, grasping the edge of the table with my fists and shaking with anger. I gasped for breath, struggling to fill my lungs, dizzy and lightheaded from the effort it took to breathe.

Tommy laughed and went to work on the rest of the library, shoving the books from the shelves and wailing in a high-pitched scream. The other children froze, glancing from Tommy to me in horror. And I just squeezed my eyes shut and started to rock back and forth, begging this nightmare to be over. I wanted to be anywhere but here, dealing with this shit. Right now, I felt like I wasn't even in my own body. Complete mayhem was happening around me, but all I could do was pant and rock, pant and rock.

"What on Earth is going on here?" the head teacher, Mr Farnsworth, shouted. His voice bellowed over the noise of the library, but I didn't look up. I couldn't. "Children, go back into class. Miss Boot, will you take Tommy to the nurture room? I'll deal with him later," he said to one of the other teaching assistants that must've been walking past at the time. "Miss Yates, you need to come to my office. Now."

I tried to stand up, but I couldn't. My brain and my body weren't fully aligned. Inside, I wanted to shrivel up and die right there on the spot. I could feel my muscles compacting, my limbs freezing up. My body felt heavy, empty, devoid of the energy it took to even move. In my head, there was a sea of emotions I was drowning in. I had no control. I couldn't even deal with a wayward child. I had totally lost it. Every thought was like a tumbling mess, a waterfall of confusion. I couldn't think straight, and I felt like I was dying.

Suddenly, the weight of warm, strong arms around me and voices telling me it'd be okay broke through the cracks in my soul. Female voices that were soothing and giving me the gentle encouragement I needed to lift myself up off the chair I was slumped into.

"I'll make a cup of tea. You shouldn't have come in today, love. It's all too much." That was Sue, one of the older teaching assistants, who everyone saw as the mother of the school. Along with Grace, a learning support assistant, she led me into Mr Farnsworth's office then scuttled off to make the strong tea she said would make me feel better. I took a tissue from a box on the desk to try to clean myself up, but inside I was hollow. It was as if I was stuck in a dark well with no chance of escape. There was no rope to pull me out and no light of hope, only darkness.

A few minutes later, Sue reappeared, clutching a mug of steaming hot tea, and Grace followed with a packet of chocolate biscuits that she told me she'd kept hidden in her locker for emergencies like this. If only my problems could be solved by tea and biscuits. I smiled and thanked them, knowing I wouldn't be touching any of it.

"Thank you, ladies." Mr Farnsworth came in and stood at the door as they fussed around me then took the hint and left.

He closed the door behind them then pulled a chair over

to sit opposite me. I couldn't look at him. I probably wouldn't have been able to look at myself if he'd put a mirror in front of me. I was a shell, an empty vessel. Here in body, but my mind was checking out.

"I think it's best if you take a bit of time off, Harper. A leave of absence. You've been through a trying time, and as a school we want to support you. But we can't have what happened just now happening again. I have to think about the welfare of the pupils as well as the staff. You aren't fit to teach at the moment."

My head shot up. All I heard was, *you aren't fit to teach.*

"Are you firing me?"

"No. But I am going to refer you to the occupational health team. I think they're best qualified to assess whether you're fit for work. They offer excellent counselling services. Take some time out to get yourself well again. You're no good to us if you're like this."

I shook my head. He *was* firing me. He wanted me out. I'd made a mistake. One fucking mistake in all the time I'd worked here, and he was forcing me out.

"You can't do this. I love this place. I live for this job." I couldn't stop crying, rocking on my chair and sobbing hysterically. The thought of losing everything was all-consuming. My whole life was crashing down around me and there was nothing I could do to stop it.

"I know how hard you work. That isn't in question here. But you're not well-"

"I'm fine. Please…"

I wasn't fine. I was the furthest from fine that I'd ever been. I was broken, and I didn't know what to do. I was lost.

"Harper, let me call Janice in the office and see if she can give you a lift home. I'll speak to occupational health and get someone to call you today to talk about your options."

I jumped up from my seat. I didn't want to hear any more. I knew the children would be spilling out of their classrooms in five minutes, heading for lunch, and I didn't want to be here. I didn't want them to see my tear-soaked face or witness my breakdown.

"I'm fine. I can drive myself." I opened the door to leave, still quaking as I sobbed.

"Please, Harper. Let me get someone to take you home. You can't drive like this." He went to follow me, but I turned, walking away and calling over my shoulder that I'd be fine.

Fine.

Fucked up more like.

I'd lost my brother, my job, and now my sanity. I didn't know how many more knocks I could take before I gave up altogether.

I raced through the corridors, past the office and out to the car park. Once I was in my car, I slumped onto the steering wheel and let it all out. I cried so hard and so loud, but I had to. I had nothing now. Nothing but the wreckage around me. Somehow, I had to piece my life back together from all of this and I had no clue where to start. Rock bottom was cold and lonely, and I wasn't sure I'd survive.

–

I don't know how long I sat in the armchair in the living room, staring out towards the trees in the garden. The cup of tea I'd made myself when I got home was still full to the brim, but it was stone-cold. It gave me something to hold, but I couldn't stomach the thought of eating or drinking. My mind that'd been so noisy and overwhelming this morning was blank now. A dark hollow cave of nothingness, just like me.

My phone buzzed with another text message from one of my colleagues. No doubt I'd been the hot topic in the staffroom at lunchtime, and as word got round, they were texting to offer their support. I didn't want to message back. They didn't want me there, so why should I waste my energy?

I heard the front door open and then Mum and Dad's voices as they bustled into the kitchen, carrying what sounded like shopping bags.

"Harper, you're home early. Is everything all right, love?" Dad had seen me sitting in the living room as he walked past, and he backtracked to come in and talk to me.

I went to speak, but my throat constricted, and I couldn't stop the floodgate holding back my tears from opening up. How the hell was I supposed to tell them what a monumental fuck up I was, and that I couldn't even manage a session teaching six children in a reading group?

Mum must've heard the commotion because she

barrelled into the room next, and when she saw me crying, she started too.

"I knew it was too soon. They sent you home, didn't they?" She always did know what was going on before I could tell her, and if Brodie was here, he'd have filled in the extra gaps. I never did have any secrets in this house.

"They don't want me," I managed to splutter through the sobs. "I can't do it anymore." I meant that I couldn't keep holding it all together, but from the petrified look my mother gave me, she thought I was checking myself out for good.

"Harper, love. You need to see someone. I know you think you're coping, but you're not." Mum was clutching at straws to try and make me see things her way, and Dad was crouched down next to me, giving me a side hug as I tried to reciprocate but pulled away at the same time, wanting to right myself. "It will help to talk to someone about what happened. I know it was a shock after they told us about the aneurysm-"

I shut down, hearing that conversation start up again. I knew what I saw that night. I knew why my brother died. I didn't need to hear about the complications that'd happened afterwards. It was hard enough getting my head around the fact that he was gone, let alone hearing about brain aneurysms and all the other medical jargon they filled my parents' heads with at the hospital afterwards.

I sipped my disgustingly cold tea to give me something to do and then, when mum had got her little rant off her chest, I told her about the head teacher referring me to occupational health.

"That might be a good thing." She gave me a sad smile. "They have their own counsellors, don't they? If you don't want to see Meredith with me, maybe someone there could see you?"

I shrugged. If it'd help to relieve some of the stress for her, I'd play along.

"Maybe. I'll ask them."

She seemed happy enough with that answer and let it go. I was glad. I had absolutely no intention of arguing this point any further.

–

Later that night, I sat up on my bed, afraid to go to sleep in case I missed my night stalker, or even worse, fell into another Brodie dream, reliving his death over again. The sun had set hours ago, and now the shadows of the trees outside danced across the walls of my room like sinister dark strangers that were slowly becoming my only friends.

I had my window open and I focused on the rustle of the breeze as it blew through the trees. The simple sound helped to soothe the sting from the barbed-wired heart inside my chest that pierced me every time I took a breath. The chill of the air numbed my heavy, twisted lungs. These were aches I'd never be truly free from, I knew that, but zoning out helped to dull them somewhat.

"You'll never be alone. You were born with a best friend.

Even in the womb you had your other half, always there, always looking out for you."

My grandma's voice echoed in my ears.

"Do you remember the time Brodie cut your hair so you'd look just like him?"

I heard her laughter reverberating through my mind and immediately an image of my mum, looking totally horrified, sprang forth. And there stood a five-year-old Brodie, grinning from ear-to-ear with the kitchen scissors in his hand.

"Harper looks just like me now. We're proper identical twins."

He'd laughed, Mum had screamed, and Dad tried to calm everyone down and assure Mum my beautiful blonde hair would grow back eventually.

Suddenly, I jolted awake, feeling my neck crick as a result of falling asleep in such an awkward position. All too soon, the surge of pain overwhelmed me again and I stood, walking over to the window.

And there he was.

Skulking in the shadows, hiding in the dark with all the other fucked-up creatures that only came out at night. Vermin, that's what he was.

The grief I felt in my zombie-waking state turned to fury. I spun around, flinging my door open and barrelling down the stairs.

He didn't get to come here and lurk in the night, scaring us and making us feel like prisoners in our home. He had no right to walk into our garden, intimidate us, and flaunt the fact that he was still alive, still breathing air into his traitorous body. He didn't deserve any recognition, any acknowledgement, and I wanted him gone. He'd taken my brother's life, wrecked mine, and now I was spiralling out of control. On a fairground ride that I couldn't get off, and he was driving. Forcing me to the brink of insanity.

When I got to the back door, I ripped it open, making the handle bang off the wall, but I didn't give a damn. I just stalked outside, ready to face whatever hell he wanted to unleash.

"I know you're out there," I bellowed into the darkness. "You don't get to win this time."

I didn't care what happened to me. I wasn't thinking straight. All I wanted to do was face him. Stand in front of him and tell him how much I hated him. No, despised him. Hate wasn't a strong enough emotion for what I felt when it came to Brandon Mathers. I wanted to pound my fists into *his* face this time. Make him hurt as much as I did.

"Come out and face me, you murderer. Come out from your hiding place, like the scum you are."

I stood in the middle of the garden shouting down to where I'd seen him before, but he wasn't there. Like always, he'd run away.

"You can run, but you can't hide. I'll find you."

As I walked towards the edge of the garden where the trees were, the ground underneath my feet went from soft dewy grass to hard stones and dirt. I didn't care. The pain beneath my feet was nothing compared to the pain in my body and my mind.

"I saw you. Where are you?" I shouted, pushing the leaves of the fir trees to the side. I dropped to my knees, scrambling around on the floor to find something, anything that'd give me a clue to where he was.

"Harper, what on earth is going on?"

I heard my parents behind me, but I stayed where I was, dragging my fingers through the dirt and trying to focus through my tears.

"He was here," I said without turning around.

"Who was here, love?" Dad crouched down to where I was, trying to pull my hands away from the soil, but I shook my head. I wouldn't be deterred that easily.

"He was here. I saw him. He watches me."

"Oh, God. She's lost it, Andy," I heard my mum say. "We need to call the doctor."

"No doctors, Tanya. We'll deal with this ourselves," my dad snapped back. "Come back inside, Harper. There's no one here. If it makes you feel better, I'll go over every inch of this garden, but there's no one here now. You're only hurting yourself out here. Please, just come inside."

My dad put his arms around me and scooped me up like I was still a child. I had mud under my fingernails, and I couldn't stop shaking. But I knew what I'd seen. I wasn't going insane.

TORTURED SOULS

He was watching me.

He wanted to break me.

Trouble was, I was already broken.

CHAPTER

BRANDON

I hated them for what they'd done to me. I had no one I could call on. No one was on my side. Like a piece of trash, they'd thrown me away. It was easier for them to forget I ever existed. Why would anyone want a fuck-up like me in their lives?

But I watched them.

I watched how they went about their lives with fucking smiles on their faces. Not a care in the world.

Emily was living with Ryan's family, and the pair of them made me sick. Their little displays of affection whenever they went out made my stomach turn. It didn't matter to them that they'd royally screwed me over to get what they wanted. I'd put everything on the line for them, and how had they repaid me? By making me look like a fucking fool, shitting all over my feelings and turning their back on me.

Had I really told my best mate's girlfriend that I loved her?

Because at the moment, I could barely stand to look at

either one of them.

I wasn't done with them yet, though. I wanted to make them pay. My best friend and the girl I thought I loved needed to know what they'd done. Their happiness came at a price I wasn't willing to pay.

As for Zak and Finn, they were happy enough to wipe out my existence as well. Go about their business and start the parties up again. I'd have expected more from them, especially Finn. I'd always gone out of my way to help him, nurture him, build him up in a way no one had ever done for me when I was at rock bottom. I suppose Jensen fucking Lockwood had been right. I was born in shit and I'd die in shit. I certainly had the shittiest friends of the lot. And now, every night, when I laid down in my piss-stained sleeping bag in the squat, I pictured each one of them in my mind and gave myself comfort thinking of all the fucked up ways I was going to have my revenge.

My time would come.

I wasn't going to fade into obscurity to suit their agenda.

I had a plan.

Multiple plans, in fact.

The Lockwoods wouldn't escape my wrath either. They probably thought they'd beaten the pride out of me years ago, but they hadn't. I was only getting started when it came to their fucked-up crew. But the one thing that ate away at me the most was Brodie and Harper Yates.

I lost everything because of them. My childhood, my

friends, my stake in the parties, and my fighting. I was a living ghost, surviving in the shadows. I couldn't go home, couldn't make anything right whilst she was there, haunting my dreams and taunting me every hour of every day.

I wanted to make her suffer.

I wanted her to lose everything like I had.

Her brother wasn't the innocent man she made him out to be. He'd come at me in that fight, ready to take me out. I took him first. That was the deal. Now? She was going around town painting me as some kind of villain. A devil not worthy of anyone's time. Saint Brodie was being immortalised, and for what? For being a bully? An abuser? A fighter with no morals and no credibility? Because that's what he was. He was the scum, not me. He deserved everything he had coming to him that night.

Do I sound like a fucking psycho?

Probably, but that's because I am.

I'm pissed at the world. Pissed at my friends. Hell, I'm pissed at the whole fucking town of Sandland. But most of all, I'm pissed at Harper Yates for whitewashing what was a fucking set-up.

I was set up.

I was framed for a murder I didn't commit.

I wanted to make her pay, and so I watched her. I hid in the shadows and used the darkness as my friend. I wanted to see her suffer. Make her feel like she was losing her mind just like I was. I had plans for her, and I was biding my time.

Waiting for the moment I could strike and finally break her.

But it turns out, fate was a cruel motherfucker.

Who would've thought it?

Harper Yates was even more fucking broken than I was.

CHAPTER Five

HARPER

I thought I'd hit rock bottom when Brodie died. I thought the funeral and everything that came after it was the bottom of the fucking barrel. I was wrong. Turns out, rock bottom has a basement, and that's where I was, lying on the cold, hard floor with no way out.

After my epic meltdown in the garden, my dad had brought me inside, and I spent the night in their bed with Mum, whilst Dad slept in the spare room; close enough that he could hear us and come in if we needed him, but far enough away to give us the space we needed.

I was a fucking mess. Even I could admit to that.

Was I seeing things?

Had he been there watching me at the bottom of the garden?

Or was my mind so focused on revenge it'd sent me spiralling into some fucked-up alternate universe where I didn't know which way was up and which was down?

I didn't know.

I didn't have any of the answers.

But I knew I couldn't go on like this. Hell's basement was lonely and played tricks on your mind. I'd had enough of those games to last me a lifetime.

"Harper, love, we need to talk to you about some things, but we need you to stay calm, okay? It's important that you listen and take this all in. I know you'll want to react, we all do, but we don't want you hearing this from anyone else but us." My dad was back to being his cryptic self at breakfast.

I stared at him blankly over the breakfast table, nibbling on my toast but struggling to swallow. My eyes were puffy and sore from lack of sleep. I had managed to get some rest lying next to Mum as she tried not to let on that she was crying. I didn't get a lot though. The nights were always the worst. Even the good dreams about Brodie made waking up that much more unbearable. Like a cruel reminder of what I no longer had dangled in front of my eyes and then ripped out of my grasp when I awoke. Awake, asleep, it didn't matter; life pretty much sucked ass and then some.

"I'm not made of glass. You can tell me." I glanced between them. Mum was biting her lip and looked rougher than I did, like she was continually balancing on the edge of an emotional cliff, ready to dive off. And Dad? He was right behind her, ready to jump in after.

"We're trying to hold it together as best we can," she said, taking steady breaths to help her get through what she wanted to say without breaking down. "We lost your brother, and that is the single most painful thing we've ever been through... well, are going through, in our lives. But we still have you, Harper. We need to stay strong for you. We can't lose you as well." Her voice broke and she came to sit next to me at the table, reaching over to take my hand in hers.

I knew what she was saying. They thought I was breaking. That I'd end up following Brodie and leaving them both childless, but I was stronger than that. How can you be a loser when you never quit? I would never quit.

"I'm not going anywhere, Mum. I might be struggling to get through, but I'm not down for the count." They both paled at my use of the boxing term. "I just need time. Everything is tough at the moment. I just have to ride it out, I suppose."

Dad tensed up, dropped his head forward and then stared at his hands in a daze as he spoke. "It might get a bit tougher before we find ourselves firmly set onto that road to recovery." Another deep breath. "The police rang us yesterday. We didn't want to tell you after what'd happened at school. We didn't think you could take anymore. But if we don't tell you, someone else might, and we need you to hear this from us."

I braced myself and waited for him to continue.

"They've taken all the statements they need, seen all the mobile phone footage from that night, and they've decided to drop the charges."

I gasped, feeling like the walls I'd built around myself for safe-keeping were crumbling away with his words, creating irreparable damage faster than any wrecking ball.

"They said all the evidence points towards accidental death. He took the hit, he moved away, stumbled on the uneven ground and fell. The fall damaged his skull and... Well, we know the rest. We lived it. The aneurysm must've given Brodie blinding headaches for months, but he never told any of us. Throw that into the mix and it just fortifies the case for the defence. His balance was off. He tripped."

"It's bullshit. If Brodie had an aneurysm, I'd have known about it. I'd have felt it." I could feel the rage bubbling up inside of me. I didn't care. I didn't want to keep that shit down. "I saw what happened. He didn't trip. He was murdered." It didn't matter what anyone else's mobile phone footage showed, the film reel in my head was as clear as day. He went down because of that punch.

"We can't prove that. *They* can't prove that. Harper, I know you want justice for Brodie, but he wouldn't want this." Dad looked over at Mum as he spoke. "I think as a family we need to face up to the fact that he stepped into that ring, he agreed to the fight, and now we have to deal with the consequences of his actions."

"We face the consequences, but his murderer gets off scot-free? What kind of fucking consequences is he facing, huh?"

I couldn't believe what I was hearing. Every day there were hurdles appearing in front of us, like potholes in a retro platform computer game ready to trick us and call game over.

It was a fucking joke. We didn't stand a chance. All the odds were stacked against us.

"He's probably suffering in his own hell," Dad said. "I'm damned if I know. I hope he is. The police still have no clue as to his whereabouts, and I hope he never shows his face in Sandland again. But we need to accept there won't be a trial. There'll be no one we can pin our grief and anger onto. Not publicly, anyway."

I slammed my fist down on the table, making my parents jump at my outburst. I couldn't believe Dad was giving up so easily. Where was the hunger to fight back? Brodie was a fighter, and so was I. So, why were my parents lying down and taking this?

"There is someone to blame and he needs to answer for what he's done. He can't get away with it."

"Harper." Mum squeezed my hand to get me to look at her. "It's not healthy to think like that. You have to let this go, or at least try, for all our sakes. It'll be hard for me and your dad too, but as a family, we have to. For our sanity."

I shook my head vehemently.

"No. No, I won't. I can't, Mum. I can't just get on with my life and pretend that fight never happened. Pretend Brodie wasn't killed at the hands of someone else."

Mum glanced across at Dad and he ran his hands over his face in exasperation.

"We aren't saying to forget," he said quietly. "We know it's harder for you. You were there. You saw it all. We can't begin to imagine how awful that was for you. But if you keep that anger inside, then ultimately, it'll destroy you. I won't let that happen."

"I wasn't the only one there. What about Jensen, Chase, and the others? Weren't their statements taken into account? They saw it exactly the same as I did."

The Lockwoods held a lot of power, even I knew that. Surely their word meant something in this case?

My parents looked at each other again, exchanging a strange glance that I couldn't read.

"They retracted their statements," my dad admitted, not able to look me in the eye.

"What? But that's insane. Why would they do that?"

This wasn't making any sense.

"We've got no idea. Maybe they felt differently afterwards. They could've felt under duress or had drunk too much to know what they were saying. We don't know. Their solicitor dealt with it, apparently. We couldn't get a straight answer out of Don Lockwood when we called him last night. Not that we expected to. He'd always put his family name before anything else."

I wasn't used to hearing my dad speak like that about someone he considered a friend. Don Lockwood, Jensen and Chase's dad, was an aloof, hard-faced man, but I'd never taken him for a coward. Dad was right though. The Lockwoods looked after their own, but before all this, that'd included Brodie.

What had happened to change that?

"I'm gonna go see Jensen. I need to hear him tell me exactly why he's protecting that piece of shit. Why he's not standing up for his best friend when he needs him the most. Brodie would never have done this if the tables were turned. He always stood by his friends."

I went to stand up, but my mum grabbed my arm, making me stop and sink back down into my chair.

"I don't think you should be going out today, Harper. Not after everything. You're vulnerable."

I gave a low laugh and then looked at my dad for back up. I didn't find it. He was as stubborn about all this as she was.

"Your mum's right. You need to stay here and focus on your well-being."

"I'm not about to do a Britney; shave my head and start attacking people, Dad. If I want to go out, I will."

I wasn't being totally truthful. If a Britney-style meltdown were required, I'd probably have done it, just to get my voice heard. I wasn't ruling anything out at this point.

"Fine. We won't lock you in your room. Not yet, anyway." He gave me a smile to try and show he was being jovial, but I didn't return it. I didn't doubt for a second that padlocks and chains would come into play if they had to. I'd still fight it, though. Bring it on. I'd lost my twin, my other half. I felt manic and unstable, and somebody needed to pay. Right then, anything was possible, and I was starting to realise that in this quest for justice, I was on my own.

–

Thirty minutes later, and I was banging my fist like a mad woman on the black, highly polished double front doors of the Lockwood house, blowing blonde wisps of hair out of my face and hoping I didn't look as savage as I felt. I say house, but this place was a bloody mansion. The upkeep for the topiary in the front garden alone probably cost more than most people made in a month. We weren't poor, but the Lockwoods were real money; old money.

I prayed it'd be Jensen or Chase that opened up. I didn't mind their mum, Karen, either. She'd always been nice to me whenever I'd seen her. But I didn't like Don. I felt on edge whenever he was around. Like he'd stab you in the back then shake your hand and ask you to thank him for the privilege. You couldn't even call him a wolf in sheep's clothing. He didn't hide his disdain for other people and the world around him. He wore his wolf status with pride.

He'd also been the first to back away from Emily's dad, Alec Winters, our local M.P., when all the shit came out about his dodgy dealings and what'd happened with his son. We didn't know the Winters family all that well, but they knew the Lockwoods, and before Mr Winters had been arrested and charged with fraud and manslaughter, they'd been so far up each other's asses you didn't know where Don Lockwood started and Alec Winters ended. I guess the saying was right;

fake friends are like shadows, always there on your brightest days, but nowhere to be seen in your darkest hours. Not that I condoned what Winters did. But it didn't take a genius to guess that Don Lockwood probably knew a lot of what was going on, and he'd been happy enough to turn a blind eye for all those years. Corruption breeds corruption, after all.

I lifted my hand up to knock again, then let out a grateful sigh when Jensen opened the door. He didn't look pleased to see me, but he soon painted on a fake smile to hide it.

"Harper, hey. How you doing?" He didn't stand back to let me in. His greeting wasn't that welcoming.

"What the hell is going on, Jensen? Why did you retract your statement?"

He glanced behind him, making sure no one else in his house had heard me rant, then he stepped onto the porch area and closed the door behind him. He tried to put his hand on my elbow and escort me down the steps to leave, but I shrugged him off and stood my ground.

"I want to know. What. The fuck. Is going on?"

He blew out a slow breath and leant against one of the sandstone pillars, crossing his arms over his chest and looking anywhere but at me. People were making a habit of that. Acting like I wasn't there or talking to me like I was an inconvenience. I was sure if there was a block Harper app he could download, he'd have done it.

"It's complicated, Harper. We had to think about what was best for us, for the family." My eyes bugged out of my head as he said that. I huffed and his voice went lower. "I've gotta think about my career, my future. Dad didn't want a court-case dragging the family name through the mud."

He was un-fucking-believable.

"So, it's okay to stab your best friend in the back. Your *dead* best friend. You know, the one who was murdered in front of you. Doesn't that mean anything to you?"

"Of course it does," he hissed, and then gave another nervous glance at the door as if he expected to find his dad standing there glaring back at him. "But this goes higher than just us. It's a Pandora's box we don't wanna open. We can't. You need to drop it."

"Drop it? This is Brodie we're talking about. The guy who saved your ass on more than one occasion. You'd be in court yourself if he hadn't covered for you when you first started fighting. Remember that?" I sure did, and I was more than happy to hold that little nugget over his head.

"I'll never fucking forget it. But you need to. I mean it, Harper. Give it up."

"And what about Chase? Is he following your lead like a fucking sheep too?" His eyes took on a more lethal, venomous edge when I mentioned his brother. At least we agreed on one thing; we'd protect our sibling no matter what.

"We both saw the same thing," he said through gritted teeth. "Brodie tripped and fell. It's the same story everyone's given. The videos back it up too." He shrugged like he hadn't just driven a massive knife through my chest with his words.

"Mobile phones don't show shit. You were there. You know he hit him. He knocked him backwards and Brodie died."

"Look, I know you want Mathers to pay. We all do. And he will. But we'll do it our way. No police. No courts. Our way."

It was always a control thing with Jensen. He liked to think he controlled Brodie, and now he was trying to do the same with me. But I wasn't going to be dictated to by anyone.

"I don't think I like your way of doing things. Forgive me, but why should I trust you?" I cocked my head to the side, giving him my most penetrating stare so he'd know that I meant business. "It didn't take you long to stab my brother in the back. If Brodie were here now, he'd kick your ass."

"Yeah, he probably would. Wouldn't change anything though. As far as the police are concerned, we saw nothing." He bent down and said the last part right into my face like it was a fucking threat, spraying me with a mist of spit as he did. He made me sick. I leant away, sneering at him in disgust.

"I hope that bus you threw us under swerves right back around and hits your ass. I will get revenge, but not because you've decided when and where it happens. I don't do things on your terms." He laughed at me, but it only spurred me on further. "Watch your back, Jensen. I hope you sleep well at night knowing what a low-life, back-stabbing cunt you are."

"Oh, I sleep just fine, sweetheart. And I'd be careful who you're firing your threats to. I don't take kindly to intimidation."

"Unless it's your father, then you get intimidated real fast."

He grabbed my arm then and dragged me down the steps and along his driveway. I followed, but only because he was stronger than me, so I had no choice.

"You need to leave. Don't come here again. I mean it." His jaw was clenched, but seeing the hurt and anger in my eyes, he softened a little. "If you need anything, anything at all, we'll help you. But you need to stay away. Don't ask questions. Trust me. You won't like the fucking answers."

I was done. I couldn't stand another minute of listening to his bullshit excuses. I'd never trusted Jensen, but Brodie did, and I'd assumed he'd always have his back. How wrong was I? When push came to shove, we could only rely on ourselves to get the job done... Or our twin, if we were lucky enough to have one.

CHAPTER

HARPER

I got into my car and drove away, so focused on my rage that I didn't have the first clue where I was going, not until I pulled onto the forecourt of Hardy and Son's garage. I wanted answers, and I knew they were hiding something, or rather someone.

I parked and got out of my car. There was a guy I didn't recognise working under a bonnet, but I couldn't see anyone else outside. He gave me a backwards glance and then carried on with his job. Probably expected me to go straight into the office. What he didn't expect was for me to march into his workshop and grab the nearest tool I could find. I didn't expect it either, but it was happening.

I picked up the wrench as he started to call after me.

"Excuse me, miss. You can't just come in here and take that. That's our property. Miss-"

I walked right over to the white van parked out front and lifted the wrench high into the air before crashing it down onto the windscreen. Seeing the glass crack and shatter was surprisingly satisfying. I lifted it up again, smashing down hard on the glass and feeling some of the tension from earlier trickle out of me as I pounded out my aggression. Maybe Britney had it right all along. This certainly felt better than sitting around twiddling my thumbs and waiting for karma to do its shit for me.

I didn't feel anything other than overwhelming, all-consuming rage. Pound after pound I could sense the anger mutating; changing into something I could control and channel. Maybe I was more like my boxer brother than I realised. Violence felt good.

But then, all too soon, it was over. I was being lifted into the air from behind and voices were shouting all around me. I saw an older man, probably Mr Hardy, grabbing fistfuls of his hair and pointing to the van, saying, "Mr. Gale is coming to collect his van at five. What the hell am I supposed to do now? I can't let him see that."

The mechanic that I'd seen when I'd arrived was covering his mouth and looking between me and the rest of them who'd spilled out onto the forecourt after hearing my outburst. I spotted Emily Winters walking towards me with fake concern in her eyes. She was speaking softly, but I couldn't make out what she was saying over the ringing in my ears. Then Ryan's voice boomed loud like a fucking tannoy, obliterating my anger-induced haze and yanking me into the present. He'd been the one to pull me away, and he was holding me, trying to shake my hand and get me to drop the wrench.

"Put it down. For fuck's sake, Harper. Put the fucking wrench down."

From the fear in his voice, I guessed he thought I was going to hurt Emily, so I dropped it. As soon as I did, he let me go and reached down to get it, sliding it across the ground as far away from me as he could.

"What the hell is all this? Ryan? Can you tell me what's going on?" The older guy was still tugging at his hair, looking like a broken windscreen was the worst fucking thing to ever happen in his life. Lucky him.

"Dad, this is Harper Yates," Ryan said, and his dad's face fell in recognition. "Don't worry about the damage, Dad. It's just the glass. The bodywork is fine. Kieron can fix it and I'll pay for it out of my wages." He turned to face the other guy that was still gawping at me. "Kieron, mate. Can you fit a new windscreen before five? I'll pay you extra?"

Kieron nodded like it was nothing and headed back to the workshop.

"I'll pay for the damage," I said, suddenly finding my voice. "I thought it was *your* van." I glared at Ryan as he put his arm around Emily.

"We don't want your money," Ryan spat, and then he went to walk away, but Emily stopped him.

"Harper, will you come inside and talk to us? Just for a minute. I can make you a coffee and you can tell us why you came here today."

What the fuck did she care? Her dad was about to go down for a stretch, and her mum was the biggest fuck up in Sandland. Well, she was until I started vying for that role.

Why were my problems so important to her?

Did she get off on playing the role of the saint?

Probably.

My shit probably helped her to forget about her own.

"She didn't come here to talk, Em. She came here to cause trouble." Ryan eyeballed me like I was the enemy.

"As if I'd get any answers out of you, anyway. You're all as bad as each other."

"How do you know if you don't at least try? Ask us the questions and we'll try to answer. After the last few months, we're all about honesty." Emily looked at Ryan then back at me. "At least let us try to help. We could all use a friend sometimes."

"You're not my friend and you never will be." I stood there as Emily, Ryan, and his dad stared blankly back at me.

We could all use a friend?

Her words rang in my ears and the heat of tears welled up in my eyes.

Friends.

I didn't have any. Not really. Sally had been a friend, but after dating Brodie and going through a messy break-up, she hadn't spoken to me. Not for ages. She didn't even reach out when he died or come to his funeral. Brodie's friends had been my friends. And now? They'd closed ranks. Gone into hiding and turned their backs on me.

In that moment, I realised I had no one. No one I could talk to about any of this. I couldn't tell my mum and dad about the nightmares that plagued me. They had their own grief to contend with. I couldn't tell anyone about my secret stalker, and if I did, they probably wouldn't believe me anyway. I'd driven here for a reason, and these people owed me. I needed answers and I needed to offload.

"Fine," I snapped. "But don't think this changes anything."

I picked my way over the broken glass on the floor and followed Emily and Ryan inside. Mr Hardy stayed where he was and gave me a sympathetic smile. I couldn't look at him though, because despite my unbridled anger, I also felt shame. Shame for the way I'd behaved on his property. That wasn't me. I didn't hurt people, and I didn't cause trouble. What the hell was happening to me?

The Hardy's house was next door to the garage, and Emily led us into the kitchen and clicked the kettle on. I sat down at the small wooden table in the middle and fiddled with my fingernails, while Ryan leant up against the kitchen counter next to Emily. His arms were folded over his broad chest and his muscles were tensed like he was getting ready to defend her. I didn't know what to say. Should I apologise? I didn't want to. If Mr Hardy was in front of me, I might have done, but I didn't want to use the word sorry to Emily or Ryan, because I didn't feel it. If anything, they should have been apologising to me.

Emily put a black coffee in front of me then placed a sugar bowl and some milk on the table. Ryan watched her every move, and when she sat down next to me, he joined us.

"Let's just get straight to the point. You have a problem with Ryan. Me too, I suppose. I don't know why. We weren't there that night, when..." She sighed and looked guilty. "Anyway, we don't know where Brandon is. We've tried looking for him. We've looked everywhere, but he's gone. If we knew where he was, we'd tell you."

"I don't believe you," I snapped. I'd heard this all before. I didn't come here for the rerun.

"Why would we lie?" she answered, and it was on the tip of my tongue to reel off a million and one reasons. I went with the obvious.

"Because you're his friends. Cheaters help other cheaters. You covered for him that night and you're still covering for him now."

"No, we're not. We didn't even know he had a fight that night. He hadn't told any of us." She glanced at Ryan before she said the next part. "We had a falling out and Brandon went off on one. If any of us had known he was heading to the barn to fight in the headspace he was in, we'd have done everything we could to try and talk him out of it, but we didn't know."

She'd just handed me the single biggest piece of evidence to show Mathers was guilty without even knowing what she'd done.

"What do you mean, headspace? What happened?"

Her eyes bulged slightly as I leant forward, waiting to see how she'd worm her way out of this one.

"He was angry, hurt, and probably wanted to lash out."

Then Ryan butted in to defend his friend.

"He wouldn't have gone into that fight with the intention of killing anyone. He isn't like that. He might be a shady fucker sometimes, but he's not a murderer."

Like he'd say anything different to me.

"How would you know?" I could feel the spite and anger rising to the surface again. I knew coming in here would be pointless.

"Because I know him better than anyone else. We've been friends since we were four years old. I know exactly what he's capable of, and whatever's been said about him, its bullshit."

He needed to take off his rose-tinted glasses. The Brandon Mathers he knew was a million miles away from the one I saw that night.

"I was there, remember? I know what I saw. People lie, but eyes don't. Mine saw the truth."

"Grief can do things to us," Emily chipped in, like she'd read my mind and was trying to argue that my sense of reason and truth had been distorted.

"Are you calling me a liar?"

"No. Not at all," she bit back sharply. "But your

adrenaline would've been through the roof that night. I've watched Brandon fight, and even I lose all sense of reality. I can't even begin to imagine what it'd be like to watch a loved one up there."

"You're right. You can't imagine, so please don't try. You're just embarrassing yourself." I went to stand, but Emily's desperate tone stopped me.

"We aren't going anywhere fast. Please, Harper, just listen. If we find out anything, we will tell you. You will be the first to know. You can trust us."

Could I? Could I really trust her to put my feelings, a complete stranger, above those of her boyfriend's best friend? I doubted it. That was why I kept my little night-stalker bombshell to myself. I figured if I told anyone, they'd commit me for sure.

"Trust." I laughed. "I can't trust anyone. Even Jensen has retracted his statement."

They both gasped in shock. I stopped myself and took a breath, surprised they were only just finding this out.

"You're fucking kidding," Ryan said. "He retracted his statement? Why? What the hell is that fucker up to?"

"He said it wasn't in the best interest of his family to pursue the case. Said he didn't want the family name being dragged through the courts."

They both exchanged a knowing glance and Ryan rolled his eyes.

"You mean his dad didn't want that. Bloody hell. I knew

he was a bastard, but I didn't realise he'd shaft his best mate like that. Sorry, Harper. No offense." Ryan dropped his gaze into his lap in embarrassment at his outburst. I hadn't taken him for the shy type.

"None taken. What do you know about the Lockwoods?" My own intel was limited to what Brodie had told me. I'd never really been in their circle at school. My friendship with them came later, when we were old enough to forge our own social lives. Mine had been an extension of Brodie's. I had no idea what had gone on before then, but I knew they were held in high esteem by everyone in Sandland. Not as high as the Renaissance men were now, but high enough.

"I know they aren't to be trusted." Ryan turned to Emily. "I bet if we looked deeper into their shit, we'd find more than we bargained for. Maybe we should start digging. See what corpses they've got hidden under their patio." His eyes snapped back to me. "Jesus. I'm sorry."

"Again, no need to apologise. I can handle you using the word corpse. What I can't handle is my brother's death being used as some sort of cover-up."

Emily reached across the table to take my hand in hers. I didn't like the contact, but I gritted my teeth and accepted it.

"No one could handle that," she said with a sad recognition in her eyes. "I know better than anyone how much that hurts. Like I said before, you'll get honesty here. It's how we work."

"Yeah, I know. I heard about what happened with your dad at the community centre. Sorry about that."

Emily turned to Ryan and sighed. He reached over and gave her hand a squeeze, taking her attention away from me, thank God.

I hadn't been at the community centre when her dad had faced his trial by public humiliation. But there were enough people there who had been, and the footage was all over the internet for everyone to see. Guys dressed all in black, hiding their faces with bandanas and hoodies, had kept her parents prisoners on the stage whilst a premade video played out to the audience, telling them all that Alec Winters, Emily's dad, had been laundering money through businesses in Sandland for some pretty shady people. They also exposed his part in his son's death.

Apparently, he'd picked his son up after having a few too many whiskeys and then crashed the car. His son died right there in the passenger seat, and Mr Man-of-the-people had used an accomplice to move Emily's brother's body into the driver's side and left him there. His own son, and he'd deserted him when he needed him the most in favour of his political career. A career based on lies, seeing as he also had a long-term mistress and a daughter hidden away in the capital. I suppose, when you really thought about it, Emily's life was as much of a train wreck as mine.

"We've all got our ghosts to contend with. Some of us more than others," Emily said, breaking through my reverie.

"Ghosts. I'm seeing a lot of those recently." I clamped my mouth shut. I needed to get out of there before Emily's soothing voice and sympathy had me spilling all of my secrets.

Emily stood up and went over to her handbag that was lying on the kitchen counter behind us.

"I think we're more alike than you care to admit. I didn't like talking to people about my brother, Danny, when he died. I didn't see the point. It wouldn't bring him back. But for some reason, I kept these. They weren't much use to me, but they might help you."

She handed me a bunch of leaflets. I thumbed through them, seeing grief counselling, ways to deal with the loss of a loved one, and other titles that all blended into one. She continued making her point as I flicked through them.

"I never could stomach seeing a counsellor, but I did try some of the online forums and chats. If you prefer chatting online as opposed to face-to-face, it might help." She reached forward and pulled a leaflet up from the pile to show me. "This one has a chatroom for teens and young adults that have lost a sibling. It's probably the best of the lot. I used to spend quite a few nights letting off steam in there. The guys in that chat, they get it. They don't judge, and they sometimes say stuff that'll help. It's no miracle cure, but it's a chance to have a voice, to be heard. I think you need that, Harper. You need to be heard."

I sat, dazed, turning the leaflets over and over in my

hand.

"I'll give it a try," I said, looking up at her.

I stood up and walked back towards the door. Then I stopped and turned to face them both.

"I'll pay for the damage. I shouldn't have done that." It wasn't a sorry, but it was a start.

"Kieron's probably already fixed it by now. Don't sweat it," Ryan said, opening the door for me to leave.

"Harper," Emily called out, making me stop on the path and turn to face her. "We're here for you. Anytime you need to talk, just come over. Even if you want to ramble a load of nonsense, we'll listen." Then she lurched forward and grabbed me in a hug. I took it, but I didn't return the sentiment, just left my arms hanging limply at my side as she clung to me.

"Anything," she reiterated as I pulled away.

I nodded absent-mindedly and then wandered back over to my car. I was a walking zombie in an apocalyptic post-Brodie world, where Renaissance men and their girlfriends hugged me and offered me tea and sympathy, and people I thought were life-long friends treated me like complete and utter shit.

CHAPTER Seven

BRANDON

I had one foot in the mortuary and one still stuck in the fucked-up place I used to call home.

Sandland.

Half the population lived hand-to-mouth, while the other would cut your hand off if it meant they could buy another car to go with the ones that sat gathering dust on their massive driveways. The class divide had never been so wide. But I was a class all of my own.

No family, apart from my nan. I pushed envelopes full of money through her door most weeks; whatever was left over from the cash-in-hand jobs I did on the building sites I walked every morning.

No home, unless you counted the derelict high-rise covered in shit, piss, and graffiti that'd made Finn, Sandland's own Banksy, have sleepless nights. A cold hard floor and a sleeping bag were my home now. Even the rats didn't show up anymore, preferring a better class of shithole than the one I lived in. But it kept me hidden, and I didn't get soaked in the rain. Well, not much, as long as I stayed away from the broken windows when it really poured down.

As for my friends? I'd thought I was a rich man a few months ago. A man who has friends he can count on, that he can trust with his life, is a rich man indeed. Turned out I was as piss poor in that respect as I was financially. And that was why I spent most days watching them, trying to see if there was a hint of remorse from either one of them. Those days, when there was no work at the building sites, I usually camped out in Sandland. Chose one of them to watch as they went on their merry way, enjoying their shitty little lives without me.

Not her though.

I saved my visits to her for the night-time. I liked knowing she was in her house, thinking she was safe, but she wasn't. None of them would ever be safe again. Not if I had my way.

I sat with my hoody down low over my face as I swigged on a can of cheap, knock-off Coke and sat on the wall a few feet down from Ryan's garage. They never noticed me. I'd sat here a few times, sometimes for hours, watching them working, laughing, joking about like they didn't have a fucking care in the world. They didn't though, did they? They didn't have the law coming after them, ready to send them down for a crime they didn't commit.

Bare-knuckle boxing wasn't illegal in our country, so why the fuck was there a warrant out for my arrest? The last time I'd spoken to Pat Murphy, the guy who'd organised the fight, he'd told me to lay low. Told me it wasn't worth showing my face around Sandland. That'd been weeks ago, and I was still hiding like the freak she was painting me out to be. Enough was enough. Shit had to start changing real soon, and I was going to change it.

I watched as a car pulled onto the forecourt and then she got out, her blonde hair whipping in the wind as she stomped over to the workshop where Kieron was.

What the fuck was she doing there?

I leant forward as she took something off the workbench then marched over to a van parked in front of the office and started banging the shit out of the windscreen.

This chick was crazy.

Fucking nuts.

I couldn't stop myself from laughing at her. What the fuck was she doing, kicking off at the Hardys like that? I thought *I* was mental, but she definitely had a screw loose. Face of an angel and temperament of a psychotic bitch. I had to admit, deep down, it turned me on. In a fucked up, I'd never go there, she's completely insane, kind of way. But still, it did something to me. The girl had balls. I liked girls with balls.

She lifted her arm up to hit it again, and like a crap reality T.V. show, I couldn't bring myself to switch off or look away. This shit was too entertaining.

Then Ryan, Emily, and Ryan's dad, Sean, charged out of

the office. Ryan grabbed her round the waist and moved her away from the van, shaking her hand until she dropped the tool she was holding. Sean looked mortified, grabbing his hair and shouting, but I couldn't make out what he was saying. I could guess, but I was just that bit farther away to hear it. I liked Sean; he'd always been good to me. Treated me like his fourth son, and he'd always done everything he could to help me and my nan out. So, seeing him get shit on by the likes of Harper Yates didn't sit well with me. Sure, I'd laughed at first, but she'd crossed a fucking line giving Sean grief. This wasn't his battle to fight.

Harper had her back to me, but I could see her shoulders sag. Defeat was taking over. About fucking time too. And then I bristled with anger. What the hell were they doing taking her into their house? Was this some kind of sick joke?

I gritted my teeth and held myself back, when what I really wanted to do was go over there and tell them all what I thought about them. The girl had ruined my life, was bad-mouthing me all over Sandland, and they were inviting her in for tea and biscuits?

I always knew Ryan was a pussy for Emily, but Harper too? Was he looking to start his own harem for all the broken girls of Sandland?

I bit my nails and waited. Only my nails were non-existent, so I was just biting the skin around where my nails used to be. This feeling of being helpless, of watching and not being able to act, made me feel pointless, worthless even.

I decided there and then that I needed to pay Kian a little visit. Maybe Finn too. Out of all of them, they were the ones I trusted the most. Finn, because he got me. He always had, and he barely spoke anyway, so nobody would be quizzing him for what he knew. And Kian? Kian could hack into anything if you asked him. If I wanted anything sorting that was technical and I wanted to bypass our resident computer whizz Zak, Kian was the man. He would sort me out, no questions asked. I wouldn't tell the fucker anything though. He was a good kid, but he never knew when to keep his mouth shut.

About a half hour later, the door to Ryan's house opened and Harper came out, looking saner than she had when she went in. Emily called out to her and she turned around, then I watched as Emily hugged her. Fucking hugged the bitch that had ruined my life and destroyed everything. So, she smashes up a van on Sean's premises, tries to get me put away for life, and she gets a fucking hug? I make one mistake, and I'm out. No passing go, no collecting two hundred pounds. Just fuck off, Brandon. We want to forget you even existed.

No way.

I wasn't going to take this lying down. I would have my say. If she could fuck shit up for Sean, I'd fuck shit up for her.

Watch out, little Yates. I'm coming for you.

CHAPTER Eight

HARPER

"Oh my word. I can't believe it. What on Earth is happening to this lovely town?"

Mum looked up from her phone to give Dad a worried glare over the breakfast table.

"I think we need to move house, Andy. This place is going to the dogs."

"What happened?" Dad was picking over his eggs, but any fool could see he had zero appetite.

"Someone set fire to the Lockwood's cars last night. They think they were petrol bombed on the driveway while the family slept inside. They're lucky they didn't target the house too. Who would do that?"

I knew who.

Dumb move though. Everyone knew they had CCTV in every corner of that estate.

"Have they caught them?" Dad asked. "Don's security is pretty tight all over that place. I can imagine the police are on that today."

"Yeah," I huffed, rolling my eyes. "They'll chalk it down to high jinks and close the case. Hard policing isn't exactly the forte of the Sandland police."

Mum ignored my dig and shuffled over to sit next to Dad to show him the photos on her phone.

"Karen sent me these. Police have no clue who did it, although they have some suspicions. A dark figure spray-painted over the security cameras at the front of the house, and any cameras that weren't vandalised were offline. It's like they had a perfect window to do whatever the hell they wanted, whoever they are."

Criminal damage and tampering with technology? Sounded like the fallen saint of Sandland had weaselled his way back into the good graces of the Renaissance men. There were only two guys I knew of who could tap into systems like that, and they were both in that crew.

"I shouldn't say this," Dad said in a low voice, like the Lockwoods were in the next room. "But Don has enough enemies to fill Wembley Stadium. I think they'll have their work cut out for them sifting through that black hole."

Mum hummed in agreement then leant forward to look at me.

"Maybe you should reach out to Jensen and Chase? They haven't had an easy time of it lately. We need to stick together in these trying times. Plus, safety in numbers. I do worry about you being on your own sometimes, Harper. Sandland isn't like it was years ago. These gangs are-"

"You don't need to worry about me, Mum," I said, cutting her off. My own safety was the least of my worries. If someone wanted to come for me, I was ready.

"All the same," Mum added. "Those boys might not be going through the grief we are, but they are going through a lot."

I tried to look contrite and empathetic, but I wasn't. They'd had cars burnt. Cars that would probably be replaced today. A minor inconvenience for them. They had insurance. They also had people on the payroll who'd deal with that annoyance for them. They wouldn't be phoning companies or getting quotes, organising salvage and recovery. That was beneath them. So why should I feel sorry for them when all they'd done was fuck us over? They deserved a bit of payback. Unbeknown to my parents, they weren't grieving Brodie like we were. They'd moved on.

Suddenly, I felt tired of the scrutiny being thrown my way. Mum had sensed something wasn't right, and I wasn't ready to discuss it. I certainly wasn't prepared to tell them about my little visit to the Lockwoods yesterday, or my own crazy blow out at the Hardy's garage.

Shit.

I'd caused criminal damage, hadn't I? Did that mean the police would suspect me of burning those cars? I mean, I had an alibi. I was at home all night. But I also had a motive. A pretty fucking big one.

"I need some fresh air," I muttered, suddenly feeling

nervous. I grabbed a piece of toast from the rack so they wouldn't pester me to sit down and eat, then I wandered over to the patio.

When I opened the door and stepped out into the garden, the icy chill made me shiver. The dew on the grass was a blanket of glittering frost, and I was thankful I had my Converse on this time.

I made my way to the bottom of the garden, the grass crisp and crunching delicately under my feet. I pulled my hoody tighter around my middle and hugged myself, trying to find comfort in my body heat.

And then I froze.

In between two fir trees, right where *he* liked to stand, was a collection of white pebbles, arranged to spell out the letters RIP. Underneath was a single white rose laid there like some sick homage. The fact that it was a white rose, like the one I'd thrown down to rest on Brodie's casket, made me realise that he'd been there that day. He'd seen me. And he wanted me to know he had. This was another one of his sick and twisted games.

"You won't win," I said in a low, angry voice to nothing but the open air around me. "Play all the games you want, but you won't win with me. I'm not fucking scared of you. You're nothing, do you hear me? You. Are. Nothing."

I kicked the stones until no evidence of their message remained, then I picked up the rose and stalked back towards the house. I stomped up the steps and headed for the bin, shoving the rose into it and then stormed back inside. I was done playing his hide and seek twisted shit. If he wanted to come onto our property, he needed to be man enough to face me. No more skulking in the shadows. No more secret messages and stalking. We both wanted revenge. We were both fighters. But only one could win. And that would be me.

CHAPTER  Nine

BRANDON

I held my breath as she came out of the house, looking dazed and confused. No doubt she'd heard about my visit to the Lockwoods last night and it'd spooked her.

She knew I was coming for them and she was scared.

I liked her best when she was scared.

The way her skin paled and the brightness of her eyes. I wondered what it'd be like to have her close to me and feel that fear first-hand. The shivers and the way her skin would react to mine. The gasps that would feed into my own, and the taste of her... of her terror. I wanted to taste it. This girl was getting under my skin in so many ways I'd lost count. Like a needle feeding me the hardest drug. She was becoming an obsession. Crawling into my warped, broken soul to set up home there. I couldn't go a day without watching her, following her, knowing what she was doing. But it was getting worse. I needed more. Her anger and her grief mirrored my own. She fed into my demons and made them hungry for more.

I stayed hidden in amongst the trees as she came nearer, so near that I could hear her deep breaths. She pulled her hoody closer around her, but it didn't help. She shivered like a lost puppy and I couldn't look away. Watching her so vulnerable, knowing I could step out at any moment and do whatever the fuck I wanted made something stir within me. Something I'd never felt before. For the first time in years, I felt alive.

She made me feel alive.

When she saw my tribute laid out on the floor, she gasped. I smiled, waiting for the tears to flow, but they never came. My feisty little thing was a warrior. She wouldn't take my shit lying down, and I stood taller watching her, knowing she felt power from seeing what I'd done. I made her strong. I gave her strength.

But don't get too cocky, little one. I can take it away again too.

And then she spoke, and hearing her soft voice calling to me made every single hair on the back of my neck stand up. She looked and sounded like an angel, even though her words were anything but angelic.

"You won't win."

Maybe not, but I'll enjoy the fight.

"Play all the games you want, but you won't win with me. I'm not fucking scared of you."

And that's your first mistake, angel. You should be scared of me... Of what I can do. Even I'm scared of me.

"You're nothing, do you hear me? You. Are. Nothing."

Yeah. And people who are nothing have nothing to lose.

I watched her kick the stones and grab the rose. The way she huffed and flipped her hair made me smirk. Little Miss Feisty was playing right into my hands. I couldn't wait to toy with her some more.

I had all sorts of surprises up my sleeves.

And she was never going to see them coming.

CHAPTER Ten

HARPER

It was hard to know who I could trust. My inner circle consisted of my parents and me, and even they didn't know about half the stuff that had been going on. I think they thought I was going a little crazy. Okay, a lot crazy, after my night-time garden breakdown. I felt like I was carrying the weight of the world on my shoulders and then some. Staying quiet about my midnight stalker was making me die a little inside every single day.

I scrolled through my phone, wondering who I could reach out to, to offload and share some of the burden. I'd always had Brodie before. He was my go-to person if I needed help with my emotional overload. He took it all. But that support system wasn't there anymore. It certainly wasn't there with the Lockwoods. They were the last people I'd turn to.

Suddenly, I remembered the leaflets Emily had given me, and went to my bag to fish them out. Maybe a stranger was what I needed. Someone who would listen without prejudice and offer help and support without judgement. I didn't have to speak or tell anyone anything I didn't want to. Hell, I could just sit back and read their stories. Maybe that'd make me feel better, hearing that someone else was going through the same kind of bullshit I was.

I heard my mum close the front door, heading out to another one of her appointments with Doctor Meredith, so I took advantage of the quiet and headed to my room.

Once inside, I locked the door and powered up my laptop. I had no idea what these forums would be like, but I opened up the leaflet for the one Emily said she'd used and found the web address.

I typed it in and then scrolled down, reading about how they could provide support in a variety of ways, from one-on-one counselling with a professional, to peer help groups and online forums. They listed their charity ethos in five bullet points. They seemed to be a professional outfit.

Number one in their five-point plan stated that it was good to share your experiences. Peer support was one of their key successes when bringing people together. Hearing from and sharing with others about their loss. Where people who had gone through what you had could offer guidance on how they coped. I highly doubted anyone else on here had been stalked by their loved one's murderer, but I'd keep an open mind. I was willing to try anything at this point. My emotional well was overflowing, and I was crippled under the weight of it all.

Second, they wanted everyone to know their feelings were normal and valid. That it was part of the grieving process to be faced with a host of emotional and physical challenges. I guessed I wasn't the only one considering doing a Britney then. I certainly didn't recognise myself anymore. I don't think my colleagues at the school did either, but I was beyond caring about that. Maybe I'd get some tips on how to challenge my aggressive energy. Or maybe even a few revenge plans. Mathers would never see me coming when I finally hit him hard. I already felt reckless and unpredictable, and I hadn't even started.

Next, they highlighted that my bereavement wouldn't have a set time limit. I could have told them that already. There never would be a time limit on how devastated I was. I'd feel it every day of my life until I took my last breath. Brodie was a part of me, like a limb. His death wouldn't change that. Instead, I'd have to learn to live without said limb, and life would eventually take on a new normal. But my grief would never end. I was clear on that. The pain inside was a pain I'd have to endure forever.

Their fourth pledge was one of continued support. They promised they'd be there for everyone through every stage of their grief. That there would always be a safe space for anyone that needed it, whatever time of the day or however desperate they were. I liked that. A twenty-four-seven friend, a listening ear in the early hours. They'd probably regret that pledge once they'd heard what I had to say at three a.m.

Last, they explained that their charity was run by the members for the members. Any topic was up for discussion. There was no agenda. This was for us.

At the bottom was the membership sign up, and I hovered my mouse over it, still feeling apprehensive about taking that leap into the unknown. Then I thought, 'Fuck it. What do I have to lose? Not a lot at the moment.' And I clicked to join.

For the purpose of anonymity and to partake in the chat on the forums, I had to give a username. I wracked my brains for something that'd fit, looking around my room for inspiration. When I glanced up at the bookshelf above my desk, I had my lightbulb moment. I loved *Game of Thrones*, and what better character to base my name on than the one who represented my current state of body and mind.

Lady Stoneheart.

A shell of a woman who was vengeful and had no mind for the consequences of her actions or what it would mean for the future; she could only focus on the here and now, much like me. She was a character that could barely speak after a brutal attack and had to cover the wound in her throat to be heard. I might not have a wound people could see, but the pain was there, and it made it difficult for me to speak too. And like Lady Stoneheart, I would be relentless in my plight for revenge for my family. At least, that was the original plan, but now, I felt like my main plight was to survive to see another day. One thing was clear though, I wanted to show *him* what he'd done to me when he took away the most important person in my life. He needed to know about the pain he'd caused.

I typed in my handle *LadyStoneheart23* and clicked send on my profile. Instantly, a list of chatroom titles popped up, each one referring to a different type of bereavement. There was the lost my parents, lost my mum, lost my dad, lost a grandparent. They even had one for lost my pet. Then I found what I was looking for; lost a sibling. I clicked to enter, and the chat opened up.

LadyStoneheart23 has joined the chat

EmoGirl- I think the people who tolerate you on a daily basis are the real heroes, Fucking_Alan.

JoeNotExotic- I doubt he leaves his parent's basement very often. The only action he gets is from Pam… You know, Pam of his hand.

EmoGirl- Hey Lady, welcome to the madhouse.

JoeNotExotic- Hi Lady!

Fucking_Alan- Lady, I hope you are one. These douche canoes are roasting me today.

HangingWithMyGnomies- You brought it on yourself, Alan. Hey Lady!

I'd obviously joined the chat at a crucial point in their stage of grieving. I was intrigued to find out why they were all hating on Alan, although his username did kind of give him away. I didn't want to type anything yet though. Even though a few had said hi, I wasn't ready to jump in.

Fucking_Alan- Gnomio, you wish you had my way with the ladies. I know you only log on these days to hear about my exploits. Looking for tips are ya?

HangingWithMyGnomies- Pretty sure the earth revolves around the sun not you, Alan. The only tip I'd accept from you would be in pound sterling, mate.

Fucking_Alan- Jealousy isn't a good look on you.

EmoGirl- Alan, your date climbed out of the bathroom window after you told her if she ate much more, you'd be rolling her home. I don't think he needs those kinds of tips.

Fucking_Alan- It was a JOKE, people. Do chicks not have a sense of humour these days?

JoeNotExotic- Dude, if you're trying to improve the world you should really start with yourself. Nothing needs more help than you do.

Fucking_Alan- I don't need help. I'm perfect as I am. In the immortal words of the great Mac Davis, 'Oh Lord, it's so hard to be humble, when you're perfect in every way. I get frightened to look in the mirror, 'cos I get better looking each day.'

EmoGirl- I'd be frightened to see how fat your head was. You should change your username to elephant man.

Fucking_Alan- Now that's just rude, EmoGirl. Not to

mention disability-ist or whatever they call it. To know me is to love me. And I'm one hellova man.

JoeNotExotic- You're one hellova something. Maybe I shouldn't type it on here. This is a public chatroom.

Fucking_Alan- Joe, knock yourself out. No, really. Go and knock yourself out *Insert punch emoji* and do us all a favour. Just joking! Before you all jump on the troll express. Joe, you know I love you.

HangingWithMyGnomies- Careful, Joe. Sounds like he wants to take you on a date next.

JoeNotExotic- Lol. I'm JoeNotExotic, otherwise known as the troll king, the gay, keyboard warrior nerdy kid... not a mullet in sight over here. I'd chew you up and spit you out, Alan. Still want a piece of me?

Fucking_Alan- Which piece are you offering?

EmoGirl- Fuck's sake. New girl, lady, must think we're a bunch of weirdos.

Fucking_Alan- Speak for yourself, Emo.

EmoGirl- Jesus loves you, Alan. Everyone else thinks you're an asshole.

Fucking_Alan- I'm thinking of changing my name to CaroleBasketcase, just so we look like a couple, Joe.

JoeNotExotic- To be honest, we'd never work, Alan. I'm a unicorn and you're a donkey. I'm majestic and you, my dear, are just an ass.

I couldn't believe what I was reading. This wasn't what I

was expecting when I logged on. Not one of them had mentioned a lost brother or sister. I guessed this was what the charity had meant when they said it was run by the members for the members and no subject was off limits. Looked like Alan had brought an extra large spoon into the chat with him so he could stir shit up.

I saw a few private chats pop up along the bottom of my screen and hesitated, wondering if I should open them or not. I clicked on the one from EmoGirl first. She seemed like one of the saner members of the group.

EmoGirl- Hey. Don't let Alan put you off. Everyone is really cool in here. Alan is a knob, but you'll get used to him.

LadyStoneheart23- I gotta admit, this wasn't the chat I expected when I came on here.

EmoGirl- It can get darker. We try to keep it light. We all have our demons in here and most of us prefer to suppress them. You okay?

I stared at the cursor blinking back at me. Was I okay? I guess I needed to be honest.

LadyStoneheart23- Not really.

EmoGirl- Wanna talk about it? No pressure.

LadyStoneheart23- I lost my brother a few weeks ago.

EmoGirl- That's tough. So you're still in those early stages? Must feel pretty raw, huh?

LadyStoneheart23- Yep. He was my twin.

EmoGirl- Ouch.

LadyStoneheart23- What about you?

That was as much sharing as I was ready for at that moment.

EmoGirl- I lost my half-brother about a year ago. I never really knew him, but it still hurts. I missed out on a lot and it sucks that I'll never get a chance to get that back.

LadyStoneheart23- I'm sorry to hear that.

EmoGirl- I'm working through it. Coming on here helps. If ever you need to offload let us know. Joe is really cool. Hit us up if you ever need to chat. Might wanna stay out of the private chat with Alan though. First time I came on here he private messaged me to ask me how I liked having Rod Hull's hand shoved up my ass every day. Emo... Emu. Guy was referring to the bloody puppet. Ruined my childhood in one message.

LadyStoneheart23- OMG. I'll be on my guard then. Thanks.

EmoGirl- Yeah. His chat can get a bit much. You have to know when to beat him back down, like a whack-a-mole.

LadyStoneheart23- I'll keep my hammer handy!

I minimised the chat and saw another one waiting to be opened from Fucking_Alan. Guy was persistent, obviously.

Stupidly, my curiosity got the better of me and I opened it.

Fucking_Alan- Hey, lady. Nice to meet you. I'm sure if you give me a chance I can turn that stone heart to fire.

LadyStoneheart23- Fire, once you crash and burn. Thanks, but no thanks.

If I wanted a dating app I'd have gone on one.

Fucking_Alan- That's harsh, lady. I'm guessing Joe or Emo got to you first then? As Flavor Flav would say, don't believe the hype.

LadyStoneheart23- Public Enemy?

Fucking_Alan- Don't I know it. They're always hating on the good looking dudes in this chatroom.

LadyStoneheart23- No, I meant the group. SMH. I make my own judgement. One look at your username and I knew right away what you were in here for.

Fucking_Alan- Lmao. Okay. It's the name my parents use. The first one and the last. I lost my little sister to cancer six months ago, but it didn't stop them from hating on me. No worries though. We're all here to help. It might look like Joe, Emo, and I don't get on, but they've been my lifeline these past few months. You ever need anything, just holler.

LadyStoneheart23- I appreciate that. Thanks Alan. And for the record, I think you should change your username. Although CaroleBasketcase might not be the best choice.

Fucking_Alan- Anything that gets Joe going is a good choice in my books. Trust me.

I clicked the window closed and left him hanging. As I did, I noticed the group had started to get serious. Joe was talking about his older brother committing suicide and I read on for a little while but logged off when he started to go deeper. I couldn't handle his misery too. But as I shut the site down, I realised that I'd actually done something I hadn't done in a very long time.

I'd smiled.

CHAPTER

BRANDON

I knew exactly where he'd be. Hiding under the underpass where he went most days to work on his secret masterpiece. This was graffiti he'd never show anyone else, least of all her, because he was too chicken shit to put himself out there.

I picked over the broken bottles and discarded beer cans, a few little silver gas canisters and all the other shit down there. The whole area stank of piss, stale beer, and weed. There was even a filth infested sleeping bag rolled up and dumped behind a bush. I wasn't judging. I was homeless myself. But even I had standards on which shithole I put my head down in each night. This was a drug dealers' paradise, a druggies' haven, and Finn Knowles's studio of choice.

I stood back silently, leaning against the damp moss-covered wall of the subway and watched as he went to work adding fucking highlights to her hair. Last time I'd been here, he'd only done the outline then threw his stuff down and left, storming off and muttering something about it being a waste of time. Now, he was touching it up like it was his version of the Sistine Chapel. A ten-foot spray-painted image of the girl he loved, but he'd never tell her. I couldn't blame him. Women fucked you over and left you dead on the ground. He *was* wasting his time. She'd never look twice at a guy like him.

I took another step forward, knowing the crunch from the shards of glass under my feet would alert him to my presence. I'd hidden in the shadows long enough. Today was my resurrection, as far as Finn was concerned, anyway. The rest of them could rot in hell, for now. He spun round when he heard me and dropped his arms by his sides.

"Jesus. Fuck. Brandon. Where have you been? We've all been worried about you, mate." He stayed rooted to the spot and watched me like I was a wounded animal and he wanted to tend to me but was fearful that I'd strike out in my pain-induced haze.

"*Mate.*" I laughed sarcastically. "Don't you think it's a bit late for you to call me that? Mates don't shit all over each other." I folded my arms and stared him down. I'd always been good at controlling him, using my words and my actions to mould him into what I wanted.

"I never shit on you. None of us did. It got out of hand, but if you'd stuck around, we could've sorted it."

Finn put his spray can on the floor and showed he was getting fucking brave when he took a step towards me. I matched his bravery with my own and took a step into him. He looked tired and his eyes were dark and hollow. He probably thought the exact same about me.

"Too late." I gave him my signature evil grin. The one I usually saved for the ring. "I'm not sticking around to get crucified by this town. Fucking punk-ass motherfuckers can go to hell."

"Mate... Brandon," he corrected himself. "We want to help. Ryan saw Harper yesterday, and-"

Hearing her name spoken by him made me want to tear bricks out of the walls with my bare hands.

"Save that bullshit for someone who gives a fuck," I spat, feeling ready to do some artwork of my own with someone's intestines.

"But you don't need to stay away. Harper said-"

Again with the Harper bullshit. I didn't want to hear that name come out of his mouth. I didn't want anyone to say her name.

"I couldn't give a fuck what *she* said. Bitch is out to ruin me. I'm gonna ruin her first."

"She doesn't deserve that. Whatever you're thinking, she doesn't deserve it." He shook his head, looking green, like it was his sister I'd just threatened. Dude needed to calm the fuck down. She wasn't his to defend. Was this girl intent on infiltrating every inch of my life? First Ryan, and now Finn?

"I'll be the judge of what she deserves. Now, do you want to do me a favour or not? I thought *mates* helped each other."

"They do and I will. What do you need?"

Good old Finn. I knew I could rely on him.

"I need a phone. Get some minutes and data on it too. Can you sort that for me now?"

"You know I can. But aren't you coming back? After the Lockwoods withdrew their statements, the police dropped the case."

A lightning bolt shot through my skull at what he'd said. But it didn't make sense and I didn't trust it for a second. If anything, this was a set-up to lure me out of hiding. Shit was always shady where the Lockwoods were concerned, and I'd had my fair share of bullshit off them over the years.

"The fuck? Why would they do that? What's in it for them?"

I frowned, my head starting to hurt from thinking about what those fuckers were up to. Harper too. My feisty little one was growing bigger claws, but she needed them clipped. She needed to be put in her place.

"On second thoughts, don't answer. They're up to something. They always are."

Finn nodded, but I knew he didn't agree. He always saw the best in people. It was his biggest downfall and the reason he needed me around. I trusted no one.

"So, when can you get me the phone?" I asked, growing impatient. I'd been there for three minutes already and that was too long. "I don't want to be hanging around for much longer, *mate*."

"I'll head into town now and get one. Can you give me a couple of hours?" Finn started gathering his gear together, ready to leave.

"I'll give you one hour, then I'm gone. Don't let me down."

He looked up at me, trying to hide his anxiety. He knew I meant it.

"Oh, and Finn? Don't tell anyone else you saw me. I came to you 'cos I know you can keep your mouth shut."

Forty minutes later, Finn came back to the underpass with the latest iPhone and a shitload of free data. I knew there was a reason he was my favourite. If you asked him for a pound, he'd give you two and ask if there was anything else you needed.

"Will you at least tell me where you're staying?" he asked, looking genuinely concerned.

"I'm okay. I have a roof and four walls. That's all you need to know. When I'm ready to tell more, you'll be the first person I come to."

He seemed happy with that answer and gave a weak smile.

"They miss you, you know. We all do."

And I call bullshit.

"Didn't stop them doing the gigs again though, did it? Those parties were my idea. I deserve a cut." It still stung that they'd done that without me. Those were my events. Damn it, I was the fucking event. People only came to watch me fight.

"And if you come back, you'll get a cut." He sighed. "Do

you need any money? I don't have much, but whatever I've got you can have."

I needed to start teaching him to defend himself again. Weak fucker was gonna get his ass kicked for being so damn nice.

"I'm good, but thanks."

"For what it's worth," he added. "They didn't want to start it all up again without you. And to be honest, it's just not the same. We needed the extra cash though, and we've been chipping in to help your nan."

"Yeah, she told me." I let slip and then covered my mouth, realising what I'd said.

"We guessed she knew where you were. Didn't push it though. She's your nan. Be careful though. I think the Lockwoods are watching her."

Fucking Lockwoods could watch all they wanted. If I got my hands on them going anywhere near my nan, they wouldn't have eyes to watch her with. Burning their cars was just the start as far as I was concerned.

"I'm not an idiot. I wouldn't get caught. I'd never put her in danger and I'd never let them hurt her either," I stated, as if it needed saying. Finn knew me. He knew what I was capable of.

"Cool. Well, you know where I am if you ever need me, bro."

"Yeah, down here mooning over a ten-foot portrait of Effy fucking Spencer."

He went bright red, like I hadn't guessed who it was he was painting. Dude was flogging a dead horse with that one.

"If you want my advice, you'll give it up. Fuck them, but never let them get their claws in and never stick to one girl."

"Effy's not like that."

I laughed at his naivety.

"They're all like that. Trust me. You come first."

And with that little nugget of wisdom, I left him to brood over his artwork and the hopelessness of his case.

CHAPTER

Twelve

HARPER

I didn't want to be here.

If it wasn't a stipulation from my workplace that I attend, I wouldn't be.

I sat twiddling my thumbs as the counsellor from occupational health wittered on about the merits of grievance counselling and the statistics for successful phased returns to work after a breakdown like mine. He said all the right things. They were there to support me. They wanted what was best. But spending a rainy Wednesday afternoon in this guy's stuffy office, bobbing my head like a nodding dog in the back window of a granny's car wasn't helping at all. He was speaking and I didn't want to listen.

"Everything we say here is strictly confidential. Unless you tell me something that I feel could or would cause you harm, then I'll need to report it to other agencies."

So not confidential at all then.

"But I will always ask for your permission to share anything. You can trust me, Harper."

Yeah, no. I was jumping through his hoops because I had to. I had no choice. But if he thought I'd open up to him after sitting there for ten minutes, he was kidding himself.

"Do you want to tell me a bit about what happened?" He sat forward in his chair, his focus trained solely on me.

"My twin brother died. Well, I say died, he was murdered." I shrugged like it was nothing. It fucking wasn't.

"Murdered? Do you want to elaborate? I understand if it's too difficult at the moment."

He started to scribble down notes, and I stared at the wall opposite with its framed awards that meant absolutely nothing.

Did I want to elaborate?

I guessed it wouldn't hurt to put out there what was already common knowledge. Everyone in Sandland knew about Brodie.

"He was in a fight. The guy hit him, and he went down, banging his head off the concrete floor and fracturing his skull. He bled out on that floor. A filthy barn with hay and shit everywhere. It was degrading."

Counsellor guy stopped writing and looked up. Despite what I'd thought only moments ago, I was starting to open up. I had to offload. The whole sordid saga had built up inside of me, like bile that clung to every inch of my soul, stagnant, and damaging for far too long. I needed a release.

"I held him in my arms as he died. I've still got the clothes I wore that night too. They're covered in blood, but I can't bring myself to get rid of them. I need to keep them."

"Why do you need to keep them, Harper?"

I looked at him like he was an idiot.

"Because they remind me of what happened and what I need to do next."

"And what is that?"

Did he really need to ask?

My need to impress this guy had long since flown out the window and I couldn't hold back from blurting out what truly lay in my heart.

"Get revenge. He needs to pay for what he's done to us, what he did to Brodie that night. He can't just get away with it. No one else seems bothered about making him pay, but I am, and I will. Make him pay, that is."

Counsellor guy huffed out through his nose, like what I'd said had offended him. I couldn't care less.

"Do you think it's healthy to hold on to that anger and use it in this way? Anger is a valid reaction to your grief, and it's natural to attach that anger to someone else. But the way you're talking now? The fire that's suddenly ignited in you? You seem consumed by this other man and the want for revenge. This is the first time I've seen you get animated today. But negativity breeds negativity, Harper."

"Consumed?" I started shaking. I couldn't believe he was arguing with me. "He killed my brother. I'm consumed by thoughts of what I want to do to him to make him suffer."

"But you'd never act those out, would you?" He was

staring at me now, notepad discarded, and he was poised, waiting for me to say the wrong thing. He was trying to trick me.

"Why not?" I said, holding my chin higher in defiance.

He shook his head.

"I think you could benefit from some one-to-one counselling. You are placing a lot of your energy into something which is ultimately going to destroy you from the inside out. Do you understand what I'm saying?"

Yeah, I do, and I want to tell you to fuck off. If I want revenge, I'll get it.

"Harbouring anger, guilt, all of that is normal. But to seek out revenge is something else entirely. It's not healthy."

I flipped, feeling backed into a corner by his fake sincerity.

"So, he can terrorise me, but I have to take it? I can't fight back?"

He started to root around in his folder, then he pulled out a piece of paper to read from.

"I have a note here that says you thought you saw someone in your back garden." He looked back up at me. "Are you seeing things like that a lot?"

The ringing in my ears intensified. My throat dried up, and I reached for the plastic cup of water to help me speak.

"That was a private matter. My parents swore they wouldn't tell anyone."

My inner circle of trust was dwindling fast. In fact, I

doubt you could call one person a circle. The only person I could trust was me.

"They only told me after we booked this appointment. They want to help you. They want *us* to help you. We can only do that if we have all the facts. Do you see things? Do you hear voices?"

All the fucking time.

"No. I didn't see something that wasn't there, if that's what you're implying." I left it at that. I doubted he'd take my other sightings of Mathers seriously.

"I think you're giving this man way too much power over you," he said, looking at me with kindness in his eyes. "The key to healing is letting go of some of that anger you're bottling up. I'm not saying that'll happen overnight, but we can help you with that, with intensive counselling."

Nobody had power over me. Least of all Brandon fucking Mathers. I'd never bow down. No matter how much he taunted me.

"Why would I want to let go of the anger? It's all I've got."

"Because it's hurting you way more than it'll ever hurt him." He sighed. "I have read a little about what happened to Brodie. I also know the police aren't pressing charges. It's being recorded as accidental death, is that right?"

"That's bullshit. The whole brain aneurysm and Brodie tripping himself, it's all complete and utter bullshit. I know what I saw."

"And no one is trying to take that away from you. What we want is to get you well. And you're not well, Harper. For the next few months, we need to make your mental health the main focus. You are the most important person in all of this. Not him. Not the murderer. You. Do you think wherever he is now that he's thinking about you?"

I knew he was.

"No, he's not," he said, interrupting my thoughts. "He's living his life. We need to find a way back so that you can do the same."

This guy was clueless, but I knew I wasn't being heard. I was getting nowhere fast.

"I will go to counselling," I said to get him off my back. "My mum is seeing Doctor O'Neill. I've already told her I'll go and see her too." I wouldn't, but I wasn't about to let him book me in with one of their quacks.

"Ah, Meredith. We know her. She's one of the best."

Fucking great. Now I had to hope he didn't contact her asking for updates. Mind you, he did say he'd need my permission to talk about me.

"I know," I answered, giving him a fake smile of hope. "I also have a few leaflets my friend gave me." I grabbed Emily's brochures out of my bag to show him, feeling proud that I had something with me to make it look like I was trying to jump his hurdles. "These really help too."

"That's very good, Harper. Great that you have a friend who's supporting you and finding these avenues of support for you. Have you rung any of them? Made any appointments?"

"No. I have been online. I went on the chatrooms... On this one." I showed him the pamphlet. "The people on there seemed nice. Genuine."

"That's... great. But you need to be careful. Some of these chatrooms aren't as safe as they seem. People online are different to how they would be in real life."

Here we go again.

"I know. I'm not a kid. We teach about e-safety in school. I'm not about to start typing in my personal details or arranging to meet up with anyone. I do have a neutral username. I know what I'm doing." I shoved the leaflets back into my handbag, feeling embarrassed that I'd opened up and shown them to him.

"But that's the problem," he said. "In grief, often we don't know what we're doing. We can't make good judgement calls and we act out of character. You're vulnerable right now and I'd hate to see someone take advantage."

"I know I need to be on my guard. I only went online to read the chats. They're funny. They made me laugh." I was seconds away from standing up and leaving. I didn't need to justify myself or my actions to this man.

"Well, that's good. As long as you keep it that way, you shouldn't have to worry."

I frowned. Why would a charity set up to help people dealing with bereavement have chatrooms that were unsafe?

Surely someone policed them. I asked him that very question, feeling like I needed to vindicate myself.

"I'm sure they do. But my priority is your wellbeing, so I'm always going to tell you to exercise caution. Maybe get out with real friends more. Being with other people, getting outside, is far more beneficial to your mental health than any online community. Just be careful. That's all I'm saying."

I didn't agree. I had no friends to call on. Plus, that forum had made me laugh for the first time in weeks. If I wanted to go on there and ask them how to make a bloody bomb to blow up Sandland, I would. No one would tell me what to do. This was my life. I would live it how I wanted. And after the past few weeks, I wanted to live it for Brodie. To do the things he couldn't. I knew what he'd do if he was still here, and it wouldn't be pissing about in a counsellor's office or chatting with fake friends over coffee.

Thirty minutes later, and I was sprinting out of that counsellor's office like my life depended on it. I couldn't escape fast enough. The air in the building was stifling, and it wasn't to do with their lack of air conditioning. I'd had about all I could manage for one day.

I stomped over to my car parked towards the back of their cramped car park and stopped dead in my tracks when I saw it.

A single white rose lay underneath my windscreen wiper.

He was here.

Anger bubbled and coursed inside me, but it didn't make me weak. It burned a fire in my soul. My broken, bruised, and battered soul. He thought he could play me. Intimidate and scare me into submission, to do what? Take me further down than I already was?

Too little, too late, *mate*.

I was dancing with the devil, on first name terms with the guy, and had him in my back pocket. He was playing on my team now. The battle lines had been drawn all those weeks ago in a shitty, rundown barn. Now, he was over-stepping the mark and he needed to be taught a lesson.

I plucked the rose out of its holding place and held it to my nose, smiling like a fool. Anyone watching would think it'd been left by an admirer with the way I was grinning. I opened my car door and threaded the stem into the front dash panel so it sat up proudly on display.

"Thanks for the rose," I said in a cool, calm voice. "I hope you rot in hell."

Then I drove off, my rose standing tall for everyone to see. I'd get rid of it when I got home, but I knew he'd be watching, and I wanted him to know he wasn't getting to me.

Leave all the roses you want. This lady's stone heart is numb, frozen, and ready to fight back.

CHAPTER
Thirteen

HARPER

I was fired up and couldn't relax. Driving back home, I decided I needed to offload some of my tension, so I decided to make a detour to the Lockwood's house. Mum had said I should call in, pay my respects for the loss of their... cars.

Fucking jerks.

As I pulled up to the kerb, I spotted Jensen and Chase on their driveway, arms folded over their chests and looking over two brand spanking new Range Rovers, one black, one white. I supposed these were their new rides and they could take their pick, deciding which one to use every day. Black for their traitorous hearts or white for the fake image they were currently projecting all over Sandland. I'd have thought yellow would've been more their style, to match their cowardice.

They both turned at the sound of my car pulling up and Jensen's jaw tightened as he muttered something to Chase. A warning, I'd bet.

Don't say anything.

Cover your tracks.

Protect the family name.

"Harper," Jensen said through gritted teeth as I got out of my car.

He walked towards me, extending his arms like he expected us to hug. After our last meeting, I was going to struggle with a handshake.

"How are you?"

He saw that I wasn't there to play nice. My shitty expression gave it away, and he went back to folding his arms over his chest in a defensive manner.

"Sorry to hear about your cars." I nodded over to Chase as I spoke. He gave a strained smile but stayed back.

"We know who did it." Jensen turned to glance at Chase, who grimaced on cue. "When we find him, he's a dead man."

"So, you'll kill him over a fucking lump of metal, but not for my brother?" These guys were unbelievable.

"It's not that simple." Jensen took a step forward then bent down to sneer into my face. "I told you to fucking drop it."

I grinned back, trying my best to look unhinged and deranged.

"See, that's where you're wrong. I won't *drop it*. I won't ever give up. If getting to Mathers means outing your shady shit then buckle up, boys. You're in for a bumpy ride."

The veins in Jensen's neck looked like they were ready to pop. His jaw was clenched so tightly he'd probably do permanent damage to his teeth.

"I'm not fucking around, Harper."

"Neither am I." I took a step into his space this time and made him lean back. Good. I liked having the upper hand in his intimidation tactics. "You were there that night. Your statements hold a lot of weight in Brodie's case-"

"What case? There is no case."

"Oh, there's a case. And I'm gonna make damn sure it stays open. You've got something to hide, I know that. But I think you're underestimating me. Brodie had the brawn, I have the brains. I'll find out what it is, and when I do, I'm taking you down with him. Do you hear? I'll take you, Chase, Mathers, hell I'll take your whole fucking family down if I have to. Better warn your second cousins I'm coming for them."

"That's big talk from a little girl," he snarled on a low growl.

"Wasn't it Shakespeare who said, 'she might be small, but she is fierce?' He liked his tragedies, and when I'm finished, that's what you'll be living." I kept my manic grin in place. I was on a roll.

"Yeah, and that quote comes from *A Midsummer Night's Dream*. Just like your threats... all a dream. It will never happen. Leave it be or live to regret it."

Just at that moment, Don Lockwood strolled out of his front door, giving me the stink-eye but smiling his fake smile.

"Harper. How are you?" He strode down the steps onto

his driveway as if he were the Godfather, all bravado and menace. I half expected a few goons to come strolling out after him, carrying tommy guns and chewing matchsticks or whatever it was they chewed. "It's good to see you getting out and about. How are your parents? You will send them my regards, won't you?"

"Yeah, thanks," I replied, coming across like a stroppy teen. I eyeballed Jensen and hissed, "This isn't over." And then flounced off to my car without another word.

As I slammed the door shut, Don's face took on an evil sneer and his lip curled up as if he was threatening his sons. It should've made me feel sorry for them, but it didn't. They needed a wake-up call. The people of Sandland were fed up with the bullshit, and my shit list, which was growing longer by the day, had them toying for first place.

Mathers or Lockwood?

Who would I take out first?

–

Once I got home, I threw that bloody white rose in the bin and then safely ensconced myself in my bedroom.

My haven.

I logged my computer on and clicked into the bereavement chatroom. I needed a bit of light-hearted banter after the day I'd had. I was done with people who thought they could walk all over me.

LadyStoneheart23 has joined the chat.

Regina_Phalange- Mate, you know it's a fucking bad day when the dog shitting on your bed is the least of your worries.

JoeNotExotic- I hope you fed him dry food last night.

Regina_Phalange- Did I fuck. My whole house is getting fumigated. Hey lady!

JoeNotExotic- Welcome back, lady. Glad we didn't scare you away.

HangingWithMyGnomies- Hi lady, how's it going?

My fingers hovered over the keys, but I stayed silent.

Regina_Phalange- Anyway, enough of my… shit. Lol. How was counselling yesterday, Joe?

JoeNotExotic- Ugh. Fucking pointless. He wants me to keep a diary of every time I feel angry about my brother's suicide. I don't think they make notebooks big enough to write all my anger in to. Guy has no fucking idea. It'd be easier to list all the times I don't feel angry.

Regina_Phalange- I hear you.

LadyStoneheart23- Me too.

I'd done it. Typed my first line in the group chat and it was shit. But I understood what he was saying. Anger was the norm for me these days.

EmoGirl has joined the chat.

Legion has joined the chat.

Regina_Phalange- What's your story, Lady?
HangingWithMyGnomies- Don't feel like you have to tell us.
*JoeNotExotic- What he said. ^^^*
EmoGirl- Afternoon, guys.

I took a few deep breaths. Like the counsellor guy had said earlier, I didn't know these people. I had to be on my guard. Yet, I wanted to tell them. I felt like I needed to spout a bit of this shit to get it off my chest. Like a release for the pressure valve that was compacting my overworked brain.

LadyStoneheart23- It's okay. I lost my twin brother. He was murdered, and not a day goes by where I don't want to hunt down his killer and make him suffer.
Regina_Phalange- Shit, that's deep. Do you know who it was?
LadyStoneheart23- Yeah, I do. The fucker has been stalking me for weeks. Thinks he's clever, leaving me little warnings, like he's coming for me next. Watching me. Standing in my garden at night.
Regina_Phalange- Fuck.

HangingWithMyGnomies- Sounds like something from a horror movie.

EmoGirl- I don't like the sound of that. Do you wanna DM me, Lady?

JoeNotExotic- Yeah, I think a DM with Emo would be good. Have you told the police? That is some real shit, lady. You shouldn't have to deal with that.

LadyStoneheart23- The police don't care. They don't do anything. And thanks, but I can handle it. I should've made my Game of Thrones inspired username Aria or A Girl With No Name. That's what I feel like. I have my kill list ready to go and I'm adding to it every single day.

EmoGirl- I understand you're angry and hell knows I'd be shit scared too if I was you. But you need to get the authorities involved. Stalking is some next level shit.

*JoeNotExotic- What she says! ^^^*

HangingWithMyGnomies- I would definitely be backing away and calling the cops. How do you even leave your house? Do you leave your house?

LadyStoneheart23- He doesn't scare me. If he wants to come for me, I'm ready for him.

EmoGirl- I don't agree. Lady, you need to get help. I mean that coming from a place of love. Don't put up with this. We don't want to see you on the front page of the newspapers tomorrow.

JoeNotExotic- If it was me, I'd be moving house, city… Damn, I'd leave the country. I've no idea what this murderer did to your brother, but they sound crazy as fuck if they're after you too. Ring the police and get help. Now.

Legion- I disagree.

EmoGirl- Why????

JoeNotExotic- He would say that, he's a legion. He thinks we're all fighting with an army.

Legion- On the contrary, the definition of my name doesn't come from the dictionary. Try the bible. As for the police, they do fuck all. If you want revenge, Lady. Do it yourself.

EmoGirl- Legion, I'm guessing you're a guy. It's a bit different for us girls… And it's a hell of a lot different in the real world.

Legion- Oh, I live in the real world, Emo. I've seen shit that'd make your head explode.

EmoGirl- Nice. But Lady has a real problem. A stalker. Save the exploding heads for your computer games, Legion.

JoeNotExotic- Legion, if you're going with the biblical definition it sounds pretty fucked-up. A guy possessed by demons? My name is Legion, for we are many? That's some twisted shit, dude.

Fucking_Alan has joined the chat.

Legion- What can I say? I'm a complex guy.

Fucking_Alan- Complex. Sounds like you're in the right place, my friend.

Legion- No one could bind him anymore, not even with a chain, for he had often been bound with shackles and chains, but he wrenched the chains apart, and he broke the shackles into pieces. No one had the strength to subdue him. (Mark 5:3-4)

Fucking_Alan- Legion, you're stealing my crown, dude. I'm the king of cool quotes in here.

LadyStoneheart23- I like that quote. Kinda sums up how I feel. I won't be shackled anymore. I want to let my rage out.

Legion- Then do it.

JoeNotExotic- Wasn't legion a shitload of demons exorcised from a possessed man? All sounds a bit dark, mate.

Legion- Isn't that what this chat is for? To exorcise our demons. To go to the dark places other people don't want to hear about. Not in the real world, anyway. A freaks playground.

Fucking_Alan- He's right. We are all a bit freaky in here.

EmoGirl- Speak for yourself, Alan.

JoeNotExotic- Naming yourself after a bloke who was possessed by thousands of demons is as dark as they come.

Legion- Feared by many, loved by few. That's me. But then, I've always lived by the motto, 'It is better to be feared than loved, if you cannot have both'.

EmoGirl- Machiavelli

Fucking_Alan- Dude, enough already. You're making me look bad.

EmoGirl- Alan, these quotes would go over your head anyway. Nineties rap and your mums record collection are the extent to which you go.

Fucking_Alan- And who doesn't love a bit of nineties rap? I've got ninety-nine problems but a stalker aint one.

JoeNotExotic- Low blow, dude. Low blow.

I saw a private chat pop up along the bottom of my screen, and thinking it was from EmoGirl, I opened it. It wasn't.

Legion- Burn them to the fucking ground. That's what I say. Burn them all, then rise like a phoenix.

One chat and I already felt like this Legion guy got me better than anyone else I knew. He got my situation, anyway.

LadyStoneheart23- I plan to.

I replied, then shut the window down, smiling to myself. At least someone had faith in me.

CHAPTER

Fourteen

BRANDON

My insane hunger was turning into an unquenchable thirst. I'd hungered for redemption for so long it'd become an everyday emotion for me, a need that burned deep. But now, since her, I needed to know more. I was thirsty for knowledge. I wanted to know more about her. What made her tick?

I'd seen her cry at her brother's funeral. I'd watched her rage and go wild at Ryan's garage. And I watched her swing from fear to defiance at my little calling cards. And through it all, I couldn't ever get a handle on the girl. I could never second guess her. Like yesterday, she'd gone into that office building to do whatever the fuck it was she was doing, and when she came out and saw my rose, she smiled like it'd been left by her fucking boyfriend.

I used the car I'd hot-wired to follow her, expecting her to go straight home, but no. She'd rocked up to the fucking Lockwood's of all places, and then totally blew my expectations out of the water when she started getting arsey with them. I could see she was arguing with Lockwood, and when his dad came out, she turned on her heels and left, flying down the driveway like a bat out of hell and looking like she was ready to go nuclear on all their asses.

She wasn't like anyone I'd ever met before. She was unstable, unpredictable, and slightly psychotic. It was like looking in the mirror at a daintier, blonder version of me. Hell, she *was* me. A female version of me, anyway, and I needed to find out more.

That was why I'd ventured a bit further over the line tonight, coming out from the shadows where I usually stood. I was on her back patio, looking up at her bedroom window. I knew it was hers. The glittery pink skull in the windowsill gave it away.

The window was open, and it crossed my mind to climb up the drainpipe at the side of her house. Maybe use the flat roof of the extension to help me get across and through into her window. But I didn't. Instead, I tried the patio doors that led into her dining room, and sure enough, they'd been left unlocked. Pretty stupid when you considered all the criminal damage that'd been going on around Sandland over the past few weeks. You couldn't trust anyone these days. The Yates's obviously thought they were safe. Looked like I wasn't doing my job properly. I'd have to do something to rectify that.

I stood at the door for a few seconds, letting my eyes adjust to the dark so I could pick my way around the furniture by the light of the moon without making a noise or waking anyone up. I'd have hated to have to up my plans so soon and start using violence to get my point across. Best they all stayed asleep. The bogeyman works better when he's left alone to do his bidding.

They had an open-plan kitchen diner, and I made my way around the table towards the breakfast bar, ready to leave my next surprise for her. The electrical buzz from the kitchen appliances gave the house a comforting feel, and I could smell the vanilla from the plug-in candle thing her mum had next to the door, wafting over me like it was trying to calm me down. Must be nice to live in a house that pumps out a fresh scent even when you're asleep and can't smell that shit.

I laid the white rose I'd stolen out of the next-door neighbour's garden on the work surface and took the paper out of my back pocket, tucking it underneath. Then I got an apple from the fruit bowl and placed it on top of the paper, just to make sure it didn't blow away when a door opened. I wanted her to see it. I couldn't wait for her reaction, knowing I'd been inside her house. Would it scare her to know I could get to her anywhere? Or would it give her a thrill? I had no idea, but I'd enjoy finding out.

Standing in her kitchen, power coursed through my veins, and I didn't want to leave yet. I hadn't quenched my thirst for all things Harper. So, I walked over to a sideboard that ran the length of the wall opposite the kitchen area. I took my mobile phone out from the pocket of my jeans and clicked the flashlight on. Probably a shit move if the neighbours saw it, but I wanted to get a better look at what lay in front of me.

There were framed photographs of the family on the top of the sideboard, lots of them. I loved my nan, and she'd done the best job she could at bringing me up, but we didn't have framed photos in our house. The only photos I'd seen from my childhood were faded, curled at the edges, and kept in a shoebox at the top of my nan's wardrobe, like she was trying to hide away the reality of our shitty lives.

In this house, there were photographs from holidays; skiing, at the beach, and trekking in the mountains. I hadn't seen the sea until I was ten years old and we went on a school trip to Brighton. I'd certainly never been skiing. Our lives were worlds apart, whole galaxies even.

In the photos, every one of the Yates's was smiling. The photos I had weren't like that. Most of the time I was grimacing into the lens, or I wasn't even looking, too engrossed in whatever I was doing as my nan made a feeble attempt to document my life on film. I was never dressed for the occasion like these pictures either. In our photos, I usually had mud all over my knees, a dirty face, and clothes that looked like they'd seen better days. Mostly homemade by Nan, using fabric that was already threadbare.

I picked up a photograph of Harper and Brodie with their heads together, grinning into the camera, and then I noticed a smaller frame that'd been hiding behind it. It was of Harper on her own. It looked recent, and in it she was sitting on a rock, surrounded by hills and little wooden houses. It didn't look like it'd been taken in this country. It was probably

Switzerland or somewhere posh like that. The style of the houses looked European; pretty. But she... she was fucking stunning. Her blonde hair that framed her face made her glow like an angel. The light in her eyes was mesmerising. I'd never met this Harper. Sure, I knew Brodie had a sister before that night, and I might have caught a glimpse of her in a darkened room or at one of our parties, but I'd never seen this side of her. The side that shone like a fucking beacon.

I'd done that.

I'd taken the light out of her eyes. I'd made her the shell she was today. And looking at the photograph, I realised I hated myself for it.

I should have walked away. I should have taken the fucking rose, my message, and my fucked-up self and left her alone. Finn was right, she didn't deserve this, and yet, I couldn't. The force that drew me to her was too strong. I couldn't walk away now even if I wanted to. But I knew one thing, looking at the angelic face staring back at me from the photograph. I wanted her to get some of that back. I knew she'd never be the same after losing her brother, but she wanted to feel powerful. She wanted back control of her life. I could give that to her. Even if it was in exchange for my own. Maybe, just this once, I could do something selfless.

I kept hold of that photo frame. It was mine now. A reminder of what my new plan was. There were people in this town I was coming for, that'd never change.

But her?

I was going to save her.

CHAPTER
Fifteen

HARPER

Good morning, flower.

Good fucking morning, flower.

That was the message he left for me in my kitchen. I was thanking every lucky star that I'd woken up first and found it. Having to explain this to my mum and dad was another ball ache I could do without.

I guess he thought he was being funny, leaving a note with a flower and calling me fucking flower. But his passive-aggressive bullshit was starting to grate on me. Not to mention the fact that he'd overstepped so many boundaries coming into my home. How the fuck did he get in? I couldn't see any signs of forced entry.

Shit.

I hoped he didn't climb through my window. Mine was the only one left open the night before.

Fuck.

The thought creeped me out, made me shiver, want to take a bath in bleach, and scrub my skin off. I felt so violated.

I shoved the white rose and the note to the bottom of the bin, hiding it under the gross vegetable peelings and other shit in there so no one would see it. Then I took the apple and binned that too. Like I'd eat anything he'd touched.

I glanced around, suddenly feeling like I was being watched. What if he hadn't left at all and was hiding in our pantry? My life was turning into a horror movie, but I wasn't the dumb blonde everyone thought I was.

I stomped over to the pantry door which was ajar, but when I flung it open, all I saw were the shelves full of cereals, tinned food, and other groceries my mum was stocking in preparation for the zombie apocalypse. I slammed it shut, then marched over to the patio doors. I pushed the handle down, and sure enough, the door opened.

Shit.

It must have been like that all night.

I'd need to start checking all the locks and bolts myself before I went to sleep. Dad was dropping a big fucking ball leaving us open and vulnerable to the likes of Brandon Mathers and his psychotic ways.

I shut and locked it back up, giving the handle a good yank to double check it was secure. I didn't even trust myself with my safety anymore.

Mum walked into the kitchen just as I was throwing myself against the door again one last time for good measure.

"Are you okay, love? Did you manage to get any sleep?" She smiled at me, trying to look bright and refreshed, but the bags under her eyes were dark and heavy. When she stifled a yawn, I could tell she'd had as restful a night as I had. Just my shitty luck that the time I was asleep was the time he'd made his night-time visit.

"I got a bit of sleep," I said, sitting up at the breakfast bar and taking an apple out of the fruit bowl. Then I remembered that Mathers had had his hands all over the fruit and I put it back again, grimacing.

"No appetite again?" She sighed. "What do you have planned for today?"

I shrugged. What kind of stupid question was that? I was doing the same today that I did every day.

"Nothing. Just gonna hang around here."

Mum was busying herself making coffee, but she stopped to give me one of her stern motherly expressions.

"Maybe you should try to get out. It's not healthy to lock yourself up in your room all day."

"Hold on." I wrinkling my brow in confusion. "You said I shouldn't be going out. That I was too vulnerable. Now you think I shouldn't be staying in? Which one is it, Mum? 'Cos I'm starting to get really confused."

I shouldn't have taken my frustration out on my mum, I knew that. It wasn't her fault we had a crazy guy breaking into our house and leaving roses on the counter when we were asleep, but I couldn't think straight.

"I think you should be seeing your friends more. Sal hasn't been round for ages. You two used to be inseparable.

Why don't you hang out with her today?" Mum asked as she filled the coffee machine and fussed over wiping the already pristine counters down.

"Mum, I haven't spoken to Sal in months. You know, since she broke up with Brodie. Do you even remember that? Do you know anything about my life?"

Obviously not, otherwise she'd know to drop this right now.

She stilled and threw the cloth into the sink, rubbing her hands over her tired face as she sighed.

"I forgot. I'm sorry. What can I say? Since losing your brother, my memory has been all over the place. I went to see Meredith with my slippers on yesterday and left the car running in the car park throughout the whole hour-long appointment. I'm lucky I still had a car to come back to when I got outside. I'm hopeless." She pressed the button on the coffee, but she'd forgotten to put a cup underneath and the scalding liquid poured out all over the countertop and onto the floor. "Oh, shit. Look. I can't even make a bloody coffee." She started to tear up as she grabbed a handful of paper towels to soak up the mess. I hopped off my stool to help her.

"I think we're all a bit hopeless, Mum." I felt guilty that I'd just snapped at her. "We're all trying to get through this the best way we can."

"I know." She threw the sopping wet towels into the bin and then turned to face me. "But if you go out, Harper, it'll help. Get yourself into the real world. I know it's hard at first.

I hated it too, but we have to start living again, or at least trying to."

"Fine. I might head into town later. I'm running low on hair products. Maybe I'll meet up with someone and go for a coffee too while I'm there."

I couldn't give a shit about my hair, and God knows who I'd meet for coffee. Maybe I could buy two coffees-to-go, head to the park, and leave one in the bushes for my stalker. He was the only person who seemed interested in following my life these days.

"That's the spirit, love. A day with a friend will do you the world of good."

"I'll make sure I leave my slippers at the front door." I grinned and gave her a hug, then left her to make a more successful cup of morning coffee.

I headed up to my room, still feeling the anger from his break-in coursing through me. I needed to find out where he was hiding. Maybe pay him a few visits of my own. He wasn't the only one holding a grudge.

I locked my bedroom door and gave an involuntary shiver as I thought about him wandering around my home. Like a nervous child, I double checked the lock, even though deep down I knew I was safe. It was morning, and creatures like him didn't come out to play in the light.

I made my way over to my desk. It was still pretty early, so I doubted there'd be many people on the group chat, but I logged on anyway. I needed to do something to take my mind off the violation of being broken in to. This chatroom was slowly becoming my lifeline. It made me feel less alone.

LadyStoneheart23 has joined the chat.

Regina_Phalange- Lol. I am fucking dying here.

Fucking_Alan- That's it, Reggie, laugh at my misery.

Regina_Phalange- Only you, Alan. Only you.

JoeNotExotic- Come on then. Give us the low down. You can't tell us that and leave us hanging.

*EmoGirl – *Runs to get popcorn**

Fucking_Alan – We matched on Tinder. What can I say? She looked hot and her messages were dirty as fuck. I arranged to meet her at a bar in town.

JoeNotExotic- Didn't you check out her Facebook or Insta account?

Fucking_Alan- We hadn't got that far. I only knew her first name.

EmoGirl – Rookie mistake, Alan. Lol.

Fucking_Alan – Well, I know that now! Anyway, I rocked up feeling pretty excited to meet her. She was a sure thing, and she was hot as fuck in her Tinder photos. My night was sorted.

JoeNotExotic- And???

Fucking_Alan – She had no fucking teeth.

Regina_Phalange – Oh my God. Bloody priceless.

EmoGirl – Maybe she had an illness?

JoeNotExotic – Always positive thinking, Emo. I love you, girl.

Fucking_Alan – A bloody illness? Girl was sick if she thought I'd be going there. She had like three teeth in her head. Three. My nan has more than that.

Regina_Phalange – Was she a good friend of your nan's?

Fucking_Alan- Come again?

Regina_Phalange – I have images of you turning up to a date with an eighty-year-old. So funny.

Fucking_Alan – She was in her twenties. I'm no octogenarian-phile or whatever the opposite of a pedo is. Calm your tits, Reggie.

Legion has joined the chat.

JoeNotExotic – I'm really gonna regret typing this, 'cos I'm gonna sound like Alan, but at least she'd give good head.

EmoGirl – Joe, I'm disappointed. ROFL

*JoeNotExotic- Me too, Emo. *Hangs head in shame and gives an evil laugh**

Fucking_Alan- I'm so glad my dating exploits amuse you.

Regina_Phalange- Every fucking time, mate.

Fucking_Alan – When I got home, I looked at her Facebook and Insta.

EmoGirl- She actually gave you her last name?

Fucking_Alan – Last name, phone number, social security number… This chick was desperate. When I looked online, she wasn't smiling with her mouth open in any of those photos. Even if I had cyber stalked her, I wouldn't have known. Girl duped me. I dated a fucking gummy bear… Well, the female version of Albert Steptoe. Nothing is advertised properly these days.

EmoGirl – Speaking of stalking, how you doing, Lady?

LadyStoneheart23- Better for coming on here and hearing about Alan's toothless date.

Fucking_Alan- Yep. There'll be plenty of 'gaps' in her diary from now on. I'm not bitter though. I hope she succeeds. You know, like a toothless parrot. Sucks seeds. Get it?

JoeNotExotic - *Watching the tumbleweed blow past*

EmoGirl – Alan's tinder dates get excited when they hear he has a corner office with views of the city, drives a half a million pound vehicle and gets paid to travel. But it kinda sucks when they find out he's a bus driver.

Fucking_Alan – I used to be a bus driver, but I got sick of people talking behind my back. Ba dum chhh…

EmoGirl- Anyway, enough about Alan's toothless wonders. How you really doing, Lady?

LadyStoneheart23 – You really don't want to know.

TommyTank has joined the chat.

Fucking_Alan –Tommy! Mate. Do I have a story for you!

Regina_Phalange- Hey Tom!

I heard the ping of a private message popping up at the bottom of my screen and I saw it was from Legion. Seeing as this Tommy guy was taking over the feed, I decided to click the chat open and see what Legion had to say.

Legion – I want to know.

LadyStoneheart23- Is Alan's dating drama not doing it for you this morning?

Legion – If he thinks that's a bad date he should have been in my house growing up. My mum's dating history reads like a Stephen King novel. Pure fucking horror.

LadyStoneheart23 – That bad, huh?

Legion – I didn't come with a complimentary bong, syringe, or a spoon to cook her shit up. I was a totally useless son. So yeah, it was that bad. Enough about my fucked up childhood, though. What's happened?

LadySytoneheart23 – He broke into my house last night.

Legion – And?

LadyStoneheart23 – Isn't that enough?

Legion – Did he hurt you?

LadyStoneheart23 – Not physically, no. But he was in my house. My fucking house, Legion. That's another level of fucked up.

Legion – You need to wind it back for me. What's the deal here?

LadyStoneheart23 – He murdered my brother and now he's after me.

Legion – Yeah, I got that part from the last chat, but how did he murder him?

LadyStoneheart23 – My brother was a boxer. He was in a fight with him that turned nasty. He hit my brother, my brother stumbled, fell and cracked his head off the floor.

Legion – So I take it this was no boxing ring then?

LadyStoneheart23 – No. It was bare-knuckle boxing. I fucking hate it too.

Legion – Excuse me for being cruel here, but why is that guy to blame? Sounds to me like he hit your brother, your brother tripped, fell and the rest is mother nature or fate, whatever.

LadyStoneheart23 – You sound like the rest of my town.

Legion – I'm not trying to invalidate what you're saying, just trying to paint a picture here. Why? What are the town saying?

LadyStoneheart23 – That it was an accident. The police too. Apparently, my brother had an undiagnosed brain aneurysm but I don't care what they say. I don't care about complications in surgery or mobile phone footage. It was murder.

Legion – What about the police reports? Statements?

LadyStoneheart23 – They've dropped the case. My brother's so-called best friends all retracted their statements and I'm on my own.

Legion – Sounds harsh. I'm sorry to hear that. Sometimes being alone is better though. More clarity and less noise from other people. If you want revenge it's easier to think and plan without every fucker in your ear.

LadyStoneheart23 – That's what I thought. They don't understand anyway.

Legion – I get it.

LadyStoneheart23 – I know, which is totally insane since I don't even know you. Anyway, I've added my brother's best friend to my shit list.

Legion – Why?

LadyStoneheart23 – Because he's a pussy and a coward.

Legion – Say what you really mean, Lady.

LadyStoneheart23 – I always do. He's hiding something and I'm gonna find out what it is. He won't help me press charges or get the case reopened. He's threatened me. Said if I push it, I'll live to regret it and told me it's a Pandora's box I don't want to open.

Legion – Sounds like a great friend. I hope I don't meet him in a dark alley.

LadyStoneheart23 – Me neither. I'm coming for him. I just haven't decided who I'm taking down first. The stalker or the coward.

Legion – Sometimes it's the devil who hides in plain sight, acting the part of the angel, that turns out to be the most evil fucker of all.

LadyStoneheart23 – Exactly. I hate Mathers, but at least I know what I'm getting with him.

Fuck.

In my erratic, angry state of mind, I'd typed his real name without thinking about it. I couldn't take it back now though. I'd hit return and put it out there.

Legion – Better the devil you know, right?

LadyStyoneheart23 – Exactly.

Legion – I like it. People always spout shit about karma. I say fuck karma. You want shit done? Do it yourself. That way, you get to watch when it all goes your way.

LadyStoneheart23 – That's what I'm hoping!

Legion – So, he died in a fight. What was your brother like?

LadyStoneheart23 – To me, he was everything. My best friend, my brother, my hero. I miss him every day.

Legion – And how do you feel now? Right this second?

LadyStoneheart23- Like I want to burn the whole fucking town down. Smoke out his murderer and give him every last ounce of my pain and misery. Let him carry this instead of me.

Legion – You don't think he's hurting too?

LadyStoneheart23- No

Legion – Why not?

LadyStoneheart23 – He's laughing. Leaving me bloody

roses just because they're the same flower I left on my brother's grave. Watching me, breaking into my garden, my house. It's all a game to him.

Legion – You want control. You want the upper hand.

He wasn't asking. This was a statement, and yeah, I did.

LadyStoneheart23- Damn right I do.

Legion – Then you need to do something to draw him out.

LadyStoneheart23 – Like what?

Legion – What's the one thing that'd piss him off the most?

LadyStoneheart23 – I've tried bad-mouthing him around town. His reputation was in the gutter anyway so it did no good.

Legion – Guys don't give a fuck about shit like that. What does he care about? Come on, Lady. You can do better than this.

LadyStoneheart23 – Fighting.

Legion – And?

LadyStoneheart23 – And his friends.

Legion – You said you felt alone. Maybe you need to start making some friends. Friends who can help you.

LadyStoneheart23 – You think I should start hanging out with his crew and piss him off? Make him come out of hiding 'cos I stole his friends like we're back in high school?

Legion – Maybe not quite like that, but I guess you could do with a friend or two. If it makes him step out from the shadows then it's a win-win.

LadyStoneheart23 – I'll think about it.

Legion – Good. And while you're at it, think about how fucking awesome you've been to stand up to all the bullshit that you have.

LadyStoneheart23 – There's been a lot of bullshit to stand up to.

Legion – Yeah? And you're a fucking warrior. My little warrior.

LadyStoneheart23 – Thanks. Nice to know someone has my back.

Legion – back, front… it don't matter. I've got you.

LadyStoneheart23 – Thanks Legion.

Legion – Stay safe, little warrior. If you ever need me, come on here. I'll have your log in saved on my desktop like the fucking bat signal.

LadyStoneheart23 – My own Bruce Wayne.

Legion – Something like that.

LadyStoneheart23- Thanks.

Legion – Always.

I smiled and logged off my computer, feeling more empowered than I had done in weeks, months even. Maybe a visit to the Renaissance crew was in order. Perhaps I could use them to get what I wanted. No more hiding behind my bedroom curtains or relying on pseudo friends with no backbone to do a one-eighty and help me out. Legion had given me a better plan. Play the monster on his own turf. Set the rules myself. He might have thought he was the king of Sandland, but he wasn't here, and that crown was going to get mangled under my feet. That, and every other thing in his life that was good. I was going to fucking destroy him.

CHAPTER

HARPER

The sun was beating down as I parked up in town. It was busy and I was lucky to get a space. The parking gods were on my side for once.

I used my phone to pay for the parking online and then headed in the direction of Sandland's one and only shopping centre; a precinct filled with approximately six shops in total. Welcome to Sandland. The heart of complete nothingness.

I kept my head down and strolled along, oblivious to the outside world. When I got nearer to the coffee shop, I heard someone call out my name. On a lovely day like today, they'd always put chairs and tables outside, and when I glanced up, I saw Emily Winters waving at me. She was sitting having a coffee with two other girls. Reluctantly, I waved back and went to walk on, then I remembered what Legion had said, and I stopped and headed over to their table. Maybe I could use this to my advantage.

"Harper. Come and sit with us. Have a coffee," Emily said, radiating goodness as she pulled out a spare chair next to her.

"Erm... Okay. Maybe just one."

I sat down, trying to look sane even though I felt like a freak. I didn't know how to act anymore. I couldn't stop shaking.

"Harper, this is Liv and Effy. Girls, this is Harper."

I gave them a forced smile.

"You're Brodie's twin sister," Liv blurted out, her eyes like saucers.

"I think she already knows that, Liv," Emily snapped and then turned to me. "How are you feeling?" She reached out and rubbed over my hand. This girl liked physical contact, which was something I'd always struggled with. Even before losing Brodie.

"I dunno," I said, keeping my eyes on my lap and shrugging. "I get up. I get through the day. Then I go to bed. That's pretty much my life right now."

Shit. I was being way too honest.

"You're so brave to come out today," Effy said, then blushed as if she was supposed to wait to be addressed before speaking to me.

"My mum wanted me to get out. I forced myself."

I didn't know why I was opening up to them. I didn't know them from Adam. What did they care about my life?

"You should be proud of yourself. That's a big step." Emily reached over and squeezed my hand again. I sat there, dumbstruck. What else was I supposed to say? My conversation skills were seriously lacking, and I didn't want to make the effort. I needn't have worried though. Emily and her friends could talk the hind leg off a donkey.

"I'll go get us some more coffees. What are you having, Harper?" Liv asked.

"A latte would be great. Thanks." I went to grab my purse to give her some money, but she brushed me off.

"I'm not taking your money. Put it away. You can get us a drink next time."

Was there going to be a next time?

"So, what've you got planned for tonight then? Spill!" Effy said, turning to Emily.

"Ryan is taking me out. It's our date night. We don't get much privacy these days. Don't get me wrong, I love living at Sean's, but we have to get creative with our alone time, if you know what I mean. Connor doesn't care, but I don't like doing stuff when Sean's about."

"Show Harper your dress." Effy grinned then turned to look at me. "We just went to try on dresses and Em bought the cutest outfit for tonight. Show her, Em."

Emily stiffened slightly.

"I don't think Harper is bothered about my dress. She has more important things on her mind."

I did, but I shrugged. Maybe a bit of normality was in order.

"I don't mind. I'd like to see it. I can't remember the last time I bought a dress. I live in ripped jeans, hoodies, and

Converse these days."

"Nothing wrong with that. I love a good pair of Converse." Emily gave me a wink. Then she pulled out a chiffon and silk blue baby doll dress covered in delicate glitter. It was so pretty and unlike anything I'd ever wear. But I liked it. It suited Emily down to the ground.

"Now that is a fucking dress," Liv said, placing the tray of coffees down on the table. "Doubt it'll stay on long though. Good job it's not a tight bodycon, hey. Better access, if you know what I mean." She cackled at her own innuendo and the other two blushed.

I sat watching them, fascinated by the dynamics at play. Liv seemed to be more confident and louder. Effy was quieter and more reserved. And Emily? She was a mix of the two. Not in your face, but welcoming all the same. I was starting to warm to her. Only a little bit, but it was something.

"Do you know where he's taking you?" Effy asked.

"I couldn't care less," Emily replied. "I don't need anything fancy."

"What? You bought that dress so he could shag you on the back seat of his van?" Liv rolled her eyes.

"No. Maybe." Em chuckled.

"Ugh! I'm so jealous." Liv threw her head back and groaned. "At least one of us is getting some action. I could make a joke about camel toes and being as dry and barren as the Sahara Desert, but I won't gross you out while you're all drinking."

"Yeah, thanks for that image, Liv. Nice one." Emily laughed, almost choking on her latte.

"You know you can get creams for that," Effy whispered, and then went bright red again.

"I was joking, Eff. You know me. If I'm getting no action, I'll make my own. Speaking of which, did you see the photos of those new vibrators I sent you on WhatsApp? Bloody amazing." Liv started to tap on her phone and show Effy what she'd already sent her. Effy pretended to look interested, but she just looked awkward.

"Put your dildos away, Liv. Harper didn't come to sit with us to find out about your latest purchase."

"She saw yours." Liv shrugged.

"It was a dress not a twelve-inch rubber cock," Emily blurted out, and I couldn't hold back my laugh.

"It's silicone not bloody rubber. Anyway, maybe Harper would prefer dildos to dresses. You get more use out of them."

I sipped my coffee to avoid having to answer and let them prattle on, talking about anything and everything. They chatted for ages, and even though I didn't contribute all that much, they didn't make me feel bad about staying quiet. I quite liked playing the role of a girl with no worries for a while. This was all new for me.

After a while, I said my goodbyes and left, telling Emily I hoped she had a good date night, and Liv that I hoped she enjoyed her special purchase too. Emily sprang out of her chair to hug me before I went. I'd never really been a hugger, but I didn't push her away. I didn't want to be rude.

As I walked back to my car, the sick feeling that was always heavy and stagnant in my stomach felt less overwhelming. I was proud of myself. I'd gone out, had coffee, and made some conversation. Maybe I wasn't a total freak after all.

When I got home, I made my way upstairs to my room and logged onto the chat.

LadyStoneheart23 has joined the chat.

HangingWithMyGnomies- I feel like that some days. Sometimes it's enough that you made it to the end of the day, mate.

Regina_Phalange – Alan, I lost my sister two years ago and I still cry most days. Coming on here is the release I need sometimes.

Fucking_Alan- Fucking sucks.

Regina_Phalange- Whatever gets you through the day. As long as it isn't illegal or harmful to your health, that is.

Fucking_Alan- Today's a fucking right-off. I'm gonna log off and do a John Wick marathon. Or maybe I'll go old school and do The Matrix.

HangingWithMyGnomies- You do you, bud. Always here if you need us.

Legion has joined the chat.

My heart jumped into my throat when I saw his name pop up and then the private chat box appeared below.

Legion – You okay?

LadyStoneheart23 – Yeah. You weren't joking about that bat call, were you?

Legion- Always here when you need me. So, what's up?

LadyStoneheart23- I took your advice. Went out and had a coffee with his best friend's girlfriend of all people.

Legion. How did it go?

LadyStoneheart23- Surprisingly… not awful. She's actually really nice. She made me feel welcome and… normal, I guess.

Legion- Do you like feeling normal?

LadyStoneheart23- That's a weird question. But actually, I don't think I'll ever be normal. I always felt a little bit crazy even before my brother died.

Legion- Good. Normal is overrated. And what is normal, anyway? One guy's normal is another guy's crazy.

LadyStoneheart23- I'm thinking you lie further in the crazy camp than the normal one.

Legion- What gave me away?

LadyStoneheart23- Apart from your name meaning you're possessed by demons? Lol. The way you seem to not give a fuck.

Legion- I don't.

LadyStoneheart23- I like that.

Legion- Makes life a lot simpler.

LadyStoneheart23- I need to take a leaf out of your book. I want to not give a fuck.

Legion- But then you wouldn't be being true to yourself. You're the little warrior. Warriors who don't give a fuck are dangerous.

LadyStoneheart23- I want to be dangerous.

Legion- I think you're better off being smart. Leave the danger to knuckleheads like me.

LadyStoneheart23- You're not a knucklehead.

Legion- I am.

LadyStoneheart23- Knuckleheads don't quote the bible and Machiavelli.

Legion- This one does.

LadyStoneheart23- Why are you helping me?

Legion- I like you. You have a voice that needs to be heard. Power that needs to be unleashed. I want to help you with that.

LadyStoneheart23- You don't know anything about me.

Legion- I know you loved your brother and you'd do anything to avenge his death, so that makes you a loyal sister. I know you take time to sit back and listen, read about how others are feeling on here and you choose your words carefully. That shows you're kind and thoughtful. You take time out of your day to speak to a no-mark like me, so that means you're selfless. And each day you wake up, not knowing what shit the world is going to drop on you. That makes you brave beyond belief. See? You're my little warrior. I know more than you realise.

LadySyoneheart23- Erm… speechless right now. That's some of the nicest shit anyone has ever said to me.

Legion- Meh. I'm a smooth-talking knucklehead too.

LadyStoneheart23- And I know nothing about you. Tell me something about yourself. Something that no one else knows.

I sat and watched the blank screen, worried that my question had scared him off. He didn't reply for a while and then a message popped up and I let go of the breath I'd been holding.

Legion- The last memory I have of my mother is her screaming into my face that she hated me and wished I was dead.

LadyStoneheart23- Fuck. That's brutal. I'm so sorry.

Legion- I was three years old.

LadyStoneheart23- She must've been high. No mother would ever truly think that about their child.

Legion- She was high, but she meant it. She hated me.

LadyStoneheart23- I'm sure she didn't. How did you get over that?

Legion- I didn't.

LadyStoneheart23- Oh, God. I actually wish I could

climb through my screen and hug you, and I hate hugging.

Legion- That's not the worst memory either, just one I've never shared with anyone.

LadyStoneheart23- If you ever want to share some of the worst, I'm here. I'm no counsellor but I know what it's like to keep shit bottled up. It's not good.

Legion- I don't think anyone is ready for that kind of darkness, least of all you, little warrior. We're supposed to be focusing on building you up, not loading more onto your shoulders.

LadyStoneheart23- But it might help you heal.

Legion- Heal. I resigned myself to the fact that I'll never heal a long time ago. I have scars on my body but it's the ones inside, the scars that people don't see, that hurt the worst. They're the ones that'll never heal. They'll never go away. I've got a lot of those. I'm a lost cause. A tortured soul.

I felt my chest grow heavy with sadness, imagining some disfigured guy sat at a computer somewhere pouring his heart out to me. A guy who felt ugly inside and out. But it didn't matter to me what he looked like. Beauty came in all different forms. For me, it came from inside. And right then, he was the most beautiful person because of what he was doing; trying to make me feel good about myself and being a warrior himself too.

LadyStoneheart23- I think you should wear your scars

with pride. They're your battle scars. Proof that you're a survivor.

Legion- I had to survive a lot more than just my mother.

LadyStoneheart23- Oh?

Legion- And that is a conversation for another day.

LadyStoneheart23- Little steps.

Legion- Little steps indeed. You did good today. Smile. Hold your head high and fuck them all.

LadyStoneheart23- I'm glad you messaged me.

Legion- I'm glad I found you. Goodbye, little warrior.

I had a secret.

His name was Legion.

And slowly but surely, I could feel myself starting to open up to him; to the idea of him. He made me feel hopeful for a new day. Excited about when our next chat would be. And gave me butterflies just by reading or whispering his name.

He was my secret.

Just for me.

Only me.

CHAPTER

Seventeen

BRANDON

I'd waited long enough.

I was tired of living in the shadows.

Every dog has its day and mine was about to get wild. I bloody loved it.

The police weren't pursuing my case, and after a quick chat to Pat Murphy on the phone the night before, I was itching to get back. Pat said he could offer me fights, pay me really good money too. I wanted that. I missed the adrenaline rush and the high I got from boxing. Getting casual work on the building sites went someway to channelling my pent-up aggression, lifting the heavy bricks and shit, but it wasn't enough. I needed that raw, electric buzz of energy. The shouts from the crowd. The feeling that nobody, not one fucker in this town had beaten me. Life might've kicked my ass when I was a kid, but now I was the one taking it by the balls and showing everyone who was boss.

I followed Ryan to the old waterworks across town. The place had been bought by a local building contractor and they'd already started cleaning out the place. Good job. The last time we were here, scoping it out for one of our parties, it smelt like shit, and anyone stepping their foot through the front door would've been knee deep in it too.

Not today though.

The floors had been cleared, plastered over, and there was stuff lying around; scaffolding and materials from the builders. The fencing around the place warned trespassers to stay out. There was danger on the premises. Advertising that was like waving a red rag in front of a bull for the likes of us.

Danger?

We lived for it.

I watched Ryan pick his way through the rubble, and tentatively, so as not to alert him to my presence, I followed him. When he came to the open warehouse area at the back of the works he stopped, and I heard him greet Finn and Zak like they were visiting dignitaries and he wanted to make a good impression. I should've known they'd be here. Well, at least my resurrection would be an epic one. Finn had got the prelude, now it was show time.

"The new flooring is gonna make it easier to set up in here," Zak said, keenly looking around and probably picturing himself as the fucking king residing over proceedings from his decks.

Don't get too comfortable, mate. I'm back now.

I couldn't wait any longer. I stepped forward to make myself known and started to do a slow clap of my hands. All three of them spun around, and surprise, surprise, not one of them looked pleased to see me. Well, Finn looked slightly less pissed off, but he was still frowning.

"The fuck?" Ryan spat, crossing his arms over his chest and giving me an evil glare. He stood with his legs wide in a predatory stance, obviously feeling cocky and ready to face off.

Bring it on, fuckers.

"Pleased to see me?" I laughed. "You all look like you've seen a ghost."

"A ghost that should've stayed dead," Ryan sneered and eyeballed me like a motherfucker. Didn't he know that even in death I'd still wanna be heard? I was going nowhere.

"Ryan, let's hear him out, okay?" Zak cut in, patting Ryan on the chest.

"Yeah, *Ryan*. Hear me out. Listen to your bitches."

He didn't like that, and I couldn't give a fuck.

"Fuck you, Brandon," Zak scowled at me like the bitch he was.

I laughed. I liked stirring shit up like this. I'd missed the banter. I held my hand up to my ear, pretending I was deaf to mock him. "Fuck me, was that? Or fuck me over? 'Cos the three of you have been doing a really good job of that lately."

Ryan charged forward, panting like a rabid dog. If they could, his nostrils would've been blazing fire.

"You fucked yourself over, mate." He held his arms up like he was the fucking boss. "So, tell us, what are you doing here? It's a bit of a coincidence that you've chosen today of all days to come back. Checking to see how your secret revenge plan is going, hey?"

I had no fucking idea what he was on about. What was special about today?

I didn't take the bait though. This meeting was going to progress on my terms, not theirs.

"Mate, if I had a revenge plan for you three fuckers, you'd know about it. No secrets here. I'm as honest as shit about how much I fucking hate you and what you did to me. But as usual, I have no clue what you're on about. Are you that scared of me you're starting to make things up in your head now?"

I saw anger then exasperation wash over each of their faces, and it spurred me on to know I was getting to them.

"What we did to you? What exactly did we do to you?" Ryan narrowed his gaze at me. He was doing a really good job of looking like a clueless twat.

I ran my hand over my jaw and gave them my signature smile. The one that told them I didn't take any shit.

"We had a fight over a girl. I can handle that. We lost our heads over a bit of pussy and we went crazy." I shrugged like it was no big deal.

"You fucking cunt." Ryan went to launch himself on me, but Zak and Finn held him back.

"That's it, bitch. Let your guard dogs keep you in check." I smirked, knowing I was driving him insane and loving every minute.

He pointed his finger at me, leaning over Zak's shoulder as he shouted. "You call Emily a bit of pussy again and you'll regret it."

I pretended to look like I gave a damn, shaking my head and trying to stifle the grin that wanted to break free.

Maybe it was a low blow?

But he'd got a few blows of his own in the last time we went toe-to-toe. It was my turn for a bit of payback.

"I call a spade a spade."

"Yeah, and you're a fucking knobhead," Ryan said, spitting venom. "What do you want? Say your shit and get out of here. We've all been better off since you left."

"Ry, that's bullshit," Zak interrupted. "Let's at least hear what he's got to say."

Ryan yanked his arm out of Zak's grip, giving him a dirty look. Then he took a step back and turned to face me.

"Go on then. Enlighten us. What are you here for?"

"You know what? I fucking hate you right now." Not my best comeback but it was how I felt.

Ryan lifted his chin, acting all smug and defiant.

"Can't say I like you all that much either."

Good. The feeling was mutual.

"We fell out over Emily. That's cool. I'm over it. But what I can't get over is how you three fucked me over after. You." I pointed at Ryan first. "We've been mates for years. You were like a fucking brother to me. I was closer to your family than

I was to my own. Okay, so you've got your girl now. Fair play. But you couldn't help yourself, could you? Rushing off the next morning to make your statements at the police station about the fight. You couldn't wait to throw me under the fucking bus. Did it make you feel like a man? You'd hit me, told me what a worthless piece of shit I was, won the girl, and then off you went spilling your guts to the police about what a fuck up I was that night."

His eyes went wide. He didn't know I'd been watching them that morning. I knew more than I'd ever let on. Knowledge was power, after all.

"My statement was nothing like that," he said, shaking with anger as he spoke. "I told them I hadn't seen you. I also told them that I knew you better than anyone else and that I'd stake my life on it being an accident. I'd go to court and say that shit too. So, don't come in here with your bullshit accusations and try and paint me out to be something that I'm not. Both me and Em stood by you. We always would. There's nothing that we've done in these last few months to go against you. I don't care what you think you've seen or what you think you know. I know the truth." He banged his chest with his fist in confirmation. "And my conscience is clear, *brother*."

I took a moment to collect my thoughts. There was stuff I still needed to get off my chest, and I was struggling to see things as clearly as I did before. Ryan's little speech was fucking with my brain.

"And you," I said, getting my shit together fast and

turning to face Zak. "All you've done is strut around town with your over-gelled hair and your stupid grin. You couldn't wait to get those parties started again, could you? You had the spotlight all to yourself. You liked that, didn't you, *mate*? You didn't have to vie for the attention anymore. No more crowds heading down to see me fight and leaving your shitty D.J. act so it'd flop like Lockwood's limp dick. You could shine all on your own. When I was around, you didn't stand a chance. I was who they came to see. I *was* the fucking event."

"And we all miss having you around," Zak replied, sounding humble. "So, I like a bit of attention." He shrugged and grinned to himself. "But I never felt jealous when you got it too. You're talking out of your arse, mate. If you came back now, we'd welcome you with open arms."

"Would we?" Ryan said, cocking his eyebrow.

Zak turned to face him and frowned.

"Yeah, you know we would. Takings have been down since Brandon left." Then he looked back at me. "We'd have you back and we'd have your back. We always have. I don't know why you're coming at us with all this shit. We're the ones who should be mad."

What the fuck was he on about now?

"And why should you be mad? Come on. I could do with a laugh."

"Where do we start?" Ryan shook his head, grinning smugly to himself.

Finn had stayed pretty quiet so far, and I couldn't tell if

he was measuring us all up or he was scared to admit he'd already seen me.

"Start at the beginning, bro. I've got all day."

I was the one to spread my arms out wide this time, showing Ryan that I was the boss around here, not him. I was ready for them to come at me and whine like little bitches about how I'd abandoned them. Bring it on.

"You pissed off without telling anyone where you were going." Ryan started right where I knew he would. "You got into a fucking fight that's been hanging over all our heads for the last few months. Cops have been grilling us. Following us everywhere to try and find you. But don't worry about that. Don't worry about fucking up our lives, as long as you're okay, right?"

As long as I'm okay? He needed a fucking wake-up call.

"You think I've been okay since I left? You think it's been easy for me? Do you think I liked watching you go about your business as if nothing fucking happened?"

I could feel the anger rising up again. I was ready to explode.

"Then why didn't you reach out to us sooner? We'd have helped." Finally, Finn had spoken.

I knew they were visiting my nan and I was thankful for that, but I wasn't going to kid myself.

"You'd have ratted me out first chance you got."

"We wouldn't do that. You know you can trust us," Finn replied, and from the contrite look on his face, I almost believed him.

"He can trust us, but can we trust him?" Ryan piped up.

"You can trust that I'll knock you the fuck out if you've got the balls to come over here and say that again," I snapped.

"Yeah? You daring me?" Ryan goaded like he was ready to throw down with me in this shithole.

"Woah. Hold on a minute. Let's hear what he's got to say about the text messages," Zak said, playing referee again.

"What text messages?" I asked, looking each one of them in the face.

"The ones you sent us last night. We know it was you."

Ryan pulled his phone out of his back pocket and started to read from it.

"We know what you've done. It's payback time. We are coming for you." He held his phone up and snarled at me. "What is this shit? Do you think this scares us?"

What the fuck?

"I didn't send that."

"Like fuck you didn't." Ryan stared straight at me, his accusation as clear as day. I didn't take my eyes off him once when I answered.

"I didn't."

We stood silently for a few seconds, looking between each other. The only sound was the drip drip of the pipes above and our heavy breathing.

"If he said he didn't send it, I believe him," Finn said, breaking the silence.

"Me too," Zak added.

"Well, if he didn't send it, who did?" Ryan pocketed his phone and gave the others a pointed stare. Something was going on and I wanted to know what it was. I hated being left out of the loop.

"Let me get this straight. You got a text message last night-"

"We all did," Ryan butted in.

"And you think it was me? Mate, I didn't send shit to you. Honestly. On my nan's life. And I wouldn't fucking swear on her life for just anyone, but I will. For you. I. Didn't. Send it."

"Okay." Ryan threw his head back and let out a groan. "Looks like we've got more shit to deal with than we thought."

"Why the fuck are you letting a bloody text message get to you? Block the number. It's not hard. Who gets spooked over a text? It's probably kids messing about. Have you lost your balls since I left as well as your street cred?"

"We haven't lost anything, and we're taking it fucking seriously because what we did was some serious shit. Do you have any idea who those people were that we pissed off when we exposed Winters? We're playing with the big boys now. This isn't a fucking joke." Ryan always did take everything to heart. He needed the likes of me around to keep him grounded.

"If they're that hell bent on getting to us, a text message should be the least of your worries. It's a threat, but it's a weak one. A coward's way of doing business."

"Us?" Ryan scoffed. "You make it sound like you're on our side." Ryan crossed his arms over his chest, flexing his muscles as he did. He should know by now, that didn't scare me.

"It could be the Lockwoods? They're the biggest cowards around here." Finn suggested. "Maybe they found out Zak was snooping after what you and Emily said about them dropping the case and threatening Harper."

"Come again? They threatened her?" Heat coursed through me and I clenched my fists. My rage levels were spiking again. Even hearing her name made me feral.

"Don't." Ryan went back to wagging his finger at me like a high school teacher. "Leave her out of this. That girl has been through enough."

I squared my shoulders and took a step towards him.

"If I want to talk about her, I will."

Ryan sneered over at me.

"You can't even say her name out loud, can you? Feeling guilty?"

Like I'd ever admit that to him. I couldn't even admit it to myself.

"I've got nothing to feel guilty about."

"You had a fight with her brother. He died. Okay, so he didn't die solely because of your punches, but they fucking helped." Ryan was flying a little too close to the wind on this one.

"It's bare-knuckle boxing. What did he expect? Could happen to me one day," I said, not giving a fuck.

Ryan shook his head in disgust at my response.

"Are you still gonna fight?" Finn asked me, steering the conversation away from Harper.

"Pat has fights lined up for me. The pay's pretty good too."

Ryan gave a low chuckle then stopped and glared at me.

"So, you're coming back. Are you gonna just rock up to Sandland like nothing's happened? Leave it to us to break the news to Harper? That girl's sanity is hanging by a thread as it is."

"Don't fucking say her name!" I shouted.

"Why? 'Cos you can't handle it? Can't take the blowback, mate?"

I was seconds away from reminding Ryan why I was the undefeated fucking champion in our town.

"No," I hissed through my clenched jaw. 'Cos she isn't yours to talk about. So shut your fucking mouth."

"What?" Ryan glared at me and gave a fake laugh, but Finn cut him off.

"You'd fight for Pat and not us?"

"Why would I fight for you?"

"I don't know. Because we're friends? We stick together. Ryan might be pissed, but if you want to settle your differences with your fists, I'm sure he'll get over it after." Finn did have a point.

"I don't need to fight him. I have an important meeting with the college tomorrow. It won't look good if I rock up with a face covered in bruises," Ryan replied.

"College?" Had I heard him right?

"Yeah. I'm doing a business and accountancy course. Hoping it helps to grow the kit car business," Ryan said, suddenly losing the bravado and talking to me like he used to.

"Cool. I'm happy for you."

And just like that, the atmosphere started to shift.

You see, that's what we did. We fought like brothers. Said shit that most people wouldn't and then we took a step back. I took that step back and realised that the guys standing in front of me were the only family I had. I'd been pissed at them, but if I was honest with myself, I knew they'd done their best given the circumstances. Could they have done more? Probably. But then I wasn't always easy to deal with. I knew that.

"If I come back, would you let me fight again?" I asked, knowing what Zak and Finn's answers would be, but it was Ryan I wanted a response from.

"Yeah. That's what we want," Finn said.

"I'll miss the limelight." Zak smirked. "But yeah. The fights were our unique selling point. Anyone can put on a party."

"Not like us they can't," Ryan stated proudly.

"Whatever. But no one can put on a show like Brandon. Those fights were the shit."

174

Yes, Zak. Yes, they were.

"Well, that's two votes," I said, folding my arms and standing tall. "Am I going to have to veto you, Ry, or am I back in?"

He took a deep breath and stared me down.

"We want honesty."

"Yeah," I shrugged and then nodded in agreement.

"No bullshit," he added.

"Cool," I replied, trying not to smirk or look smug. I knew this was a big step for Ry. It was for me too, and I didn't want to jeopardise this truce we were slowly building.

"And you leave Emily and Harper alone."

He said it as a statement, not a question. I could've guessed that'd be Ryan's last deal-breaker.

"I don't want to upset your missus," I answered honestly.

See, I was abiding by his rules already.

"Looks like the crew is back in action again then," Ryan declared, and the other two smiled.

I put my arm out to shake Ryan's hand and he took it. We'd made progress. It wasn't at all what I'd expected when I came in here. In reality, it was better. I'd thought I was entering a warzone. I'd braced myself for battle. But the cold war was thawing already. Blood might run thicker than water, but our brotherhood ran stronger than anything. The Renaissance men were a team. A team I was proud of. And now we were getting back on track. We could go back to being unstoppable.

"You'd better prepare your statement for the police though," Ryan added. "They might've dropped the case, but they'll still want to haul you in."

"Oh, don't worry. I've got plenty to say to them."

"I don't think we want to know," Zak said, smiling. "We've missed you, man."

He walked over to me and gave me a hug, patting my back as he did.

Finn grinned.

And Ryan?

He muttered something about telling Emily before anyone else found out I was back.

That's right, motherfuckers.

Brandon Mathers was back.

But I hadn't forgotten why I left. There were still a lot of people on my ever-growing shit list, and not everyone was going to be hanging the flags out when I returned. I'd find out who sent those texts. I'd find out what the Lockwoods were up to too.

And Harper?

That was unfinished business I would take great pleasure in wrapping up.

CHAPTER Eighteen

HARPER

"Harper, love. There's someone here to see you."

Mum walked into the living room and I muted the television, having absolutely no idea who'd be visiting me at home.

Then Emily Winters appeared, craning her neck from behind Mum's back to greet me and give me a shy smile.

"Hey. I hope you don't mind me dropping by unannounced like this."

"Of course she doesn't," Mum answered for me. "Emily, would you like a tea or coffee? Or a cold drink, perhaps?"

"A tea would be lovely. Milk, no sugar. Thank you, Mrs Yates." Emily sure was good at talking to parents. She already had my mum eating out of the palm of her hands.

"Call me Tanya," Mum said over-enthusiastically, batting her eyelids and grinning down at Emily like she was the second coming.

She scuttled off to the kitchen and Emily sat down on the sofa a little way down from where I was. From the way she was fidgeting I guessed this wasn't a social call.

"How have you been?" she asked as she wrung her hands in her lap. She seemed nervous. That didn't bode well as far as I was concerned.

"I'm okay. Today is... bearable. Just." I smiled, hoping I sounded jovial and trying to put her at ease. It didn't work. She just nodded and stared at the muted T.V. screen.

"I've heard they set a date for your dad's trial. That sucks," I added. A pretty lame attempt at a conversation, but it was something.

"Yeah. I'm not sure I'll be going to the court unless I have to. Kind of want to avoid the press and all that crap."

Now it was my turn to nod and stare absent-mindedly. Should I put the T.V. volume back up or would that be too rude?

"I tried that website you recommended," I said, in a desperate bid to fill in the awkward silence.

"Yeah? What did you think?" She brightened up a little and swivelled in her seat to face me. You'd think I'd just given her the best news she'd heard all day.

"It's not at all what I thought it would be. It actually makes me laugh."

"I felt the same. Some days the chat would go darker, but there was always someone in there to lighten the mood. Does Alan still go in there?" She smirked, and I could tell she probably had a few Alan anecdotes to share from her own visits to the forum.

"Fucking Alan? Yeah. He's a one-off, isn't he?"

"That's putting it politely."

We both laughed nervously.

"Do you ever go in there now?" I hoped she didn't. I didn't want to share this with anyone else. I liked having it all to myself. My secret haven. The thought of Legion chatting with her made me uncomfortable.

"No. Not anymore. But it helped me at a time when all I was capable of was talking online. I liked the anonymity."

I felt a little lighter hearing that.

"Me too," I admitted.

Mum strolled back in with a tray loaded up with mugs of tea. She'd also added some Kit-Kats and Chocolate Mini Rolls.

"Help yourselves, girls," she said and took her own mug off the tray then left us to it.

"Your mum is lovely. If we were at my house it'd be china cups, plates of biscuits, and *don't slouch while you're sitting on the sofa, dear*. I love a Mini Roll." Emily leant forward to grab one off the tray. Then she sipped her tea and started to peel the wrapper off.

"It's lovely to see you, and thanks for thinking of me, but I've got a feeling there's something you want to tell me and you're stalling," I said, as Emily averted her eyes and shoved more chocolate into her mouth to give her some thinking time.

"Well, I was thinking of coming to see you. You know, to

check on how you are. But you're right, there is something I need to let you know about. I wanted to tell you before you heard this from anyone else."

I put my mug down and sat forward.

"Spill it. What's going on?"

Emily took a deep breath and fixed her eyes on me as she spoke.

"He's back."

She didn't need to say who *he* was. I knew. And hearing her say he was back made the bottom of my stomach drop out and a wave of nausea engulf me. I started to shake, as if he was going to walk through the door at any minute. It was crazy because, in my mind, when he'd invaded my thoughts, my privacy, and my fucking home, I'd wanted him to come out and face me. I wanted to stand in front of him and give him both barrels. Destroy him with the force of my anger. But hearing he was back, actually living and breathing, walking around Sandland like Brodie never existed, that bothered me. I didn't want to see him, not really. I didn't know what I'd do if and when I did. Was he laughing about us? Did he think this was all a big fucking joke?

"Have *you* seen him?" I asked.

"No. Not yet. But Ryan has and he said he's pissed but he wants his life back."

"He wants his life back." I shook my head, exasperated at what she'd just told me. "He's lucky he has a life to come back to. My brother doesn't. Neither do I most days."

"Oh, Harper. I'm so sorry." Emily scooched down the sofa to sit right next to me and take my hand in hers. "If it's any consolation, Ryan told him he has to stay away from you. He warned him. You are off-limits. It was part of their agreement for his return."

I knew that was bullshit. If Mathers wanted to get to me, he would. No one told Brandon Mathers what to do.

"It's fine. Well, it's not, but I'll survive." I slipped my hand out of hers and sipped my tea, but it hurt to swallow with the golf ball of anxiety in my throat.

"Ryan said he can tell he's full of guilt. For you, I mean. He feels guilty about what happened."

"And he should be."

"I know. I just don't want you to think he's waltzing around town with that swagger of his and giving it the big I am. He isn't the same. That's what Ry said, anyway." She shrugged. "And there's one other thing you should know. He's going back to fighting."

I never expected he'd stop. That man was a walking weapon of mass destruction and his fists were locked and loaded. I felt sorry for the next sucker who ended up in the ring with him.

"He hasn't learnt his lesson then."

"Nope."

"It's all about the money and the notoriety with him, isn't it?" The guy's bravado would always overshadow any guilt he might be putting out there. In fact, I reckoned the guilt was all for show. Something he felt he had to do to be accepted back into the fold of his little fucked-up crew. Once the gossip died down, he wouldn't show an ounce of remorse, only swagger.

"Actually, that isn't why he fights, but it's not my place to talk about that." Emily blushed and went back to fidgeting again, wringing her hands in her lap and biting her lip.

I should've known Emily would be on his side, keeping his secrets, and trying to defend him. I wanted to challenge her on it, but I didn't have the energy. She'd think whatever the fuck she wanted to. It didn't matter what I had to say.

"I don't care anymore." I sighed. "He can take all the hits he wants, as far as I'm concerned. That man is dead to me. I don't ever want to see him. I hate him and everything he stands for."

Emily hummed out some weak form of agreement and we sat there, finishing our tea in silent contemplation. Eventually, Emily piped up first.

"If you want to get that first meeting over with, there's a party next week at the waterworks. Brandon's doing his first fight there. You should come."

"Why would I want to meet him? Why would I put myself through that?" I couldn't believe they were laying the bloody red carpet out for him like that. Making his return something to talk about. He left for a reason. He didn't deserve any recognition for his comeback. I certainly wasn't going to be there to see all that fake fanfare.

"I just thought it might be better on your terms. You wouldn't have to go up to him or speak to him. But maybe seeing him in a crowded room might help fight some of those demons you're wrestling."

Like it was that easy to get rid of my demons. The devil appeared in many forms, and in Sandland, his face was one of them. Why would I purposely put myself through that?

"I appreciate the offer, but I'd rather avoid him completely. Thanks though."

I thought that'd be the end of it, but she wasn't giving up easily.

"I hear what you're saying, but you won't be able to avoid him forever. Sandland's a small town."

Just watch me.

"You're talking like he has some effect on my life. He doesn't. He wasn't a part of my life before it all happened and he isn't now. I'd rather forget he exists."

I was lying, of course. Brandon Mathers consumed ninety-nine percent of my thoughts. Actually, since chatting with Legion, it was probably slightly less, but still, he was dominating my life. Forgetting he existed would be like forgetting to breathe.

After a while, Emily stood up to leave. She'd achieved what she came to do; she'd told me about his return. But she seemed disappointed that I didn't see him the way she did. She obviously had empathy for whatever it was that made him tick. I just saw that tick as a time-bomb ready to go off and destroy everything that I loved now he was back.

I followed her out of the living room and down the hallway.

"I'll send you details of the party, in case you change your mind," she said, opening the front door.

"I won't change my mind," I answered firmly, but Emily wasn't listening. She was cooing over something on the front step.

"Oh my God, these are beautiful. There's no card though. Are they for you or your mum?" She leant down to pick something up, and when she straightened up and turned to face me, I saw them. A bouquet of white roses wrapped in cellophane. No note. No RIP message. Just the flowers this time. But I knew who they were from. This was his 'I'm back' message.

Emily placed them in my arms, and like a dumb fool, I stood there and took them without saying a word.

"Looks like someone has an admirer." She winked and then waved her goodbyes as she left.

I watched her get into her car and drive off, then I looked around. I knew he was there somewhere, watching me. I could feel him. He wanted to see how I'd react to the news that he'd returned. How I'd respond to his flowers. They were beautiful; Emily was right. But I didn't want them in my house. They were his sick way of reminding me what I'd lost. Him trying to control and frighten me.

I walked over to the side of the house, opened the lid of

the bin, and dropped them in. They belonged in the trash, and so did he. I grinned, looking down at them, knowing they would die in that dark, filthy box. A fitting end for something beautiful that he'd touched. He tainted everything.

Satisfied that I'd given him the show he'd come to watch, I turned and marched back into the house. When I shut the door, I leant my back against it and squeezed my eyes shut. I didn't know how much longer I could hold it all together. I felt like the pressure gauge in my head was building again and I needed a release.

–

LadyStoneheart23 has joined the chat.

EmoGirl- I don't know if they were his favourite flowers, but I left them on his grave. It's the first time I've been there.

JoeNotExotic- That's a big step for you, Emo. I'm proud of you, hun. I know you don't really have much to do with that side of your family.

EmoGirl- It's not through choice, Joe. I don't know them. They don't know me. I should make more of an effort, I suppose. It's not like I have a lot of family around me at the moment. I could do with a bit of extra support sometimes.

JoeNotExotic- Take it at your pace, babe. At the end of the day, if they wanted you in their lives, they'd be there for you. I'll always be there for you.

Fucking_Alan- Is it wrong that I wanna sing the 'Friends'

theme tune now?

JoeNotExotic- Alan, we'd expect nothing less.

EmoGirl- I need cheering up, Al. Tell me about the worst date you've ever been on.

JoeNotExotic- I think we've heard about them all already.

Fucking_Alan- There's always more, my friend. I am a veritable Wikipedia of dating don'ts. Okay, which one do I go with?

I've got it…

It's gotta be the notorious Felicity.

She turned up at the bar steaming drunk. It was six o'clock and this girl was paralytic. So wasted she could barely stand up. I asked her why she'd had a drink before she came out and she told me she was nervous…

Tommytank- Had to get shit-faced just to date you, hey, Alan?

Fucking_Alan- Lol, Tom. No. She said she'd liked me for ages and she needed a little something to calm her nerves. Two minutes later, she threw up in her handbag and then lurched forward and tried to kiss me. Grossest kiss I've ever dodged. Pure filth.

EmoGirl- OMG.

Fucking_Alan- That's not even the punch line, Emo. Turns out she had her two kids in the beer garden waiting on us. I didn't even know she had kids. Don't get me wrong, I'd happily date a MILF. But one who shows up comatose with her kids at the pub? Nah. I'll pass.

Legion has joined the chat.

EmoGirl- Perfect place to jump in, Legion. Alan was just telling us all about barf-gate.
Legion- How will I ever recover from the loss of hearing that story?

When I saw his name, my heart did a little happy dance. He was here. He was always here when I needed him. The private chat box appeared and I clicked without hesitation.

Legion- Little warrior. How's it going?
LadyStoneheart23- All the better for being on here.
Legion- Tell me something you did today that made you smile.

I was going to type, coming on here and chatting to you, but that sounded way too cheesy.

LadyStoneheart23- I took a bouquet of flowers from my fucked-up stalker and dumped them in the trash.
Legion- And how did that make you feel?
LadyStoneheart23- Like I was giving him the finger. I knew he was watching me. I'd have preferred to shove the flowers up his ass. Those thorns would be a killer. Lol. But

the trash was the next best thing.

Legion- You, my little warrior, are a girl after my own heart.

That made me smile.

LadyStoneheart23- Tell me something that made you smile today.

His response took a while to come through, but when it did, it warmed my heart.

Legion- Knowing my little warrior gave someone the finger today and took back some of her power.

LadyStoneheart23- Quiet day in the Legion household then if that's your high point.

Legion- Quiet in the house, noisy in my head.

LadyStoneheart23- Talk to me. You always say you're here for me, but I want to know more about you. I'd like to think I could help you too.

Legion- Why?

LadyStoneheart23- 'Cos that's what friends do. And I want to help. It makes me feel good.

Legion- You're one of those do-gooders then, yeah?

LadyStoneheart23- I just wanna be a good friend.

He didn't reply and I felt like he was backing away from

me.

LadyStoneheart23- I know you said I wasn't ready for your darkness, but nothing fazes me. I've been told I'm a good listener.

Still nothing.

LadyStoneheart23- Tell me something that made you feel powerful.

I sat back, watching and waiting for the screen to come to life. I was desperate for more.

Legion- Really not gonna give up, are you?
LadyStoneheart23- Nope.
Legion- Okay… Are you sure you're ready for this?
LadyStoneheart23- Born ready.
Legion- When I was eight years old I was bullied at school. It was bad. Really bad. I have no idea why these guys chose me. Well, I do, kind of. I was the poor kid. The runt of the school. At that time, I was an easy target.
Anyway, this one day, the teacher asked me to take a message to the head. I left the classroom and didn't think anything of it. I gave the note to the head teacher's secretary and when I was heading back to class I got yanked across the hallway and pulled into the boys' toilets. They must've

seen me walk past their classroom and they managed to get out of the room to hunt me down. They weren't in the same class as me, you see. They were a few years older.

My heart was in my throat reading and I couldn't bring myself to interrupt him.

Legion – They started to hit me, knocked me to the floor and got a few kicks in. It was nothing new. They did this most days. But this time, the main one straddled my lap and forced my shirt up. They'd been doing woodwork and they'd sneaked a craft knife out of the classroom. The second guy pinned me down as the main one spat in my face then told me he was gonna give me a mark I'd never forget. He said he hoped I'd bleed to death as he pushed the knife into my stomach and started to carve something.

It was his initial.

He laughed while he did it too.

I lay there trying to kick and thrash them off me, but I wasn't strong enough. The pain from the knife made me shiver and sweat and I swear I was close to blacking out that day. Fucker even punched me after 'cos I'd bled too much and it got on his uniform.

They swapped roles and then the other one got to work, slicing me up. Then they laughed at what their initials were, after they'd branded them on me. I didn't understand what they were on about at the time, but they told me it was something my mum was good at.

I could barely read through the tears. This was his moment of power? What the hell was this?

LadyStoneheart23- I don't know what to say. Didn't a teacher help you?

Legion- No. I stayed in the toilets for ages but they never noticed I hadn't gone back to class. The blood was everywhere, but I used paper towels to try and stop it. I didn't want anyone to find out. Not even my friends.

LadyStoneheart23- How did this make you feel powerful?

Legion- Because once the bleeding died down I went out, changed into my P.E kit so the teacher wouldn't see the blood, and then I found both of their lunch boxes on a trolley in the hallway.

LadyStoneheart23- And?

Legion- And I pissed all over their lunch and then watched them eat it in the playground, scrunching up their faces 'cos their sandwiches were soggy and smelt off. Best fucking feeling ever. Apart from when the cuts stung me when I tried to laugh. That part was shit.

My heart was breaking for this boy. He thought he'd got the upper hand even though they'd maimed him like that. Probably scarred him for life.

LadyStoneheart23- I wish I could go back in time and help you. Those bullies sound like the biggest pieces of shit to ever walk the earth. If you'd been at my school I'd have stepped up to stop it.

The screen went silent again.

LadyStoneheart23- Did the scars fade? It wasn't too deep was it?

Legion- It's still there, I can feel it. But you can't see it now. I had a tattoo to cover it up as soon as I was old enough to get in the artist's chair. Well...until I got a fake I.D. to get me an appointment.

LadyStoneheart23- What tattoo did you get?

Legion- A lion. Its not just any lion though. It's a lion wearing a headdress. Kinda symbolises who's the chief now.

LadyStoneheart23- I love it. Now that is power. I'm so sorry you had to go through that though. You're one of life's fighters too. Obviously, you always have been.

Can I ask you one more question? Say no if you don't want to answer.

Legion- Hit me with it, little warrior.

LadyStoneheart23- What were the initials they carved?

The cursor flickered and dots danced about to tell me he was writing.

Legion- B and J. Get it, BJ? They thought it was fucking funny to carve that into me. I had no clue what it even meant at the time.

LadyStoneheart23- Fuck. I'm so sorry.

Legion- Don't feel sorry for me, little warrior. I've had my day. It's all good. Life throws these things at us to test us. Only the strong survive. Me and you, we're strong. You hear me? You are a fucking warrior. And whatever happens, you will survive.

LadyStoneheart23- I will knowing I have people like you on my side.

Legion- Always. Whatever you need, I will always be here.

And I wholeheartedly believed him too. He'd been there every time I'd needed him.

He had never let me down.

CHAPTER *Nineteen*

HARPER

I spent the next few days avoiding any contact with the outside world unless it was through the chatroom. I didn't want to go out and risk seeing that man. I wasn't prepared. Not mentally, anyway. I knew I couldn't avoid him forever, and I didn't feel totally safe in my own home after the last few flower messages I'd received. But in my room, there was only me and whoever I wanted to invite in.

That was usually Legion.

He'd opened up to me so much more since telling me about the attack in the school bathroom. Turned out he'd been a target for those bullies for years, and he barely left his house growing up. If he did leave to get something for his nan from the shop, they usually found him, and they'd beat the shit out of him. It was always unfair odds too; him on his own and them in a gang. He said he learnt to socialise online or on the rare occasion that his nan allowed it, he went to a friend's house to play on his PlayStation. He was one of the lucky ones. He had a few close friends that he trusted, and they tried their best to look after him. But it wasn't until his twelfth birthday that things started to change for him.

He had a set of dumbbells bought for him as a birthday present. He'd told his friends he wanted to get fitter; stronger, and they'd clubbed together to buy them. He told me how he used them every day and night religiously to build himself up. Then, when he was old enough to get a paper-round he used the extra cash to pay for entry to a local gym and used their equipment. The bullies laid off him once he'd created enough muscles to overpower them. He'd grown taller too. See, that's the thing with bullies. They always target the weaker, smaller ones. It makes them feel big to have power over someone like that, but once they meet a tougher opponent, they crumble. Bullies are cowards hiding behind a front of fake strength. When all is said and done, they are nothing. I told Legion as much and he agreed.

Legion- Don't ever worry about me, little warrior. Every dog has its day. I've had more than my fair share. I don't take shit anymore. They run and hide when they see me nowadays.

LadyStoneheart23- Do you still see them?

Legion- Not all of them. The main one still comes around every now and then. When he does, I love taunting him. He's got years of retribution coming his way. I dish it out in small doses though. I like keeping him on his toes. He'll never get too comfortable 'cos he'll never know when or where I might strike next.

LadyStoneheart23- You said the main one. Two of them carved their initials into you. Where's the other one?

The screen went silent and I waited.

LadyStoneheart23- Do you still see the other one too?
Legion- Not anymore.

He changed the subject pretty quickly after that.

Legion- You've been coming on here a lot more lately. Is there any reason why you're hiding out on here?
LadyStoneheart23- I prefer being here to being out there.
Legion- Is that because you're avoiding facing your fears?
LadyStoneheart23- Why should I have to face anything?
Legion- You shouldn't, but locking yourself away isn't good for you, little warrior. Remember what I said. You are strong. You are powerful. No one can take that away from you.
LadyStoneheart23- You come on here as much as I do.
Legion- Ah. But am I sitting in a bedroom, or in a café chatting to you on my phone? I could be anywhere.
LadyStoneheart23- Are you? At a café, I mean?
Legion- Not this time. I'm in my bedroom. Alone. Talking

to you.

I don't know why, but my stomach flipped. He was alone, in his room, talking to me. A totally innocent statement and yet I felt a little tingle of something.

Ladystoneheart23- I'm alone too. In my room.

Stupid statement, Harper. He already knew that.

Legion- When was the last time you had a guy in your room?
LadyStoneheart23- A long, long time.
Legion- I'm flattered.
LadyStoneheart23-You should be. I don't open my doors for anyone.
Legion- But you have for me.
LadyStoneheart23- Yeah. I feel safe with you.
Legion- And what if what I wanted to do wasn't safe?
LadyStoneheart23- Well, that depends.
Legion- On what?
LadyStoneheart23- On whether I'd enjoy it.
Legion- Oh, you'd enjoy it.

I couldn't type fast enough. I'd never been this excited, nervous and turned on before. Well, not for a long time, anyway. I had a feeling Legion had more wicked intent than he let on, and I was intrigued.

LadyStoneheart23- *Tell me more.*

Legion- *You want to know what I'd do if I was there now, in your room?*

LadyStoneheart23- *Yes.*

LadyStoneheart23- *Tell me.*

Legion- *First of all, I'd make sure the door was locked. I wouldn't want anyone interrupting me.*

LadyStoneheart23- *Good. You take precautions. ;)*

Legion- *Lol. Sometimes. I do like taking risks, but not with you.*

LadyStoneheart23- *So, we're safely locked away. What next?*

Legion- *I'd watch you. See how my being so close affected you. The way you breathe; will it be slow and shallow or deep and wanton? I'd study you. Enjoy the flush in your cheeks, how your skin goosebumps as I take a step nearer. Your eyes would grow wider but you wouldn't know whether to be scared or excited.*

LadyStoneheart23- *I wouldn't be scared with you.*

Legion- *You might be. I can get intense. I would be with you.*

LadyStoneheart23- *I like intense.*

Legion- *Good. I'd stroke my finger along your shoulder or down your face. You'd shiver from the contact and I'd smile. I'd like that I affected you.*

LadyStoneheart23- You do.

Legion- You'll open your mouth slightly to gasp and I'll look at your lips. I'll want to taste you, feel what it's like to have my tongue slide against yours, my mouth on yours.

LadyStoneheart23- Then do it.

Legion- Oh, I will. But it won't be a gentle kiss. I'll thread my fingers into your hair and pull you to me. I'll kiss you hard and take what I want.

LadyStoneheart23- I like that.

Legion- You'll groan into my mouth and it'll be so fucking hot. I'll push you against the wall without breaking free from our kiss and you'll feel what you do to me. How hard you make me.

LadyStoneheart23- God. I want this.

Legion-You'll try to wrap your legs around me, and maybe I'll lean into you a little, give you a bit of that friction you're so desperate for, but I won't be finished with you. I'll want to go further.

LadyStoneheart23- I will too.

Legion- I'll break away from our kiss and leave you panting. You'll touch your lips like you can't believe what we've just done but you'll want more. So will I. I'll always want more of you.

LadyStoneheart23- You're really good at this.

Legion- You have no idea.

Legion- I'll lead you over to the bed and make you lie down. Then I'll climb over you and push your legs apart to sit in-between them. You'll look nervous but you don't need to be, babe. I know how to take care of you. I know what you need.

LadyStoneheart23- I'm so fucking turned-on right now.

Legion- Me too, babe. Me too.

Legion- I'll lift your dress and you'll sigh. Maybe you'll try to cover yourself up, but I'll give you a look to tell you that you should never hide from me. I want to see what's mine.

LadyStoneheart23- Only yours.

Legion- I'll hook my fingers into the side of your knickers and pull them down slowly, looking in your eyes as I do. Then I'll tell you to relax, open your legs wide for me and you will. You'll want me to see every part of you.

LadyStoneheart23- Fuck.

Legion- I'll stroke my fingers along your legs, up and down your thighs but I won't be able to take my eyes off how fucking beautiful you look lying there ready for me. I'll want a taste. I'll want it so fucking bad I won't be able to focus on anything else.

LadyStoneheart23- Neither will I.

Legion- You'll moan as I lower myself between your legs and run my tongue along your pussy. You'll taste even better than I imagined, and I'll lick and suck your clit into my mouth. I'll write the fucking alphabet with my tongue onto your clit to get you off. I'll use my fingers too. One to start off with. I don't want to hurt you. You're so tight and I want you to enjoy every single second. Then, when you're so fucking wet and ready,

I'll use two maybe more, and I'll curl my fingers inside you. You'll arch your back off the bed 'cos you're so turned on, and you'll grab my hair, pulling on it so I'll fuck you harder with my mouth and my fingers.

LadyStoneheart23- This is insanely hot.

Legion- You'll start to shake. I can tell you're close. I'll suck your clit and use my tongue to bring you to orgasm and you'll come all over my fingers and my face. You'll rub your little pussy all over me and I'll keep licking and sucking, bringing you back down to Earth. I'll do it with the biggest grin on my face.

LadyStoneheart23- And then I'll want more.

Legion- You'll always want more. My greedy little warrior.

LadyStoneheart23- I'll want you. I'll want to feel what it's like to have you inside me.

Legion- So what will you do next?

LadyStoneheart23- My heart will be beating out of my chest and I'll probably be shaking like a leaf after what you've just done, but I'll beg you. I'll tell you that I need you. That I need more.

Legion- You've gotta work for it, babe.

LadyStoneheart23- I'll pull you up towards me and yank the buttons of your jeans open. You'll watch me and your breaths will be deep, panting almost. You want me to touch you.

Legion- I do.

LadyStoneheart23- Then I'll pull your jeans and your underwear off in one go. You'll have to help me, but once they're gone, I'll look down to see how hard you are. Long, hard and ready.

Legion- So fucking ready.

LadyStoneheart23- And I'll want to taste you too.

Legion- Fuck yes.

LadyStoneheart23- I'll push you back and kiss down your stomach, and then, when I'm there, I'll lick over the head of your dick, around and underneath. You'll be the one gasping then and I'll love it. I'll smile up at you then suck you like a lollipop, using my hand at the base to stroke you and make you moan. You'll taste so good and you'll love the way it feels when I moan as I'm sucking you.

Legion- Will you suck my balls?

LadyStoneheart23- Lick them. Suck them. I'll use my tongue to tease them and drive you wild.

Legion- Fuck yes.

LadyStoneheart23- You'll tell me you're close and I'll take your dick back into my mouth.

Legion- How far will you take me?

LadyStoneheart23- All the way down my throat.

Legion- Fuck. Will you let me come down your throat?

LadyStoneheart23- Yes. I'll swallow every drop you give me. I'll take everything you've got to give, and I'll love it.

Legion- If you suck me off like that I won't be able to stop myself from grabbing the back of your head and fucking your face. I'll want to come so badly inside you.

LadyStoneheart23- You will. You'll come in hot spurts down my throat and I'll swallow you down.

Legion- Fuck. I think I'm gonna come right now.

LadyStoneheart23- You won't be finished though. You'll want more.

Legion- Damn fucking right I will.

LadyStoneheart23- Would you let me take charge? Would you let me ride your dick while you lie there?

Legion- I'm not sure I could hold back, babe. Maybe on round two or three I'd let you ride my cock, but not now. Now, I'd need inside of you and I'd need it hard, rough, and fucking fast.

LadyStoneheart23- So, what would you do?

Legion- I'd throw you onto your front. Pull your ass up into the air and force your head down into the mattress. You'd have your ass on show for me and I'd fucking love it. I'd settle myself behind you, holding your hips with both my hands and then I'd slam my cock into your tight little pussy. I'd thrust into you so hard you'd have to grab onto the bed post to steady yourself. I'd fuck you roughly from behind and you'd reach down and rub your clit to make yourself come harder for me. And when you do come, your pussy will squeeze my cock so tightly I'll lose control myself. I'll fill you so full of my cum and then, when I pull out, I'll watch it trickle down over your pussy and your thighs.

LadyStoneheart23- That's so sexy.

Legion- That's just for starters, babe. I've locked you into this room. I've got all night to play with you. You'll come so many times you won't be able to stand up the next day.

LadyStoneheart23- I think we just overstepped the forums guidelines on decency.

Legion- I couldn't give a fuck. I'd do it all again. I love talking dirty to you.

LadyStoneheart23- Typing dirty.

Legion- Same thing. Did you touch yourself when I was typing and make yourself come?

I could feel myself blushing just reading his question.

Legion- Don't lie to me.

LadyStoneheart23- I felt embarrassed to. But I'm so wet and turned-on I may have to log off to take care of business.

Legion- Will you think of me when you do?

LadyStoneheart23- I always think of you.

Legion- How do you picture me?

LadyStoneheart23- I'm a massive Chris Hemsworth fan, so I'm kinda picturing Thor whenever I think of you.

Legion- A superhero. I like that.

LadyStoneheart23- How do you see me?

Legion- I see you all the time.

LadyStoneheart23- You know what I mean.

Legion- I'm guessing blonde hair maybe?

LadyStoneheart23- Yeah.

Legion- Blue eyes.

LadyStoneheart23- Should I be worried?

Legion- A kick ass body and a smile that'll melt my heart.

LadyStoneheart23- A smile especially for you.

Legion- Everything will be just for me.

The screen went silent for a while and I thought he'd left the chat. A thought suddenly came into my head and I typed it, not sure if he'd be there to respond.

LadyStoneheart23- I forgot something.

Seconds later the cursor flickered to life and he responded.

Legion- What did you forget, little warrior? Is it the sex toys in your top drawer? Remember, I said we've got all night.

LadyStoneheart23- Your scar. The one on your stomach that the lion tattoo covers. I'd find it and I'd kiss you there.

Legion- That's cute, babe. Why?

LadyStoneheart23- Because as long as there is breath in my body no one will ever hurt you again. Think of it as a kiss to make it all better.

Legion- Babe, you're killing me. Talking to you on here is doing things to me.

LadyStoneheart23- Good things?

Legion- *The best things. You're my girl, little warrior. You make my life worthwhile.*

LadyStoneheart23- Same here.

Legion- *Good. Now go. Log off and take care of business. That's what I'm gonna do. And Warrior? Think of me.*

LadyStoneheart23- Always.

CHAPTER Twenty

BRANDON

She wasn't leaving her house. I knew why. She didn't want to see me. She was doing everything in her power to block me out. But she couldn't stay hidden forever.

When Thursday came, her self-imposed quarantine ended, and I watched her walk out of her house for the first time in days. She kept her head down, her long blonde hair covering her face like a veil, and she stared at her feet as she walked with determination. At first glance, you'd think she was timid; hunched over through fear. But looking at the defiance on her face, I could see she was on a mission. Her strides were strong and purposeful. She knew where she was headed, and she was pumped and ready for whatever it was she thought she was facing. Me probably.

I followed her, staying back so as not to alert her to my presence. I was getting good at stalking. The silent shadow, always there even when the sun wasn't shining. It hadn't shone for a long time in my world. But that was all about to change.

She turned into a familiar road and I watched her walk towards the Lockwood estate. Jensen must have seen her approaching from a window inside the house, because he rushed out of the front door to try and intercept her. She wasn't easy to ignore. My girl stood out wherever she was, and in this quiet suburban street the little hellcat was like a screaming banshee even though she didn't make any noise. It was obvious Jensen was trying to keep her presence quiet.

I watched him drag her down the side of his house into a high-walled alleyway. I didn't like the way he yanked on her arm, making her flinch and pull away. It made me want to head over there and put myself between them. He was manhandling her, and it didn't sit well with me.

Instead, I stood on the other side of the wall in his neighbour's driveway, listening. Something told me I needed to hear what was about to go down.

"I thought I told you not to come around here again. Are you fucking stupid? I don't know what you think you're gonna achieve by this, but you need to go, Harper. No good can come from you being here."

Jensen was talking in a low, gruff voice, but he was threatening her and walking a thin fucking line as far as I was concerned. Considering this was his best mate's sister, he was showing a hell of a lot of disrespect. The guy needed a lesson in manners. Those were my favourite subjects to teach when it came to assholes like him.

"He's back. Did you know that?"

She sounded angry and it made me smile. I loved the fire in her. I loved that I did that to her.

"Everybody knows that. So? What do you want me to do? Hold a gun to his head and get him to confess to killing Brodie? Make him admit he went into the fight with the sole aim of knocking your brother to the ground, smashing his head open and killing him?"

Even from a distance I could hear her intake of breath.

"You didn't need to put it like that, but yeah. It'd be a start. You've done fuck all else for him."

Some fucked-up brotherhood they had. When shit hit the fan, they bailed on each other. I could've predicted that though. Lockwood always was a no-good piece of shit.

"It was an accident, Harper. Get over it."

It was, but he was doing a crap job at helping her see that.

"What? So, you're just over it, are you? All those years of friendship? Shit. Brodie treated you like a brother and you're just gonna let it go?"

Their brand of friendship was a fucked-up one even in my books, and I'd dealt with a truckload of fucked-up shit in my life.

"What else do you want me to do?" Lockwood hissed like the pussy he was.

"Help me! We could go down to the barn where the fight was. Check out the flooring. Christ, anything would be better than the radio silence you've given me since the funeral."

"But it was an accident! I already told you and you just need to deal with it."

I didn't like the change of tone in his voice.

"Harper, there isn't a judge or jury in this whole town who'll see it any different. You're fighting a losing battle. And I'm never on the losing team," he hissed.

"At least I'm fighting. It's a damn sight more than you've ever done."

She sounded so desperate. Why did hearing that do something to me?

"Listen, I'm going to put this in really simple terms, just so you understand. I am not getting involved. Brodie fought and he lost. He paid the price for going into a fight without being match fit. End of. I suggest you drop it too. There's other forces at play here, Harper, and if you carry on, you're gonna find a fuck load of trouble at your door."

They'll have to get through me first.

"Are you threatening me?" she said, trying to sound confident. She wasn't. I could hear the slight hitch in her voice.

"If that's what it takes to get rid of you, then yeah, I'm threatening you."

My rage levels were hitting full capacity. We weren't the best role models, but we'd never speak to a woman like that. Money doesn't buy you class or manners, it would seem. So, he wanted to get rid of her? Bigger forces were at play? I wanted her to push harder. Whatever he was hiding needed to be exposed if his family was as corrupt and twisted as I guessed they were.

"You're the biggest piece of shit. Do you know that?"

Good, my girl was standing her ground. It made me proud to hear her fight back.

"Yep. Still not gonna lose sleep over it, sweetheart."

You will when you're lying in a hospital bed being fed through a fucking drip. Sleep through that, motherfucker.

"I'm not leaving. I'll scream this bloody street down if I have to."

I heard some commotion going on and I didn't stop to think. My instincts kicked in and I flew into action. After the way he'd been talking to her, it was time for me to shut him the fuck up. I charged down the drive and turned into that alleyway. When I saw them, I lost it completely.

Jensen had his hand over Harper's mouth, and he'd pinned her to the wall. Her eyes were bulging, and she looked petrified. He was hissing and spitting out threats, but I couldn't hear what he was saying over the blaring in my ears. No one puts their hands on a woman in my presence and gets away with it, least of all him.

I was about to grab his shoulders and pull him off, but I was too late. He stepped back and smacked his fist into her face, sending her crashing to the floor. The blood that was boiling in my veins became a volcano of pure, unadulterated rage.

"You fucking bastard." I slammed him against the wall

and smashed my fist into his face. He didn't move away; he was too dazed from seeing me come out of nowhere. "You ever touch her again and I will fucking kill you," I shouted, holding his face in my hand and feeling like I was about to explode. I hadn't felt anger so viciously for a long time.

He didn't even attempt to fight back, the fucking coward. He took one look at Harper, laid out on the floor clutching her cheek, and he pushed me off and ran back towards his house. I always knew he was a cunt. All mouth in front of his mates, but when he came up against a worthy opponent like me, on his own, he pissed his pants like a punk ass little bitch. I didn't care who heard me in that stuck-up, snobby neighbourhood. I shouted down the alleyway to let him know his days were numbered. Me torching his cars would be the least of his problems once I got my hands on him.

"That's it, Lockwood. Run away, just like you always do. You can't hide forever though, you fucking piece of shit. I'm coming for you."

I turned to look down at her lying on the floor. Lockwood could wait. I had more important things to deal with, like making sure she didn't totally lose her shit from seeing me.

I put my hand out in an effort to help her, but she just glared at me wide-eyed and pushed herself up on her own.

We stood facing each other, both panting. Me, from the effort it'd taken to give Lockwood the best right hook I could manage, and her from the anxiety of seeing me for the first time since that night. So many emotions were playing across her face, but not the ones I wanted to see.

She lifted her chin, trying to speak confidently, but there was a crackle of vulnerability in her voice.

"Why couldn't you just crawl away and die? Why are you here now, making my life hell? Does it give you some kind of twisted kick to watch me?"

She had no idea what sort of kicks I'd been getting lately.

"Aren't you glad I did?" I folded my arms over my chest and gave her the smirk that I usually saved for the ring. Fuck, why did I do that? It was like I couldn't control my body or my thoughts around her, so I reverted to asshole mode, grinning at her like she was my next victim. "If I hadn't been here, your mate there would've done a number on you. I think a 'thank you' wouldn't go amiss."

She narrowed her eyes at me in disgust.

"Thank you? Are you joking? I curse the day you were ever born. I'm not thankful, glad, or in any way pleased to see you reappear out of the shadows you've been lurking in. I hate you."

Her pretty little face was all screwed up as she spoke, making her look even hotter. Defiant Harper was a turn-on, but feisty Harper might just be my favourite.

"Not really liking myself much at the moment either," I said, going for the humble approach. See, I could be humble when I tried, and I really wanted to try with her.

"Good. So leave. Why are you back here? No one wants you here."

Like I'd ever leave her now.

"It's my home. I belong here." I took a step closer to her and she took a step back. It made me smile. I liked that I affected her.

"Thanks for the flowers, by the way." She stared straight in my eyes and made my stomach flip.

What was up with that?

I hadn't felt that before.

"Did you bother to leave any for my brother? You know, at his graveside."

"I really don't think now is the right time for us to talk about what happened that night, do you?" I didn't want to get into a fight with her. Not when I couldn't take my eyes off her mouth and my mind out of the gutter.

"Why? You've dodged it for months. Is it still raw for you? Do you find it hard facing up to what a monster you are? Because that's what you are. A monster."

Oh baby, you have no idea.

"You're hurt. You need to get some ice on that cheek," I said, pointing to her face and forcing the conversation down a route I could cope with.

"Don't pretend you care. You've destroyed my life, you've persecuted me for your own sick thrills, and now what? You're going to stalk my every move until you push me over the edge?"

She thought she was goading me. But every word out of her mouth was doing the opposite. This angry talk fucking turned me on, and I needed to put a stop to it, now.

"I'm here to get my life back."

She scoffed at my response. Little did she know that by me getting my life back, I was trying to give her hers back too. I wanted her to accept what had happened, move on, and become stronger, because of me. I wanted to have that power over her, but right then, she was the one holding all the power.

Why couldn't I stop shaking and sweating?

"And you couldn't do that somewhere else? Away from me and my family? You just had to come back here."

"My family is here too," I snapped.

"You have no family. What did you think you'd achieve by coming back here? No one wants you."

That hurt. But I swallowed my initial response down and took a breath to gather my senses.

"I'm not looking for your forgiveness."

"Good, because you'll never have it." She gritted her teeth, standing taller.

"What happened wasn't right. I know that."

This was the closest thing she was ever going to get to an apology. I surprised myself at the words coming out of my mouth.

"It wasn't right," she said with a fake laugh. "Which part? The part where you hit my brother and killed him? Or the part where you've tried to drive me insane?"

"I wanted to help you," I blurted out. My brain was shutting down and my fighter instinct was starting to take over.

"Help me? By leaving me flowers and threats? How does that help me?"

"I gave you fire in your belly, didn't I? A reason to fight back. I stopped you from wailing on the floor like a broken, weak mess. You had a purpose, a reason to get out of fucking bed every day because of me."

"I never wanted to fight! I hate fighting! I hate what it does to people; what it did to my family and to Brodie. How can you stand there and make out that you did me a favour? Is that your way of justifying yourself? Does that help you sleep at night? To know you broke me?"

The sadness in her eyes damn near destroyed me. I wanted to reach out and touch her; take that pain away.

"I made you the little warrior you are. Don't ever forget that. You are a fucking warrior. You're not broken. You're the strongest woman I've ever known."

Her eyes went wide and mine did too when I realised what I'd said.

"What did you call me?"

The panic on her face made me want to rewind. Go back in time and make everything different. Even when I tried to do something to help her, I fucked it up.

"Little warrior. I called you my little warrior."

She leant forward and grabbed her stomach, covering her mouth as she cried into her palm. I went to touch her, let her know it was okay, but she jolted away from me like I'd got the fucking plague.

"Oh my God. Please no. Please, tell me it wasn't you."

I didn't know what to say. When I'd got Kian to hack into her laptop, I only ever wanted to see what she was doing; maybe get more dirt on the Lockwoods. I hadn't expected to find my little warrior on there. To feel something I'd never felt before for any other human being. Despite what I'd said earlier, she *was* broken, and so was I. But together we'd gone some way to fixing each other, hadn't we? Or was I so totally clueless that I'd read it all wrong. I wasn't the best at putting my feelings out there, but with her, online, I'd told her things I'd never told anyone else. I'd been myself. Now, she knew it was me. I was Legion, and she didn't like what she saw. It was Emily fucking Winters all over again. I just had to face facts. Girls like her were never meant to be with boys like me. And boys like me never did get the happy ever after.

I knew after this it was all going to crumble at my feet. But I stood firm and answered her truthfully.

"It was me, and I'd do it all again. I said the things you needed to hear. Well, I typed them, anyway."

She pushed past me, not ready to hear anymore, and ran down the alleyway. But this wasn't over. There were so many things I still needed to say. Things she needed to hear. She thought I was her enemy, but I wasn't. If anyone was on her

217

side, it was me. I wanted my little phoenix to rise from the flames, even if she burned me to the ground doing it.

So, I followed her. She could try and avoid me all she wanted, but I wasn't going to be ignored. We'd ripped a band aid off just now, but the wound still needed cleaning and there was no time like the present.

–

I trailed her back to her house. I was going to catch her up in the street, but I figured she'd feel more comfortable talking to me if she was in her own home. Not that I expected her to let me in, but I could hope.

She charged through her front door then slammed it shut. I ran up the steps and knocked, expecting her to fling it back open. But it wasn't Harper who answered, it was her dad.

"Can I help you?" he asked, eyeing me up like I was about to rob the place. Shame he didn't have the same vigilance when it came to locking up at night.

"I need to talk to Harper." I stood my ground and stared straight back at him.

"And you are?"

Fuck. He didn't know who I was. If I told him, this could go downhill very fucking fast.

"He's someone who needs to leave," Harper stated, appearing behind her dad and glaring at me with disdain.

Her dad looked between the two of us and his nostrils

flared as he put two and two together and came up with five.

"Did you do that?" He pointed at the red mark on her cheek. "Did you hurt my daughter? Because if you did, you can try going up against me next. You might not be so lucky though."

I fought back the smirk that wanted to break free at the thought of this overweight forty-something trying his luck in a fight with me. Instead, I lifted my chin and told him, "No, sir. That would be the work of another one of her *friends*."

He turned to give Harper a questioning look, but she avoided his gaze and kept her glare on me. If looks could kill, I'd be kicking back in hell with the best of them right now.

"Its fine, Dad. I'll get rid of him."

He turned back to me and gave me a threatening look as he said, "I don't want any trouble."

"You won't get any trouble from me, sir."

He nodded but didn't look convinced.

"Well, at least you have some manners." He looked me up and down. "Maybe appearances are deceiving, after all."

Story of my life. But then again, I didn't have the best track record and most of the time my appearance was in alignment with my intentions; in your face and ready for violence. But not with her. Never with her.

Her dad left us, and she came to stand on the porch with me, closing the front door so no one would hear us. She wrapped her arms around herself like she was trying to form a protective barrier from me or whatever I might say.

"Why have you followed me here?" she asked. "Haven't you done enough?"

"I'm not leaving it like that," I said, taking a step towards her.

"Like what? Me feeling totally betrayed, embarrassed, and violated yet again. I don't have anything to say to you." She shook her head, and from the glisten in her eyes I could tell she was close to tears.

"Well, I've got a lot to say to you. You don't need to feel embarrassed about anything. And how exactly did I violate you?" I didn't like being painted as some kind of pervert. That was Lockwood's domain. I'd never forced her into any of our chats. Okay, so she didn't know who I was, but now that she did, surely she could see I wasn't all bad?

"You broke into my house, Brandon. You watched me from my garden and stalked me online. Fuck. I don't even want to think about what I said to you."

All true and I'd own it.

"I don't regret any of it."

"I wouldn't expect you to." She huffed and then peered up at me, and I could tell from her face she wanted to hurt me with the next words out of her mouth. "You'd have to have a conscience to feel remorse. You don't have that. You're soulless."

I couldn't argue with that. A few months ago, I'd have told them to dig a hole for me next to her brother, because I was as dead inside as he was. But that was then. Now, I'd had a spark ignited inside me and a fire burned just for her. Only a fool would walk away from something like this and I was no fool.

"Maybe I was soulless back then. But since I met you, I haven't felt the darkness dragging me under quite as much as it used to. Since I got to know you, life's been... interesting."

I felt proud of that speech. I'd really put myself out there. But when she grimaced at me, I realised it still wasn't enough.

"You don't know me, Brandon. You've watched me and we've had a few random conversations online."

I couldn't understand her. How could she say I didn't know her when we'd shared parts of ourselves in that chatroom? I'd seen her at her worst, and I was still fighting for her. I'd fought for her more than any of her friends had. What else did she want from me?

"You know more about me than anyone else in my life right now," I told her. I felt so confused. I didn't know what else to say to make this right.

Her eyes drifted to my stomach, where the scars were now well hidden by my tattoos.

"You tricked me."

"I tried to save you."

"You were the one who broke me." She fisted her hands in her hair and gave a little growl. "You broke me, Brandon. I'm this fucked up mess because of you."

"Was it all me though? I mean fuck, Harper. In all this,

doesn't Brodie get to take some of the responsibility too? Did I force him into that ring? Shit. It was an accident, okay? I didn't want it to happen. I didn't want any of this."

She clenched her eyes shut and took a deep breath.

"I don't even know what I think anymore. I can't remember the night that well. It's all just a blur; a series of snapshots of the horror that's my life now. But you don't get to tell me how to feel about any of it." She stabbed her chest as she talked, and I could see that the defiant little warrior was back.

"I'm not trying to tell you how to feel, but I'm not the devil you've been painting me out to be."

I didn't want her to hate me. Not really. But I didn't know what to do to change it. I thought knowing I was Legion would make her see me in a different light, but it did the opposite.

"Oh, you're just a born-again saint, aren't you? So, all the stalking, the flowers, and messages, that's the actions of a sane and guilt-free person, is it? I don't know what fucking planet you're on, but in my world it's not okay to do that. You scared me. You made me feel like I was going insane."

"I made you feel alive again," I said through gritted teeth. I felt agitated that she wasn't getting this.

"So fucking what? How can I be alive if I'm scared to leave my house?"

"I'd never hurt you. Not like he just did. It's your friends who're your enemies, not me."

I was losing control. Losing the grip on this exchange with every word that came out of my mouth.

"There's more than one way to hurt someone, Brandon. You did it in the worst way, without ever using your fists. You hurt me in here." She thumped her chest and then she tapped the side of her head. "And in here. That shit does more damage than anything. You knew what you were doing, but you did it anyway. You didn't care."

"I did... I do care. Please, Harper. Try and let me explain. I know I sound fucked-up, but I only did what I did to get closer to you. I wanted to help heal you."

She shook her head and backed away from me, putting her hand on the door handle to show she was almost done with this conversation.

"You're really good at pushing yourself forward, aren't you? Making yourself heard. But you don't listen."

I had no idea what that meant.

"Then tell me. I'm listening now."

"I don't want you here. I don't want you following me or leaving me anything in my garden, kitchen, or anywhere else. That chatroom... it was a lifeline for me. You've destroyed that."

I was her fucking lifeline, not the bloody chatroom. Didn't she realise that?

"We can still go on there," I said, trying to make her see that it wasn't all totally lost. "If that's the way you want to talk to me for a bit, then we can use that."

"We're not friends, Brandon. I don't want to talk to you. Not in real life and certainly not in that chatroom." She sighed. "You might be listening, but you aren't hearing what I'm saying. I don't want you in my life. You're the reason my life is the shit heap it is. The only thing you can do to make that better is disappear."

She may as well have stuck a knife in me with those words. The last thing I wanted to do was disappear. It was never going to happen.

"I'm not going anywhere," I said defiantly.

"Then maybe I will."

I froze. She wouldn't leave Sandland, would she?

"You'd leave here because of me?" I couldn't explain why, but there was a lump forming in my throat, making it difficult to speak.

"Anywhere would be better than being here watching you act like nothing ever happened."

Whatever I did next, I had to make sure she didn't leave. I needed to say the right thing. Whatever that was.

"Fine. You want space? I'll give you some space."

"I don't want space. I want to be left alone."

I bit my tongue, knowing whatever response I gave would hurt one of us. Instead, I took my own step back and in a low voice I told her, "This isn't over."

"It is," she replied, opening her door and slamming it shut behind her.

I stalked down the driveway feeling like my heart was

being twisted and contorted in my chest. I was close to breaking point. I didn't want to walk away from her, and I couldn't give her fucking space; I didn't even know how. I was so wound up I needed to offload. I knew Finn would be fucking useless. His experience with women was zero to none and he wasn't the chattiest fucker. Zak would give me some flowery bullshit, and despite his proven record of success with women, I doubted he'd know what to do with a girl like Harper. No, I needed a dose of brutal reality from my best friend who'd always give it to me straight. So, I headed to Ryan's garage. I knew he'd know what I should do next, because me? I didn't have a fucking clue.

CHAPTER
Twenty One

BRANDON

"There he is! Where've you been hiding then, son?" Sean walked over to me, grinning and holding out his arms for a fatherly hug when he saw me coming across the forecourt of the garage.

"Just took a bit of time away, Sean. But I'm back now."

He held me tightly, giving me a proper hug to show he'd missed me. Then as he pulled away, he patted my arm.

"It's good to have you back. Don't leave it so long next time, okay? You're a part of this family, Brandon. We've missed having you at our table."

"I've gotta admit, I've missed Connor's Sunday roasts." I joked. I'd missed the family more.

"There'll be a plate with your name on it this weekend, lad. I'll tell him to do extra Yorkshire puddings, just for you." He rubbed his hands together. This man knew the quickest way to my heart.

"It's a date. Is Ryan in the office?" I asked, pointing towards the building.

"No, it's his day off. He's in the house," he replied, nodding over to his home next door. "You might want to knock first though. He's with Emily." He winked and then laughed as he sauntered off back to his workshop.

I hadn't seen Emily since that night. I suppose now was as good a time as any to get that meeting over with.

I didn't bother with the front door, I never had. Instead, I opened the side-gate and walked into the garden and then gave a little knock at the back door. I saw Ryan walk through into the kitchen, and when he saw me his face dropped, then he righted himself and waved me in.

"It's already open, mate. Come in."

I went in, flicking the kettle on as I walked past it, and grabbed some mugs out of the cupboards. You see, Ryan's house was like my own. In fact, growing up I felt more at home here than I did at my nan's.

"You want a coffee?" I asked him as he sat at his kitchen table, eyeing me with suspicion.

"Yeah. There's some of those latte things that Emily likes in the cupboard too. Maybe make her one while you're at it?"

I opened the cupboard again, grabbing the box but not having the first clue what I was doing with them. I took a coffee pod out and went to tear open the lid, only to hear Emily shout out, "Not like that. You've gotta put it in the machine first."

I turned to watch her take it out of my hands and then give me a smile. There was a new coffee machine on the side that hadn't been there the last time I'd visited. Emily got to work setting it up and making her own drink. I just stood there, staring, feeling like a complete fool. It seemed to be a running theme for me.

"Sorry. I'm shit at making hot drinks." I shrugged.

"It's okay." Her smile grew wide and it still lit up the room, but it didn't make me feel the way it used to.

Emily's smiles used to give me a warm feeling inside. Now... not so much. I mean, she was still nice to look at, but she was my best friend's girlfriend. Watching her stir her coffee while he looked across the room at her like the sun shone out of her ass made me realise that me and her would never have worked. She was always Ryan's girl.

Ryan must've mistaken my staring for something else because he cleared his throat, and in an irritated tone, he snapped, "What do you want, Brandon?"

"I'm lost, mate." I never had any filter when it came to the lads. I always said it like it was. "I fucked up and I have no idea what I'm supposed to do next."

"Brandon, you've fucked up so many times I'm surprised you even notice the difference these days," he said, and Emily tutted at him.

"Ryan! Brandon's come here for help. I don't think he needs to hear that."

"Whatever." Ryan rolled his eyes and then he leant back in his seat. "Come on then. What's happened this time?"

He motioned for me to sit down, and so I did.

"Em, babe. Give us a few minutes, yeah?" he said, dismissing Emily. But I didn't want her to go. I figured she'd have just as good an insight into what I should do as Ryan would.

"She can stay," I told him.

"You sure?" He looked at Emily as he said it. I think he was worried about how she'd feel staying in here with me.

"I think Em might give better advice than you, mate," I said to justify her presence at the table.

He laughed and Emily smirked as she sat in the chair next to him.

"Come on then, big man. Give it to us," she said.

I took a sip of my coffee and then hung my head as I let it all spill out. I told them about watching Harper, the flowers, the messages. I told them everything; the online persona I'd used to get closer to her and how I'd followed her to Lockwood's house. I didn't want to look up and see the pity in their eyes, so I kept my focus on my coffee and gave them every last sordid detail of what had happened after I ran Lockwood off. I told them what Harper had said and how I didn't know what I should do next but staying away was not an option for me. I wasn't a quitter.

"It isn't about being a quitter," Emily chipped in. "Giving her space isn't necessarily a bad thing."

"Mate, I told you she was off fucking limits." Ryan rested his elbows on the table and scrubbed his hands over his face, sighing. "Why did you do that? Don't you think she's been through enough? Just leave her the fuck alone."

"I couldn't! I can't!" I argued back. "I needed to make it right."

"You can't make it right. It'll never be right," Ryan shouted, but Emily reached out and rubbed his arm to calm him down. At that moment, I was ready to stand up and walk out. I didn't like the answers he was giving me. He wasn't seeing things the way I was.

"You made it right with Emily," I argued. "And look what we did to her dad."

"He was a crook and he deserved to go down for what he did. And yes, Brodie was a bully growing up. But everything that's happened since, that's something you've got to walk away from."

"Not gonna happen." I could feel my temper rising again.

He went to speak, but Emily butted in.

"Could you give me and Brandon five minutes alone?"

Ryan's eyes widened and he stuttered over his response. "Why?"

"Because I want to talk to him. Do I need to say anything more than that?" She gave him a look and he grimaced and then stood up.

"Fine. I'll be in the next room if you need me." He kissed the top of her head and gave me a threatening glare in warning. I glared back. Did he really think I was still a threat?

Emily watched him leave, and once the kitchen door

closed, she turned to me and sighed.

"First off, I need to give you an apology," she said, and I frowned at her. "The way I spoke to you that night, what I said, it was mean and unkind. I'm so sorry. I should've taken your feelings into account and I didn't."

I suddenly felt embarrassed that she was bringing this up again. The fact that I'd told my best friend's girlfriend I loved her all those months ago made me want to kick my own ass. What kind of friend does that?

"You had a lot going on that night. I can see that now." This wasn't what I'd expected her to talk about, and I wasn't sure how comfortable I was dredging it all back up.

"I know. I think my head was so screwed up that I forgot my manners. I didn't mean the things I said."

"I'm sure you meant some of them." I smirked.

"You're a good guy, Brandon. You deserve to hear that. You're a little intense sometimes, but that's just you. It's who you are. If I ever made you feel worthless, then I'm truly sorry." And she was. I could see it in her eyes.

"Em, I should say sorry too. I messed up with us. I said shit about Ry too to try and break you up. It was all so fucked up that night. He's always loved you. I loved you too, but now-"

"But now, you realise you aren't *in* love with me, and there's a big difference. I think if you're really honest with yourself, you were in love with the idea of me. But I was never the right girl for you. And I think you know that because you've met the one now, haven't you?"

I nodded and stayed quiet.

"Brandon?" She reached over and put her hand over mine. "I'm saying this from a place of love, so please don't go off on one, but you do act like a bull in a china shop over most things. You have the kind of intensity that can sometimes be intimidating. You never take no for an answer. You're head strong to the point of insanity, and you've always done whatever the hell you want. And that's been fine, for now. Most of us didn't call you out on it, and those that did, you just shot them down."

I laughed at her honesty.

"What happened to the apology I just had? Feels like you're pissing all over that now, Winters."

She couldn't hold back her own chuckle. "I like that you're calling me Winters again. Kinda feels like old times."

We both smiled, and I decided to do what Harper had told me I never do; I listened.

"With Harper, you need to do things differently. She isn't like the other girls you've been around. She's tough, but she has a vulnerability at the moment that you need to respect. She's confused, about a lot of things. Her life has changed immeasurably in the last few months. I know what it's like to lose a brother. It's devastating. But to lose a twin? That's the next level of heartache."

"She didn't know him as well as she thinks she did," I said, with the images of the Brodie I remembered swimming around in my consciousness.

"Do any of us ever know anyone? At the end of the day, he was her twin brother. He died and she's heartbroken. Now, she's trying to find her way back. She has to figure this out on her own, Brandon. You can't do it for her. I've been to visit her. I've chatted with her about it all, and I think, deep down, she knows it was a tragic accident, but she has to come to that conclusion in her own time. You can't force it. Nothing you say or do will make it happen. You have to give her space. Time is a great healer and if you can give her that, and it's meant to be, she will come to you."

A great speech, but I still wasn't convinced.

"She won't. She hates me."

"She hates what happened. She doesn't know you, Brandon. Not like we do."

"I don't think I can stay away." I told her because what was the point in lying? I was here because I needed help.

"I know it's not in your nature to take a back seat, and trust me, I'll go and see her, put in a good word for you. But you have no choice here. You have to let her find her own way."

I trusted Emily, and if she was going to see Harper, and talk to her, then I guessed that was better than nothing. I still wasn't sure I could be totally silent though.

"You're really good at this, aren't you? You should consider a career in counselling. I think I'd keep you busy for years if you took me on. I'd probably help to get yours and

Ryan's kids through college too with my fees."

"But I'd never charge you. We're friends. It's what friends do. Listen, concentrate on your fight this weekend. Put all your energy into that. I know you're good at channelling your demons into your boxing, so do it now. Give Harper space; she needs it. And if you need to vent, come to me. Sometimes, another woman's perspective helps. Ryan is too similar to you. You both have cavemen instincts when it comes to your women."

"Nothing wrong with a caveman," I said, sitting taller.

"No, there isn't. But clubbing her over the head and dragging her back to your cave isn't going to work with this one. You need to play smarter."

"Smarter, huh? I guess I can try that."

There's always a first time for everything.

We heard Ryan shuffling about impatiently in the living room. He obviously didn't like being away from her for too long, or didn't like me being close to her. So, we both stood up at the same time and then Emily wrapped her arms around me. My second hug of the day and it was another genuine one. But hugging her back, I realised everything she'd said was true. My body didn't react to her in the same way it did with Harper. I wasn't in love with Emily Winters. My heart and mind belonged to a girl who couldn't stand the sight of me.

My little warrior.

I just prayed that eventually she'd see what I saw. That we'd been brought together by the worst thing imaginable, but things happened for a reason, and maybe she was mine. Maybe she was my reason to try to be better in this world.

That's if she'd have me.

CHAPTER
Twenty Two

HARPER

I couldn't go on like this anymore. I was tired. Exhausted from carrying around so much anger, guilt, frustration and grief. Like a broken record playing on repeat, I could hear Brandon's voice in my head, chipping away at my walls.

It was an accident.

I didn't want it to happen.

I didn't want any of this.

I didn't want it either, but it'd happened and now I had to find some way to deal with it before it totally destroyed me.

I'd never read any of the reports on the fight. I hadn't looked at the newspapers, or the stories online. I hadn't even read the police report or anything from the hospital. I couldn't face it before. But I realised that I was a hypocrite. I'd accused Brandon of not listening, but I was refusing to listen too. I didn't want to hear what the doctors, the police or my own parents were telling me. Maybe now it was time to open myself up and face the reality of Brodie's death.

I found the folder my Dad kept hidden in our sideboard in the kitchen diner, filled with every piece of information he'd gathered about that night, and I took it up to my room. Then I sat down, and I read every single thing I found in there. It wasn't easy to read, and as I delved deeper into the facts, I became angry.

Doesn't Brodie get to take some of the responsibility too?

I thought about what Brandon had said, and I felt my chest ache with the realisation that Brodie was to blame as well. He'd put himself at risk. He'd ignored me when I begged him not to fight and did it anyway. He was as focused on winning as Brandon was.

Only Brodie wasn't well, was he?

He'd hidden that from all of us, and it made me angry. Why hadn't he told me? Why had he gone ahead with it knowing he wasn't at his best? In all his bravado, he hadn't ever put us first. He hadn't thought about what it'd be like for us to live a life without him. He hadn't taken care of himself. His pride had trumped everything else, even me.

I placed the documents back into the folder and opened my laptop, ready to do some research of my own. A subarachnoid haemorrhage was what the doctors called it. Looking at all the articles online, I realised that Brodie's chances of surviving something like that would've been slim. If he had survived, his life would never have been the same. I didn't even want to picture what that would've meant for him, but I knew it wasn't pretty. I also knew Brodie wouldn't have wanted to live like that.

My heart felt heavy as I trawled through websites to try and get my head around it all. My whole body was shaking, but finding out about it, seeing it in plain English, written in black and white, that was something I'd had to do. I needed this to help me move on and begin to accept what I couldn't change.

The more I read, the more mixed up and helpless I felt, and I realised I wanted to reach out to someone. I needed help. I missed the Legion I knew before I realised who he was.

I tried to save you.

Did he really believe that? Did he honestly think that watching me had been a way to help? I couldn't work out what had been going through his mind, and in all truth, I don't think he did either. He was as mixed up about all this as I was.

I'm not the devil you've been painting me out to be.

I'd always said the devil appears in many forms. Legion himself admitted he was plagued by demons. Then it hit me. His demons had taken hold the day his mum left him. They'd magnified when he was abused and bullied to the point of being brutally scarred. And those scars? They were real, and I couldn't bury my head in the sand anymore.

I knew Jensen had bullied kids in school, but he'd always taken a particular dislike to Brandon. My brother had followed Jensen like a damn puppy dog, and in those years, I'd been the annoying sister he'd wanted to ditch at every opportunity. He'd even got Mum and Dad to move me into a different class so he could be free. I covered my mouth and held in the sob I felt rise up in my throat. Those initials that'd been carved on Brandon were the work of Jensen and my brother. I couldn't hide from that anymore. And it was no wonder Brandon hated them like he did. They were the reason he was the way he was.

I took a few deep breaths. Trying to come to terms with the fact that my brother wasn't perfect was tough. He was my twin. I was supposed to know everything. But I realised I didn't. Or maybe I'd had a clue and I just didn't want to acknowledge it. If that was the case, then I was guilty too. Guilty for letting that abuse go on for all those years when I could've stopped it. In my eyes, that made me as fucked-up as Brandon. He had his demons and so did I. But at least he owned them. Me? I was in denial.

Well, not anymore.

I still felt unbearable grief. I probably always would. I loved my brother, and whatever he'd done in the past wouldn't change that. But I had to find a way to move forward with my life. To actually live my life. I couldn't stand these chains anymore. I needed to feel free.

I couldn't stop myself from clicking onto the website and heading to the chatroom. I tried to convince myself that I needed to hear another stupid story from Fucking Alan to lighten my mood, or maybe have a heart-to-heart with Emo Girl to try to make sense of everything and possibly feel like I wasn't alone. But who was I kidding? I knew what I really wanted. I wanted to see if he'd been on there. In some cruel, twisted way, I needed to have that connection with him.

LadyStoneheart23 has joined the chat

I could see a few familiar names on the main chatroom, but that wasn't what drew me in. It was the private message waiting for me at the bottom of the screen from the sender, Legion.

My hand was shaking as the mouse hovered over it. I knew I'd open it, there was never any doubt about that, but I still had to brace myself for whatever lay behind that one click. Then, I took the leap of faith and I opened the message.

Legion – Harper,

I know I said I would give you space, but let's be honest here… When have I ever done anything I'm told to do?

I know I shouldn't be contacting you on here. You probably won't even see this anyway. You'll take one look at my name and delete this, but whatever. I need to get this off my chest. I'm not the kind of man to shut up and take all the crap that's being thrown his way. I did that for years and now… I can't do it. I have to be heard. Maybe I'm a narcissist? Or a psychopath or something? Hell, the fact that I'm even asking myself that shows what a twat I can be sometimes. I know I'm not like most guys out there. But I'm trying to change. I want to change. For you.

No one should have to change. Not for anyone. I bit my lip, feeling nervous as I read on.

I've never said this to anyone before. I've never felt the need to justify myself for anything in my life, but with you, I do. Harper, I'm sorry. I'm sorry for what happened with your brother. I'm sorry that anything I did after that night scared you or made you feel like you couldn't cope. What can I say? I was fucked up in the head. Probably still am if I'm being honest.

I'm sorry that my being here makes you feel like you don't want to be. I hate that. I don't ever want you to leave. Not because of me.

But most of all, I'm sorry that you're hurting. I want to take it away, but I don't know how. Everything I do or say seems to make it worse, and I'm lost, little warrior. I'm lost here.

I don't know what else to tell you right now, but I hope that one day you'll find the happiness you deserve. I pray that one day I get to see it. All I want is to see that sparkle in your eyes again.

I've attached a video link. I guess it says how I feel better than any words I could use. Watch it. And when you do, know that this is my message to you. I'm not a good guy, but I want to be. I haven't always done the right thing, but with your help

I hope I'm learning.

Be strong, little warrior. One day, it'll all turn out right.

Brandon x

I was shaking and the tears were streaming down my face. His words were unexpected and just so beautiful.

I had no idea what the YouTube video would show me. I'd never heard of the song Demons by Imagine Dragons, but I put my Air Pods in and clicked on the link, and I watched and really listened.

Holy shit.

I thought I was crying when I read the message, but the video damn near broke me. I replayed it over and over again. I even Googled the words and cried harder at what they were telling me. He was a broken boy, and I was a broken girl. He wanted to heal me, but he didn't know how.

I wiped away my tears so I could see the screen of my laptop. I tried to stop my hands from shaking so I could type a sentence.

LadyStoneheart23- Tell me something that made you smile today.

I didn't know what else to say. But this was my way of reaching out to him. My own olive branch. I couldn't just leave the message as read and not respond. I wasn't totally heartless, despite feeling like my chest was a hollow void of nothingness most days. There was still something there, and he'd just ignited a small spark within me.

The dots instantly started dancing about to show me he was responding. I held my breath, waiting for what he'd say.

Legion – You.
You made me smile.
Thank you for reading my message. X

I stared at the screen, not sure what I should type back. I was lost for words, drowning in a sea of emotions and feeling totally and utterly drained.

LadyStoneheart23- Every journey starts with a single step. I took a step today. You did that for me. Thank you. X
Legion- Anything for you, little warrior. Anything. X

With a heavy heart, I logged off. I didn't want to go into the main chat. I'd got what I came for. I'd needed to share and unload some of my grief. But instead, he'd shared a piece of himself and that was enough. His honesty had given me what I'd needed. It was okay to be angry, to not know how to react. But I needed to remember that in my darkest times I wasn't alone, and I could do this. I could find my way back. It was time for me to try and start living again.

CHAPTER
Twenty Three

BRANDON

This was what I'd missed. What I'd grown envious of to the point of wanting to fuck shit up over.

Our parties.

Knowing the lads had started them back up without me had hurt, I couldn't deny that. But tonight, it was all about my comeback. This was what I'd been waiting for and I might sound conceited, but I couldn't give a fuck. It was what the people wanted too.

I hadn't expected to see Emily chipping in to help set things up, but she did. The girl swept the floor in the main area of the waterworks like she was preparing for a visit from the queen. I kind of felt sorry for the broom with how hard she was working it. I guess she was trying to distract herself from her Dad's trial. It was into its second week and the publicity on that thing was brutal. The press was dragging her dad, Alec Winters, name through the mud, and Emily's too. But Ryan was doing a good job of taking her mind off it. Ryan, and the broom she was currently abusing.

"I think you missed a spot," I said, tutting and pointing to the part of the floor she'd swept for the twenty-fifth time.

She stopped and wiped the sweat from her brow and blew her hair out of her face.

"Don't you have a bag you should be punching somewhere? Or a person? Maybe you could practise on yourself?"

I threw my head back and laughed.

"Nice to see you still have some fight left inside you. I missed sparring with you, Winters." I held my fists up and punched the air and she huffed out a laugh.

"I missed it too. I like giving my brain a workout, thinking up new ways to insult you."

"I like a woman with brains." I shrugged.

"You like a woman if she's breathing. Brains doesn't even come into it."

I faked a shocked look and went to give her a cheeky response, but Ryan cut me off.

"I've just got another text."

I turned and watched Zak and Finn walk towards us, getting their mobile phones out of their pockets.

"Yeah, me too." Zak sighed and rubbed his hand over his face in exasperation.

"I changed my mobile number three days ago and they're still texting me? Why?" Finn asked, sounding exhausted. I think the paint fumes were getting to him. He needed to take a break from his Effy masterpiece.

"Because, like it says, we need to pay for what we did," Ryan said, then turned to look at Emily. "I'm sorry to say it, babe, but your dad is in on this. I just know it."

"Did you get a text?" Emily asked, spinning round to face me. All four of them pinned me with an expectant stare.

I took my mobile out of my back pocket and tapped the screen, but there was no message. I knew it'd look suspicious, but I wasn't about to hide the truth from them. Not anymore. I'd had enough of hiding.

"Nope. I got nothing." I held my phone up as if to show them, not that they could see anything from where they stood.

"Why are they texting you three and not Brandon?" Emily was asking the million dollar question that was on all of their minds.

"Because whoever is sending these texts thinks Brandon is innocent?" Finn offered, looking hopeful and giving a shrug. I liked his optimism.

"Or they don't know he was involved?" Zak replied, and Ryan groaned at both of their lame responses.

"Or our friend here knows more than he's letting on." Trust Ryan to go straight for the jugular.

"What are you trying to say, mate? You think I sent those? You think I don't have anything better to do than send shitty texts to my best friends. Fuck that and fuck you if you don't believe me."

I didn't have time for this shit. Our energies would be better spent on trying to figure out who was sending them.

That, and my awesome comeback fight.

"I believe you," Emily stated firmly. "Ryan, I think you do too," she said, giving him the side-eye. I guess he didn't like the prospect of sleeping on the couch as he shrugged and nodded in agreement.

"Zak, haven't you been able to get a breakthrough on it? Come on. Tech is your thing, man. If anyone can find out who's sending them, it's you," I added, taking the heat off me for a while. "Or maybe you don't want to say anything 'cos you know who it is already and you're protecting them."

Zak bustled forward like he was going to teach me a lesson, but Ryan stepped in his way and tried to calm him down.

"Zak's tried," Ryan said, looking between the two of us. "We don't know. Do you think we'd be standing here wasting time if we did?"

"Maybe you should let Kian take a look. I know he's got a mouth the size of the Blackwall Tunnel, but he knows his stuff."

I knew Kian had skills. He'd tapped into Harper's internet fast enough. Maybe he could help out here too.

"A fresh pair of eyes might help," Emily replied, looking ever hopeful.

"Maybe. But for now, we keep this between us. The less people that know, the better. We watch our backs, and we watch each other. If someone's out to get us, they'll have to go against all of us." Ryan folded his arms over his chest and stood tall.

"Damn fucking right," I replied, lifting my chin to show them that I was right there with them. You hurt one of us, you hurt us all, and that included Emily.

–

Five hours later, and the grey empty space we'd been stood in before was transformed into the hottest event within a thirty-mile radius. Zak's strobe lights and thumping bass made the atmosphere electric. The people were packed in; wall to wall bodies that were dancing, drinking, smoking, and living life the way they wanted to live it. That was the fucking point of all this, after all. We were giving our two fingers to the establishment. They could try taming us and slap all the restrictions they liked around the town, but if we wanted to party, we would fucking party.

I stood to the side and scanned the area. I didn't know why I was looking for her, but I was. Stupid, really. Why would she come to a thing like this? She'd barely left the house since I'd been back.

I couldn't deny I felt a twinge of disappointment that she wasn't here though. In some twisted way, I wanted to share this with her. It was my big moment, and I was pumped and ready for it. Brandon Mathers was back in business.

"Don't look now, but Lockwood just walked in," Emily said, coming to stand next to me and nodding to the far end of the building.

"Which one?" I asked, not really giving a shit.

"Both of them." She raised her eyebrows at me, obviously unsure what my reaction would be.

"They came to see a decent fight. A fair fight." I shrugged. "That's something they don't usually take part in."

I already had my arsenal fully loaded for when I saw Lockwood. I knew he'd give me a wide berth though. This was my territory he was on, and he was outnumbered, outskilled and outsmarted. He'd never choose to go against me, not in front of everyone. His defeat would be too humiliating. He was saving himself for a time when I'd be alone. Thing was, I was never alone. The demons he'd given me all those years ago followed me everywhere, and retribution was what they fed on. I'd always be ready for him.

I made my way to the back room, where Kian was hyping the crowd up for my first fight. I was so ready for this. I was going to give them a show they'd never forget. The words that Lockwood had said to me all those months ago still rang in my ears.

"You're a wannabe Tyson Fury without the charisma. You're less gypsy king and more shitty king. You know, like the shit they found you in when your mum left you to bone every drug dealer she could get her hands on."

When he'd said that before, I'd snapped. I'd let my anger get the better of me and I'd lost my head. But not today. Today that memory was spurring me on.

No charisma?

I was going to fucking ooze the stuff.

I couldn't give a rat's ass what he said about my mum. She was a piece of crap. But every time he spoke, every time he showed the world what a low-life cunt he was, hitting Harper like he did, it fuelled the demons inside me. It gave me even more reason to focus, channel my energy, and release that tension in the best way I knew how. Through my fists.

Finn had already taped up my hands, and when I got into our custom-made ring, with its hay bales and the usual crowd of familiar faces hanging off the edge, I smiled.

I fucking loved this.

The smell of the sawdust and the hay, the buzz from the masses; this was what I was made to do. I was a fighter. I'd always be a fighter. This was my world, my life. If I didn't have this, then what was the point in anything?

I was fighting some kid from a few towns over; Callum Kendall I think his name was. Kid had a similar build to me, but that didn't mean shit. From the look on his face he thought he had this all wrapped up. But I'd enjoy teaching him a lesson in manners.

I was the fucking king around here.

The crowd began to cheer and shout as I took my t-shirt off and started to roll my shoulders and jab the air with my fists. My adrenaline was through the roof, but I was good at keeping myself in check. I couldn't let ego get in the way of my performance. Well, not yet, anyway.

I painted on my trademark evil grin and stared at Kendall before I turned to the crowd and held my arms up.

"You thought I wouldn't show up? Thought you'd seen the last of me?" I shouted over the noise with a wicked smirk on my face. "Now, why would I piss around? I came here 'cos I'll throw down with any motherfucker who talks shit about me in this town."

The crowd started chanting my name, and I could see Kendall gritting his teeth. He knew he was getting stitched-up and I fucking loved it.

"Did you miss me?" A few called out *yeah*, while the rest told me to shut the fuck up and get on with it. "Of course you did. What else would you be doing on a Friday night but watching me smack the shit out of this little fucker here?" I thumbed to Kendall and laughed. The crowd was fucking lapping it up and I was on a roll.

"I'm undefeated," I shouted, flexing my arms and giving Kendall a wink. "But you're welcome to have a go. You see this?" I pointed at my fist. "Weapon of mass destruction. You'd know all about that, wouldn't you, Lockwood," I said, turning back to the crowd. The booing that ensued told me they already knew what a piece of shit he was.

"I know you're hiding in here somewhere. But I'll find you. You need payback, and I'm not talking about the shit that went down with me and my brothers. See, this is what *we* do for our women, Lockwood. We throw parties. You? You throw your fucking fists, you absolute bellend." I nodded to myself, feeling that anger starting to surge forward.

"I know you, Lockwood. You can't hide from me. You've put on a bit of timber since we last met, and they do say you are what you eat. Well, you must eat woman beating pieces of shit 'cos that's exactly what you are." The crowd erupted into jeers and angry catcalls.

I'd done that.

I'd shown everyone who didn't already know what he was really like.

I pointed around the crowd and then turned to face Kendall, still pointing but giving him my last smirk of the night before I fell into my zoned-out, crazy motherfucker, fighting mode.

"I'm Brandon fucking Mathers, and that means something around here. Can you smell that?" I sniffed for dramatic effect. "That's the smell of your own fucking fear."

He shook his head and spat on the floor. This little shit was more disrespectful than I thought.

"Come on then. I'll let you have the first punch," I said, tapping my chin. "But after that, it's your fucking funeral."

The boos and shouts I heard didn't faze me. I knew what I'd said was controversial, considering what'd happened at my last fight, but I wasn't gonna give anyone the impression that that had affected me. I needed to show them I was still the hardened bastard they thought I was. No fear, no mercy. Get the job done and give the people what they came to see. Me, doing what I did best.

The ref gave us the run-down of the rules and wished us both good luck for the fight. I didn't need luck. I had talent and determination on my side.

I kept my promise. I let him hit me and I braced myself as I took that blow. It was fucking hard, and he caught my ribs good and proper, but I righted myself soon enough and went in on him, raining blow after blow like he was my own personal punching bag. Kendall leant against the hay bales holding his sides as the ref separated us and checked he was okay. If he was floundering already, this was going to be easier than I thought.

I stood firm in the middle, with my fists up to protect my face, and my muscles clenched, ready to attack. Kendall stepped forward, ready to restart the fight, and a few of the crowd shouted our names in encouragement. My eyes were on him though, reading his thoughts, working out his next move. I liked to think I was a clever fighter. I tried to outmanoeuvre my opponent in speed, strength and skill. Anyone can throw punches, but me, I threw tactical moves with my hits, and that took focus and ability. A fucking God-given gift, that's what I had.

I smiled and beckoned him on with my left hand. I knew the crowd would love that. It was all part of the show. He smirked back at me and just as I was about to duck his left-hook I saw something out of the corner of my eye that took the breath right out of my body and totally pulled my concentration from the fight.

She's here.

It was her long blonde hair that I saw first, then the way she was clenching her hands in front of her face and biting her nails. Her eyes were wide, scared even, and she was looking straight at me like she might keel over at any second.

My little warrior.

And then I felt it. The thud as his fist connected with my head. My whole body shuddered as I felt the dazed confusion from the force of the punch that hit me. Any boxer will tell you that a blow to the head is the worst. And I'd just done something I'd never done in all the years I'd been fighting. I'd lost my concentration and let the other guy get the better of me.

The crowd started to shout as I staggered to the edge of the ring. I looked up to where she'd been standing, but she was gone. I couldn't see her anywhere. I suddenly felt desperate. I had to get out of there, but I also needed to win this fight. I wasn't about to go down for the first time ever on my comeback appearance.

I shook my head to right myself, pictured Lockwood and Yates in that bathroom back in school, and I got my fucking shit together.

"Are you okay to carry on?" the ref asked me.

I nodded and stalked over to Kendall, threw my fist back, and smacked him in the face. He hadn't expected me to come back at him so hard, and he did a crap job of protecting himself. I gave him a few more steady left and right hooks and he was down and out for the count before I could come up for breath. The ref came over to hold my arm up and declare me the winner, but I couldn't bask in this glory, not after she'd left like that.

Fuck.

Had she heard me say it was his funeral?

I'd really fucked up. She was never going to forgive me after this. There I was being hailed as a champion and I felt like the biggest loser. There was no golden wave of glory radiating through me. No rush of adrenaline making me want to punch the air. All I felt was shame. Shame and worry.

Where was she?

I didn't stand on ceremony or give the crowds the victory speech I had prepared in my head. Instead, I grabbed my t-shirt and forced my way out of the ring and through the throngs of people who were patting me on the back as I passed. I headed to where she'd been standing, and as I stopped to scan the crowd, I saw Emily making her way over to me.

"Are you okay? I've never seen you lose it like that before."

"That's because I've never lost it like that before," I replied through gritted teeth without sparing a look her way. I was too focused on trying to locate a certain blonde.

"You saw her, didn't you?" she said, and I turned to face her.

So, she'd seen her too.

"I didn't know she'd be here, Brandon. If I did, I would've told you."

I knew she meant that.

"She found out some way."

"I gave her the details but I never in a million years thought she'd show up. She said she wanted to stay away from you. I was as surprised as you when I saw her across the room. Trust me. I wouldn't do that to you. I know how important tonight was, and I also know how hard it would've been to see her watching you like that."

I pinched the bridge of my nose, even though my fingers hurt like hell. I was numb inside and out.

"She looked frightened," I said. "I don't think she was with anyone else. You need to give me her number so I can call her and see if she's okay."

Emily frowned, as if she was thinking about it, then she huffed out a smile.

"I love you, Brandon. But I'm not giving you Harper's number. She'd never speak to me again."

"Fine. You ring her. But we can't let her go. She's... vulnerable." I was too, and I needed to know she was okay.

"Wow." Emily's eyes went wide. "Never thought I'd hear you say that about a girl. You're really worried about her, aren't you?"

I leant down to speak low in Emily's ear.

"I'm not a totally heartless asshole, Winters. Not to everyone, anyway. Now bloody ring her before I tear this whole fucking place down."

She rolled her eyes at me and reached into the pocket of her jeans. I watched her pull her phone out and tap the security code in. When she did, I grabbed the phone from her and stalked away.

Emily followed me, shouting angrily for me to give it back, but I carried on scrolling through her contacts until I found Harper's number. I hit the call button and turned to face Emily, putting one finger over my mouth to shush her and then holding her back with my arm.

The phone rang once before it was answered, and a frantic-sounding Harper spoke first.

"Is he okay? Emily? Has something happened? Is he all right? Please, talk to me!"

I couldn't answer.

I was stunned into silence for the first time in my God-forsaken life.

She was worried about me.

She was scared for me.

Her first thought had been if I was okay. What was I supposed to say to that?

I stayed silent and passed the phone to Emily, who snatched it from my hand and gave me an evil glare for my troubles.

"Hey, Harper. Yes, he's fine. He took a hit, but it didn't knock any sense into him. He's still an arrogant twat."

I smiled as she spoke, but my heart was beating faster

than it had done only minutes ago during my fight. And that adrenaline rush that I always felt after a match? That was through the fucking roof. I didn't want to hope for anything. Hope usually ended badly for me, but she had me on her mind and that had to mean something, surely?

"He did see you, yeah. I think it distracted him. Oh God, don't apologise. You're the last person who should be apologising. Listen, ring or text me when you're home so I know you're safe. Everything is fine. He won. Okay? It's over."

Emily said her goodbyes and ended the call. All I could hear was, *text when you get home.*

"She's not home yet? You should've asked where she was. It isn't safe for her to be out on her own at night."

"Who said she's alone?" Emily said nonchalantly, and then she smirked. "Cool it, Rambo. She's in a taxi, on her own, and she'll be home in five minutes. Jeez, anyone would think you really liked this girl." She winked.

"Maybe I should go after her?" I went to walk away, but Emily grabbed my arm.

"Don't. I think tonight was enough of an eye-opener for her. Give her time, Brandon."

What did that mean? An eye-opener? She'd seen her brother fight before. Why was my fight any different? If anything, it would've been therapy for her, surely?

"She probably didn't expect to feel the way she did when she saw you tonight." Emily elaborated. "It can be quite intense watching you up there. I hate it and I'm not as emotionally invested. She snapped her mouth shut and flinched. She'd said something she felt she shouldn't have.

"What do you mean, emotionally invested? Have you spoken to her about me?"

Emily shuffled her feet. She was crap at hiding her true intentions.

"We had a few chats on the phone. I just read between the lines. Don't go reading too much into what I say, big man." She breathed out a sigh of relief when she saw Ryan and Zak coming towards us. "Now, go. Be with your adoring fans and make the most of tonight. It's not every day you're made to feel like a living legend."

"You haven't lived my life, sweetheart." I winked, but the bravado I was putting on was for her benefit. Inside, I was a tortured mess of anxiety, and this was the last place I wanted to be.

CHAPTER
Twenty Four

HARPER

I don't know why I went. In some perverse and twisted way, I'd needed to do it to expel a demon that was sitting on my shoulder. What would it be like to see Brandon fight again? Would he show any remorse? Would he be different and more humble, maybe? After what had happened, would it affect him and make him a more guarded fighter?

From the minute he walked into that makeshift ring, he was larger than life. A showman. He had every single person in that room eating out of the palm of his hands, even the ones who were heckling him. They loved him. He loved them. But I hated it. I hated the atmosphere, the overdose of adrenaline and testosterone filling the air, the shouts and catcalls that made me flinch. But most of all, I hated how utterly helpless it made me feel to stand at the sidelines again and watch a fight, feeling like my whole world was about to implode.

I hadn't expected to feel like that. I thought seeing him would make me angry, and fire up my thirst for revenge, but it did the opposite. It made me nervous, crippled me with anxiety, and just like when Brodie fought, I had to practise my breathing and force myself not to storm forward to stop it all. It was fucking barbaric and it was tearing me apart, still. I couldn't stand it.

Would I feel like that watching two strangers?

Probably.

But knowing what lay behind that tunnel vision of fury that fired Brandon up made it worse for me.

I cared.

There. I'd admitted it to myself, albeit in my head, but I did care about what happened to him. He'd been through so much; I didn't want him to have the same ending as Brodie. I couldn't bear to lose someone else to that sport. If you could call it that. I wanted him to find peace in a different way. I knew he'd be as stubborn as Brodie if he was ever asked to stop fighting. But I hoped that in time, he would find something else that meant more to him than fighting did. He was worth more than that.

I fired a text off to Emily to let her know I was safe. Then I crept through the house, hoping I didn't wake Mum and Dad, and headed to my room. When I closed the door, I flopped down onto my bed, hoping sleep would take hold and quieten the voices in my head. Voices that I found unsettling, because I didn't fully understand the emotions they were creating inside me.

Emily text back moments later and told me she'd ring me tomorrow. I didn't answer. I didn't feel like engaging anymore with the outside world. I couldn't comprehend myself or my feelings at the moment, so I didn't want to burden anyone else.

What was this guy doing to me?

He'd smashed into my world like a wrecking ball, but the reverberations of his hits just kept on coming. What had started out as destruction all those months ago had turned into something else entirely. He'd forced his way into my life, given no thought to my sanity, and yet, after everything, he was making me feel. Okay, most days it was angry, hurt, and pissed off. But tonight, I'd felt fear, worry, concern. I thought those kind of emotions were dead to me. I thought caring about another human was something I'd struggle to do after having my heart broken. But I guess that's where I was wrong. I wasn't the shell of a woman I thought I was. I still had empathy and the ability to show compassion. The fact that I'd shown it to Brandon tonight was a big fucking deal for me.

He'd seen me in the crowd. I'd distracted him and he'd almost got injured because of me. How did it make him feel when he saw me? Did the memories suffocate him? Or was it something else?

I couldn't stop myself from climbing off the bed and going to my laptop. In all my confusion, one clear thought kept pushing itself to the forefront of my mind. I needed to reach out to him. Even if it was just to make sure he really was okay.

LadyStoneheart23 has joined the chat.

EmoGirl- I did think about going, but I don't think they're ready for me yet.

JoeNotExotic- She's your sister. You could both be missing out on a fab friendship there. You never know, Emo.

EmoGirl- Half sister. And I don't even know if she wants to speak to me. Mum told me to leave it, but I can't. Maybe I should send her an email? I found her email address on Facebook.

JoeNotExotic- But you have her real address. It's always better to meet face-to-face.

EmoGirl- Is it? It wasn't the best meeting the last time I was in a room with her.

JoeNotExotic- She didn't know who you were then.

EmoGirl- Hey, Lady. You're up late. You okay?

LadyStoneheart23- Yeah, I'm good. I think I turned a corner recently.

Legion has joined the chat.

My heart jumped and my hands started to shake.

EmoGirl- That's always a good thing. Sounds like you've made a few breakthroughs then, Lady.

LadyStoneheart23- I had a little help along the way.

Legion- You don't need anyone's help, little warrior. All

your goals are yours to celebrate.
    JoeNotExotic- True, Legion. Very true.

I swallowed my pride and opened up a private chat with him. It was the first time I'd ever private messaged anyone on here without getting a message through first. I really was starting to walk a different path.

    LadyStoneheart23- Are you okay?

I clicked send then cursed myself when I reread my message. It sounded so lame. Like I was a parent checking in on him. Guess he'd never had that though, growing up.

    Legion- Never worry about me, little warrior. I'm big enough and ugly enough to take care of myself. But the next time you want to leave like that, tell one of us. I don't like to think of you getting into a taxi on your own.

After taking a beating and winning a fight like that he was online chatting to me and stressing over my ride home.

    LadyStoneheart23- I can take care of myself.
    Legion- You shouldn't have to.

I didn't know what to type back in response.

LadyStoneheart23- I liked what you said about Jensen tonight. He is a piece of shit.

Legion- His time will come. I'm gonna make him regret the day he put his hands on you, believe me. But I'm sorry for what I said about it being that guy's funeral. I didn't mean to break open old wounds. I wouldn't have said that if I knew you were there.

LadyStoneheart23- It was a show. I get it. A circus. It's fine.

Legion- It's not. It was thoughtless and I'm sorry.

He'd said sorry. It wasn't lost on me that Brandon rarely said something like that. He obviously meant it.

LadyStoneheart23- I'm glad I spoke to you tonight.

I knew I'd sleep slightly better knowing I had made the effort. The nightmares would probably still come but lately, they were getting less. Little steps.

Legion- Me too, little warrior.
LadyStoneheart23- Night, Brandon. X
Legion – Night, Harper. X

I logged off and then shook my head.

What was happening to me?

Maybe I did need to see someone, like Mum with Doctor Meredith. I didn't recognise myself lately and I felt like I was stumbling through each day. Was this some weird Stockholm syndrome without the captivity? Because it was bloody confusing, that was for sure. The man who used to stoke the fire of my revenge was now able to calm the flames, all through a simple online chat. Maybe his method of therapy was helping me more than I realised.

CHAPTER
Twenty Five

HARPER

For the next few days, Emily was pretty relentless in her texts and phone calls. She even offered to come round a couple of times, but I'd gotten good at making excuses. It was nice that she cared so much, and I did feel guilty for not reciprocating her enthusiasm. So, after a lot of persuasion on her part, I eventually agreed to go on a girls' night out with her. In reality, I wasn't that fussed about doing the whole socialising thing. I liked my own company, but Emily had it all planned out and I didn't like to keep letting her down. There was only so much a person could take before they turned their back on you forever, and I needed all the friends I could get.

But once that night rolled around, the nerves well and truly set in. What had I agreed to?

Emily told me she'd pick me up at seven. I didn't have a choice. I also didn't have a thing to wear, but I settled on ripped skinny jeans and a tight black tank top. I wasn't really in a dressing-up state of mind yet. Not like I used to be. Those little black dresses would be hanging in my wardrobe for a while longer yet.

When the doorbell rang and Mum opened the door to let Emily in, she hugged me. I pulled away feeling awkward and then reached for my Converse, but she flew forward and yanked them out of my hands.

"No way. Not tonight. Wear these heels." She grabbed my black stilettos that I hadn't worn in months and threw my Converse to the back of the shoe cupboard. "Converse are great, but tonight is a heels night. Let your hair down, Harper."

Mum just chuckled at my distress and sauntered off to the living room, leaving me to argue this one on my own.

"I don't even know if I can still walk in those," I moaned. Having blisters for the next week really wasn't worth the hassle.

"After a few drinks you won't care." She laughed back and threw them to the floor in front of me to put on. I didn't feel like hashing this out anymore, so I did as she'd asked.

Standing up, I remembered how tall and powerful heels made you feel. It actually felt good. Maybe Emily had been right on this one.

I picked up my clutch bag and we headed out to her car. Emily told me that Liv and Effy were going to meet us at the bar. I smiled, but I felt so nervous at the thought of walking in there. Would everyone be looking at me? Feeling sorry for me? I knew I'd need a few drinks just to calm myself down. I was over-thinking everything. What would I even say to these girls? I barely knew them. This was so far out of my comfort zone.

I stayed quiet on the drive over. Emily filled the silence with stories about the Hardy's and how excited she was to find a new place for her and Ryan so they could have more privacy. I smiled and gave the appropriate responses, and in a way I felt jealous. Emily seemed to have it all figured out. She had Ryan, they were planning a new life together, and she was doing well in her college course. Where was my life heading? My job didn't even want me there, I had no boyfriend, and I still lived with my parents at twenty-three. But then she started to open up a little about her dad's trial and I realised she hadn't always had it easy. The happiness she was living now had been one she'd fought for. Maybe that's what we all had to do. Fight for what we wanted. Life wouldn't just come to you. You had to make it happen.

When we got to the bar, Liv and Effy were already inside and had secured a table for us. There was music playing through the speakers, but it wasn't too loud or busy and I let my shoulders relax slightly as I scanned the room and realised that there was no one here I recognised.

"Has Ryan gone on a boys' night?" I asked her as we ordered our drinks.

"That's what he said. I bet they don't even make it out of Zak's living room. It'll probably be a few games of FIFA and a couple of beers." Emily rolled her eyes but smiled. The way she lit up whenever she spoke about him was infectious.

We carried our drinks over to the table to join the other two, and I found myself joining in more than I thought I would. None of them tiptoed around me, and it was refreshing. At home, my parents spoke to me like a child sometimes, and it grated on me, but I couldn't get angry at them. They didn't deserve that. I also understood why they did it. I hadn't been the most stable person to live with over the last few months.

We were just chatting over our third round of drinks when Liv let out a huge groan.

"For fuck's sake. He can't leave you for five minutes, can he?"

Emily glanced to the door and then swung back round to face us, putting her hands up in defence.

"I swear, I told him to steer clear of this place. I don't know what he's thinking. I'm so sorry, girls. I'll go and ask him to leave."

She went to stand up, but Liv grabbed her arm to stop her.

"It's fine. Let them stay. As long as he doesn't steal you away."

I peered over my shoulder and sure enough, there was Ryan at the bar with Zak Atwood, Finn Knowles, and Brandon. They were all wearing jeans and dark t-shirts, but Brandon's tattoos made him stand out in the group.

He stood tall and appeared arrogant as he looked

around the room. When his eyes landed on me, the arrogance I thought I saw was replaced by apprehension. He swallowed and then turned to take the drink that Zak was offering him.

"Are you okay?" Emily whispered. "If you feel uncomfortable and want to leave, we can."

"No. It's fine," I said, trying to convince myself as much as her.

She gave me a look that told me she wasn't buying it, but she let it slide.

"Okay. If at any time you need to leave, just say the word and we'll go."

I was touched that she was taking my feelings into consideration like this. I know that given the chance she'd probably want to be with Ryan over us, but she didn't show it.

"You can go and say hi. We won't be mad at you," Liv said, sipping her cocktail.

"I see him every day. It's fine." Emily waved her hand nonchalantly.

"Do you want to go over and say hi to Finn?" Liv turned to nudge Effy and she blushed, taking a sip of her drink to try and hide it.

"I'll go over in a bit. Don't want to look too eager, do I?" Effy huffed, and Emily and Liv raised their eyebrows at each other.

"Trouble in paradise?" Liv asked.

"What paradise? He barely speaks to me when he sees

me. I think you two see things that aren't there half the time." Effy didn't sound too happy about whatever it was that was going on between her and Finn.

"He's shy, Eff. Don't be too hard on him," Emily replied, giving Effy a kind smile.

"I'm shy too," Effy argued and stuck out her lip, pouting.

"There's shy, and then there's Finn Knowles," Liv said, pointing at him across the room. "That boy needs a kick up the backside if you ask me."

"We didn't," Effy replied, quick as a flash.

"Maybe I can work my cupid magic on him." Liv tittered.

"Leave it, Liv. I'm not ready for you to start meddling in my love life." Effy rolled her eyes, looking over at Emily, and the two of them shared a knowing look.

"Bollocks to that. If I hadn't pushed Em towards Chase Lockwood, Ryan would never have got his shit together."

I almost choked on my drink.

"You dated Chase Lockwood?" I asked Emily, feeling shocked that she'd go there. Even I'd heard the rumours about Chase and his... how should I say this, man-whoring ways.

"No!" she stated with a look of disgust on her face. "Liv tried to set it up, but I have standards." Then she became embarrassed and started to blush. "Sorry, Harper. I know the Lockwoods are friends of yours. I didn't mean to offend you."

"They're not my friends. Not anymore," I snapped back a little too brusquely.

I could tell they were itching to ask me what had happened, but bringing up anything about those brothers was the last thing I wanted to do. I had a good buzz from the drinks, the girls had made me laugh, and Brandon was in the same building and I hadn't freaked out. Tonight, I'd made real progress.

It got busier as the night wore on and the atmosphere in the bar ramped up a gear as the music started playing louder. There was no dancefloor; people just let go and danced where they stood, making the most of it.

Despite her earlier protestations, Emily had gone over to talk to the boys, but to her credit she didn't leave us for long. Effy grew quieter the longer the night wore on, and she couldn't stop herself from glancing across to where Finn stood and sighing. I made a conscious effort to try and avoid catching Brandon's eye, but I felt him everywhere. Knowing he was here made the skin on the back of my neck prickle and my stomach churn with nervous energy. He was like a magnet I was trying to avoid being pulled towards. Did he feel it too?

Emily and Liv headed off to the toilets and Effy turned towards me.

"I don't know what I did wrong?" she said, not looking at me, but peering over my shoulder at the bar area. "One minute I think he likes me, the next he does everything he can to avoid me. Why are boys so hard to figure out?"

"Maybe it's not you. Maybe it's something else." I offered, not having the first clue what was going on with her.

"I asked him out once. Only for coffee. He looked like I'd slapped him round the face and couldn't make up excuses fast enough to get away from me. The next day he posted an envelope through my door with a note inside. He'd drawn a picture of my dog by hand. It was beautiful." She shook her head sadly. "He's a complete mind-fuck."

"That's really sweet. He obviously likes you."

"Does he?"

Effy jolted forward in her chair as some woman behind our table, who'd drunk way too much, fell backwards and knocked into her. She didn't complain though. Effy was too polite for that. I glared at the woman, but she just laughed and announced to the men with her that she wanted to dance on the tables. I really hoped she didn't mean ours.

I watched as the woman climbed up onto the table next to us and almost broke her neck when her heels got caught in the grooves of the wood. She was shouting the lyrics to the song and swaying, and the men watching her just laughed, clearly enjoying the show. The woman needed a strong coffee and a new set of friends, in my opinion.

I saw Liv and Emily coming back across the bar, and when they spotted the woman, they both raised their eyebrows at her. She didn't have a care in the world. She also had zero control and no balance whatsoever. She was an accident waiting to happen.

We all watched her, stunned and holding our breath in anticipation for the impending fall. But suddenly, the air around us became stifling and I tensed when I saw Ryan and Brandon standing next to us, both of them with faces like thunder. Zak and Finn were a bit further back, but from their expressions, shit was about to go down.

"You need to get down," Brandon shouted to the woman over the music.

The woman did the most unsteady looking slut drop I'd ever seen and ran her ridiculously long nail under Brandon's chin. I didn't like that. I didn't like her touching him.

"You're a big strapping man. Why don't you make me?" she purred back, but instead of sounding sexy, she sounded deranged.

"I'm not joking. Get down. You're gonna hurt yourself," he hissed, but loud enough that we could all hear him.

"It's so cute that you care. Why don't you come up here and join me?" She beckoned him on with her scrawny finger. Brandon just glowered back.

"You need to sober up and go home."

We all sat watching, frozen in shock at how this was all playing out. Anyone could see how furious Brandon was, and it made us all hyper-alert, dreading what would happen next.

"I'll go home with you, baby. If that's what you want," she said in a husky voice, leaning back down again and running her hand down his chest. He grabbed her wrist and pulled it away, grimacing at her touch like she'd just scorched him.

"You have no idea who I am, do you?" he shouted, and a

few people nearby moved away, probably frightened of getting caught in the crossfire. I could tell by the way Brandon's jaw was clenched that he was close to losing it.

"Should I? Do I know you?" She laughed. "Did we fuck already?" She covered her mouth, pretending to look shocked. "Damn, I would've remembered you."

"It's Brandon," he snapped.

"Brandon who?" She had absolutely no clue who he was, and Brandon was growing more irritated by the second.

"Brandon. Your son."

What the fuck?

That was the last thing we'd expected him to say. This was Brandon's mother? The cheap hooker dancing on the tables looking like she didn't have a care in the world was the same bitch that'd screamed into a little boy's face and told him she wished he was dead.

"I don't have a son." She shrugged. "Oh, wait. Yes, I do. But he's a skinny little shit who fucked up my life."

I shot up out of my chair, but Emily and Liv were closer, and they managed to get in her face quicker than I could.

"You're un-fucking-believable... *Mum*," Brandon said, folding his arms over his chest and doing a really good job of keeping himself in check.

"You're a fucking disgrace," Liv spat at her.

"You need to leave." Emily went to move forward, but Ryan held her back.

"Fuck off, Pam. Don't you think you've done enough

damage for tonight?" Ryan said, snaking his arm around Emily protectively.

"I'll do whatever the fuck I want," Brandon's mother sneered, but she wasn't smirking for long. Liv lurched forward and grabbed her arm, pulling her off the table.

"You're upsetting my friends. Grow up, bitch, and get a fucking life."

Brandon's mother just swayed on her feet and cackled at the way Liv was manhandling her.

"Worst thing I ever did was have him. I should've aborted him when his dad gave me the money for it. I could've done us all a favour."

The next thing I knew, I was standing in front of her and my hand connected with her face. She reeled backwards and covered her cheek, scowling over at me.

"What was that for?"

For being the biggest piece of shit as a human and a mother.

For destroying your son's life.

For ever showing your face in Sandland.

For still breathing.

I didn't get a chance to say my piece though. The girls, Ryan, Brandon, Zak, and Finn stood in front of me like they were my protection, and a doorman marched over, ready to read us all the riot act.

"Okay, Pam. Party's over. Come on. I've got a taxi waiting out the back for you," the doorman said, giving

Brandon a sympathetic look.

"Why the back? You're such a spoil sport," Brandon's mother slurred. Her eyes were glazing over, and I felt sure she'd probably already forgotten the scene she'd just created, she was that drunk.

"'Cos I don't want you putting off any more of our customers." The doorman sighed, and as he started to lead her off, she stumbled into him and he caught her as she almost fell to the floor.

"You could take me back to yours," she said, grinning up at him as he held her up by his side. "I could do that thing you like with my tongue."

He just turned to look at Brandon and said, "I'm so sorry, man." Then, without waiting for a reply, he carted her off and left us all to deal with the aftermath of what'd happened.

–

Brandon didn't stick around for long. His mother wasn't even halfway across the room when he said, "Fuck this shit." And stormed off out of the bar. The rest of us stood there stunned into silence. No one knew what to say or do for the best.

"I should go after him," Finn piped up, and Ryan went to go with him, but I shocked even myself when I jumped in front of them.

"No. I'll go," I said, leaving the rest of the group gawping at me, speechless.

I darted to the exit, and when I got outside, I looked left and right, but I couldn't see him.

"I think he went that way," one of the doormen said, pointing down the road.

I thanked him and started to walk the way he'd suggested, but I couldn't see Brandon anywhere and it made me feel anxious to think of him out here alone with his demons.

I stopped next to an alleyway to gather my bearings, and when I peered down into the darkness, I saw him, leaning against the wall with his head hung low. He looked lost and broken, and it made my heart hurt to see him like that.

I stalked towards him like I was approaching a wounded animal. I didn't know what frame of mind he was in and I felt like I needed to be cautious. When he heard my footsteps, he looked up and the way he sighed so deeply made me want to reach out to him and make it better. I don't know when it'd happened, but Brandon's happiness seemed to be tethered to my own. His feelings affected mine.

"I'm sorry you had to see that," he said, shaking his head and staring at the floor like he wished it'd open up and swallow him whole.

"You don't have to apologise for anything."

And he didn't.

Whatever that woman had done in her life, it was no reflection on him. He'd come out relatively unscathed considering what a major fuck-up she was. I doubt many people would survive a childhood with her playing a starring role. No wonder he had issues forging relationships when that was what he had to base his experiences on.

"I can't believe that... woman back there gave birth to me. I feel ashamed."

I felt another flip of my heart, hearing him sound so tortured and alone.

"Don't ever be ashamed of who you are, Brandon. She's the one who should feel shame, not you."

I didn't know if he was hearing what I was saying. He could barely look me in the eye, preferring to glance down the alley or at the floor than look at me.

"She's probably forgotten me already... Again," he said on a whisper. And I knew in that instant that it didn't matter what she did or how many times she denied him or put him down. He'd always want her approval; her love. He was a boy who'd never felt a mother's love. That had to hurt harder than anything in life. Maybe just as much as losing a twin.

Maybe.

"Then that's her loss. She doesn't deserve to have a family. She doesn't deserve a son like you."

"A son like me? What, a fucked-up head-case who stalks girls he likes. Who's only skill in life is hitting people and causing absolute fucking mayhem."

And that was it. My heart was well and truly gone.

"You like me?"

He smirked and shook his head.

"That's what you took from all that?"

"Brandon, I'm not gonna pretend I understand anything you've done in the past, but in a way, after seeing *that* tonight, I kind of get it. You haven't had the best family life."

And you have absolutely no idea how to handle your emotions because of it.

"Other people have it worse."

And a lot more have it better too.

"You're forgetting who you're talking to. I know what she said to you when you were little. I know the damage she caused." I couldn't stop myself from reaching forward and brushing my fingers over his stomach, knowing what lay underneath that t-shirt. Feeling his warmth on my fingertips made my whole body heat up. That magnetic pull he'd had on me back at the bar was still as strong in this alleyway. "I know what damage they all did… And I'm sorry. I am so, so sorry."

His eyes never left mine as he held his breath, then he looked down to where my fingers were touching him and let out a deep sigh.

"We can't take on the sins of our relatives," I said, willing him to look at me. "I think we both know that."

"I know. But it doesn't stop the guilt, does it? I could've done more."

"What more do you think you could've done?" I asked, peering up into his eyes.

"I ran." He rubbed his hands over his face and groaned.

"I bottled it and I ran away. I should've stayed and helped you."

"I wouldn't have let you."

"Will you let me now?"

He hung his head and the look on his face made my heart ache for him. He looked so lost, hiding here in the darkness.

"I know you like to hide this part of you. A bit like you're hiding now. You don't want people to see the darkest parts. But I want to see them. You've seen mine. You've seen me bent over in the dirt, broken and crying."

"Because of me." I heard the hitch in his voice. This was the rawest I think I'd ever seen him. He was putting himself out there, letting it all go, for me.

"I broke because I lost my brother and I couldn't handle it. Neither could you. What can I say? We have shit coping mechanisms." I gave a low laugh, trying to make light of the shitty situation we were in.

He chuckled back and it made my heart hurt less to see him open up to me somewhat.

"I have no coping mechanism. I just am. I learnt from an early age that you have to be there for yourself, 'cos no one else is going to help you."

"You helped me. At least you tried to. In your weird fucked up way." I grinned, hoping he saw how I meant it.

"And look how that turned out."

Nope. He wasn't getting it.

"Yeah, look. I'm out for the first time in months, drinking with friends, having a good time, and standing here in the dark with you. Who'd have thought this would've happened a few months ago?"

He bit his lip and then looked right at me.

"Can I ask you something?"

"Sure."

"Will you ever forgive me?"

And that was the million dollar question.

"It isn't about forgiveness, Brandon. What happened, happened. It could've been anyone in that ring with him that night. I know that now." I sighed. "It's about finding peace. I'm getting there, slowly. But I'm not sure you are."

"I don't think I'll ever find peace. I'm used to living in my head with the constant noise and feelings of shame, inferiority, guilt, disgust... the list is endless." And that list I could see etched into his face, in the wrinkles on his brow, the clench of his jaw and the pain in his eyes.

"You've lived with that all these years? How are you still functioning?"

"I don't. I fight. That's the only time I feel any sort of calm. Well, it was."

He clenched his fists at the side of him and I could feel the tension in his body.

"And after the accident, you lost all that. You don't feel that calm anymore, do you?" I knew the answer, but I asked the question anyway

"No. That's not what I'm saying." He frowned and leaned towards me. "I feel the calm, but I have another outlet now. I have you."

My heart skipped a beat.

"I don't know what to say to that."

"You don't have to say anything. I know the way I feel. I also know you'll never feel that way about me and I'm okay with that. I'm used to rejection. I've lived my whole life with disappointment. It's second nature..."

I didn't give him the chance to utter another word. I leant up and planted a kiss on his lips. A soft, gentle peck that told him he didn't need to keep making excuses. That messed up, confused but calm feeling he was experiencing, I felt it too.

I pulled away but stayed close to him, looking deep into his eyes. He blew out a low breath and whispered, "You don't have to feel sorry for me."

"That's not what this is."

"Isn't it? I don't want you to use me for some kind of fucked-up therapy, Harper. A way to prove to yourself that you're moving on."

"I'm not."

He reached forward and cupped my cheek and I leant into him. His hands were rough and calloused, but I liked the way they felt against my skin. The rough with the smooth. I looked up at him, seeing the confusion in his eyes, the way he was toying with his emotions.

"I have thought about you every day since that night," he said. "You are the first thing I think about in the morning and last thing on my mind at night. I lie awake and wonder if what I did will ever get any easier for me to deal with."

"It will, if you let me help. We can help each other."

He placed his forehead gently against mine.

"I think I'm beyond help."

"You don't know if you don't..."

I was the one who didn't get to finish this time. Brandon kissed me, grabbing the back of my head and crashing his lips hard onto mine. He sent my mind into freefall.

I kissed him back, opening my mouth and groaning as our tongues laced together. I'd never been kissed this way before. Raw and electric; that's the only way I could describe it, because he lit up my whole world.

I reached up and wrapped my arms around his neck, pulling him even closer, and he spun me round so my back was against the wall. Then he lifted me up by the backs of my thighs and I clamped my legs around his waist.

We stood against that wall in the shadows, finding ourselves in each other. The warmth of his body made me melt. The heat of his kiss set me on fire. I never wanted it to end. I wanted to live in the darkness forever, with him. He made me feel alive.

I ran my fingernails across the back of his head, and he moaned into our kiss. I threaded my fingers through his hair and tugged lightly as he squeezed my ass and ran his hands from my waist to my thighs and back again. And all the time, we were grinding our hips against each other. Needing more.

Brandon was the first to pull away, but he kept his forehead pressed against mine and panted as he said, "I don't want to end this, but I'm not fucking you in an alleyway, Harper."

I blushed at the crudeness of his words. "I didn't think..."

"I want to, but you deserve better." He sighed as he dropped my legs and let me stand on my own. "I'm not saying I don't want this. I do. Trust me." He quirked an eyebrow and looked down at his trousers with a smirk and then back up at me. I couldn't keep the smile off my face at the obvious bulge he was sporting.

"You like me," I said like an idiot.

"I more than like you."

He gave me another kiss and then he chuckled to himself.

"I guess my mother was good for one thing after all. I never thought my night would end like this." Then he full-on laughed. "I can't believe you slapped her."

"She asked for it. And for the record, that's the first time I've ever hit anyone."

He reached down to take my hand in his and lifted it up to kiss my knuckles.

"Good. I'm the brawler around here, not you," he said, then playfully knocked his fist against my chin and laughed again.

"Your mum got us together. What are the chances?"

"Are we? Together, I mean?" He bit his lip and looked at the floor, shuffling nervously and kicking stones that weren't even there.

"We're something. Let's not label it just yet. Let's see where this thing takes us," I suggested, and he seemed happy with that.

"I can do that."

"Brandon?"

"Yes, little warrior?"

"You ever creep into my garden or my kitchen again to stalk me and I'll kick your ass."

He threw his head back and roared with laughter.

"What if I'm doing it to sneak into your room? There have to be exceptions to the rule?" He winked.

"I suppose I could overlook certain exceptional circumstances," I said, pretending to look serious about it.

"Good, because I'm not staying away. I want to be everywhere that you are."

CHAPTER

Twenty Six

BRANDON

I'd been a gentleman the night before and taken Harper home. Not my usual M.O, but then I was trying to be a better man for her. I managed to get another kiss at her front door, but I didn't want to push my luck. I wanted this to work, and I also had Emily bloody Winters sat on my shoulder the whole time, telling me I had to treat Harper differently. She wasn't like most girls I'd been around. She wasn't like any girl I'd ever met before.

But today, I was pumped full of aggressive energy and wound up to the point that I wanted to punch a wall. After the run-in with my egg donor and then holding back from doing what I really wanted to do with Harper last night, I was like a tightly coiled spring. I needed an outlet, and I decided there was a better target I could aim for than a wall.

Jensen fucking Lockwood.

I'd left it far too long to teach that prick a lesson, and I needed him to know she was off-limits. Payback for him putting his hands on her was long overdue.

I stormed up their ridiculously extravagant driveway, smirking at the matching Range Rovers they had parked up.

Did they know it was me who torched the last lot?

I bloody hoped so.

I wanted them to know that no matter how much time passed, I'd never give up getting my revenge on them for what they did to me. Chase might not have used his fists like the others, but in the later years, he'd stood and watched. He was as guilty as they were.

I banged my fist on their door and kept the demonic smile on my face. I wanted him to see what my intentions were the minute he opened that door. The Joker had nothing on some of the crazy shit I wanted to do.

When it finally swung open, and Chase stood there gawping at me, I tried not to let my smile falter. If I had to knock him out to get to his brother, I would. His smug-ass face deserved a beating.

"Where is he?" I asked, putting my foot forward to stop him from closing the door.

"He isn't here." Chase folded his arms over his chest, trying to look tough, but I noticed the way his hands were shaking. The fucker was scared.

"I'll wait then." I took another step forward, so I was standing in the doorway. I wasn't going to be pushed out. I was going to be heard. "Are you gonna invite me in for a drink? Or do I have to sit outside on your driveway all day? 'Cos I will. I'm not going anywhere."

Chase took a furtive glance down the hallway then whispered, "I don't know where he is. He won't be back here today. I can't help you. You need to leave."

He tried to move towards me, maybe hoping I'd back off and he could shut the door in my face, but that was never gonna happen. I stood my ground.

"You know where he is."

"Honestly, I don't. He left the night of the party. Your party at the waterworks. Nice touch, by the way, making him out to be a pussy in your little speech, but my brother doesn't hit women."

"Are you sure about that? 'Cos I know what I saw and the bruise on Harper's face told me a different story."

His eyes went wide, and I could tell he believed me. He didn't want to, but he did.

"I don't know what you're talking about." He couldn't look me in the eye when he spoke.

"Your brother hit Harper and he needs to pay."

And I'm here to collect on his debt, with my fists.

"If my brother hit her, then I'd punch the fuck out of him myself," Chase said, holding his chin up and doing a shit job of looking like a stand-up guy.

"Don't pretend to be self-righteous with me. I know you, remember. I know what your little crew are capable of. He hit her, but he won't ever do it again. When I get my hands on him, he's gonna regret it. Trust me."

Chase narrowed his eyes at me suspiciously.

"Why do you care? It's Brodie's sister... oh... wait, are you and her? Fuck... That is something I did not see coming."

I wanted to give him a smart answer, wipe that smug smirk off his face, but I was interrupted.

"What is going on here?"

Don Lockwood strode towards us looking like his wife had shrunk his underwear in the wash as he grimaced in annoyance.

"Brandon's just leaving," Chase stated, trying to usher me out of the door again. He needed to stop getting so fucking close. If he carried on poking the lion inside of me, he'd get a scary fucking wake-up call.

"I'm here to see Jensen," I said firmly, making sure both of them knew I wasn't fucking about.

"Jensen is out of town." He shrugged. "He's away on business. Why do you want him?"

I didn't trust Don Lockwood one bit and I didn't like the way he was eyeballing me. This guy was twice my age, but I could tell he fancied his chances. I also knew he'd been involved in the whole money laundering bullshit that Emily's Dad was on trial for. We could never pin anything on him, but he was knee deep in the shit. The fact that he'd got away with it and ghosted Alec Winters ever since must've made him feel untouchable. But as far as I was concerned, nobody was unbeatable. If he came at me, I'd come back even harder.

"I didn't expect to see you here today. Not at the trial?" I asked, hoping to get a rise out of him.

He gritted his teeth as he reluctantly responded.

"That trial has nothing to do with me or my family."

"Shit always floats to the top, huh?" I glared back at him, daring him to fight back. He didn't like that I wasn't cowering away.

"I wouldn't know," he said, putting his nose in the air like he was better than me. "There's no room for cheats and liars in my world."

"But lies don't stay buried for long."

We stared at each other for a few seconds until the tense moment was broken by his wife, Karen, coming out into the hallway. She took one look at me and she gasped.

"Oh my God. You look just like…"

She didn't get to finish what she was saying. Don Lockwood spun around and charged over to her, grabbing her arm aggressively and marching her away from where we stood.

"I'd appreciate it if you'd leave our house," he snapped over his shoulder. "We have nothing for you here."

My back went up at the way he dragged his wife away. Guess that's where Jensen got his sadistic streak from. Like father, like son.

"I thought my family were freaks." I laughed. "But yours take the fucking cake. Enjoy living your lies, Lockwood. Tell Jensen I'll be waiting for him."

He didn't reply, just stood gawping at me like the fool he was.

I turned and walked away, but all I'd achieved through my visit was a larger chip on my shoulder and an even stronger urge to hit something.

–

When I got to the gym, I headed straight for the boxing area, bypassing the weights and the cardio machines. Since coming back to Sandland, I'd used the place to work out and train for my comeback fight, but they didn't employ me anymore. After bailing on them following the incident with Harper's brother, they gave me my cards. But luckily, I hadn't burnt every bridge, and Ken, the manager, still let me use the facilities. It was a good job too, because I was wired and ready to explode.

It was busy, but I found a free punch bag towards the back of the room. I took my t-shirt off, and after one of the guys helped me to tape up my hands, I got to work, imagining Jensen's face as I pounded the leather. I was so engrossed in hitting the bag with as much force as I could, I didn't notice anyone close by, not until I felt a hand tap my shoulder. I stopped and pulled the headphones out of my ears.

"Brandon. It's good to see you." Pat Murphy clapped me on the back like he was a proud father.

"Pat." I nodded, feeling too zoned-out to give him anything more.

"You're in good shape," he said, looking me up and down.

"Thanks." I went to put my headphones back in, but he put a hand on my arm to stop me.

"I know you're back to fighting for your boys again, but hear me out, okay. I still want you to come and fight for me."

I shook my head. I'd already made my mind up on this. It wasn't up for discussion again.

"I already told you, I'm not interested. I made a promise to my friends and I don't let people down."

"I understand that, and I'm not saying you can't still fight for them, but if you fight for me too, we could really make something here. You should be fighting on a bigger stage. Punching for the big bucks not for fucking bets. What do you even make on those nights? Hundreds? If you fight for me, I could add a zero to that number."

Pat was a good guy, but I wasn't born yesterday.

"What's the catch?"

"No catch. I need the best fighters on my books. You're the best I've seen in years. I have contacts in the U.S. and I'm setting up a few fights. Bare-knuckle boxing isn't legal over there like it is here, but there's ways around it. Don't you want to be a champion?"

He thought he could reel me in with fake titles and bullshit about fighting in the states? He'd need a damn sight more than that if he wanted to entice me.

"I don't need a title from anyone."

I started to punch the bag again, effectively dismissing him, but he wasn't giving up.

"Brandon Mathers. U.K. bare-knuckle champion, does have a certain ring to it, doesn't it? And I'm sure you don't want to be living with your nan for the rest of your life. Just think what that kind of money could do for you. For your future. The more fights you get under your belt, the bigger the pay cheque."

He did have a point. I couldn't live with my nan or sofa surf for much longer. And the thought of buying my own place was a dream I wanted to make a reality.

"So, I'd still be able to pick my own fights?" I asked, grabbing the punch bag as it swung towards me.

"As long as it didn't jeopardise your fitness or clash with any of my bookings. Just think about it, okay. You have my number."

I had to admit money had been tight lately, and a bit of extra cash would've helped. Maybe a few fights for Pat wouldn't be so hard. I hadn't met a guy yet who could beat me. Perhaps now was the perfect time to start branching out? Try tougher opponents. We'd had to throw the net wider to find the last fighter, and even though I'd had that lapse in concentration, Callum Kendall was no match for me. It was like taking candy from a baby, and I didn't want my fights to grow stale.

"Fine. I'll do it," I said before I could change my mind.

"Good lad." Pat slapped me hard on my back. "I'll be in touch. We'll need to think about diets, fitness, and your daily training regime. That sort of stuff."

"I train just fine. I don't need any help." I frowned, not liking how this was going already. I didn't take orders well, not from anyone.

"For what I have planned, we'll need to turn you into a fucking machine. Don't worry, son. I have it all planned out. Once we're finished, the world of boxing won't know what's hit it."

CHAPTER
Twenty Seven

BRANDON

Had I just made the worst fucking decision of my life? I had no idea. My brain was fried. I could barely think straight. And after using up my energy at the gym, I needed to find some clarity. That's why I was standing in the Hardy's living room, pacing up and down as I recalled everything that had happened in the last twelve hours at the Lockwood's house and then with Pat Murphy.

"We were worried about you last night, mate," Ryan said, interrupting my incoherent rambling. "Are you okay? You know, after everything with Pam?" He stared at me like he expected me to flip out at any second.

"My egg donor is an attention-grabbing whore. It's the story of my life. I should be used to it by now, but it still gets to me."

Ryan understood, and he knew me well enough to know when to drop the subject. I hadn't come here to talk about Pam fucking Mathers, the woman who didn't deserve the title of mother.

"I didn't expect Harper to be the one to chase you down. I've got to admit, it shocked me." He smirked.

"You and me both." I couldn't stop myself from grinning, even though my insides were tangled up in knots. Things were finally starting to look up for me... At least I thought they were. If I could get my head around everything.

"Not sure what she'll think about you fighting for Murphy though. Wasn't he training Brodie before he died?"

I'd heard those rumours too, but I didn't want to dwell on whatever had gone on between Pat and Yates. That was his business, not mine. All I knew was, Pat wanted the best. He'd badgered me for months to join him. Now, he'd got me. The rest wasn't up for discussion. Well, not Brodie's involvement, anyway.

"I'm not sure I'm gonna tell her." I shrugged, trying to convince myself that it wasn't a big deal.

Ryan sighed and leaned forward in his chair.

"I don't think you're gonna be able to keep something like this quiet, mate. You know what this town's like; gossip spreads like wildfire. Look, I know I said to stay away from her, but even I can see there might be something there between you two. If you want to make a go of it, you need to be honest."

I didn't think I was being dishonest. I didn't need to answer to anyone. I'd always been my own man. I made my own decisions.

"It's just boxing. It's what I do."

"But it's not just boxing to her. It's what destroyed her life. She won't take it well if she hears it from someone else. Don't you think she should have a choice on whether she gets thrown back into that world again?"

If she chose to be with me, and I really fucking hoped she did, then surely she'd already made that choice? I frowned, trying to get my head around the way Ryan was thinking, but I was struggling.

"I am that world," I stated plainly.

Everyone in Sandland knew what I was. And if I was honest, when I came to discuss Pat's offer, it was because I wanted Ry to tell me it'd be the best thing to ever happen to me. That I was going places. I didn't expect him to throw more spanners into the works. He really wasn't helping.

"But are you? Really? The world Pat lives in and the one we created are two completely different things."

"He told me it wouldn't affect our business," I argued, feeling my shoulders tense up as I folded my arms.

"And you believed him? You really think he'll invest time and money into you to sit back and watch you piss it all down the drain by fighting some chancer from a council estate?"

"I don't lose."

Ryan was skating on thin ice now.

"You might lose her if you carry on being an asshole about this." Ryan gave a low, frustrated sigh. "I'll say one thing though, life is never boring with you around."

Emily chose that exact moment to walk in, and the tense

atmosphere became slightly more bearable.

"Boring is not a word I'd use to describe Brandon," she said, after hearing only half of what Ryan had said.

"It's all fun and games with me around, Winters." I gave her a wink and sat my ass down. With Emily, I could spin the conversation towards something else which was bugging me.

"Hey, Em. You're a chick."

She laughed and rolled her eyes at me. "Yep. Last time I looked I was a... chick. Although we prefer other terms, like girl, woman, female-"

"Yeah, whatever." I rubbed my hands together, trying to think how best to word this. "What sort of things should I do if I wanted to be... I dunno... romantic and shit?"

"Romantic and shit?" She shook her head, looking at me like I'd spoken a foreign language.

"I wanna do something nice. You're a girl. You know what girls like."

"I'm assuming this is for Harper?"

My face grew hot hearing her name. Emily glanced at Ryan and then smiled, cuddling into his side.

"Flowers are always lovely. Ryan bought me peonies on one of our first... times together." She started blushing.

"Errr, no. Flowers are a definite no." I tensed, remembering the last bunch of flowers I sent to Harper. I think I'd well and truly pissed all over the flower giving where she was concerned. "And what the hell is a peony?" I added, frowning. "Dude, you need to take control of your balls from time to time. She's turning you into a pussy."

"I am not!" She snapped then huffed and wrapped her arms around Ryan as she rubbed against him like a little kitten. "What about a picnic? Ryan had Connor make up a picnic basket for us on our first date. We didn't eat much of it, but it was really romantic. I bet if you asked Connor, he'd do one for you."

"Do I look like a picnic kind of guy to you?"

"Do I?" Ryan answered, challenging me. "On second thoughts, don't answer that."

Emily sighed, rubbing her hand over Ryan's stomach, and I could tell I probably had about three minutes left before he kicked me out.

"Ryan buys me chocolates. Last week, when it was my time of the month-"

I held my hand up. "Yeah, I think that's a bit too much information, Em." I said, grimacing.

"What? It was sweet. I was in pain and he did something thoughtful. He's always thoughtful." She peered up at him, and from the heated stare he gave her, I knew the minutes counting down my departure were now seconds.

"Chocolate. Great. I'll do that," I said, standing up to leave. Neither one of them made any effort to get up or see me to the door, and when Ryan threaded his hand into the back of her hair and pulled her to him for a kiss, I knew my time was up. "I'll see myself out," I shouted as I banged the door closed. But once I was stood outside, I smiled.

I wanted that.

To be so consumed by another person and for them to be totally and utterly lost in me, that the rest of the world just falls away.

I wanted that with her.

So maybe I needed to start taking other people's advice. I needed to tell her about Pat, and I had to make the effort to be what she needed me to be. I had to try harder.

CHAPTER
Twenty Eight

HARPER

I was trying to keep myself busy and steer my mind away from a certain bad boy who was dominating my thoughts recently, so I decided to bake some cookies. Who I was baking them for, I had no idea. Mum and Dad had gone away for the night to some spa retreat. Dad thought a facial and massage would help bring Mum back from the zombie state she was living in. I suppose I shouldn't have mocked him for making the effort. It was a nice gesture. But it left me alone with nothing but my thoughts and a mountain of chocolate chip cookies that would probably go to waste. I'd even decided to wear one of my summer dresses too. I was channelling the fifties housewife vibes pretty damn well.

I was just contemplating boxing some cookies up to take to the neighbours when I heard a knock at the front door. I wiped my hands clean on my apron, took it off, and wandered down the corridor to find out who it was. When I opened the door, I was surprised to find Brandon standing in front of me with a confused look on his face, holding up a carrier bag.

"I bought you these," he said, shoving the bag forward for me to take and walking past me into the house. "It smells fucking awesome in here. What are you cooking?"

I frowned and shut the door. I couldn't remember inviting him in, but then, I guessed Brandon never waited for an invite. If he wanted something, he went for it.

"I was baking cookies. Not sure why though. My Mum and Dad are away."

Brandon's eyes lit up like I'd told him they were liquid gold and he grabbed one off the cooling rack and ate it, even though it was probably still hot and would scald his mouth.

"I always knew you were my ideal woman. Baking cookies and waiting for me to show up." He winked like it was some inside joke and I stared back at him blankly.

He grabbed another one, as the first obviously didn't touch the sides, and I placed the carrier bag on the kitchen work surface and opened it up to see what he'd bought for me. I frowned even harder when I saw a pile of chocolate bars. There must've been every Cadbury bar ever made in there. Why was he bringing me a mountain of chocolate?

"I don't get it?" I asked, feeling confused. "Is this a joke I don't know about? Or are you trying to give me diabetes?" I was surely missing something here.

"I wanted to do something nice for you," he said, like it was the simplest thing in the world. "I didn't know what to get you though, and Emily told me Ryan buys her chocolate when it's her... you know... time of the month and all that. She said it's romantic." He shrugged, taking another bite of his cookie. "I figured flowers were a no-go, so I went with the chocolate."

I couldn't stop myself from laughing. Not in an unkind way. It really was sweet, but he was totally clueless. So clueless it was actually endearing.

"What's so funny?" he asked, laughing along with me through his mouthful of cookie.

"You. I don't think this is what Emily meant when she said to buy chocolate. It's really sweet that you wanted to do that though," I added after seeing the way his face dropped.

"I'm trying to be different. I wanted to do something that wasn't the usual crappy Brandon effort." It made my heart hurt to hear him talk like that about himself.

"Nothing you do is crappy, Brandon. Please don't say that. And don't think you have to do anything special for me either. I'm the least high maintenance girl you'll ever meet."

"That's probably a good thing then."

I knew what he meant. He thought if my standards were low then he'd have more chance of living up to them. I was starting to be able to read him a little more clearly and it surprised me how low his self-esteem was.

"I like you, Brandon, just the way you are. I don't need you to change or try to be something you're not around me. I've had a lifetime of fake people and lies. One of the things I love about you is your honesty. There's no bullshit where you're concerned." I took a breath and watched as his eyes widened. Had I said too much? "Please don't change. I know exactly what I'm getting into here, with you. I know who you are."

He nodded and a small grin appeared on his ruggedly handsome face. I liked his cheeky grins.

"I'm a fighter. I always will be." He lifted his chin, trying to look tough, but after wolfing down half a batch of cookies and standing in my kitchen with twenty or more chocolate bars in his bag, I knew he was anything but.

"Yep. Yes, you are," I said. He liked that, I could tell, because his grin grew wider.

"And I'll fight for you too." He took a step closer to me and I stood my ground. I could feel the atmosphere in the room becoming heated... electric.

"I know you will."

"So, no more chocolate?" He nodded down to the bag and I gave a low, throaty chuckle.

"I love chocolate. But you don't have to buy up the whole shop. And I'm not on my period, so-" I raised my eyebrows at him, and he took another step towards me.

"That's good to know." I watched as his gaze travelled over my face, lingering on my lips, and then he looked me in the eyes. "No parents today?" He cocked his head to the side and bit his lip.

"No. They're away for the night. They-" I didn't get chance to finish my sentence because he crashed his lips to mine and kissed me hard and forcefully. His hands cupped my face and held me in place as he took what he wanted. What we both wanted.

I groaned into the kiss and he pushed his hips forward, trapping me against the kitchen counter. I put my arms around his neck and pulled him into me further, not that that was possible. We were already plastered together. I scraped my nails across the back of his head through his hair and he moaned, moving his hands down to wrap around my waist and then grab my ass.

I loved the way he kissed me, like he'd die if he didn't get close enough. Like I was the air he needed to breathe. He tasted sweet, like cookies and forbidden promises that we'd whispered to each other in the darkness of our bedrooms once upon a time. I'd never felt so lost in another person as I did in him. The way his lips moved against mine made me ache with want. The way our tongues tangled made the nerves spark to life inside me. I was so ridiculously turned on, so needy and horny, and I needed to move this upstairs, because my kitchen was the last place I wanted to do all the things I had planned with Brandon.

I pulled away and my heart fluttered when I saw how cute he looked with his eyes closed. His breath shallow and his mouth ready for more.

"We need to take this upstairs," I whispered into his ear.

"I don't need a bed. A wall or a table will do." He opened his eyes and grinned that wicked grin at me again.

"I'm sure it will, but we're doing things different,

remember." I slid out of his grasp and sauntered over to the door. "Are you coming? Or are you gonna stay down here and eat the rest of the cookies?"

He gave a low, raspy chuckle.

"I think you'll taste even sweeter than those cookies."

The stare he gave me made me clench my thighs together. I remembered what we'd said in our sex chat online that night. I knew what he'd promised to do. Question was, could he live up to his promises?

I walked up the stairs and couldn't keep the smile off my face as I heard him bounding up behind me, taking the steps two at a time.

"Someone's eager." I laughed.

"You have no fucking idea," he growled.

He spun me round just as I opened the door to my bedroom, smashing his lips back onto mine and walking us backward into the room.

He kicked the door closed, and as the backs of my knees connected with my bed, I stumbled and dropped my ass onto the mattress.

"Do you remember what you said to me? What you typed, telling me all the things you'd do if you were ever in my room?" I asked, looking up at him through my lashes as he stood towering over me.

"Sweetheart, I've replayed that fantasy over and over in my head at least a hundred times since then. And every time, it just gets better and better."

He brushed his knuckles lightly against my jaw and then tucked the stray hairs behind my ear. I tried to keep my breathing steady, but my heart was racing and all I could focus on was how he was making me feel, standing there looking at me that way. Touching me like I was made of glass, but he was so ready to shatter me. He was going to enjoy it. Brandon wasn't here to play gentle; he was here to claim what was his.

He turned around and clicked the lock on my door shut.

"I told you I always take precautions," he said, turning slowly back around to face me, and letting his eyes wander over my body, so seductively that I could almost feel his stare caressing my skin. Dancing over me and making me pant a little harder.

"I should hope so," I replied, not knowing how else to answer. My brain had checked out and my hormones were in the driving seat. "Come on then. Show me what you've got."

Fuck, where did this Harper come from? I don't think I'd ever been so sexually confident with a man before.

Brandon stood still, watching me as I lay there. He wasn't charging forward like I thought he would. No. He was studying me. He obviously had a lot more self-control than I did.

"What are you waiting for?" I asked, leaning back onto the bed and scooching a little further up so I was lying ready for him.

"I'm watching you. I said I would."

He took a few steps forward until he was standing over me again, and then he ran his fingers lightly up my calf and further up to brush my thighs. "Your skin's so soft, so flawless. I like the way you shiver when I touch you like this."

I liked it too.

I wanted to hold my breath just so I could concentrate on that one sensation he was creating without anything else interrupting how awesome it felt to be touched by him. How amazing it was to be warmed by his delicate, feathered touches, as soft as a butterfly's wings. I closed my eyes so every single focus, every sense was his to own. Nothing else mattered but what he was doing.

"You look so pretty like this, lying here with your eyes closed. Waiting for me. So fucking beautiful."

I gasped, but I kept my eyes closed. I liked letting go like this. I wanted to give up control. After being guarded for so long, I wanted to feel free.

The mattress dipped as he climbed on, and I felt the scratch of the coarse material of his jeans against my legs as he crawled over me. He held himself up with his strong arms, and I kept my eyes closed as his breath fanned across my face.

"Look at me, Harper. Let me see what you're thinking," he whispered, warm and low.

I slowly opened my eyes and looked up at him. The depth of feeling I saw in him in that moment made me sigh and reach up to caress his face. He was so beautiful. So complex and complicated, but I wanted to work him out. I wanted to know what made him tick. I wanted to know everything.

"Are you sure about this?" he asked, begging me with the fire in his eyes to say yes.

How could I ever say no to him?

This broken man was mine.

I was his.

We weren't perfect, but together we made perfect sense. To me, anyway.

"You are the one thing I am sure about." His eyes softened as I spoke. "I have absolutely no clue what's going on with my life. Most days I wake up not knowing how I'll cope throughout the day. But you... You I get. I want you, Brandon. I want this."

He leant down to nuzzle into my neck, and I tilted my head for him.

"You never have to feel alone, Harper. You've always got me. I'll always be here. I'm here for you."

He kissed me gently on my neck, nibbling around my ear and I closed my eyes again. I didn't realise I was gasping and moaning until I felt him lift his head.

"Those noises you make, they're such a fucking turn-on," he said, and then he covered my body with his and his hand grabbed the back of my head, pulling me into a fierce and brutal kiss.

He moaned loudly as he slipped his tongue over mine, his hips grinding into me, showing me exactly how hard he was and how much he wanted this too. Desperate, I clung to him with my hands around his shoulders like he was my lifeline.

I opened my legs and started to wrap them around his waist, but he chuckled and pulled away from our kiss. "Remember what I said about me knowing what you need?"

I nodded.

"Trust me, little warrior. I've got you." He brushed the back of his hand over my cheek and then he smiled. "I've always got you."

He grabbed my leg from around his waist and pulled it off, then sat up. He gave me a brief glance, just to make sure I was okay with everything he was doing, then he lifted the skirt of my dress slowly like he was unwrapping a present. Once my dress was up around my waist, he took a deep breath and hooked his fingers into the sides of my knickers and gently pulled them down my legs. My breathing hitched as I felt how wet I was for him, and how the simple act of him doing this was making me tingle and pant in need.

He dropped my knickers to the floor, never taking his eyes off me, then he pushed my legs open. When he saw me, really saw me for the first time, I swear I heard a growl at the back of his throat.

I reached down to touch myself and he licked his lips and moaned.

"Fuck. You are stunning. I could come just from watching you do that. You don't get to have all the fun though." He winked and lowered himself until he was settled with his head between my thighs.

He planted delicate kisses on the inside of each thigh as I used my fingers to circle and stroke myself. Then he lifted my hand out of the way. "I'm guessing that after today there won't be a single thing in this world that'll taste as sweet as you do." Then he pressed his tongue against my clit and he licked me, making my back arch and my head whip back with how amazing it felt.

"Stay still, little warrior," he commanded, putting a hand on my stomach to keep me in place. Then he pushed my leg up further and licked over and around my clit, sucking it into his mouth and then rubbing his tongue in the most delicious way.

I rocked my hips in time with the pace he had set, my hands fisting the bed clothes beside me. I couldn't stop myself from crying out as he drove me closer and closer to the edge with every swirl of his tongue. He was bloody good at this, and I begged him not to stop.

He moved further down, piercing me with his tongue and tasting me like I was his last meal and he was a starving man. I grabbed his hair and pulled it hard, needing more but not entirely sure what to do about it. Speech was pointless; all I could do was cry and moan.

He licked back up to my clit and went to work teasing me with his little nibbles and sucks, then I felt his fingers stroking, playing, pushing inside of me and making my moans grow louder, more feral. I was so close I couldn't cope with the intensity of the build-up. I felt like I wanted to ride his face, but I also wanted to feel him inside me. I needed that connection too.

I was just about to beg for him to fuck me when I suddenly cried out, falling over the edge and exploding with the most powerful orgasm I'd ever had. My legs shook and my body jerked as the spasms went on and on, the ripple effect of the orgasm sending the most exquisite feeling to every inch of my body. Brandon kept suckling, bringing me down from my high and giving a low moan as I whimpered beneath him, panting and dazed, like I'd just drifted down from the clouds. Who knew that my devil, the self-professed demon, could take me to heaven like he just had? If that was what he could do with his tongue then I wasn't letting him leave this room until I'd enjoyed the full Brandon Mathers experience.

He smiled up at me as I glanced down at him and tried to get my breathing under control. Then he placed a gentle kiss between my legs and said, "Definitely sweeter than the cookies. Maybe next time, we can bring the cookies upstairs and I can eat them out of you."

He really, truly meant that.

"Oh my God." I laughed, covering my face with my hand.

"I'm not a messy eater." He shrugged. "I won't let any go to waste."

I just gave him my own cheeky smirk and sat up, pushing my hand against his chest and forcing him to the edge of the bed.

"I think it's my turn to get a taste." I winked.

He ran his hand over my hair and said, "You don't have to."

"I want to." My eyes widened. I never thought I'd hear a guy turn down a blow job. Especially Brandon. But when he whipped off his t-shirt and quirked his mouth in that signature grin of his, I knew he was more than ready.

He slid off the bed and stood at the foot of it, his eyes never leaving mine as I crawled down to where he was. I sat on the edge of the mattress and he lifted my chin to face him.

"I hope you know how special you are to me, Harper. You're not like any girl I've ever met before. I really want to be with you all the time, and I think about you all day, and-" He started stumbling over his words, and I knew he was trying to share his feelings with me, make me see that this wasn't a one-time thing. I already knew that. As if I'd let him walk away from me now.

I let my gaze wonder from his eyes to his perfectly sculpted tattoo-covered chest, and that was when I saw it. The lion tattoo on his stomach. I ran my hand over the skin there and felt the bumps of the scar. His reminder of the evil shit that had been done to him all those years ago. I swallowed hard, feeling like I might burst into tears at any moment. I went to speak, but I didn't have the words to convey how I felt. Sorry wasn't ever going to be enough. So instead, I leant forward and kissed it and tried really hard not to let the tears fall and spoil this moment we'd built together.

"It's in the past, Harper. It's done," he said, stroking the back of my hair as I ran my arms around his middle to hold him close. "I'm not a victim. Neither of us are. We're the warriors, remember?"

I took a deep breath and looked up at him. The apology in my eyes must've been enough because he just nodded and said, "I know." And brushed his hand over the side of my face and cupped my cheek.

A wash of emotions flooded me, making it hard to catch my breath, and I felt so much in that moment that I'd have done anything for him. I wanted to be everything to him. I needed to make him feel as fucking amazing as he'd made me feel only minutes before. This wasn't the time to dwell on past mistakes. This was our future.

"Okay, big man. That's enough soppy shit. Let me have my fun now," I said, covering the hand he had on my cheek and turning to kiss the palm. "Do you remember what I said I'd do to you?"

His eyes sparkled and I knew exactly what he was waiting for.

I grinned and yanked the buttons on his jeans open and then I slid his jeans and boxers down over his ass and thighs. He reached down to pull his dick out as I did, and when I saw him for the first time, I smiled.

He was perfect.

I wrapped my hand around him. He was thick and long,

and I couldn't wait to play with him. Have him in my mouth, have him every way I could. I pumped my hand up and down a few times, slowly but firmly, loving how silky he felt, imagining how amazing he'd feel inside me. He threw his head back and gave a long, low sigh and then dropped his head forward to watch me; his eyes glazed over with lust. I saw a little bead of moisture at the tip and I licked it, moaning as I did so he'd know I loved it.

"Suck me," he begged, running his thumb across my lower lip.

I ran my tongue slowly around the head, keeping my eyes locked with his as I did, then I licked underneath, and he closed his eyes and let out a groan. Hearing a man moan for me like that was the single biggest turn-on, and I squeezed my thighs together, the familiar tingles sparking to life again.

I sucked the head into my mouth first, swirling my tongue over the sensitive underside, but it didn't take long for Brandon to grab my hair and push me further. So, I swallowed and took him deep into my throat. The guttural moan he let out was all the encouragement I needed, and I sucked him as he fisted my hair and rocked his hips forward.

I grabbed his ass as he pumped into me, then I used my hand to cup his balls and pulled back, letting his dick pop out of my mouth. He groaned in protest, but when he guessed my intentions, he didn't complain. I grinned up at him as I licked down his length towards his balls and then I went further, taking one of his balls into my mouth and letting it roll around my tongue. I sucked gently and got lost in the sounds of him sighing and moaning as I pleasured him. Then I moved to the other side and he widened his legs as he let me taste the most sensitive part of him. I'd never done this before, but judging from his reaction, I wasn't doing too badly.

His dick was throbbing, and I could tell he was close. I wanted to taste him and experience everything. So I licked back up to the head and took him deep again, and this time he went hard, fucking my face and making me pant as I breathed through my nose and sucked him.

He barely managed to say the words, "I'm coming," before thick hot spurts of cum spurted at the back of my throat, and I swallowed, keeping my pace but sucking gentler because I knew he'd be sensitive. I licked gently until his moans became sighs and his thrusts slowed down.

Eventually, he pulled himself out of my mouth and then stroked my face with so much love that I almost blurted out my feelings right then and there.

We both stared at each other, caught up in the moment, and panting to catch our breath.

"Is this the part where you flip me over and take me from behind like you promised," I asked, breaking the tense, emotionally charged atmosphere.

His gravelly chuckle made my skin prickle.

"No, sweetheart. This is where I hold you really close and thank my lucky stars that I ever found you."

"No doggy style?" I tried to hold a laugh in, but I ended

up snorting through my nose.

"That comes after the cuddling."

"Never took you for a cuddler, big man."

He quirked his brow at me as he climbed onto the bed and pulled me up with him. The fact he was naked and I still had my dress on made him frown harder, and he pulled it up and over my head, then made quick work of getting rid of my bra too.

"Are you kidding? Naked cuddles with you? That's better than sex." He chuckled to himself as he pulled me closer, but I placed my hand on his chest and looked at him.

"You are joking, right?"

"Of course I'm joking. You don't think I'm going insane over here? I'm desperate to sink my cock into your tight little pussy."

Usually, words like that would have made me cringe, but not when he said them. The way he spoke without giving a fuck was a real turn-on.

"I want that too," I said in a breathy whisper into his ear, and he growled and rolled me onto my back, sliding his body over mine. "Are you hard again?" I asked as I felt his dick pushing into my thigh.

"It would appear so," he replied, lifting his upper body away from me and looking down into my eyes. "It's what you do to me."

I opened my legs wide and he settled his hips where he needed to be. I lifted my knees and wrapped my legs around him, digging my heels into his ass and willing him to take this further.

He leant over to grab his jeans from the side of the bed and pulled a condom out of his pocket then ripped the foil. He reached down to roll it on and positioned himself ready.

As he pushed inside of me, we both cried out at how it felt. The way he stretched me was amazing. And when he said, "Fuck, you feel good." I knew he was experiencing the same level of euphoria I was.

He went slow at first; long, deep strokes that made me moan and arch my back. I moved my hips and then grabbed his ass to push him deeper into me. Feeling his ass clench as he pumped in and out was sexy as hell. He had a fucking awesome ass.

I groaned into his ear and then nibbled, kissing along his jaw and neck, moving my hands from his ass, up along his spine, and then I clung onto his shoulders, holding on tight. I was glad I did, because he started to speed up and his thrusts became harder, driving into me at an unforgiving pace.

He grunted as he fucked me into the mattress, pounding with every thrust. I reached up and held the bars of my headboard and he wrapped his arms around my shoulders. I always knew sex with Brandon would feel like this; raw, feral fucking. It was animalistic and I loved it. I loved letting go and feeling wild.

He swivelled his hips, hitting the spot every damn time, and it wasn't long before my eyes were rolling into the back of my head and I was crying out.

"I'm gonna come, Brandon. Please don't stop," I begged. But he'd never stop or pull away; he was as far gone as I was.

"I won't."

He managed to grunt into my neck, and then I felt it. The explosion inside of me.

I let go of the bed frame and clung to him, shaking and convulsing as my whole body became engulfed in waves of pleasure. My walls clamped down hard around him and I contracted over and over again.

"Oh, baby. That's so good," he moaned, and then I felt him thicken and find his own release, groaning low and feral as he rode out his orgasm.

He slowed down and eventually he stopped and lay with his body over mine, both of us not sure which planet we'd just been on or whether we were truly back on Earth.

"I think I love you, Harper Yates," he whispered into the pillow next to my head.

"I think I love you too, Brandon Mathers," I replied, snuggling into him and breathing him in.

He seemed to tense slightly, and I worried that I'd said the wrong thing. Had I heard him right?

I groaned as he pulled out of me slowly and then rolled onto his side. Gently, he edged forward and put his nose right next to mine.

"I said it wrong. I don't think I love you..." My heart fell into the pit of my stomach. "I know I love you."

And the tears I'd fought back earlier fell out of my traitorous eyes.

"I love you too, Brandon."

"You don't have to say it just 'cos I did. I know I'm not the best guy for you and I'm not easy to love, but.-"

I put my finger over his lips to stop him spouting more bullshit.

"Will you shut up? I love you, okay? And for me, it's easy to love you. You think you're not the best guy for me, but you are. You don't see what I see."

"What do you see?" he asked, pulling my finger off his lips and kissing it.

"I see a guy who has his faults. He's done some really shitty things and he's learning to live with that. But I also see a man who's honest, genuine, someone who'd go above and beyond for his friends. I see the things you do for other people, the way you put them before yourself. The way you dealt with your mother with such compassion when the rest of us wanted to slap the stupid out of her.

"You do sweet things for me, and you don't always get it right, but that doesn't matter. You try, and that's what counts. You also make me laugh, and every time I look at you, I get this warm feeling. I haven't felt anything other than lost, alone, or sad for a long time. But I don't feel that with you. You make me want to live to see another day. You make me excited for the future. To everyone else you might be the tough guy, the fighter, but not with me. I see what lies behind all of that. The vulnerability, the need for acceptance. You don't ever have to pretend with me, Brandon. I love you for you. I always will."

From the shine in his eyes I thought he might be close to tears himself, and when he spoke, I could hear a croak in his voice that he was trying to hide.

"You're the first person to ever love me and not expect anything from me. I think you're probably the only person who loves me out of choice. I'm pretty sure everyone else in my life just tolerates me."

"Well, they don't know you like I do. Like I'm getting to know you." I sighed, feeling a veil of sadness fall over us. "Brandon, you work so hard on your physical strength, training for your fights, but you need to work on your self-esteem too. You are worthy of being loved you know."

He nodded, but I knew it would take more than my words to convince him. Luckily, I had all the time in the world to show him with my actions.

"We've both been hurt, in here..." I pressed my hand over his heart. "But together, we can find the happiness we deserve."

"I hope you're right, little warrior."

"I am. I know I am," I said and gave him a soft, gentle kiss.

We'd taken another little step towards healing. Okay, I tell a lie; it was a big fucking step. Huge. But lying in his arms, I knew we'd be okay. We hadn't had the most conventional start to our relationship, but it was ours. It was us. And I wouldn't have it any other way. Who cares about the start anyway? It's the ending that everyone wants, and Brandon Mathers was my happy ending.

CHAPTER
Twenty Nine

HARPER

I woke up with a start when I heard the noises downstairs indicating that my parents were home. My heart and brain went into overdrive and I rolled over to wake up Brandon, but when I turned, I saw he'd already left. My open window gave away his preferred method of escape.

It made my heart sink seeing where he'd lay, and when I reached out to touch his side, I could still feel his warmth. He hadn't been gone long. In fact, I bet he'd heard my parents coming home and decided to do his Spiderman disappearing act. I couldn't blame him. It wasn't going to be the easiest thing to convince my parents that I hadn't gone totally bananas in my decision to be with Brandon. They were already questioning my sanity, so this wasn't going to help my case.

Still, I didn't want to hide away. I'd done enough of that for the past few months to last me a lifetime. I wanted this to be a new beginning. Lord knows we deserved it. I was fully prepared for people to say it was too soon, or that I was with him because he reminded me of Brodie. But I didn't care for gossip. Never had. At the end of the day, people would say whatever they wanted. I couldn't control that. All I could control was my happiness, and at that very moment, I was the happiest I'd been in a long time.

I heard a soft knock on my bedroom door and I sprang out of the bed and grabbed my dressing gown to cover myself. When I opened the door, I saw both Mum and Dad on the other side staring hesitantly at me as if they were trying to gauge what mood I was in.

"Hey. Did you have a good spa break?" I pulled my robe tighter around myself and prayed there was nothing behind me that'd give away what I'd been doing while they were away.

"It was nice." Mum snaked her arm through Dad's as she spoke, and for the first time in months, I took a really good look at them both and noticed how tired they were. There were wrinkles around their eyes that I hadn't noticed before and a darkness deep within that made me feel guilty. Guilty for the stress and worry I'd given them on top of everything else they were coming to terms with. Life for them was bad enough. They didn't need any extra worry.

"We're going to see Brodie in about an hour. We know you don't like going back there, but we thought we'd ask if you wanted to tag along. No pressure. Just don't want to keep anything from you, Harper." Dad took a deep breath after his little speech and peered nervously down at the floor.

He was right, I didn't like going there. But today, I felt I had to make the effort. There were things I needed to say to Brodie; secrets I needed to get off my chest. I also wanted to show my parents that I could be there for them too. It must have been hard for them to go there as often as they did. It was a constant reminder that they'd lost such a precious part of their lives.

"No, I'll go with you." Mum's eyes went wide as I spoke and Dad's face shot up in surprise.

"Are you sure?" he asked.

"Yeah, I'm sure. We're a family. You shouldn't have to do it alone."

"We're never alone." Mum gave Dad a look that radiated love and made me feel warm and hopeful. "We always have each other." Then she turned to me and reached out to squeeze my arm. "Always."

–

When we got to the churchyard, Mum got busy cleaning the leaves away and brushed over Brodie's headstone to make sure everything was up to her standards. Dad took the old flowers out and went off to collect water, striding towards the communal tap with purpose. And I stood there in a daze, watching this strange ritual they had that I knew nothing about.

"Did you want to start cutting the flowers down? I've got scissors in my bag." Mum pointed to the rucksack on the floor that she kept in the boot of the car for their visits.

When I knelt down to look inside, there were shears, a scrubbing brush, cleaning products, and everything else she'd need to keep Brodie's graveside looking immaculate.

"I did buy some fake flowers in the week. I thought I'd save those for winter though, just in case we ever get snowed in and can't make it up here." She ran her hand over the marble headstone and touched the lettering that spelt out his name. "I like to keep you looking good, don't I, Brodie?" She sighed.

I opened the bunch of brightly coloured flowers and started to trim the stems.

"Zinnias," she said, like I knew what she was on about.

"What?"

"They're zinnias." She nodded at the lively explosion of colour nestled inside the bouquet. "They last the longest. Or at least, that's what google told me. I know it's silly and he's not really here. But this is all we have now. Doctor Meredith said it helps to be able to talk to him. I like to talk to him here."

Dad came up behind Mum and bent down to kiss the top of her head. "Whatever helps to get us through the day, hey?"

We worked together in silence for a few minutes, cleaning, trimming, and arranging everything. When the last flower was set in place, Dad gathered up the discarded cuttings and rubbish and stood up.

"Shall we take these to the bin and then have a little walk around? Give Harper and Brodie a few minutes alone?" he asked Mum.

"I think that's a good idea," she replied, although she looked torn between wanting to stay and leaving us behind.

"Thanks." I stayed sitting on the ground next to Brodie's grave. I was grateful that they were giving me some time alone. The things I wanted to say I didn't feel I could say in front of them.

"We'll be over there when you need us." Dad pointed to a gazebo in the middle of the graveyard, with benches evenly placed around the edge. "No rush, love."

I watched them walk off and when I felt satisfied they were far enough away not to hear me I turned to look at the cold marble.

"I never thought I'd be talking to you like this, but then I didn't expect a lot of things to happen recently. I think I've gone through every emotion there is since you left us.

"I hated you for leaving. I was angry that you did this to us and to yourself. Why didn't you ever listen to me? I had a bad feeling that night, but you wouldn't stop and..." I took a breath. I needed to slow my racing thoughts and jumbled words.

"What's the point in hashing it all out again? One of the main things I've come to learn through the heartache, anger, loss, and guilt is acceptance. Acceptance for the things I can't change. For the life I have to live now. You were always going to do what you wanted to do and that's okay. It was your life to lead. But now, I have to lead mine."

I stroked my fingers through the soft grass and felt a calmness settle over me.

"I know you're probably looking down on me and thinking I'm making a right royal balls-up of it all. Maybe I am, but I can only go on what I feel, and after doing the right thing for so long, I want to do what *I* want for a change. What feels right for me. Choose a path that hasn't been dictated by anyone else. Damn it, Brodie, even my school years were controlled by you. You wouldn't let me be in your class. You shut me out for the most part, and now I know why."

This was the part I was dreading. Telling him that I knew what he had done and trying to come to terms with it.

"Why did you do it? Why would you want to make another person feel so shitty just to make yourself look big in front of your friends? Friends who were really crap at having your back, by the way. Do you know what Jensen did? Did you watch him hit me? Brandon did. He's also been the only person, apart from Emily and Ryan, that've stood by me through this. You have really shitty taste in friends. I sometimes find myself wondering what it'd be like if you'd been on their side, the Renaissance men, I mean. How different would our lives be now? You'd probably still be here for one. But I can't change anything and daydreaming about what ifs isn't ever going to bring you back or make anything about this feel right.

"I guess what I'm trying to say, in my rambling, bumbling way, is that I forgive you. I forgive you for the God-awful mistakes you made back in school. I know that deep down you were a good person. You did something wicked. So, so wrong. But that's your cross to bear, and if there is a heaven, I'm pretty certain you'll be doing everything you can up there to make amends."

I glanced up at the sky, the weight of guilt already drifting slowly away.

"He made mistakes too, but he's a good man, Brodie. I know you and he would've never seen eye-to-eye. You're probably pulling your hair out right now and telling me it's too soon, I don't know him, he's using me. But I don't feel that."

I took another deep breath and tried to make sense of my puzzled mind.

"I'm not here looking for your approval. I know you well enough to know you'd never give it. I'm here to tell you that he makes me happy. If he ever stops making me happy, I'll walk away. After everything I've been through, I'm finally beginning to accept my own self-worth. I deserve more. I lived in your shadow for long enough and I like having the sun on my face for a change. I'm not saying I don't miss you every hour of every day, because I do. There'll always be a part of me that feels empty and lost without you. But he makes those dark days more bearable.

"He never meant for any of this to happen. I know there was no love lost between the two of you, but he isn't a killer. If he could go back and change it, he would.

"Anyway, what I'm trying to say is I'm with Brandon now. But I don't want you to think this means I've forgotten about you, or I condone anything about that night. Life is shit sometimes, but we have to make the best of what we have. This is me making the best of it."

I couldn't stop myself from smiling, thinking about the chocolate bars, and then all the online messages, and the way he'd treated me since he'd stepped out of the shadows to face the music.

"He reminds me of you. He's a little off-the-wall sometimes, and he hasn't got the first clue about dating. He says stupid shit because he doesn't think, but it isn't because he's thoughtless. He acts before he engages his brain, just like you. He puts everyone else before himself, and he gets it wrong probably more times than he gets it right, but that's what I love about him. He's real, Brodie. What you see is what you get. He might be a little rough around the edges, a little coarse for some people, but not me. I like him. A lot. Hell, what am I saying? I love him. And I am one hundred percent dreading telling Mum and Dad about this."

I peered over my shoulder to see Mum and Dad sat huddled together on a bench in the gazebo, both of them staring right at me.

"I think I'll need to work up to that one, but coming here today and telling you is a start. Another step forward."

I pushed myself up off the floor and ran my hand over the top of his gravestone.

"I'll see you soon, Brodie. I love you, bro."

I made my way over to my parents, and Dad stood up and held his arms open, ready to hug me. I buried my face in his chest and breathed him in. There was a serenity inside of me that I hadn't felt for a long time. Whether that was because I'd lifted some of the burden from my shoulders after talking to Brodie, or because being held by my dad always made things feel less hopeless, I didn't know. To be honest, it was probably a mixture of both of those things. I was lucky I had such supportive, loving parents. Brandon didn't have that, and the thought made me ache for him. It made me want to hold him in my arms and give him that feeling that he'd missed out on all his life.

I pulled away, but my dad kept his arm around my shoulder.

"We're doing okay, you know," he said. "Our little family is doing okay."

Mum sniffed back a tear, and I smiled.

"I think I might join you the next time you visit Doctor Meredith."

Mum's face lit up.

"Are you sure, Harper? I mean, I would love that, and Meredith had reserved a space for you, in case you ever changed your mind. She's ready whenever you are."

"I wasn't ready before, but I am now. I think counselling will help me to come to terms with things and remember Brodie the way I want to."

Dad squeezed my shoulder in support and Mum stood up to give me a hug.

"This is the best news I've had in a long time," she said. "I love our little family. I love you both so much. Brodie too."

She started to cry, and we held each other. Just like we had done on the day Brodie died, and at his funeral after that. We'd hold each other up for as long as we needed to until we could each stand tall again in our own right. Because that's what a family does.

It works together.

It builds you up.

It gives you strength when you don't have any of your own. I wanted that for Brandon too. And maybe, in time, we could build that together.

CHAPTER
Thirty

BRANDON

I didn't want to leave her like I did. I stayed awake half the night, watching her sleep and stroking her hair because she just looked so damn beautiful. But in the morning, I heard the front door close, and I knew I had to get out of there. I didn't want to put her in a position where she had to smuggle me out or lie to her parents. So, I did the decent thing, and I climbed out the window. It wasn't like I was going into her garden blind; I knew it like the back of my hand.

It hurt like hell to go without saying goodbye though. I wondered if we'd ever get to a point where I could walk in through her front door, say hello to her mum and dad without them wanting to gouge my eyes out, and just be what I wanted to be to her.

Her boyfriend.

Someone she leaned on.

Her everything.

I dropped by my nan's for a quick shower, threw on a clean t-shirt and some sweats, and then headed over to Zak's place. The lads had been blowing up my phone since I'd switched it off yesterday, and they were having a meeting this morning to discuss some bullshit I couldn't even focus on. All I could think about was what her face would've looked like when she woke up and saw that I'd gone.

Would she think I'd regretted it?

That I couldn't face the morning after the night before?

I fired off a quick text to the lads to let them know I was on my way, then I sent one to Harper, hoping I'd say the right thing.

> **Brandon: I didn't want to leave you this morning. I'm sorry that I did. Thought it best to avoid your parents. I'm sorry.**

She didn't reply for a while, and I've got to admit, it messed with my head. But when my phone eventually lit up with an incoming message, every muscle in my body tensed in anticipation.

> **Harper: I get it. I understand. You've got nothing to apologise for. I know you prefer using the garden fence instead of the front door anyway.**

She added a cheeky winking emoji to let me know there were no hard feelings and it helped me to relax somewhat.

Brandon: What can I say? I'm very flexible.

I sent my response then slapped my own face at how lame I sounded. I needed better banter.

Harper: I know exactly how flexible you are. I like it too.

I chuckled. She'd added another winking emoji and I knew that would keep me going through the day. My banter I could work on. At least she didn't hate me.

She liked me.

She said she loved me, but I knew not to get my hopes up on that front. People said things in the heat of the moment. I wanted to believe that a girl like her could love a guy like me, but judging from my past history, I knew I needed to prepare myself for a fall.

When I knocked on Zak's door a little while later, Ryan answered and walked away without uttering a word when he saw it was me, leaving me to close the door myself.

"Nice to see you too, fucker." I slammed it shut and Finn jumped out of his skin.

What was his deal?

"Thought you'd gone AWOL again, mate." Ryan smirked as he sat his ass down in the seat I always claimed as mine whenever I was here. Fucker knew it'd piss me off, but he didn't care.

I sauntered across the room to stand over him. "I think you're in my chair." He just folded his arms and stared back up at me, grinning like a motherfucker.

"You can have it back when I leave. I can't stay long, anyway. Em is in court today. She's got to give evidence at her dad's trial."

I would've argued my case, but I figured he'd probably have enough stress without me adding to it. Sitting in a courtroom watching Emily's dad worm his way out of a long stretch in prison for fraud and manslaughter was enough to push anyone over the edge.

"How's that all going?" Zak asked as he tapped away in the corner on his laptop and kept his eyes glued to the screen. Ignorant fucker. I sat down next to Finn and took the can of Coke out of his hands to take a swig. He didn't complain. He never did.

"It's not going great for him, I'm not gonna lie. Her mum's due a wake-up call too when he eventually goes down for it. She's convinced he'll get off. Doesn't matter what we tell her. The woman is a nutcase."

Ryan knew as well as the rest of us that this trial was a fucking joke, a circus for the media. The odds were stacked against Emily's dad. We'd made sure of that. The sooner they locked him up, the better.

"Couldn't have happened to a nicer guy." I laughed,

handing Finn back his empty can of Coke. "So, why are we here? Did you miss my handsome mug? Is that it?"

"Make the most of it, mate. Once Murphy has you fighting for him, you'll look more like Gollum than ever before." Ryan thought he was fucking funny, but he needed to leave the comedy to the experts. I was about to tell him as much when Finn cut me off.

"You're fighting for Pat Murphy? I thought you said you wouldn't do that?"

Why did the disappointment on Finn's face hurt more than anything else? You'd think I'd kicked his puppy by the way he was eyeballing me.

"I didn't tell him," Ryan added, looking anywhere but where I was sitting. "Figured it was your news to tell. Sorry."

I rubbed my hands over my face. I knew Finn was a sensitive little fucker, but I didn't think he'd be bothered about something like this.

"It won't affect anything with us," I said, turning to face him on the sofa. "Pat's gonna schedule fights around our business. Don't worry, mate. You're still my number one." I grabbed his knee and gave it a shake like he was a kid, and I was putting his mind at rest.

"And if you believe that, you'll believe anything," Zak piped up, and I threw him a filthy look. "Pat will do what Pat wants to do. Good luck to you, though. You're gonna need it."

I huffed out on a grin and shook my head. Was he for fucking real?

"Thanks for the vote of confidence. I won't need luck, though. I have skill."

"I don't mean luck with the fight. I'm talking about the business side of it."

I could see Ryan out of the corner of my eye watching Zak and probably second guessing that I was moments away from calling him out on his bullshit advice. So he cut in, doing what he always does best; distracting me from making a dickhead of myself.

"Have you told Harper yet?"

Zak stopped typing to look up and I felt Finn's eyes burning holes into me. Ryan really was good at keeping things on the downlow. Looked like they didn't know a thing about me and her.

"Nope." I kept my poker face in check and waited for one of them to scoff at the ridiculousness of her being with someone like me.

"So, its official?" Zak asked. "You and her? You're a thing?"

"Yes. Do you have a problem with that?"

He held his hands up in defence and then smirked. I looked across at Finn and he was holding back a fucking grin too.

"I'm not pussy whipped, if that's what you mean."

"That's the last thing we'd accuse you of." Zak laughed.

"Like I said, have you told her?" Ryan sighed and pinned the other two with a keep-your-mouth-shut glare before turning to me.

"It's not that I'm hiding it," I admitted, because it was true. "Last night wasn't the right time. But she knows what she's getting into. She knows who I am, and she said as much herself. So, thanks for your concern, but we're good."

"I hope for both your sakes you're right." Ryan flicked through his mobile phone, pretending to look like he didn't give a shit.

"Whatever. I'm not here to talk about how awesome it's gonna be when I'm the world champion. Wouldn't want any of you to feel inferior." Both Ryan and Zak scoffed at me, but not Finn.

"Success comes at a price," Finn said in a low, mournful voice.

"And I've got the goods to pay," I snapped back. "Look, what is this? An intervention or something?"

Zak slammed his laptop shut, and I knew then that he meant business.

"We think Lockwood might be behind the text messages we've been getting."

I shrugged back at him.

"That doesn't surprise me."

"We got another one yesterday," Ryan added. "Told us we should think twice before putting on another event. Unless we wanted to see the whole of Sandland 'go off', that is. In other words, they were threatening some kind of explosion or something. Zak tracked the message back to a mobile registered to Don Lockwood."

"So, what are we waiting for then? Let's go and confront him." I went to stand up, but Zak gestured for me to sit my ass down and listen.

"Not so fast. I ran a check on Lockwood, and he has multiple mobile phones registered to his name and his company too. He's a dirty fucker, so we need to play clever and keep this information close to our chests, until we know exactly what we're dealing with. He is distancing himself from Alec Winters publicly. He claims he had nothing to do with the money laundering. But he's making a lot of fucking effort to try and fuck shit up for us. He's trying to mess with our heads."

I agreed with him. The Lockwoods liked their mind games. But so did I.

"Not all of our heads though," Ryan said, glaring over at me.

"Are you still not getting any messages, Brandon?" Finn asked.

"Nope."

I wasn't going to apologise for it either. Sure, I had their backs when shit went down, but I wouldn't lose sleep over the fact that Don fucking Lockwood wasn't sending me lame text messages to try and scare me.

"That part just doesn't make sense." Zak frowned as he spoke. "But that's why we have to play the long game. Wait it out and see what he comes at us with next."

I didn't agree with him.

"Fuck the long game. The Lockwoods have been pissing around for too long. I'm still waiting for Jensen to show his face around here so I can rearrange it for him."

"Aren't we all? That fucked up piece of shit has been dodging our bullets for too long now," Ryan said, showing as much anger as I felt.

"You'll have to get in line, mate," I told him. The first hit was always going to be mine.

"There won't need to be any lines. We'll be standing right next to you. He messes with one of us, he messes with us all. And that includes Harper."

That was what I loved about these lads. It didn't matter what we went through, we'd always have each other's backs. We'd always be there when one of us needed help. We weren't blood brothers; we were brothers of the heart.

"So, the plan is to pretend we don't know Lockwood is a shady fucker?" I gave a sarcastic huff and looked at each one of them to gauge their reaction.

"The plan is to stay tight," Ryan stated confidently. "Watch our backs and make sure he knows he isn't spooking us. Business as usual."

I heard my mobile ring and I slid it out of the side pocket of my jeans. When I saw Pat Murphy's number flashing back at me, I tried not to show any recognition of it on my face. I didn't want the lads to think I had any reservations.

"Yeah?"

"Friday," he said loudly down the line. "I need you match fit and ready for your first opponent. I've got some heavy hitters putting a lot of money on this one. It's the fight they've all been waiting for."

"All of my fights are what they've been waiting for."

Zak rolled his eyes at me from across the room.

"I like your cockiness, kid. Save it for Friday, though. The crowd are gonna love it. There might be some sponsors watching too. Make sure you bring it."

"I always do."

Pat hung up first and I threw my phone down onto the coffee table in front of me.

"You've got a fight booked?" Finn nodded at my discarded mobile.

"Yeah, this Friday."

"Fuck, that's soon. Are you gonna be okay?" Ryan said with genuine concern on his face.

"I'm always okay."

"Might be a good idea to tell her though. She shouldn't hear something like that from anyone else. And let's face it, news will be all over Sandland by the end of the day." Ryan spoke sense, I knew that. The other two hummed in agreement. But for me, it was a little more complicated. She might accept me as a fighter, but would she want to watch? Did I want her there? The last time I'd fought and I'd seen her I'd totally lost my head. What if that happened again?

"I'm sorting it. You look after your woman and I'll look

344

after mine." I'd reverted back to my trademark defensive response.

"You sound like a caveman." Zak laughed.

"She loves that about me." I winked, and the atmosphere became slightly less hostile.

"Whatever," Ryan said, pushing himself up off my chair. "I need to split. I said I'd pick Emily up. Take her to the court. Text me any updates."

I stood up too.

"Do you want me to come with you?" I asked. "Give a bit of extra moral support?"

Ryan patted my back as he came past me.

"That's good of you, mate, but no. I've got this. Anyway, we're going to view some apartments tonight, so it's not all bad."

I was happy for him. I couldn't wait to get my own place. I also couldn't wait to get my chair back. Plus, Zak needed to make me a coffee. I'd been here ten minutes already and he'd done fuck all.

"Black, two sugars," I said as I settled myself into the best seat in the house and grabbed the remote control. "Chop chop."

I heard Ryan laugh as he walked out the door.

"You know where the kettle is," Zak said, not moving from his seat.

"Why have a dog and bark yourself?"

I smirked when he stood up and asked Finn if he wanted

345

one too.

This shit was too easy.

CHAPTER

HARPER

Call me a crazy fool, but I missed him already. I kind of felt bad for him too after receiving his text messages earlier. He didn't want to leave me, but he must have thought he had no choice. I guess in his own way he was being selfless. Putting me first and doing a runner so I wouldn't have to bundle him out or explain to my parents why I had a tattooed bad boy in my bed.

He'd been so sweet to me lately, thinking up ways to show me he cared. I wanted to do the same. That's why I was standing on a rainy Sunday afternoon ringing a doorbell that I was sure didn't work and then knocking on the wooden door with its peeling paint to get their attention inside. There was a group of kids playing football on the grassy area opposite the house that couldn't have been older than eight or nine, but they were hollering and whistling over at me like a bunch of middle-aged drunkards. Life was certainly... different on this side of Sandland.

I was lifting my hand up to knock for the fiftieth time

when it swung open, and a sour-faced old woman stood in front of me. She had a blue apron on over her clothes and her white hair was covered with a hairnet. She scowled at me as I shivered in the rain.

"I've got no money, so bugger off. We don't buy off the doorstep round here." She went to close the door in my face, and I had to put my hand up to stop it.

"I'm not selling anything. I'm here to see Brandon."

She eyed me suspiciously, peering up at me through her glasses, and then she snapped.

"How much does he owe? I ain't got nothing, you know. So, you may as well fuck off. He doesn't live here anymore, anyway."

I frowned, trying to remember if he'd told me he was staying somewhere else.

"But Ryan said he was here. Brandon hasn't told me he's moved out."

She took a step closer and pushed her glasses further up her nose, as if that would help her decide whether to trust me or not.

"You're the girl from the photo." She pointed her bony finger and poked my chest. "You've lost a bit of weight, but it's you, isn't it?"

I had absolutely no idea what she was on about.

"What photo?" I asked, wondering if perhaps she meant something in the newspapers from when Brodie died. I didn't think they'd published my photograph, but I supposed anything was possible with some of the gutter press we'd had to deal with back then.

"The one in his bedside drawer. He leaves it out sometimes. I see it when I'm cleaning. But most of the time he hides it. God knows why. That boy has no secrets from me. I go through everything."

I bet she did.

"So, he does still live here then." She grimaced, no doubt inwardly cursing herself that she'd slipped up. "Unless I see the photo, I have no idea if it's me."

"Oh, it's you. I've got a head for faces. I remember everyone." She tapped the side of her head and smiled like she was keeping state secrets up in that brain of hers and then she went back to scowling.

"What do you want with my boy, anyway?" She looked me up and down and her face twisted like she was sucking on a lemon. "You're not his usual type."

"And what is his usual type?"

I didn't like how this conversation was going.

"I wouldn't know. He's never brought anyone home to show me."

Okay then.

It looked like I was going to be going round in circles with Grandma Mathers for a while longer yet.

"Can I come in and wait for him?" I asked, and then wondered what the hell I was doing offering to sit with this bat-shit crazy old lady while I waited for Brandon to emerge...

Whenever that would be.

"I'm busy. But you can come in if you like?"

Don't do me any favours.

"Oh, I don't want to intrude. If you're busy, I can wait somewhere else."

Grannie Mathers scoffed and stepped back, opening her door to indicate that I was welcome to come in.

"I was just about to start the season finale of *Breaking Bad*. As long as you don't tell me any spoilers we'll get along just fine."

Yeah, she was Brandon's nan all right. No doubting that.

"I haven't seen it. So you're safe."

She quirked her eyebrow at me.

"What sort of shit do you watch then? *Downton Abbey*, I bet. Although judging from the plum in your mouth I'd say you live in it too."

This woman was so rude. But I honestly don't think she knew it.

She didn't wait for my response, but as she toddled down the narrow hallway that smelt like bleach, she pointed to a door on her left.

"Kettle's in there. Make yourself useful and put it on. I like my tea strong, milk, two sugars."

I didn't bother arguing. This was probably her way of being hospitable, letting me make the tea for her.

I shut the front door behind me, and the narrow hallway was suddenly shrouded in darkness as the light from outside disappeared. I made my way down to the kitchen, filled the kettle up, and switched it on. I was just opening random drawers and cupboards to find the spoons and the mugs when I heard the front door close. Seconds later, a familiar voice said, "What the fuck are you doing? Why are you making the tea?"

I spun round to face Brandon and shrugged on a laugh.

"Your nan likes it strong. Milk, two sugars."

He marched over and took the spoons out of my hand and then gave me a gentle, loving kiss that made my heart flutter.

"You don't make the tea. Ever. She's trying it on. Don't let her frail old lady act fool you. She's as tough as old boots, my nan."

The old lady act hadn't fooled me. But the crotchety one had kept me on my toes.

Brandon pulled me into him and then buried his face into my neck.

"I missed you. It's a nice surprise to find you here," he said. "The last place I expected to see you was in my kitchen."

"I wanted to surprise you."

He held me in his arms as the old kettle started to jump around to indicate it was close to boiling. I could hear his Nan grumbling about something in the living room, but I blocked her out. No one was going to spoil this moment for me.

"Let me make this tea then we can go up to my room and talk." He pulled away and got busy making his nan a cuppa.

"Do you want one?" he asked.

"No. I'm fine."

He frowned.

"You were making her a tea and you didn't even want one yourself?" He huffed on a smile and shook his head. "I need to teach you to have a better comeback when she tries that shit again."

"I don't mind making her a drink."

"You'll set a rod for your own back. She'll have you running the hoover round next." He laughed to himself as he carried her tea through into their lounge. Then he plonked it unceremoniously down onto the table in front of her. "There's your tea, Nan. Don't ask Harper to make it again. You're supposed to treat your guests, not have them doing shit for you."

"She offered," his nan snapped back.

I hadn't.

She reached forward to grab her mug then looked up at him and tutted. "Where's my biscuits? I've got some garibaldis in the biscuit tin."

"Get them yourself," he said, and then took my hand and led me back out again, guiding me to the staircase.

"Bloody kids. No work ethic these days, that's the problem," his nan muttered, but loud enough so we'd both hear.

Brandon didn't bite back. I guessed he was used to hearing stuff like that.

I held his hand as we walked up the stairs that creaked with every step we took. The carpet was threadbare and the wooden bannister was well-worn, but it was clean. They might not have had a lot, but his nan obviously took pride in keeping her house to a certain standard.

When we got to Brandon's room, he shut and locked the door behind us. I took in a deep breath, inhaling his scent that I loved. This room was full of it. I had to hold myself back from falling onto his bed and burying my face in the sheets. I wondered then if that was how Sal felt when she visited our house and went into Brodie's room, before they broke up, obviously. I always thought his room smelt of farmyards and old socks. I figured all guys' rooms smelt like that, but not Brandon's. I could've stayed here all day.

"It's not much, but it's mine. I'm saving up to get my own place though," he said, like he needed to justify why he was still living at his nan's.

I wasn't one to talk. Twenty-three years old and I was still with my parents. I'd never felt the urge to move out and live on my own. That had never appealed to me before.

"The parties must pay well. I couldn't afford to rent a single room in Sandland on my teaching assistant wages." He tensed, and when I looked back at him, I knew he was keeping something from me. "What is it?" I asked, sitting on the edge of his bed and bracing myself for the bombshell I knew he was about to drop.

"I need to tell you something, and I don't want you to

freak out."

Oh God, what was he going to say? My stomach was in knots.

"Not that you will freak out," he added. "That's not like you, but I need you to keep an open mind. I have no idea what you're gonna think and-"

He was rambling. He always did when he was nervous.

"Just spit it out, Brandon." I swallowed the lump that was starting to grow thick in my throat and picked at the varnish on my nails in an effort to distract my racing mind.

"I've got a fight on Friday."

I looked up at him and he was staring right at me, waiting for my reaction, but his statement was so vague. I'd seen him fight before. Why was this time any different?

"I didn't know you had another party so soon after the last one."

There was something that flashed in his eyes in that moment. Something like fear, but I could've been wrong.

"It isn't a party. I'm fighting for Murphy."

In an instant, the world around me ground to a halt. My legs turned to lead, and a wave of nausea washed over me.

"Why? Why would you fight for him? You know he was working with Brodie?" My breathing sped up and I felt a tingle in the tips of my fingers. "He won't care about you, Brandon. He doesn't care. He uses people. Why are you doing it?"

Brandon came to sit next to me and took both of my

hands in his to stop me wringing them frantically in my lap. Usually, that would've calmed me down, but it didn't. The thought of Pat Murphy and his fighting ring taking someone else I loved away from me made me feel an irrational fear.

Was it irrational?

Murphy had done fuck all to help us when Brodie died. He'd done fuck all to support Brandon too. But now that Brandon was back and he'd shown he still had skills in his first fight, Murphy wanted in. He was all about the money.

"It's good money, babe. Far too good for someone like me to turn down." Brandon looked so humble as he spoke, and I hated that. I hated how he used the term 'someone like me'. It only highlighted how little he thought of himself.

"But what about your safety? There's no money in the world that can take the place of that... of you. What if-"

"I know what you're thinking," he butted in. "But nothing's going to happen to me. I'm in the best shape I've ever been. I've got this." He put his finger under my chin to turn my head and make me look at him. "Trust me."

"I do trust you. What I don't trust is for Pat Murphy to do a decent job and make sure everything goes okay. It's a dirty sport, Brandon. The fights he puts on are all for the show. He couldn't care less whether you come out the other side or not. As long as he gets his cut off the back of your pain."

"I won't be in any pain," he said, puffing out his chest. "That's the other guy's problem to worry about, not mine."

Then he lowered his head and pulled me into him so I could rest on his chest. "I didn't want to tell you. I knew you'd hate it."

"You couldn't keep it from me." I pulled back slightly to argue, but he pulled me closer.

"I knew that too. I figured the money I make off the back of these fights could help us build a decent future. I don't have anything else I can do, Harper. This is who I am."

I could have spent the rest of the afternoon talking about all the wonderful things that made up Brandon Mathers. Reminded him of what he had to offer the world that didn't involve fists and getting hurt. But I knew that wasn't the point. He didn't need to hear that from me, not at that moment. What he needed was my support.

"I know who you are." I laid my hand on his chest and felt the racing beat of his anxiety held deep within.

He took a long, drawn breath, and what he said next made my heart want to burst out of my chest and fall at his feet.

"I won't do it if you don't want me to. You'll always come first with me. Always."

I needed to add selfless to the list of what I loved about him, because right now, he was putting his whole life on the line for me.

"What sort of girlfriend would I be if I stopped you doing something you loved? A pretty shitty one, I reckon." I lifted my head up to look him right in his eyes. I needed him to really hear me. "Do I like that you'll be getting into a fight with some random guy who might beat the shit out of you? No. Will I stop you doing it? Also no."

He dropped his forehead softly against mine.

"I don't want to upset you. If this is gonna cause a problem for us or make you want to end this then I'll walk away from Pat this second. I'll ring him now."

"No. Don't." I stroked his bristly jaw and gave him a gentle peck on the lips. "This might make me a little... nervous. But it won't change the way I feel about you. Why would it?"

He screwed his eyes closed as he kept his face close to mine.

"You don't need the stress. You could find yourself a great guy with a posh office job; a career and a decent pension plan."

"What? Like Jensen?" I scoffed. "Fuck that. I don't want a *great guy*. I have the best sat right in front of me. I want you."

He opened his eyes to look at me and he smiled, making my heart do a little flip and my stomach go from knotted to fluttering butterflies instantly.

"Even if I end up with a broken nose and cauliflower ears?"

I rubbed my nose against his and put both of my hands on either side of his face.

"I'll wipe your wounds and kiss them all better."

I gave him another gentle kiss, and just as I felt like it might go deeper, he pulled away, making me give a little groan.

"Will you be there?" he asked. "I mean, would you come and watch?"

"Of course I would! Did you think I'd sit at home watching T.V. like nothing was happening? How could I, when you're going through something like that? I might hate it, but I'll be the first one to stand there and cheer you on. I'll cheer the fucking place down... Unless you don't want me there?"

"I want you there," he said, but I wasn't sure he truly meant it. He seemed apprehensive.

"Talk to me. You don't sound convinced."

"I don't want you to have any flashbacks. You know, after last time."

He really was putting me first. Taking my feelings into consideration and second guessing everything.

"I'll be fine. The last thing I want you to do when you're supposed to be focusing and studying your opponent is thinking about me and what happened. You need your head in the game. That's how you'll win, and you will win. You'll beat the shit out of whoever it is, and you'll come home to me. That's how I'll get through it. You're the best, Brandon. You are amazing. Never doubt that. I know it, Pat knows it, and soon everyone else in the boxing world will know it too. I'd never hold you back. I'll always be holding you up."

He put his strong arms around me and hugged me tightly. I hugged him back with as much strength as I could muster. Any fears I had needed to be boxed up, locked away, and buried as deep as possible, as far as I was concerned.

"You're a fucking awesome girlfriend. I bloody love you," he said and pushed me backwards onto his bed.

I fell back with my hair fanned across his pillow and I laughed. He crawled up over me and the weight of his body on top of mine pushed me into the soft, lumpy mattress.

He started to kiss my neck and squeeze my ass as his hips ground into me. I couldn't let myself go though. Not with Grannie Grim sitting downstairs.

"Brandon, your nan." I gasped as he worked his way round to that sweet spot behind my ears.

"What about her?"

"She's downstairs. We can't do anything."

He lifted his head slightly then reached over to his bedside table to grab his alarm clock.

"It's seven p.m. She goes to bingo on Sundays at seven. Give her a minute and she'll be out the door. She never misses bingo."

We both stayed still, listening out for a tell-tale sign that she was leaving, and sure enough, a few seconds later we heard the front door shut.

"See. Told you." He smiled to himself as he went back to kissing my neck, spreading goosebumps all over my body.

I could tell he had wicked thoughts and even more

wicked intentions. But so did I.

I wriggled my hips underneath him and he chuckled.

"Now she's interested."

"I'm always interested." I nipped his earlobe, and he moved his attention from my neck to my lips, taking the kiss deeper and driving me crazy with the way his tongue slid so deliciously over mine.

His lips were made to fit perfectly with mine. He was such a good kisser, and I ran my fingers through his hair, feeling like I needed to get even closer.

I heard a growl low in his throat, and he stopped the kiss to tell me, "I love the way you scratch your nails on me. Do it everywhere, baby. Mark me everywhere. I'm yours."

Hearing him say those words flipped a switch inside me, and I grabbed the bottom of his t-shirt and ripped it up and over his head.

"Damn, baby. You need me bad, don't you?" He chuckled, going back to sucking and nibbling my neck then working down to my shoulder.

"I always want you," I said in a breathy voice that made him moan and bite down on my neck then kiss over the sting. "I want you bad, Brandon."

"Only way I know how to be." He lifted himself up to look at me and the twinkle in his eyes made my lust levels go from abso-fucking-lutely smoking, to hell-would-complain-about-these-heat-levels.

"Bring it on." I grinned back and he gave an evil cackle,

settling back onto his knees and pulling my t-shirt up and over my head. His eyes burned when he looked down at me lying in my red lacy bra.

"My favourite colour," he said, leaning forward and squeezing my tits in his hands. Then he put his mouth over one and sucked me through the lace. He soon got tired of having a barrier though and snaked his arm around my back to snap my bra open and pull it off.

He kissed over my chest and groaned. "I really wanna fuck your tits." Then he popped a nipple into his mouth and sucked hard, making me hiss and arch my back. "Every inch of you is so fuckable."

I closed my eyes and grabbed a fistful of his hair, crying out for him to do whatever he wanted to me. I could take it. I could handle anything he had to give.

"It's a good job you said that." He smiled. "Because I had absolutely no intention of holding back."

He lifted himself up off me and yanked the buttons of my skinny jeans open. Then he pulled them down my legs, complaining as he did that they were, "too fucking hard to get off in a hurry. Save these for the days when we can't fuck."

I laughed and wiggled my hips to help him, and eventually he got them off and threw them over his shoulder. He licked his lips when he saw my red thong and bent down to kiss in-between my legs. Then he took the lace material in his teeth and pulled them down to my thighs, but he got too impatient and used his hands to pull them the rest of the way down.

I was laid out for him. Totally naked and very turned on.

Luckily, he had his sweats on. He'd made it a lot easier for me than I had for him. So, when I sat up and curled my fingers into the waistband, they slid off with little effort. His cock sprung out long and thick and pointed right at my face.

What was a girl to do in that situation?

I grinned and quirked my eyebrow at him, kneeling on the bed like he was.

"Are you just gonna look at it or are you gonna suck it like I want you to?" he asked in a gravelly voice.

"I'll do anything you ask me to," I answered, leaning forward and running my tongue along the underside and then across the head.

He wrapped his hand around his cock and then grabbed the back of my head with the other, showing me exactly how he wanted it. He wanted it deep, hard, and intense. He wanted me to suck him good.

I put my hands around his hips, gripping his ass and pulling him into me. His cock hit the back of my throat, but I wouldn't gag. I wanted to take all of him, every inch. So I coaxed him deeper and deeper into my throat until he moaned loudly. I sucked and let him swivel his hips as he fucked my mouth.

"You suck my cock so good, baby," he groaned, and I looked up through my watery eyes as he gazed down at me. "I fucking love it. I love you." He ran his hand tenderly under my chin and I could feel him thicken and pulse inside me. I loved that I made him feel like that.

He did a few more hard, forceful thrusts, and then he pulled out. I wiped my mouth and was about to question what he was doing when he flipped me over so I was face down on the bed.

"Ass in the air, baby. I wanna fuck you hard from behind and watch my cock sinking into your tight little pussy."

I tingled from his words alone.

"How high do you want me?" I asked, lifting up on all fours and glancing seductively over my shoulder at him as he palmed his cock and stared at my ass.

"Head down, remember. Ass as high as it'll go." I did as he told me, and he put his arm under my hips and pulled me up even higher. "Good girl."

He leant over to open his bedside table and take out a condom. I heard the rustle of the packaging as he put it on. Then I felt him run his cock in-between my legs, teasing my folds and rubbing against my clit. His breathing became deeper, more of a pant, as he started to slide slowly into me, then he whispered, "Hold on to the bed. This could get bumpy."

I reached my hand forward, and I'm glad I did, because he slammed into me hard and made me scream out loud with how fucking amazing it felt to be filled by him like this. My body jerked forward, and I cried his name as he pounded into me. The bed shook and the floorboards creaked, but we didn't care. We both wanted it hard and fast. I pushed back into him, tilting my ass to take him as deep as I could, moving my hips to get better friction. When he reached his hand around and started to circle my clit as he was thrusting into me, I lost it completely. I begged him to fuck me harder, give me everything he had. I didn't hold back and neither did he. We were like two animals that'd been lost in the wild for a lifetime. We couldn't get enough.

"I. Fucking. Love. You," he stated on every hard thrust.

"I love you," I managed to gasp in between my breathy pants.

He pounded into me and I couldn't get enough. Each thrust felt more divine than the last.

"Oh, Brandon." I used both hands to brace myself against the headboard. "I'm gonna come so hard."

"Yeah, you are," he said, working himself deeper and deeper, harder and harder.

I tried to hold it, but I couldn't. My walls contracted tightly around him and my whole body started to quiver with the force of my orgasm. I was no longer in control of my body, he was.

"That's it, baby. Milk my cock," he moaned, but he wasn't done with me yet. He swivelled his hips and kept on grinding into me, making me shake and whimper. Everything was so sensitive, so heightened. The way he gripped my hips, the feel of him slamming into me and the sound of his moans all sent me spiralling into a euphoria I never wanted to leave.

Then, without warning, I climaxed again. Wave after wave of the most amazing aftershocks rippled through me and I cried into his pillow. I'd never felt anything like it. Brandon owned me, body, mind and soul.

"So fucking perfect." He grunted and then I felt him thicken inside me and groan as he came hard. His hands held me tightly in place as he rode out his orgasm, and I turned my head on the pillow to watch as a look of pure love and satisfaction washed over him. He gazed down to where we were joined like it was the most beautiful thing he'd ever seen.

"I fucking love you, Harper," he said before he covered me with his whole frame and pulled me down to lie next to him on the bed.

We were both panting and covered in sweat, but we didn't care. We were only bothered about being close to each other, lying in each other's arms.

"That was amazing," I whispered.

"It always is with you."

We stayed entwined for a little while longer, but eventually, he had to take care of the condom, and like the true gent he was, he brought a warm cloth back to clean me up. I had plans for a shower together, but the cloth would have to do for now.

As I lay in his arms, basking in that indescribable afterglow, the memory of what his nan had said sprang clear into my mind.

"Do you have a photo of me?" I couldn't see his reaction

because I was nestled into his chest and he wouldn't let me go, but I felt his muscles clench and heard him take a breath.

"Did you look in my drawers when I was in the bathroom?"

"No. I'm not a snoop. It's just, your nan said you have a picture of a girl and she thought it was me."

He sighed and rolled me off his chest. I didn't like that. Was he pushing me away?

I watched him push up onto his elbow and then reach forward to open the drawer in question. When he pulled a familiar frame out, I gasped.

"Where did you get this?" I said, taking the frame out of his hands and then mentally face-palming myself.

The night he broke into our house, that's when he got it, dummy.

"I took it. It's my favourite picture of you. I love the way your eyes sparkle at the camera. You're so happy. When I saw that, on the night I... well, you know. I had to take it. It was a reminder for me."

"A reminder of what?" I asked gently. I knew this meant a lot to him. I could tell by the softness of his voice, and the way he looked at me like I was made of china.

"It reminds me of what you've lost. You've lost a lot because of me... But that sparkle in your eyes? I wanted to give that back to you. I wanted to see that happiness on your face again. That photo reminded me what I needed to do. I'm not giving it back," he stated firmly.

"How did we not notice it was missing?" I asked, more to myself than to him. It only highlighted the fact that both my parents and I had been walking around in a daze for so long. We didn't even notice when things went missing right under our noses. "Brodie took that photo. It was our last family holiday. We went skiing in Switzerland."

Brandon grew stiff next to me, and I knew this wasn't the right time to bring up anything about my brother.

"I love that photo," he added, before he took it out of my hands and placed it on the bedside table.

"You can keep it."

"I wasn't planning on giving it back."

"You don't need it as a reminder though. You have me. All you need to do is look at me and you'll find that sparkle again. You did that for me. You gave it back to me."

He grabbed me into a hug and buried his face into my neck. I loved when he did that.

"My forever. That's what you are," he said in a muffled voice against my skin.

"Promise?" I asked, running my nails across his scalp the way I knew he liked.

"Do you honestly think I'd ever let you go? You're it for me, Harper Yates. Bloody hate your surname though. We may need to do something about changing that soon. Mathers suits you better."

"All in good time, big man," I said, smiling and curling into him like a pet monkey. "We have all the time in the world."

He pulled away and his face faltered slightly.

"Do we though? Have all the time, I mean? If there's one thing we both know it's that life is precious. It changes in an instant. I don't want to wait around, Harper. I'm an impatient bastard. If I know what I want, I just take it. And I want you."

"You've got me." I kissed him and felt the heat between us start to rise again. Looked like Brandon's bedroom slash sex den was going to be my new favourite place to hang out.

-

After another round of energetic, toe-curling sex that'd probably really pissed off the neighbours, we resigned ourselves to the fact that we couldn't stay in bed forever, and put our clothes back on. Brandon held my hand and led me out onto the landing, and I felt torn, knowing I had to leave. I had stuff to do in the morning. But I didn't want to go.

We started to walk down the stairs and then froze when we heard a croaky voice humming from the kitchen.

"I thought you said she'd gone out?" I whisper-yelled at him.

"I thought she had."

We crept down the stairs, trying not to alert her to our presence, and partly because I was too embarrassed to face her, but that old woman could give a ninja a run for their money. I could see where Brandon got his stalker skills from.

"Leaving already?" she shouted out of the doorway as my foot hit the last step. "Mind you, sounds like you got what you came here for."

I hit my forehead on Brandon's back and let out a deep sigh. *Great way to impress the family, Harper.*

"Nan. Why aren't you at the bingo?" Brandon asked sharply, turning around to take me in his arms.

I didn't want to have to face his nan, but I had no choice. I needed to man-up.

"Bingo was cancelled this week. Something to do with the water pipes or some crap like that." The clatter of cutlery and banging of cups told us she wasn't happy.

"But I heard you go out."

"I took the bins out." She appeared at the doorway to the kitchen, clutching her bread knife a little too aggressively, and I flinched. "Don't worry, dear. I had my headphones in as soon as I heard you two going at it upstairs." My cheeks flamed with embarrassment. "I managed to get through three episodes of Sons of Anarchy too. So, it wasn't a total waste of an evening." She grinned to herself, patted Brandon on the shoulder like she was proud of him and hobbled down the corridor to her living room.

"I'm off now, Mrs Mathers. Thanks for having me," I shouted down the dingy corridor.

"Next time bring some iced buns or maybe a Victoria sponge. It'll go nicely with that cup of tea you never made me."

I laughed at her cheekiness.

"Yeah, I'll do that."

I heard her chuckle to herself then she shouted back. "And it's Elsie. Not Mrs Mathers."

Brandon's eyebrows shot up.

"She likes you. She only lets close friends and the milkman call her Elsie. Even Ryan hasn't been given the privilege of first name terms."

"Wow. I am honoured." I lifted onto my tiptoes to kiss him and broke into a laugh when I heard her bellowing down the hallway again at us.

"It'll be Mrs Mathers again if you keep manhandling my grandson at the front door for much longer."

I ignored her and gave him one last kiss. Then I headed back to my car that was parked at the end of his path.

He leaned up against the doorframe, watching my every move, and he didn't go in until my car turned the corner out of sight. But driving away, I could still feel him tugging on my heart strings, like an invisible chord tethered us together.

We might not be in the same room or building, but it felt as if we carried a piece of each other wherever we were. I felt like that, anyway. Maybe it was because we owned each other's hearts. I smiled at that thought and then a wash of dread drench me.

He was going to fight for that man on Friday.

He'd be going up against an opponent and I could do nothing but watch and hope, pray that he came back to me in one piece.

I'd never be that girl who dictated what her boyfriend

should and shouldn't do, but the nerves were already kicking in. How the hell was I supposed to keep this locked down until it was all over? I loved him. The thought of losing him was one I couldn't bear to think about. If anything happened, my heart wouldn't recover.

He was mine.

I was his.

So why did I feel like the happiness I'd fought so hard to get was starting to drift away from me?

CHAPTER

Thirty Two

BRANDON

By the time Friday rolled around, I was buzzing and couldn't wait to get into the ring again. The fight was taking place at a local boxing gym a few towns over. It was a step up from the spit and sawdust I was used to, and that fact alone made me feel powerful, more important even.

Pat assured me this was just the start for me. Once I'd got a few wins under my belt, it'd be stadiums and then arenas. The world was my oyster, and Vegas was my end goal according to him. He'd filled my head with all sorts of stories; even came round to our house to convince Nan that life was about to change for us. She told him he was full of shit. She wasn't swayed easily when it came to sweet talkers like Pat. She always had her guard up. Must be where I got it from, because even though I felt honoured to be headlining in a place like this, I couldn't help but keep my guard up too.

"There's a good crowd out there," Ryan said as he came into the changing room I'd been allocated. He looked nervous as he sat down next to me. I don't know why. I had this one in the bag. Defeat wasn't in my repertoire.

Finn was busy taping up my hands and Zak stood in the corner, biting his nails.

"It's gonna be a good fight. I'm fucking ready for this." I grinned back at them, letting them know they were in for a top night. I always delivered on that score.

"Just stay focused. Hit him hard and knock him the fuck out," Zak added nervously from across the room. Like I needed his boxing advice. Even his music suggestions were questionable in my opinion.

"You worried about me?" I laughed and flexed my fingers as Finn finished up. It'd become a tradition now for Finn to strap me up. I wouldn't trust anyone else, and he was like my good luck charm.

We heard the door open, and looked up to see Kian waltz in, carrying a crate of water bottles and banging the door off the wall as he nudged it with his elbow.

"It's fucking mental out there. Who are you fighting?" He huffed and dropped the water onto the floor next to Ryan's feet, making a dent at the bottom of some of the bottles.

Every eye in the room turned to glare at me. I knew exactly what they were thinking.

"I've no idea. Pat said it was better for me to focus on my training and go in blind." I knew it sounded like bullshit, but at that point, I didn't care. I was there for the money.

If I really thought about it though, it was shady. I liked to study my opponents, see where their weaknesses lay. But when I'd questioned Pat about it, he'd shot me down every single time. I decided it wasn't worth the hassle. I was confident enough in my ability and I trusted his judgement call. He said I'd fucking nail it, and I would.

"You know that's complete and utter bullshit, right? I've got a bad feeling about this, mate." I knew Ryan had my back, but this wasn't his call to make. I was getting sick and tired of people thinking they knew what was best for me.

"I couldn't give a fuck who I fight. I'm ready to take anyone on." And I was. I wasn't some wet behind the ears punk-ass kid. I was doing what I could to take my career further. I was a hustler, and if that meant I had to do fights like this to claw my way to the top, I would.

"What if he's built like a brick shithouse? It could be the fucking mountain from Game of Thrones for all you know." Zak always had the best advice at the best of times. Not.

I wanted to ask him if he thought I'd run away like a loser. I mean, they could have put a bloody lion in the ring and I'd still have had a good go.

"They've gotta be in the same weight category as me, dumbass." He shrugged. "Don't sweat it, Zak. I'm good to go."

"How do you know he isn't setting you up?" Finn suddenly piped up.

Truth was, I didn't know. I just had to trust in my own ability, because in reality, I wasn't sure if I could trust Pat.

"Yeah," Kian butted in, pointing his finger at me. "I heard one bloke outside say it's gonna be a blood bath. Maybe they have set you up, mate."

Jesus, these lads really knew how to build me up ready for a fight. Had they forgotten about my undefeated record? Did I need to remind them what a punch from me felt like?

"Blood bath for them, not me." I was done with this shit pep-talk. They weren't helping me get into the zone at all and if I was honest, the only person I wanted to be around right now was Harper. "Stop listening to gossip, okay? You're worse than a bloody woman."

I started pacing the room. I couldn't help it. I was like a caged tiger and everything they said and did pissed me off.

"Speaking of women," Kian answered back, totally oblivious to the fact that he was starting to outgrow his welcome. "Harper's outside with Em and the others. I told her to come with me, thought maybe she didn't know where you were, but she said she didn't want to disturb you. Something about getting into the right headspace?"

At least my woman had my best interests at heart.

I thought about my response before I answered. Part of me wanted to block out the fact that she was here. I knew she'd be worrying. But I also knew she was the reason I was doing this. I loved fighting, but I wanted to make a better life for myself, so I had more to offer her.

Ryan could see I was hovering over my decision.

"Do you want me to go and get her?" he asked, sensing my apprehension.

"Do you mind?"

He nodded and stood up, giving the other three a look that told them they needed to make themselves scarce.

"Good luck, mate." Ryan stalked past me and patted my shoulder. "I know you won't need it though. Show these tossers what us Sandland boys are made of."

I watched him leave, and he beckoned for Zak and Kian to follow him. Finn stood up and grabbed a water bottle from the floor, handing it to me.

"I... I..." He stuttered over his words, so I bypassed his nervousness and gave him a brotherly hug. Actions always spoke louder than words where Finn was concerned.

"You don't need to say anything. I already know." The lump forming in my throat wasn't a good sign, and I swallowed it down. I needed to switch into fight mode, not get in touch with my emotional side.

He nodded, staring at the floor as he broke away, and then he turned to leave. As he opened the door, I saw Harper standing on the other side. Even in her red hoody and black ripped skinny jeans she looked fucking stunning. Her long blonde hair was tied up into a high ponytail and she was biting her lip like she shouldn't be here.

"Don't just stand there, get in here."

This woman could shatter any wall I put around myself. She fucking owned me. Forget dampening down my emotions, I wanted to wrap her in my arms and show her how much I loved her. The minute I laid eyes on her, every feeling inside me intensified. I stalked over to where she was and grabbed her arm, pulling her into the room and slamming the door behind her. I need to touch her, smell her, feel her in my arms to quieten the angry voices in my head.

In the privacy of my changing room, I held her close to my chest, buried my face in the warmth of her neck, and let the softness of her breath and her steady heartbeat focus me. She clung onto me like this was the last time we were ever going to see each other. When we eventually parted, she ran her fingers lightly down the hardened muscles of my chest and stopped when she got to my lion tattoo.

"I'm only gonna say one thing, Brandon." She traced her finger over the bumps of my scar and then looked up at me through her long lashes. The hurt she held behind them almost crippled me. "Come back to me."

Damn. Hearing her say that tore a hole down the centre of my heart.

"I'll never leave you."

I pressed my forehead against hers. If I could find a way to tuck her inside of me I would. Sounds weird, I know, but she was so much a part of me that it didn't feel right when she walked away. I needed that constant contact. I wanted her with me, always. She was my lifeline.

"I probably shouldn't say this." She bit her lip again, and I reached up to pull it free, then lifted her chin. I wanted to kiss her so badly. I wanted to take her mouth with mine and steal every breath, every word. But I held back, letting her say her piece.

"What is it? Come on. Don't ever hold back on me."

She breathed deeply before she spoke again, taking a steadying breath so she could get her words out. No doubt she was deciding whether what she was going to say was right or not. But I never wanted her to second guess anything, not when it came to me.

"I lost one soulmate to this sport. I don't want to lose another." Her eyes glazed over with the tears she was desperately trying to hold back. "I shouldn't have said that, should I? I've made things worse."

I held her face in my hands and looked her in the eyes. I needed her to not just hear what I was about to say but feel it too.

"You could never make anything worse. You make everything better." She nodded, but I could tell she wasn't convinced. She tried to shift her gaze to the floor, but I wouldn't let her. I needed her to listen, to accept what I was saying. "When this is all over, I'm taking you away somewhere. Just you and me. I'm gonna treat you like the queen you are. Everything is for you, Harper. Every fucking thing."

She smiled and shook her head.

"I don't need fancy holidays or nights away, Brandon. I just want you. Maybe you could send your nan away, though. So we can have a bit of privacy."

I threw my head back and laughed at her cheekiness. Not that I didn't agree. My nan, God bless her, could be a thorn in my side at times.

"And that's why I love you so fucking much. You're the only person in this God damn world that wants me for me." I placed a gentle kiss on her forehead as she grinned and wrinkled her nose.

"And I'll kick anyone's ass if they take advantage," she said proudly, looking up at me from underneath her long eyelashes.

I loved that about her. My firecracker. My little warrior. She wasn't scared of anyone, and she probably would kick their asses. She had become my biggest cheerleader, and I don't know what I'd ever do without her. I hoped I'd never have to find out.

I couldn't hold back any longer. I grabbed the backs of her thighs to lift her up and her legs locked firmly around my waist. I slammed my lips over hers, pushing her back against the wall and plunged my tongue into her mouth. Tasting and teasing, sliding my tongue over hers and feeling my need for her grow as our teeth clattered together and we panted out the same breath. Kissing her was everything, and yet not enough. I needed more. I needed to be inside her.

I pushed my hips into her so she could feel what she did to me, how hard she made me. Even when I faced an important fight, this woman had managed to blindside me and make me her prisoner. The switch in my head that turned off most of my humanity, the one that made me the machine I needed to be to stay focused in the ring, it didn't work around her. She'd ripped the wires out and short circuited my system. I was still feral, but I needed something else to quench my thirst now. I needed her.

Suddenly, there was a loud knock at the door that pulled us from our lust-filled bubble. The door swung open, interrupting our moment, and Pat's head appeared from behind it, shouting at us.

"Showtime, lad. Put her down and get your head in the game. I've got a lot of money riding on this one."

Harper wriggled out of my hold. Her lips were red and swollen from our kiss and she smoothed her hair to try and control the stray wisps that had fallen free from her ponytail. She'd never looked more beautiful than she did now. I ran the back of my hand down her cheek and she held my hand and kissed inside my palm, then reached up on her tiptoes and placed a delicate kiss on my lips. A gentle goodbye kiss. Only it would never be goodbye, not where she was concerned. I meant it when I said I would never leave her. This was forever.

"Knock him out. For me," she whispered and then walked out, not once acknowledging Pat's presence. She slid past him like he was nothing and left me without a backwards glance. Pat and his mates stood in the doorway like a pack of hyenas ready to feast on the spoils of my victory. From heaven to hell in a matter of seconds.

I jabbed my arms out in front of me, punching the air and getting myself psyched up. As I did, I spotted Ryan, Zak, and Finn a little way down the corridor. Then my head almost fucking exploded when I saw who they were talking to.

Jensen Fucking Lockwood.

Only he wasn't dressed like the rest of them. He had his hands taped up and he was wearing a pair of blue shorts. The peace and serenity that'd cloaked me when Harper had been here was swiftly and cruelly stripped away. All I felt was pure, unbridled anger.

"It's him, isn't it?" I gestured down the corridor to where Lockwood was facing-off with my friends.

"Yeah. It is."

I turned to glare at Pat, hoping he could feel the torture of my gaze penetrate through his rhino thick skin. He hadn't stitched me up, he'd ripped a massive fucking hole through any shred of trust I might've had.

How could he keep something like this from me?

He held his hands up in defence, but his face showed no remorse, only crinkles of mirth from the way his eyes wrinkled as he spoke. "After your last fight, with all that talk, this is the showdown the punters wanna see. You've got nothing to worry about, lad. You could beat him with one hand tied behind your back."

I could beat Pat too. A prospect that was looking more inviting by the minute.

"A heads up would've been nice." My blood was boiling already.

"If I'd told you he was back in town, you'd have gone off

like a bloody firework and kicked his ass. Probably got yourself thrown into jail for the pleasure too. At least this way everyone gets to see you pound his face in, and you get paid for it. It's a win-win."

I couldn't concentrate on what Pat was saying over the pounding in my head. All I could see was *him* acting the big man down the hall. All I could focus on was getting into his face and knocking him the fuck out.

"It's a fucking set-up. Finn was right."

"It's business!" Pat raised his voice and waved his fat finger in my face. "And it's money. The people out there want this fight. You bragged about it yourself at your last match. This is what we do, lad. We give the audience what it wants. We take their bets, and we go off laughing all the way to the bank."

Some things were worth more than money.

Trust.

Pride.

Love.

"He hurt my girl."

"And now you're gonna hurt him." Pat chuckled to himself and muttered under his breath that it was a genius idea to get Lockwood on board. Whether it was genius or a fucking fool's mission was yet to be seen; for Pat, at least.

So, I guessed Lockwood already knew he was fighting me. I was the only one that'd been kept in the dark and I wasn't happy. I didn't like being lied to. I wouldn't stay in the dark and on the back foot for long though.

I let Pat walk out first, wandering off to talk more bollocks to his cronies. I waited for him to be far enough away, then I kicked the door off its hinges and marched down to where Jensen stood shouting his mouth off. He spun around when he saw me coming towards him. I was surprised he stayed rooted to the spot and didn't bolt like the pussy he was. Mind you, he had his crew behind him to make him feel like a somebody. It was a different story when he was on his own. Then, he was a nobody.

"And here he is. The man of the hour. The shitty king of Sandland." Jensen was back to his ballsy self, giving me all the bravado he could muster. He was fucking delusional. "Disappointed?"

"To see you? Always. I thought you'd have learnt your lesson by now, Lockwood. I've beaten you once before and I'll do it again." I kept moving forward, getting into his space to piss him off.

"You got lucky. But let's face it, I've beaten your ugly ass more times than you can count. I bet you still wet the bed thinking about all the fucked-up shit we did to you in school. Is that why Harper's dating you now? Does she feel guilty about what her brother did to fuck up your head? She always was a soft touch for a sob story. She's gonna love it even more after tonight when she's nursing your wounds." He turned to laugh at his friends like what he'd said was fucking funny. He'd be laughing through his wired jaw after I was finished with him. He spun back round to face me, keeping the sly smirk on his face. "If you think the right-hook I gave her was good, you should see what I've got planned for you."

I snapped, lurching forward, feeling like my whole body would implode if I didn't hit him right that second. I never wanted him to say her name, and the memory of him putting his hands on her made me vicious, totally unhinged with the intensity of my thirst for revenge. Whoever said it was gonna be a blood bath was right, I was gonna rip his fucking head off.

Ryan jumped in front of me like he was taking a bullet to save my life.

"Save it for the ring, mate," he growled into my ear as he kept himself in between me and the grinning cunt who was begging to have his whole face rearranged. "Use the anger. Channel it. Own it. Don't let it own you. If he gets under your skin, he'll win. You can't let that happen. He needs to go down."

I listened to what Ryan said. I didn't want to rein it in, but I knew I had to. For now. There was a better way to get my revenge, and Ryan was right. He always made sense. I had to own this anger, use it. Focus on the end goal and show everyone in that room that no one messes with Brandon Mathers or his woman. Years of deep-seated hatred, anger, and fury would be the fuel I needed to bring this to an end once and for all. After tonight, I never wanted to see another Lockwood in my face ever again.

Jensen backed away and headed back to his side of the corridor with his mates. Zak, Finn, and Ryan formed a wall around me and kept giving me their pep-talk, bigging me up, but I couldn't hear them. I'd started to faze them out. I was pumped, ready, and heading into that fucking zone.

Just as the announcer started speaking to the crowd over the sound system, I heard the vibrations from the guys' phones chiming in unison, pulling me out of my headspace.

"Fuck, I forgot to turn mine off," Zak said as he pulled his mobile out of his pocket. The other two swiped their screens, and when they read their messages, I saw the change in their expressions.

"What does it say?" I asked, knowing they were about to hit me with bad news.

"It's nothing. Don't worry about it." Zak was a little too quick replying. He shoved his phone back into his pocket and looked anywhere but at me. This was fucking bad.

"Ryan? What did it say?" I glared daggers at him, watching my best friend battle inside himself over whether to tell me or not. He didn't want me to know what it was, but he would never keep a secret. He was always honest. But it was Finn who eventually broke the stand-off.

"It says, tell him to throw the fight. If he doesn't, we'll hurt the girl."

Harper.

They were threatening Harper.

"And you still think this is Don Lockwood?" I pointed

down at Ryan's phone as I spoke.

"That's what the records say." Zak was a whizz at these things. If he said it was linked to Lockwood, then it was. I trusted him one hundred percent.

"It's an empty threat. He'd never hurt Harper. We wouldn't let him anywhere near her." Ryan sounded so sure, but I knew better than anyone, if someone wanted to hurt you, they would. It didn't matter how well protected you were. There was always a way.

"This ends tonight." I smacked my fists together, more than ready to take him on. No one threatened us and got away with it. First, I was gonna take out Jensen, and then I was going after Daddy Lockwood. The days of me cowering because of anyone from that family were well and truly over.

"Are you still gonna fight?" Zak asked me, and I frowned. I couldn't believe he needed to ask me that.

"Of course I'm fighting. I'll fucking kill him. And after I do, I'm going after the rest of his family."

I heard the bass from the music in the venue reverberating through the corridors and I closed my eyes, letting the atmosphere wash over me, trying to centre myself and clear my head of all the crap it'd taken on in the last few minutes. I needed to be focused to get the job done and do it well. There couldn't be any room for error. Not with so much at stake.

They called out Jensen's name and I heard the crowd roar as he went out to a hail of boos and jeers. Looked like I wasn't the only one that couldn't wait to see him get his ass handed to him.

The lads each patted me on the shoulder and told me to fucking smash it. I nodded, but I didn't speak. When they called my name, I walked in and jabbed my arms as I headed for the ring. People clapped me on the back as I went past, and I heard the shouts and cheers, but I couldn't settle, not until I'd seen where she was. There were hundreds of people in here, but all I cared about was her.

I climbed up into the ring and put my mouth guard in. Then I scanned the room for a red top and blonde hair. As soon as I saw her standing with Emily, I felt a calmness wash over me. She tried to smile, but I could see how nervous she was. This was the worst thing she could ever watch, but she loved me enough to go through it. She was putting herself through hell to be there for me.

Why the fuck was I doing this again?

Why was I putting her through this?

The ref came over and called me forward to toe the line. Jensen stood in the middle, smirking at me. The cocky bastard.

I sauntered over and glared back at him. I was gonna enjoy every minute of this.

"Right, lads," the ref shouted to us over the noise of the hecklers. "Let's have a clean fight. No biting, no holding, no butting. No hitting with an open hand and no gouging of the eyes. Yes?" We both nodded in agreement. "Good. Let's get it on then, gentlemen."

Just as the ref stepped back, Jensen eyed my chest and stared down at my lion tattoo, and then he laughed. The sound of him cackling over the chants in the gym made my demons rise up like a phantom army. Ghosts of my past ready to right the wrongs in the most vicious way they could. Most times I could control them, but tonight I had no desire to. I wanted them to run free.

"Best day of my life that was, cutting you up. Nice touch getting the lion tattoo over the top of it though. Very apt. Me and Yates always were the kings. But you? You're a fucking mess. Just like your fucked-up mother. God knows what a girl like Harper sees in you. It won't be long before she dumps your ass and finds herself -"

He didn't get to finish what he'd started to say. A red mist settled over me, just like it had when I'd been hiding down that alleyway listening to the way he talked to her. Hearing the way he disrespected her. I charged forward and pulled my head back, then smacked him hard on the face with an almighty head butt. The cracking sound of his nose breaking and the blood that splattered all over his face sent a surge of pride through my veins. The ref shouted and the crowd booed and jeered, but I didn't care. I lifted my fist up and smacked him hard in the head, sending him spiralling to the floor.

Who was the fucking mess now?

"Jesus Christ! That's a foul, son. You're disqualified. No

butting. That's the rules. Are you a fucking moron?"

I don't know who this ref thought he was, but he was close to following Lockwood on the floor of the ring if he carried on talking to me like that.

I saw a few of Lockwood's guys jump the ropes and two ran over to tend to him whilst the others charged for me. I was ready for them, but when I raised my fists to fight back, I was jostled out of the way by Ryan and a few other faces I recognised from Sandland. It looked like my foul play had turned this event into a free-for-all, and the ring was filling up with people ready to have a go. The Lockwood crew versus the Renaissance men. The unjust against the righteous. In life, they always held the upper hand with their money and status, but here we had the power. Our numbers were greater than theirs and our fury burned stronger.

Lockwood wasn't moving, he lay there spark out. His fucked-up team tended to him as best they could as anarchy reined all around them. I spun round and smacked my fist into one of theirs that was hurtling across the ring towards me, under the illusion that he could take me on. As soon as my fist connected with his face, he fell to the floor clutching his nose and howling like a fool. Ryan was kicking the shit out of a guy and I spotted Zak wrestling another to the ground. But in all the madness my first thought was for her. If anyone had laid a finger on her I'd burn this whole fucking gym to the ground. The lads could look after themselves, they all knew how to fight, even Finn to an extent, but not her. She was my responsibility. Mine to protect. I had to find her.

I glanced over to where she'd been standing before, but she wasn't there, and panic gripped my heart in an instant, thinking she might be hurt. I tried to get to the edge of the ring, pushing brawlers out of my way as they lurched and staggered around swinging punches anywhere and everywhere. I ducked my head dodging a sharp right-hook, and that's when I spotted her. Groups of people were streaming out of the gym to try to escape, but not my girl. She was pushing against the throngs, trying to make her way to the ring like she was swimming against the tide, with Emily not far behind her. She was trying to get to me, but I'd save her first.

In that moment, I couldn't give a shit that I'd probably just pissed all over my boxing career or that my friends were fighting in this ring because of me. All I cared about was getting to her and making sure she was okay. I was done with being the puppet for everyone; Pat, my Mum, the Lockwoods.

Tonight had played out just how I'd wanted.

I'd never wanted a clean fight.

Why would I?

Nothing *he'd* ever done to me had been clean or fair. I'd gone against the rules, and I wouldn't be asked to fight in a place like this again, but I'd stayed true to myself. I'd given him a dose of the Mathers comeback, and that was all that mattered.

I jumped out of the ring with the sole purpose of getting

to her and dragging her out of here, but Pat stepped in my way, blocking my path and my clear vision to where she was. He was fuming, but his anger was no match for mine.

"You're fucking finished, Mathers. You've cost me a lot of money tonight, son, not to mention my reputation, you stubborn little shit. I won't work with you again. If I have my way, you'll never box for anyone, ever."

His words meant nothing to me. I couldn't care less. So, he'd lost money. But I hadn't lost face. I'd done what I set out to do all along. I'd shown this town and everyone in it that I wouldn't be messed with, and neither would Harper.

"You don't have to threaten me, Pat. I'm done. It's all bullshit." I breathed a little easier as Harper came up beside me, and when she heard what I'd said, her eyes widened.

"Don't say a fucking word to him you piece of shit." She barged in front of me, shouting over the crowds to Pat.

She was un-fucking-believable. My warrior princess, ready to throw down with anyone who pissed her off or got in her way. I bloody loved her.

"You'd do well to remember your manners, girl. Speak to me like that again and I'll-"

"You'll what, Pat? Show her who's boss?" I wrapped my arm around Harper's waist and pulled her into me. Then I leant over her shoulder, sneering into his face. "You even so much as breathe near her and I'll rip your fucking head off."

Harper chuckled in my grasp and put her hand over mine.

"And if you go near him again, I'll rip your fucking balls off."

Fuck me.

Hearing her threaten him was the biggest turn-on.

I watched him snarl at us, then back off, sliding out of the room and away from the chaos like the vermin he was. Good riddance. For a second, I gave in to my desire and buried my face in her neck, inhaling her. Then, I snapped back to reality and the war around us. There wasn't time to waste. I needed to get her out of here. I didn't want her in this room surrounded by so much hate. I was finally done with this shit show.

We pushed through the crowds and headed back to the changing room to get my stuff. With each step, I felt my shoulders lightened, and I started to walk taller. I'd done the right thing. I knew that. I'd taken Lockwood down and put Pat in his place too. There was a twinge of guilt at leaving the lads behind to finish the fight without me, but that soon evaporated when I spotted Ryan, Zak, and Finn hurtling down the corridor towards us.

"That was mental." Ryan slapped me on the back, laughing in his adrenaline high.

"Where's Em?" I glanced around him, but she wasn't there.

"I made her leave with Kian. He's parked out front. He'll get her home safe. She doesn't need to see this next part."

Harper narrowed her eyes at me. "What next part?"

I'd kept her in the dark enough lately, so I spent the next few minutes filling her in on what'd happened with the text messages and the link to Don Lockwood. I also told her I needed to end this, once and for all. I was going to face Don Lockwood and find out exactly what his game was. Harper insisted on coming too. As if I could ever deny my little warrior what she wanted. If she was determined to stand by my side, I'd let her. He'd threatened her in that text message. He needed to see we were indestructible. No one came between Harper and me. No one ever would.

CHAPTER
Thirty Three

BRANDON

I sat with Harper in her little car as she drove us over to the Lockwoods. We didn't even attempt to make small talk; we didn't need to. I was too wound up, and she understood that I needed the space and time to think. She always got me.

I didn't know why the fuck Lockwood was sending us texts. He'd distanced himself so far away from the scandal we'd uncovered months ago that he may as well have been on fucking Mars. He also knew we were like a dog with a fricking bone when it came to shit like this. So, why was he suddenly being so sloppy? Did he think we wouldn't find him? Or that we'd shy away from calling him out on his bullshit?

Everyone knew what we were like. We didn't stay quiet, ever. Maybe he was losing touch in his old age. Or he simply thought he was untouchable. Too bad we were on our way to show him how wrong he was.

Ryan, Zak, and Finn were following us in Zak's car and when we turned into the road, the house was lit up like a bloody Christmas tree, as if he was bragging about his self-importance to us before we'd even got out of the car.

"Are you sure about this?" Harper turned to ask me as I reached for the door handle.

I squeezed her knee to reassure her and she smiled in unspoken agreement. I'd never been surer of anything in my life. The Lockwoods needed taking down a peg or two, and none so more than Daddy dearest.

"I need this to be fucking over. No one threatens you like that." She tensed at my aggressive retort, so I reached out to take her hand in mine and brushed my thumb over her knuckles. "Don't worry, little warrior. I'm on a winning streak tonight. I won't let anything happen to you."

"It's not me I'm worried about, Brandon. It's you. You've just gone through all that with Jensen. You don't need this. Not tonight."

"It has to happen tonight, babe. I'm not going another minute with these Lockwood fuckers thinking they can get one over on us. It isn't happening anymore."

"I know. I get it."

We both got out of the car. I could see she was reluctant. Like a heavy weight was draped over her shoulders and she was trying to fight it off, but I was locked and loaded. The fire of adrenaline pumping through my body helped with that. No one was going to stand in my way.

The lads parked up behind us and they got out, coming to stand by my side as whole conversations and confirmations of our brotherhood passed between us in the silence. They were here to support me, stand by me, and have my fucking back. Hurt one and you hurt all, it'd always been this way, ever since the days when they'd picked me up after a shitty day at school. They were my soldiers, we were an army, and woe betide anyone who stood in our way.

We walked as a unit towards the house and then up to the imposing double front doors that were flanked by the ridiculously pompous topiary and extravagant wall lights that illuminated the front of the house. The Lockwoods had always been about the façade. All show and no substance to back it up. They liked to project an ideal to the rest of the world, one they thought they fooled everyone with, but they didn't. Not us, anyway. They might look like the real deal, but they were shady fuckers with zero morals.

We faced the doors in an unbreakable, impenetrable line as I rang the doorbell. Harper to my left, Ryan to my right. Finn and Zak were on either side of us. We were the dog's bollocks, and when he opened the door, he'd get a load of exactly how fucking formidable we were.

Harper threaded her arm through mine as we waited for them to open up. I looked down at her and winked. I wanted her to know I was in control, or at least for her to think I was. To be honest, it could go either way. I still felt unhinged after the fight, and my adrenaline was through the roof. I was more than ready for another throw down.

When the door swung open, we saw Karen Lockwood standing there, gawping at us like we'd come down on the last spaceship. Her make-up was plastered thickly on her face and her eyebrows were so far up into her fringe that she looked permanently startled. Add in the fact that her blonde hair was pulled back into a harsh ponytail and she fitted the plastic trophy wife to a tee. Guessing her age would be like playing a carnival game; impossible to get right. She batted her spider-like eyelashes at us and smiled. But we weren't here to play nice, so I cut right to the chase.

"Where is he?" I didn't feel the need to explain who *he* was. I was antsy, impatient, and I wanted to get this visit over with. The longer I stayed on the Lockwoods' territory, the more agitated I became.

Her eyes widened as she took me in, looking me up and down like I'd come from the fucking zoo. Harper's grip on my arm tightened. She'd noticed it too. What was this woman's deal?

"Erm, Jensen or Chase?" She bit her lip and started stalling for time. "Jensen went out a few hours ago." She peered behind her. "I think Chase is in his room-"

"We aren't here for a social visit," I snapped back. "Where's your husband?" I was losing it fast.

Just as I said that, Chase sauntered down the staircase behind her and scoffed like a little bitch when he saw us. I've got to admit, I was surprised to see him. I thought he'd have been back at the gym after watching his brother get his ass handed to him. Obviously he hadn't gone to watch. Maybe he was worried he'd be next, so he'd ducked out of that one.

Fucking coward.

"What the fuck do you want?" He scowled. Little shit was ballsy when he had Mummy at his side to defend him.

"Language!" his mum barked at him and we all chuckled.

That's right, little bitch. Do as Mummy says.

"They're here to start trouble, Mum. I couldn't give a rat's ass what language I use." He tried to sound hard, but the blush on his cheeks showed him for the pussy he was.

Ma Lockwood turned to look at us and then gestured to where Harper stood.

"I don't think Harper is here to cause trouble. She couldn't upset anyone, even if she tried." She gave Harper a kind smile, which I'm guessing Harper returned. I don't know, I didn't look. I was too busy staring Lockwood mark two down and imagining what it'd feel like to smash my fists into his face.

"We don't want any trouble, Mrs Lockwood," Harper said with a kindness I knew would be wasted on people like this.

"It's Karen, dear. You know that," Mrs Lockwood replied, beckoning Harper into the house.

She stepped forward and we all followed. But I made sure to stay by her side. I wasn't letting my guard down any time soon. She might have been kind, but I wasn't. I was there for one thing and one thing only. To show these people that no one fucked with us.

"Thanks, Karen. Is Don around? We need to ask him about a few things." I let Harper take over. She'd already got us access into the house, so I figured she was best placed to get us an audience with the main man. Use the angel to lure out the devil.

"He's in his study. I'll take you through." Karen went to walk away, but she stopped suddenly and turned to face me. "Do I know you? You look awfully familiar."

Yeah, like I mixed in the same circles she did.

"I came here a few weeks ago." I shrugged. Woman obviously had a shit memory.

"Yes, I remember that, but I mean I recognised you from before then too. What's your last name? Maybe I know your mother."

I highly doubted that Mrs Lockwood knew my mother. If she did, she wouldn't want anyone to know about it. It wasn't the type of acquaintance you'd brag about.

"Mathers. My name is Brandon Mathers."

She frowned as much as her botoxed face would let her and tried to recall the name, but came up empty.

"No. I don't know anyone by that name." She laughed to herself. "Maybe it's my age. You all look a bit familiar." She grinned down at Harper, then said, "Of course, I know you. I always loved it when you came round here with Brodie. I'd always hoped you and Jensen might hit it off one day." She winked then swallowed, looking embarrassed at what she'd said.

I gritted my teeth and held back the scathing words I desperately wanted to unleash on her for insinuating anything could ever happen between Harper and him. Harper just held my arm proudly and stated, "I'm with Brandon."

"Yes, I can see that now." Karen gave a fake chuckle. I was starting to see how well she fitted in with her husband and sons. They were all as phony as each other. "How are your mum and dad? Give them my love, won't you? I know how rough it's been for them lately. Well, for all of you, after Brodie, and ..." she cut herself off and started to walk away. Her incessant chatter followed by her clamming up showed she was nervous. Either that, or she'd remembered how disrespectful her family had been to Harper and the Yates'.

We followed, assuming she was taking us to see her husband. Chase tagged along too, despite me eyeballing him. Fucker always did have balls of steel when it came to pissing me off.

When we came to a pair of oak panelled doors, she stopped and asked us to wait outside, then snuck in through the door, no doubt to warn the occupant inside of the firing squad that'd come to pay him a visit. Or were we the suicide squad? I always did relate more to The Joker than any of the other superheroes.

"I thought you had a fight tonight?" Chase piped up. "Did he beat you that fast? Or did you run away again like a little pussy?" He crossed his arms over his puffed-out chest and rocked back on his feet. I balled my fists at my sides as

Harper gave me another reassuring squeeze.

"I knocked your brother the fuck out. Didn't see the point in staying around to watch the clean-up operation." Chase's eyes flickered like he was surprised to hear what I'd said. Did he really think I'd left, or that his brother had beaten me? I didn't have a scratch on me save for the bruising on my knuckles. And to think the Lockwoods were supposed to be smart. Obviously astute observation and powers of deduction weren't their strong point. "I'm surprised you didn't come to watch. What's up with that? Afraid you'd get your ass kicked too?"

Chase flared his nostrils, but he didn't get to say anything else. The door flung open and Karen walked out looking paler than she had when she went in.

"He said to go right in." She stood against the door to hold it open for us and we filed into the warm study like lions entering the colosseum. Prowling slowly and gauging our surroundings for any possible threats.

The room was dimly lit by picture lights on the dark wood-panelled walls and a study lamp that sat on the highly polished mahogany desk. The wooden floors creaked as we moved into the centre of the room and stood in front of the roaring open fire. There was a bookcase the height of the whole room running along one wall. Had he read all of those? There must've been hundreds of leather-bound books up there. Who had time to read that many books?

The atmosphere was strangely relaxing, with its smoky

whiskey smells and the burn of the fire behind us. The soft crackle as the flames danced over the wood. But I wasn't about to let this lull me into a false sense of security. The devil that sat behind the desk in the high-backed winged chair made sure that I kept my wits about me. If we were the lions, he was the gladiator, and he carried himself with an air of importance, full of cunning and pride for how he thought he was about to play us.

He watched each of us in turn as we took our places side by side, standing on the Chinese rug laid out in front of the fire. His face didn't give anything away. If poker were an Olympic sport, no one else would compete because what would be the point? This guy had fucking nailed it.

The room was silent as he picked up his tumbler of whiskey and took a swig, then he placed it back carefully on a coaster. He leant back in his chair with his arms outstretched on his desk, tapping his fingers and sizing us up. It was like we were standing in front of a headmaster, if the headmaster was a cold-hearted sadistic liar who only thought about himself and only kept people around him if he thought they could do something for him.

He must've got bored tapping his fingers and decided to thread them together and rest them on his paunched stomach.

"To what do I owe this pleasure?" he said in a low drawl, looking at Harper then the others, but not me. He either didn't see me as a threat or he was avoiding poking the biggest beast in the room.

"You know damn well why we've come here," I said on a snarl, and he pinned me with a stare that was supposed to unnerve me. It only made me want to goad him further. I didn't cow down to anyone.

"If I knew what you wanted, I wouldn't have asked. I don't play games. I don't have time. Some of us have a serious business to run." He stayed still as he spoke, but the tic in his jaw showed he was on edge; more so than he wanted to let on.

"God forbid we should interfere with your business. Isn't that right, *Don*?" I opened my legs to stand firmer in my place and crossed my arms over my chest.

"I take it from your tone that you have something on your mind. So, spit it out, boy. I don't have all night."

My back went up as soon as he called me boy. I knew he'd said it to belittle me. But it also made me want to settle this the only way I knew how. With my fists.

"Call me boy again, and I'll show you exactly how wrong you are."

He huffed out a laugh and moved forward to lean on his desk, his fingers steepled in front of his face.

"You've got fire in you. I like that." He turned to glance at Chase. "Do you have any idea what they want? Seems like we need to play twenty questions to get it out of them."

Chase rubbed over his chin and chuckled.

"I'm guessing it's to do with Jensen. He had a fight tonight and-"

"It's got fuck all to do with Jensen," I cut in angrily. "I wanna know why you're sending threatening texts to my friends, trying to get me to throw the fight tonight and involving my girl in this. If you want a war, you come after me, not them, and certainly not her."

Don Lockwood's head whipped back around to me so fast he almost gave himself whiplash.

That's right, I'm calling you out. You come for my friends, you come for me. I would take anyone on who disrespected us.

"What the hell are you on about?" He screwed his face up in disgust. "I haven't sent you any messages. What is all this?" In his defence, not that he deserved one, but he did look totally clueless.

"We traced the phone records. The number was registered in your name," Zak added.

We had proof. We weren't going to let him worm his way out of this so easily.

"Show me. I want to see these messages I'm supposed to have sent."

Don Lockwood stood up from his chair and walked around to the front of his desk. Then he leant up against it and held his hand out for one of us to hand our phones over. Zak did the honours, and when Don started scrolling, his brow furrowed so deeply he looked like a fucking pug. We all stood firm, ready to jump into action.

"I didn't send these." He scowled at us and handed the

phone back to Zak. Then he glared right at me. "What number did they come from?"

Chase shuffled backwards as Zak read out the numbers and Don's face got redder by the second. Dude was a prime target for a heart attack at any minute.

"That's your new number, Chase," he barked. "Care to explain to me why you've been sending those?"

I threw my head back and let out a growl as I glanced at the ceiling then back at Don fucking Lockwood. All this time we thought we were dealing with some dangerous gangsters or criminals linked to him, and all the time it was his punk ass son doing his attention-seeking bullshit. I needed to kick more Lockwood ass tonight. This was getting out of hand. No way was Chase going to get away with playing us like that. He needed to pay.

"I didn't," Chase replied, doing a really shitty job of sounding sincere. The guy needed to own up to his mistakes. He was playing with fire and now he'd gotten burnt.

"Well, they came from your phone. Why did you send them?"

The room went quiet as Chase just stood there, ignoring his dad as he burned a hole into him with his glare.

Suddenly, we jumped out of our skin as Don picked up his tumbler of whiskey and threw it against the wall. "Fucking answer me! I haven't got time for this! What the fuck did you do, you no good sonovabitch?"

Chase started spluttering over his response and Don

marched over to where he stood and slapped him hard across the face, sending Chase crashing to the floor. Harper gasped and I reached out to take her hand in mine. Obviously, the apple didn't fall far from the tree. Using their fists on people weaker than them seemed to be a family trait. They were all bullies.

"Get up." Don leant down and shouted in Chase's face, spit flying from his mouth as he hissed, "Stop lying there like a pussy and get the fuck up."

Chase did as his father told him; struggling to stand as he clutched his cheek, wincing.

"Now, explain to me like the fucking man I brought you up to be." He leant right into Chase's face as he spoke through his clenched jaw. "Why did you send those messages?"

Chase took a few deep breaths and looked at us with vengeance in his eyes. "They needed teaching a lesson. They get away with everything. The parties, the fights, the bullshit they pulled on Uncle Alec..."

Don held his hand up to stop him.

"He isn't your Uncle Alec. For fuck's sake, boy, stop acting like the world owes you something. Alec Winters fucked up. And so will you if you keep up this spoilt little brat charade every time things don't go your way. Your eighteen years old. Start fucking acting like it."

We stood watching as Don Lockwood tore his son a new one. For a family that liked to keep their shit hidden, they weren't doing a very good job of maintaining that.

"They should be locked away for what they did." Chase argued back weakly, trying to justify himself after he'd made such a shitty move. "They scam people, Dad. They're the scum of Sandland. Didn't you say you wanted to clean up this town? I was helping you. I wanted to get rid of the filth as much as you did," Chase begged like the loser he was. He could see he was failing in his dad's eyes and he was desperately clawing onto anything to make what he'd done sound right.

"If you want to say something to us, say it to our faces. Don't hide behind your daddy like a little bitch," Ryan spat.

Hearing Ryan's voice gave Chase an injection of bravado and he sprang to attention.

"I'll happily tell you to your face what I think of you." He went to charge towards Ryan, but Don held his hand over his chest and pushed him back, making Chase stumble. His bravado fizzled away fast beneath the shadow of daddy's disappointment.

"Grow the fuck up. There are ways and means, son. Ways we do things. We don't hide behind messages and play games. I'm running a legitimate business here." I couldn't stop myself from scoffing at his attempt to sound like a middle of the road businessman. He tore his gaze from his son to glare at me, but I just grinned back. "I don't want the police knocking on my door because you can't control your jealousy over some cheap pussy you lost out on because of these jokers." He shoved Chase one last time, then smoothed his hands down the front of his expensive suit jacket like it'd been nothing.

Ryan darted forward, the fury rolling off him was palpable. The reference to Emily wasn't lost on him, and the fact he'd called her cheap pussy was like a slap in the face. Even I wanted to knock the shit out of him for that one. Who did these people think they were?

"That's my girlfriend you're talking about. Your ex-best friend's daughter." Ryan could barely hold back as he glared at them both, baring his teeth like a wild animal.

"Ex being the operative word," Don snapped, pacing forward to try to intimidate Ryan into backing down. "We don't speak to the Winters family anymore and we certainly don't condone what they did." He held his nose up in the air as if his shit didn't stink. The thing was, we could all smell it, and he was the biggest liar of them all. I was getting tired of their phony bullshit.

"Your filthy hands were all over that deal," Zak said, making us all turn to face him. "We know that. Everyone in Sandland knows it too. You can argue all you want in here, but we all know the truth."

Don swerved around like a monster ready to attack and focused all of his poisonous venom onto Zak.

"What happened to Winters was his fault. Nothing to do with me, my family, or my business. So, if that's all you came here to say, you can leave." He marched back to his desk to sit down and dismiss us like some kind of demon headmaster. "My son won't be texting you again. You've got what you came here for. Now go."

Like we wanted to stay for a moment longer than we had to.

"Why didn't he text Brandon?"

We all stopped dead when Finn spoke. Don's eyes grew wide as he peered over at Chase. Chase froze and swallowed nervously as if he was trying to gulp down the lies he knew would spout out of his mouth at any minute. And we all waited. Finn had hit on something here.

Suddenly, the hairs on the back of my neck stood on end and every muscle in my body tensed up as a gravelly voice at the door said, "Yeah, *Dad*. Why didn't he text Brandon?"

We all turned to face Jensen, who stood at the door to the study. His face was bloody and swelling up badly. From the way he was leaning in the doorway, I could tell he was in pain, and that fact made this shit show slightly more bearable. I couldn't keep the smirk off my face seeing how much he was suffering, but at the same time, I was pissed. He knew something about what was going on and I didn't like him holding any cards. I should've finished the fucker off when I had the chance.

"What the fuck is going on?" I asked, looking between each of the Lockwoods. From what Jensen was implying, this went deeper than a grudge between Chase and the rest of us.

"You need to go the hospital, you're a fucking mess," was all Don Lockwood said in response, but Jensen wasn't going to be deterred that easily. He hobbled further into the room and then put his hands onto his father's desk as he leant forward to speak to him. The way he leered over him to try and get the upper hand was laughable with how broken and injured he was.

"Tell them, Dad. Tell them why Chase didn't message Mathers. Why all of us were told to stay the fuck away from him."

I frowned so hard my face hurt, and I balled my fists to keep myself in check and not lash out. I needed to hear this.

"What do you mean, all of us? You didn't stay the fuck away, did you? You've done nothing but get into my face since I came back. Goading me, hurting my girl, making me fucking angry." I took a step forward and Jensen flinched and moved back. He was scared of me. Good. He fucking better be.

He shook his head and chuckled sarcastically.

I'm not here to tell jokes, you fucker. Get to the point and stop pissing around.

"All of us were told to avoid you. I didn't say we all listened." He glanced down to his father. "He warned me, Chase, he even warned the fucking *company*." He said the last part using air quotes to let us know exactly what sort of company he meant. Most likely the same businessmen who'd sold Alec Winters down the river and royally fucked him over when he couldn't wash their dirty money anymore. "They're probably the only ones that did take the order on board." He concentrated his stare back on us. "Lucky for you, they listened. You wouldn't be standing here today if Dad hadn't

410

put a ring of protection around you. You'd be right there alongside Brodie in that graveyard or rotting in a shallow grave somewhere. That'd probably be more fitting for you though, shitty king."

"That's enough!" Don banged his fist down on the table, then pointed his finger right into Jensen's face. "You need to watch your mouth."

Funny. Seemed Daddy Lockwood wasn't too happy about the truths spilling out. But I wasn't done. I needed to know everything.

Jensen grimaced and pushed himself off the desk.

"I've been watching my mouth for the last twenty years, *Dad*. I've had enough." He turned to face me. "You want to know why you didn't get any text messages?" He cocked his head then carried on, not waiting for my response. "It's because we were told you were untouchable." He took a step towards me. The motherfucker was getting cocky in the spotlight. One more step and I'd knock him out again. "And you know what happens when we go against his wishes? ... That." He pointed over to Chase who was still clutching his cheek.

Don shot out of his chair, sending it spinning to the wall on its wheels. "I told you to leave it alone. I didn't think I needed to specify which one of them to stay away from," Don said, backtracking. His statement made no sense.

"Oh, but you did, Dad. You made it very clear after we were told to withdraw our statements about the fight that we shouldn't have anything to do with Mathers. No contact, no talking, don't even acknowledge he exists, I think were your exact words."

I felt Harper's distress like it was my own. The flippant way he was talking about the fight and what'd happened back then was like prising open a still very delicate wound for her. A wound I wouldn't let them infect with their filth.

"And why was that?" she asked, speaking up in a small voice next to me. Her voice may have been quiet, but her presence drowned me like a tidal wave. She was the strongest woman I knew, and yet, I was beginning to second guess my decision to let her come. She didn't need any more stress. She'd been through enough.

"Don't get me wrong, princess," Jensen said to Harper, making me want to rip him to pieces just for using that name for her alone. "It was an accident. But there are certain... things Dad wanted to keep buried. Isn't that right, Dad? It wouldn't look good if you got dragged into a court case, and that's what you were faced with, wasn't it? Or did I hear it wrong all those years ago?"

Don went to speak, but I jumped in. I needed to hear the truth. Not some garbled riddle from this punk. I was done with all this dancing about.

"Spell it out for me, Jensen. Pretend I missed a lot of school, you know, through all the bullying, and I need things explained a little more than most."

Don glared at Jensen as I mentioned the bullying. Was

he surprised that his offspring had turned out like him? He shouldn't have been. Everyone knew what cowards the Lockwood boys were.

Jensen laughed.

"The bullying! You know, we didn't pick you because of what you wore or how bad you smelt. We didn't even pick you 'cos of the whole living-in-your-own-shit story that went around in school. *I* picked you."

He scowled as he stared from me to his father and then back again. Then he looked over at his brother and said, "I'm sorry, man. I didn't want you to hear about it like this."

"Just say what you've got to say," Chase replied, sounding as fed up with this whole farce as I was.

"Oh, I will. I was about four years old," he said, smiling like he was telling us some kind of heart-warming childhood tale. "I couldn't sleep one night, so I came downstairs. Mum was out with one of her friends. She hadn't been here to put us to sleep and Dad being Dad had just sent us off upstairs to put ourselves to bed. I couldn't rest though. So, I crept downstairs to get myself a snack."

He glanced at Don with a wicked grin.

"You had company that night, didn't you, Dad? She wasn't the usual woman you liked to invite over when Mum wasn't around though. This one was older. Rougher. She swore like a sailor and didn't give a fuck. She wasn't scared of you either, but then I guess she held all the cards, didn't she?"

Don sank heavily back down onto his chair and pinched

413

the bridge of his nose, wincing, but the daggers he secretly shot Jensen's way didn't go unnoticed.

"I don't know what you think you heard, son, but I can assure you whatever it is, you're wrong."

"Am I? Really? After all these years, you're going to go with that? Do you think I didn't do my homework? I know everything, Dad." Jensen looked smug, but from the things that were whirling around in my head, he had no right to be.

"I'd suggest you stop right there if you know what's good for you!" Don shouted.

We all stepped forward. There wasn't a chance in hell I was going to let Don put a stop to this. I needed every gory detail.

"I want to hear this." I glared at Jensen to continue.

Harper clung to my side protectively as the others stood firm beside me. I braced myself. I wasn't stupid. I knew exactly what Jensen was getting at, but I needed to hear it from him. Don just grabbed a bottle of whiskey out of the bottom drawer of his desk, twisted the lid off, and knocked it back.

"She said she had files with a solicitor. Told you that if anything ever happened to her or her grandson that those documents would go public and you'd be ruined. Your family, your marriage, your business. The whole lot. She'd expose you for the liar and cheat you really are. You offered her money to keep quiet, and she took it. Said she needed to get clothes for the boy, and seeing as you'd been the sperm donor it was only right you donated some cash towards it.

"I watched you, Dad. I heard you sorting out the paperwork for some sort of trust fund. Not much, but enough so she could put food on the table. You called him the bastard, but she referred to him by his name. That's how I knew it was him." He nodded at me. "He was my bastard brother. And that's why I chose him. That's why I bullied him so hard in school. I wanted him to kill himself. That was if I didn't kill him first. He was gonna ruin us. Break Mum's heart and destroy us all if I didn't get to him first."

The fire that scorched inside of me suddenly engulfed my heart and I almost cried out in pain. I couldn't believe what I was hearing. I didn't want to believe it.

Don banged his bottle onto the desk, sending sloshes of whiskey tumbling onto the polished wood, but Jensen didn't let him get a word in. He wasn't finished yet.

"Don't even try to deny it, *Dad*. I heard you talking about paternity tests. That woman had you nailed to the fucking cross and you knew it."

My stomach dropped and the blood boiled in my veins. Harper wrapped her arms around me to hug me and buried her face into my chest, groaning out in her pain for me, but I couldn't hug her back.

I was numb.

Paralysed.

Disgusted.

"My nan." Was all I could manage to say through the

spiked ball lodged in my throat.

"That woman will be the death of me," Don hissed.

"That's all you can say?" Jensen turned his fury on to his father. "I tell them he's your son and all you care about is that woman draining you of your fucking money."

"He didn't give her shit." I snapped, defending my nan. "And don't worry. I don't want a penny either. I'm ashamed to think I came from the same gene pool as you. You disgust me." I glared at Don, but he couldn't look at me. Instead, he addressed Jensen like I wasn't in the fucking room.

"Your mother doesn't know any of this. I'd prefer it if it stayed that way."

Jensen gritted his teeth and looked at Chase. I didn't know what he was waiting for. Permission to shred the pieces of my life a little more?

"Why would I want to rip her heart out? You'll do a good enough job of that yourself. You've probably got half a dozen bastards out there walking the streets of Sandland." He walked over to Chase and they hugged. I heard Jensen say sorry as he held his brother. They'd grown up in a fucked-up household, but at least they had each other. I'd had no one.

"I didn't mean to hurt you." Don looked over at me now. Harper dropped her arms and turned to stand in front of me, like a lioness defending her pride.

"And you didn't do anything to help him either. Have you any idea what he went through in school? What they did to him? They should be locked up for it." She bristled with hate as she addressed Don and then the brothers. She was seconds away from launching her own counter attack, I could tell.

"Your brother would be in there too then, princess," Jensen added, looking over at her with a sly, sadistic smile. I don't know how he could be from the same flesh and blood as me. He was as far removed from my world and my morals as a slug was to a reptile.

"And he'd deserve to be," she shot back, holding her head up defiantly. "Cruelty like that shouldn't go unpunished."

"Is that why you're with him? To make up for what Brodie and I did?" I went to move towards him, but Harper stopped me.

"I'm with him because I love him. He has more compassion, more warmth in his little finger than you have in your whole body. He's kind, caring, smart, funny. He puts others before himself and he treats his friends better than most families treat each other. He's the first to stand up for others. He's decent and honest and..." She took a breath to try and calm herself down. "And I'm so fucking glad he didn't end up here with you. He might not have the money or the Lockwood name, but I'm thanking my lucky stars for that. He is everything and you are nothing. You're the ones who missed out, not him." She pointed at Don as he scowled back at her from behind his desk. "You don't deserve a son like Brandon. And he doesn't deserve to have a cold-hearted bastard of a father like you."

I fucking loved her. And in that moment, I wanted to get her as far away from the vileness of the Lockwood family as I could.

"Yeah, he's so great. That's why he did that to my brother's face." Chase piped up like the little bitch he was.

Harper went to grab for my t-shirt, and I knew right away what she was doing. She wanted to expose my scars and justify why I'd acted the way I had. But I didn't need to prove myself to anyone.

"It's all right, babe." I put my hand over hers to soothe her. It broke me to see how much sadness and love she held in her eyes. I took a breath to clear my fogging thoughts and stared at the streaks of piss stood behind us. "I don't need to justify shit to you, Lockwood. Any man who puts his hands on a woman deserves everything he gets. And bullies? Let's just say karma does have a name and its Brandon fucking Mathers. I'm proud of my name, of who I am. And if you ever come near us again, I won't stop like I did tonight. I don't want anything to do with either one of you."

I turned to the sperm donor, sitting there like the fucking lord of the manor. The man had done nothing for me growing up. We'd lived in poverty; we'd had fuck all. My nan could've fed us for a week on what he spent on a single pair of shoes. Probably have some left over for a treat, an ice-cream, or something that the rest of the kids I knew growing up took for granted. He might've given her something to help pay the bills, but it wasn't because he had a conscience, it was because my nan had an insurance policy against him, and he'd do anything to keep his nose clean.

It hurt that my nan hadn't told me any of this. But if she had, and I knew I was his kid, would it have made a difference? Maybe not. If anything, I'd have probably rebelled even more, been more pissed off with the world. I guess she was just protecting me in the only way she knew how. With blackmail.

"If I could pick anyone to be my father, you'd be the last on the fucking list. Charlie Manson has more paternal instincts than you do. Probably do a better job with your family too." I gave him my signature grin.

"I left you alone," he hissed. "I thought I was doing the right thing."

This guy was shit at excuses. I was surprised he'd gotten away with it this far.

"You blocked me out. Made it like I never even existed. You weren't doing the right thing. You were taking the coward's way out. Everyone has a price though, hey, Don?"

"It wasn't about the money."

Who was he kidding?

"It was always about the money, that and your reputation. I mean, what would the rest of Sandland say if they knew you'd been screwing a fuck-up like my mother and got her knocked up? I'll bet you even got her hooked on drugs too. Was that it? You both snorted coke and fucked like rabbits behind your wife's back. Were you so high you forgot the condom? I thought your sons were the biggest dickheads in Sandland, but you? You're the worst. You're scum. The filth on our shoes. The dirt at the bottom of the barrel. Your best friend gets caught doing the same shady shit you've been pulling for years and you run and hide like a fucking weasel. You've got no backbone, and I can't respect a liar, a cheat, and a fraud like you."

The words came tumbling out, and yet I felt like I hadn't even scratched the surface on all the reasons why I hated this man so much. He was reason I got bullied. He was the cause of all the misery in my life.

"All you have in you is hate." Don sneered at me as he spoke.

"Yeah, you're right. Hate for you."

"Then I suggest you get out. I've got nothing more to say to you. There's nothing for you here."

I didn't want anything he had to offer. I was struggling to even breathe the same air as him.

"Don't worry, we're leaving. But if I were you, I'd come clean to your wife soon. She already thinks I look familiar. I'd hate for her to hear about your sordid affair from someone else."

Don shot up from his seat and slammed his hands onto his desk.

"Are you threatening me?"

"If I did, you'd know about it," I said, feeling the anger

surge forward. "She won't hear it from me, but I can't vouch for my nan. She's getting awfully forgetful in her old age. I can't be held responsible for what she tells people when she's out and about in Sandland. Oh, and if anything ever happens to her, it's me you'll be hiding from, not the fucking solicitors."

I stalked over to the door and slammed the fucker open. The door handle banged off the wall and probably left a dent in the plaster, but I didn't care. I held Harper's hand as we headed for the door. I needed to get out. Being stuck in this building was stifling me. I felt like I was drowning in the sea of lies and deception that he'd built around himself.

I wanted no part of it.

I was done with being used, lied to and deceived. It wasn't the life I wanted for myself or Harper.

Tonight, I'd heard truths I didn't particularly want to know about. But I wouldn't let it break me. That family was nothing to do with me. I had my nan, my boys, and I had my girl. My little warrior. The one person in my life who accepted me for all my flaws and loved me anyway. Not because she had to, or because we had some time-honoured bond, but because she wanted to. She saw something in me that no one else did. I saw something in her too. I saw my future.

I wanted to make a life for us. To go out to work and come home knowing she was there waiting for me. I wanted a family, kids, screaming arguments over who left the toilet seat up or forgot to wash the dishes, which would be all on me, and then fucking awesome make up sessions afterwards once the kids were in bed. I wanted holidays by the sea and weekends spent making memories. I wanted all of that, not just because I'd never had it growing up, but because I knew there wasn't anyone else in the world I wanted to be with more than her.

"I'm so sorry, Brandon. I'm sorry everything is so fucked up." She stopped next to her car and threw her arms around me.

Before, I'd wanted to set this place on fire and spark up a cigarette in the flames as I watched it burn to the ground. Now, I felt tired of it all. I wanted to get away. Focus on the good in my life. Move forward and live. With her.

"It's not that bad, babe. I have you." I kissed the top of her head and she sighed then peered up at me.

"You'll always have me."

Her words made my aching heart ease slightly. And looking down at her, I realised my own family would never suffer the way I had. I'd treat her like a queen and my kids would grow up knowing how a real man takes care of his wife.

"Brandon Lockwood. Who'd have thought it?" Zak piped up, and his words made the hairs on the back of my neck prickle in revulsion.

I pointed my finger at him and gave him my last threatening look of the night.

"You ever call me that and I'll break every one of your fingers. You'll never D.J. or type on a keyboard ever again."

He threw his head back and laughed, but he knew I was serious. I'd let that one slide, but next time, he'd regret it.

"I've gotta say, mate, I loved the Charlie Manson reference."

I grimaced but held myself back. I hadn't said anything in there for his entertainment. But right on cue, Ryan butted in. He could read me like a book, and he knew Zak was skating on thin ice.

"We need to leave. I don't think us standing in this fucking road dissecting what just happened is going to help anyone." We all nodded in agreement. "Brandon, mate. I'm here if you need me. Call me tomorrow or whenever. You know where I am."

I slapped him on the back and then said my goodbyes. Just as I opened the passenger door to Harper's car, Finn spoke up.

"We are not a reflection of our fathers. We make our own impression in this life. Remember that. The chain can be broken."

Zak frowned at him like he was speaking a foreign language, but I got it. I knew Finn better than anyone else. I also knew what he was telling me. It was time for me to break the chain. Time for my life to move on.

CHAPTER
Thirty Four

BRANDON

Six months later

"Okay, find a space and let's practise some cool down exercises."

I watched their little legs run around trying to find a space, and after a few seconds, I realised that without spots for them to stand on on the floor, they were struggling. I'd need to add that to my list for the next time I did a session like this. I pointed to a few places and helped them to scatter out as best I could, and Harper chuckled and joined in. She wasn't supposed to be taking part, but this was her school, and the kids really listened to her.

I was impressed that they'd all paid attention and copied me as well as they did. The night before, I'd had a nightmare that the school gym had erupted into total chaos with kids climbing the walls, breaking out into fights, and ignoring every damn word I'd said. But they didn't. They were hanging on my every word and every one of them was giving it one hundred percent, pushing themselves to be the best.

After a few minutes of cool down, I called them all over to sit with me. This was the first boxing and self-defence class I'd done in a primary school. I say boxing, but we'd marketed it as an anti-bullying workshop, incorporating physical training with the exercises my college course had taught me on dealing with all aspects of childhood trauma.

When I'd walked out on Pat Murphy and my dreams of making it as a boxer all those months ago, I thought my skills would be useless. I resigned myself to the fact that I'd forever be stuck on some building site somewhere, doing manual labour, and if I was really lucky, somewhere down the line, I'd get to learn a trade. But Harper woke me up to the potential that was out there for a man like me. She was the one who'd come up with the idea of starting the boxing lessons. I asked at my local gym, the one I used to work at, and they agreed to let me rent the space for an hour, twice a week. I didn't think anyone would show up that first night, but they did. And soon the fees covered the cost of the room and then some.

The boxing lessons soon turned into self-defence classes as more and more people joined. I'd asked them what they wanted to learn, and I took their feedback on board. They wanted to know how to look after themselves. They wanted to feel powerful.

One day, I had a young lad come into my class. Fifteen years old, and I knew right away that he was suffering. I could see it in his eyes. I helped him as best I could through exercise, but that kid broke my fucking heart, and after every session with him I went home to Harper and told her how helpless I felt. She did her research, found a course at the same college Ryan went to, and the following week, I enrolled in a child counselling course. Never thought I'd see the day when I was excited about going back to school, but I was. I loved it. And after finishing with a distinction, I went on to take the advanced course.

It'd been Harper's idea to expand the business. Reach out to schools and use what I knew and what I'd learnt to help younger kids. Harper had scored my first gig at her school, and seeing as she was due to return to work in a week's time, they'd agreed. Other schools in the area signed up too after I spoke to her headteacher and told him what I did. I was fully booked up for the next month and I fucking loved it. Had to watch the language though. F bombs weren't great for business when you were teaching five-year-olds.

I hadn't spoken to Don Lockwood since that night when he'd begrudgingly admitted he was my father. Funnily enough, a week after the whole showdown, a brand new black Range Rover was delivered to my nan's house, registered in my name.

I didn't want it.

I didn't want to accept anything from that bastard, but Nan and Harper had been with me when it came and they both disagreed with me. Nan said I should keep it and run him over with it. But Harper told me to sell it. Use the money for something I really wanted. As she pointed out, he owed me that much. So I did. I sold it back to the dealership and used the money for a deposit on the flat I now shared with Harper. It was the best move I ever made. Waking up with her in my arms was like every birthday and Christmas I'd never had growing up.

I sat with the kids on the floor of the school gym and I talked to them about ways they could improve their health. I explained what their mental health was and how their mind was just as important as their body. Then I touched on some deeper subjects, telling them that words could hurt just as much as punches. I called a kid over to stand next to me and handed him a tube of toothpaste. They all laughed when I told him to squeeze it all out into my hands. He did, and his giggle warmed my heart as he piled the white stuff into my outstretched palms. He thought this was the funniest thing to ever happen to him.

"That's a lot of toothpaste to clean your teeth with," one of the girls at the front said, widening her eyes as she took it all in.

"You did good, mate." I smiled, looking down at the mess he'd made. "Now put it all back into the tube."

His little face fell, and the rest of the class covered their mouths with their hands as some gasped and others chuckled.

"Don't panic," I reassured him. "I don't expect you to get it back in. But what I wanted to show you was that words are kind of like toothpaste. Once they're out there, once they leave your mouth you can't put them back. It's impossible. So, you always need to think about how you use your words. Your words could make someone's day, or they could ruin it. Use your words carefully."

The other adults in the room gave me a little clap and the children followed suit. One lad at the front asked me if he could eat the toothpaste. I told him no. Harper was right, teaching kids was like being a zookeeper at times. But I loved how unpredictable they were. This session had been the most fun I'd had in ages.

"You have a lot of tattoos," another girl said, staring at my arms like she was mulling something over.

"I want to colour them in," her friend piped up and they both laughed.

"Are you Miss Yates's dad?" a little lad in glasses asked me, and I threw my head back, laughing.

"How old do you think I am, mate?"

"Seventy?" he answered, nodding to himself like he knew he was right.

"Miss Yates has gotten really fat," a rough-looking kid at the back said.

"Tommy, that's rude!" the teacher said to him sternly.

Ah. So, this was the infamous Tommy.

"I'm not fat, Tommy. I'm pregnant."

The other teachers all smiled at her while she rubbed over her little belly. I was surprised she was showing as much as she was at three months. But then again, I suppose you did get bigger with twins.

Yeah, we weren't doing things by halves. There were two little bundles of joy in there and we'd found out last week that it was two girls. The guy who'd spent half of his life being totally clueless about women was about to be surrounded by them. God help me.

Her parents hadn't been happy about her being with me, but after hearing about the pregnancy they were slowly coming around. I knew they'd probably always harbour a resentment towards me, and I could deal with that. As long as they treated my girls right. That was all that mattered to me.

"Are you the daddy?" Tommy asked me outright. I liked him all ready. He had no filter, I could tell.

"Yeah, mate. I am."

"My daddy says you're the best boxer in Sandland. He said you could beat anyone."

Yeah. I liked him.

"Does he like boxing? Your dad?"

Tommy's face fell and he started to fidget in his seat.

"He doesn't hit other men like you, but he can hit. Really hard too."

I saw the change in expression on every adult's face in the room. One of the teaching assistants stood up and started ushering the children out, making sure they said thank you to me as they left. But Harper, the teacher, and I kept our focus on Tommy. He didn't move. Just stayed rooted to the floor.

"Does Daddy hit anything in particular?" Harper asked on a whisper as she struggled to kneel down on the floor. I went over to her and sat down with her.

"Mummy. He hits Mummy."

I put my arm around Harper as I saw the tears well up in her eyes.

"Tommy, does he... does he..." She couldn't speak, and the teacher, Mrs Turley, had started to cry behind him. So, I jumped in to ask the question she couldn't get out.

"Mate, does your dad hit you?"

"Sometimes. But I'm tough. I can take it."

He shouldn't have to take it.

"That's not right. Your dad shouldn't be hurting you. You haven't done anything wrong, okay?" I made sure to look him in the eye so he knew what I was saying was true.

"He doesn't hurt my brothers though. Just me and Mum."

"You did the right thing today, telling us this." I heard the door open behind us and I saw the head teacher walk in. "Do you think you could tell Mr Farnsworth too? He can help your Daddy. He can help all of you."

Tommy nodded and when Mrs Turley held out her hand for him, he took it.

"Mr Mathers? Will my daddy go to prison?" Tommy asked me over his shoulder. My throat clammed up. I couldn't lie to him. I could never lie to a kid like that.

"The police will need to speak to him, Tommy. But they're the good guys. Remember that for me, yeah? They want to help you. Don't be scared to tell them the truth."

He seemed happy with that answer and he went off to face whatever hurdles he had coming his way. Five years old and he was already facing problems that most adults would struggle to cope with.

"It's no wonder he always lashed out. He must've gone through hell," Harper said on a sob. I pulled her onto my lap and held her close. "We always suspected there was something going on at home. But that's the first time he's ever opened up to anyone. You did that, Brandon. You helped that little boy. He'd have never asked for help if it wasn't for your workshop and the trust you built up with these kids today."

I buried my face in her neck as I let her cry.

"I fucking love you," I whispered, making sure the f-bomb was for her ears only.

"You're going to be an amazing daddy." She lifted her head up and the smile she gave me through her tears tore my heart open.

She knew I was apprehensive about what sort of a father I'd make. I hadn't had a Dad growing up, but I'd seen how good Sean was with Ryan and his brothers, and that's who I wanted to be like. Whether I'd achieve that remained to be seen, but I wanted to be the best that I could be. The fact that Harper believed in me meant everything. With her by my side, I felt like I could do anything.

"Don't worry about Tommy," I said, as I brushed her tears away with my thumb. "The school know now, and they'll help. I don't want you worrying." I rubbed over her stomach and smiled. "We have our own two to think about. We can help where we can, but we can't save the world."

She sighed and then nodded her agreement, placing her hand over mine. I stood up and then helped her up too. We gathered the equipment we'd used and I chattered away about how I needed to invest in spots for the floor and some other things to make the next workshop even better.

I picked up all our things and grabbed my mobile phone out of my rucksack as we headed for the door. Instantly, it vibrated with an incoming call and I saw Ryan's name flash up.

"You alright, mate?" I answered, as I balanced my phone on my shoulder and carried the two bags full of equipment through the back doors of the school gym and headed towards the car.

Things had been stressful for them since Emily's dad had been sent down. He got sixteen years for fraud and manslaughter. It'd hit Emily hard, harder than we thought it would, but we'd all been there to support her. It was what we did. We were a family.

"Where've you been? I've been calling you non-stop." He sounded out of breath.

"I've been doing that workshop at Harper's school. My phone was on silent. Why? What's up?"

I saw Harper pull her phone out of her bag and turn it towards me to show the thirty odd missed calls from Emily and a string of unread text messages.

"You need to come to the hospital." My stomach lurched. "It's Finn." Sickness washed over me. "He was found early this morning at the back of a bar in town. He'd been badly beaten, and he was unconscious."

"Jesus fucking Christ. I'm on my way. Is he going to be okay?" I couldn't even hold the car keys to open the door, my hands were shaking that badly.

Harper came to take them off me, and she pushed me to go round to the passenger side. I threw the bags into the boot and wandered round to the other side of the car in a daze.

"They don't know yet. He's in for tests. Mate, it was fucking bad."

I stood back as Harper opened the passenger door from inside.

"I'm on my way." I shut the call down and jumped in. "We need to go straight to the hospital. It's Finn. He's been hurt." She didn't press me for answers, just started the car and pulled off.

I had a bad feeling about this, so I opened my Google app and typed his name in. The first link that came up was about the court case and then a link detailing his early release.

Fuck.

"What is it?" she asked, picking up on my tension.

"Let's just say if you thought my childhood was brutal, it

was nothing compared to Finn's. I don't think I can tell you any more than that, angel. It's not my story to tell."

But I knew it.

Every dirty, sordid detail.

I was the only one he'd told, to my knowledge, anyway. We'd been there for each other, back in the days when there were other people who held all the power in our lives. I'd experienced hell on a daily basis, but Finn, he'd fucking lived there.

"Should I call Effy? Emily said in her texts it was just her and Ryan at the hospital. She'll want to know."

Harper had got friendly with Effy over the last few months, and I knew she was just looking out for her friend, but so was I. And I didn't think he needed any more stress at the moment.

"No. Don't. He won't want her seeing him like that."

He won't want anyone seeing him like that.

"But she'll want to be there. I'd want to be there if it was you. She loves him."

I didn't doubt that. But he needed to focus on himself. He didn't need to take on her grief too. Effy wasn't strong like my Harper.

"It's not that simple."

"Isn't it?" she snapped back.

"He can't love her until he can learn to love himself. He wants to, but now isn't the right time."

"I don't agree. I think now is the perfect time. He needs

her."

"He needs her to be safe too. Please, Harper. Don't push me on this one."

She bit her tongue and dropped it. And I tried to focus on how I was going to be there for her and my best friend, because he was going to need me. He was tough, but what he was facing was enough to destroy anyone. His nightmare had returned from the dead and this was a battle he couldn't face alone.

Hurt one and you hurt us all.

Only these scars ran deeper than the flesh wounds I had. They were burned deep into his soul. Tattooed into his heart and branded across his brain.

There was a reason my best friend didn't speak very often; why he chose his words so carefully. The things he'd seen had rendered him speechless. The life he'd endured had drained him of hope. He'd learned to stay in the shadows, to be quiet for his own good.

But I wouldn't stay quiet.

I'd be his voice if he needed me.

The war that was started when he was left behind that bar to bleed out on the cold, dirty pavement was a war I would finish.

I might not have been able to help him like I wanted to back when we were kids, but I was more than able to now.

I was ready to burn this town to the ground, smoke the evil fucker out of his hiding place, and show everyone what a low-life scumbag he really was for hurting Finn.

It was time for Finn's voice to be heard.

Time for his retribution.

EPILOGUE

FINN

The broken boy.

That's what they called me in school.

I didn't speak.

I couldn't.

What was I supposed to say?

Words wouldn't help me.

Nothing could.

I lived a life of chaos, but on the surface, I was a picture of calmness. Serenity. Silence.

Kind of like a swan. Everyone sees the perfection, the grace. No one thinks about the effort it takes to keep that up. The work that goes on below the surface to maintain the illusion.

My life was full of illusions.

The loving parents who couldn't figure out why their son wouldn't talk.

The puzzled professionals who tried everything in their journals and research to try and coax me out of it.

I was a riddle they couldn't figure out. And after a time, nobody wanted to.

I was the tree that fell in the middle of the empty, barren woods. Nobody heard my branches break because no one wanted to acknowledge the real problem.

I was the forgotten boy.

Until them.

The Renaissance men.

They accepted me for what I was. They didn't push me to be anything else. If I wanted to draw fucked up shit that would've had my Mum screaming and running off to the nearest psychologist, they let me. There was no judgement. I could finally be me.

But life likes to knock you back down sometimes. Remind you there is no happy ever after for boys like me.

I wanted to be free to love her.

But how could I?

When there was a devil breathing down my neck.

A devil from my past, who was ready to take the last shreds of my life and crush them in his deceitful, ugly, pain-riddled grasp.

I'd spent my whole childhood living in his hell. Now, he wanted to drag me back there and I had the fight of my life ahead of me to try and survive the unspeakable.

Would I survive?

I didn't think so.

All I could do now was pray.

Finn's story is coming in Early 2021.

Thank you so much for reading. If you enjoyed Brandon and Harper's story, then please spread the word and leave a review.
Leave a written review if you have the time, or just click on those stars that too will be fine!

AUTHOR
Acknowledgements

Writing this during a global pandemic and being in lockdown was certainly challenging. I need to say a huge thank you to my family for letting me escape the crazy world we live in and indulge in the crazier minds of my characters. You are my rocks and I would be lost without you.

Next, I need to give a massive shout-out to my book besties who have kept my sanity in check and pulled me off the ledge more times than I care to admit. Lindsey Powell, Ashlee Rose, L. G. (Lauren) Campbell, and Robyn Warner Greenwood, you ladies are amazing. You make me laugh every day and I value your friendship so so much. Thank you for always being there and for beta reading Tortured Souls. If you haven't read their books yet, you need to. They are amazing authors.

Robyn, the best PA ever! Thank you for being totally awesome and organising everything. Without you, I'd be lost. Your teasers are to die for and you work so hard to get our books out there. You're an angel, and I'm truly grateful for your hard work and friendship. If you aren't following her, then get to it. You'll find her at @books4days_with_robyn or @robynpa_

A special thank you to Karen and Leanne for being utterly brilliant and polishing this story for me. I'm so glad I found you. You've helped to make my little book shine brighter. Thank you ladies.

To Michelle Lancaster, for taking the perfect photograph of my character inspiration, Brandon. Chase Cassels for being that inspiration. This cover is freaking hot. And last but not least, Lori Jackson, for designing a kick ass cover. You guys rock!

I will always be indebted to the hard work and support of all the bloggers and bookstagrammers on social media. Your posts and graphics are amazing and you always go above and beyond. Thank you for every single post, share and comment. It means the world. Special thanks to Natalie @allireadislove, Suny @bookslover09, Natalie @fromreader.withlove, @enchantedreads_ and many, many more for the amazing teaser graphics. You guys are always the first to share anything. Thank you! Also Annie @emotionallyunhingedromantic. Your videos blow me away every single time. You are awesome! And of course the fabulous Robyn @books4days_with_robyn. I wish I could list everyone. You all do such a fantastic job.

To the indie author community, I love how encouraging, supportive, and utterly amazing you are. I feel proud to be a part of such an amazing community. #indieauthorsrock

Last but not least, to all the readers out there who've taken the time to download, read, and review my book. Thank you for taking a chance on me. I'm always immensely grateful for every read and review. Reviews are the lifeline of every author, especially us smaller indies. You guys make my day and make it all worthwhile.

Thank you for reading Brandon and Harper's story.

Lots of Love
Nikki x

Chloe Ellis

What you're about to read is my story, my truth. A truth that spans over twenty years of a love for two brothers. A love that was cruel, sometimes harsh and raw, but for me always honest and true. An adopted little sister to one, but to the other so much more. Ours was a love that defied all reason. It pushed us to our limits. It was never easy, but nothing worth having ever is; and Luca Marquez is so worth having. He's mine, he always has been and no one will take him away from me.

Luca Marquez

I've loved her forever, but I couldn't make her mine. Not until the day she walked into my club and needed my protection. She brought light into my darkness and warmed my stone-cold heart. Chloe Ellis is my whole world, but she doesn't know that yet.

Luca's world stops on the day his precious Chloe is taken from him. Faced with an impossible situation, he will stop at nothing to save her. Even if that means slaughtering anyone who gets in his way, or tearing down whole cities to find her. He'll do anything for her and he'll never let her go again.

Ryley

Don't trust the fairy tales. They trick you into believing true love will appear on the back of a white horse, in the form of a perfect, handsome Prince Charming. Most of the time, Prince Charming turns out to be even more deceptive and evil than the wolf himself. I thought I'd met my soul mate at high school. Turned out my Mr Wright was so very wrong.

Jackson

I live in a cruel and unforgiving world. I learnt from an early age how vicious life can be, but I'm a survivor. Life may have dragged me down to the depths of hell, but I know how to dance with the devil. Sometimes bad things happen to good people for no other reason than to remind us that this life is cruel. Sometimes good people are pushed to do very bad things to right the wrongs of another. But when all is said and done, we need to ask ourselves... how far would you go to protect the ones you love?

Ryley thinks she has her whole life mapped out. Her

happily ever after with her high school sweetheart, Justin, is already planned down to the very last detail. But life doesn't always work out the way we expect it to. And when demons from Justin's life threaten to destroy everything they've built up, Ryley finds herself thrown into a world of deception, lies and confusion. Truths get twisted, love and hate walk a dubious thin line, and the enemy you think you know isn't always what they seem.

This book serves as a reminder that the first Prince Charming to cross your path isn't always the hero in your happily ever after.

*An enemies-to-lovers, second-chance novel. Although this story isn't a dark read, there are elements of darkness within it, so please take note of the trigger warnings. There are also cameos from Luca's story in this book. However, you don't have to read Luca to enjoy this; it can be read as a standalone.

**Warning: 18 years + recommended reader age due to sexual content. This story also contains scenes of drug abuse, suicide and sexual violence that may be upsetting to readers. Please proceed with caution.

Hurt
TO LOVE

After darkness, always comes the light.

The darkness is where I've lived ever since they took me all those months ago. Dragging me into the shadows to play their sick and twisted games. I don't know why they took me. They talk about an eye for an eye, but I don't know these men. How can I be punished for a sin I know nothing about? A sin I didn't commit.

They love to watch me suffer, they live to make my life hell. I thought my life was over.

Until him.

He blazed through my darkness like a lightning bolt, shining through the void of nothingness. He was a force to be reckoned with.

They thought they'd broken me. That somehow, they'd won. But they didn't expect him. I know I never did. And now, my life will never be the same again.

Ella

Once bitten, twice shy. Isn't that how the saying goes? Only, this man looks like he wants to do more than just bite me. He'll devour me whole, given half a chance. Trouble is, I don't think I've got the willpower to stop him. Not when he's looking at me like that, with those hypnotic grey eyes. He's a God amongst men, but his desires are anything but Godly. He's pure devil wrapped in a designer suit.

Joe

All good things come to those who wait, and boy have I waited a long time to find a woman like her. If she thinks I'll let her walk away, she's in for a surprise. She thinks I'm the spider to her fly, but she's wrong. I'm the one caught in her web, and I've got no plans to break free.

Following a chance encounter on the opening night of a new club in the city, Joe Madden sets his sights on the beautiful brunette with the fiery temper. The only problem is she's had enough of bossy, overbearing men. So what do you do when the woman of your dreams won't even give you the time of day?

You get creative.

Joe pulls out all the stops to get Ella to notice him and win her over. However, hidden forces are at play, working against Joe and his pursuit of a happily ever after.

Is this perfect playboy everything he seems or are the smoke and mirrors covering a dangerous lie?

This is an extended novel told in two parts, and it does end on a cliff hanger.

Book two, 'Forever Yours' is the concluding part of Joe and Ella's story and is available for download on Kindle Unlimited.

Made in the USA
Las Vegas, NV
14 May 2022

48893137R00267